USA *TODAY* BESTSELLING AUTHOR
molly o'hare

JUST A BATTER OF TIME

MOLLY O'HARE

Molly O'Hare
Be You Publishing, LLC
First Print: Sept 2022
ISBN: 978-1-959120-00-1

www.MollyOHareauthor.com

DEDICATION

To all the amazing wonderful people out there. YOU matter. I see you. Thank you for being here. This book is dedicated to you. The world is better because YOU are here.

Also, to Theresa Styles, without you, who knows if this book would have even seen the light of day.

JUST A BATTER OF TIME

MOLLY O'HARE

"Hell to the freaking yeah!" Riley O'Neil pumped her fist in the air as she did her regular celebratory dance party like she did at the end of every night. With her lips curled up into a contagious smile, she flipped the lock on the door and switched the sign to Closed. Another day well done, if you asked her.

Even though it was the end of the night, a surge of adrenaline rushed through her. How could it not? This was her dream come true. Trying her best to hold in her excitement, Riley brushed her hands down her apron before spinning around to face the front of her bakery.

"Day six-forty-eight done and dusted!" Riley's feet bounced as her excitement grew. Her dance party was now in full swing by the time she moved back to the front counter, her smile somehow more infectious than before.

Her eyes sparkled with pride as they moved to the glass display case, causing her plentiful hips to do another swing.

Who would've thought she would be where she was right now?

Closing *her* bakery.

That's right. *Her* bakery.

Holy freaking moly!

Riley O'Neil owned her own damn bakery!

She did another shimmy as she moved her hands through the air to the joyful beat that played in her head. No matter how many times she tried, Riley still couldn't believe it.

Riley O'Neil was not only working in her dream career, but she was also the proud owner of her own freaking bakery.

Her smile morphed into a full-blown toothy grin as she slid her hand across the glass display case housing her creations.

Who said hard work and determination wouldn't pay off? 'Cause that was a damn lie. I did it. No cheating someone out of something or fake promises. This is mine, built from the ground up.

Riley high-fived herself.

Before she could stop, her mind briefly drifted to her parents. Quickly, she pushed those thoughts to the back of her head. There was no way in hell she would let them dampen her mood.

She was the owner of a bakery, no matter what her parents thought.

Riley's nose scrunched. Okay, well... she wasn't the *sole* owner, but that was neither here nor there. She was just going to skip past that tiny technicality and move on to the important part.

Pastries & Paws was *her* baby.

The bakery that catered to humans and their fur-babies alike. Because why not? When she first imagined the idea, she knew it was a little out there, but when she thought about it, and really thought about it, she realized it was exactly what she wanted in her life. Animals were just as much a part of the family as anyone else, and they deserved pet-friendly treats every once in a while, as well.

Just because she couldn't have a fur-baby of her own with the bakery taking up all her time didn't mean she couldn't dote on them and make goodies for them. It was her dream to one day have a house full of animals, especially since she wasn't allowed to have any growing up.

Not with how her parents were.

And until that day, when Riley knew she could have a home of her own and as many pets as she wanted, she would do the next best thing.

Thus, her grand plan of creating Pastries & Paws was born.

Riley had it all figured out. Save as much money as she could, and once she was halfway to her goal, take out a loan for the rest.

At least that *was* the plan when she mentioned it to her older brother Patrick.

How was Riley to know Patrick would end up telling his best friend Liam and then boom, stuff started rolling sooner than she could wrap her head around.

Her head spun whenever she thought about the sequence of events that led her here.

Holy freaking moly.

Riley's hips did another shimmy as she glanced around the small seating area, trying to ignore her train of thought.

The chairs were on the tables. The floor was mopped and everything was good to go for tomorrow. She had to admit; after doing this for almost two years now, she'd gotten pretty good at it. At this point, she pretty much had everything down to a science.

See, hard work and determination did *pay off.*

Riley flicked her eyes to the ceiling as she made her way toward the back. Once she made it behind the counter, she did a quick double-check to see what items she was running low on.

Of course, she would have to make her usuals. Her morning rush always wiped her out of cinnamon rolls, croissants, blueberry muffins, and a few varieties of bagels.

Once Riley was done taking inventory of the human side of her display case, her eyes glanced toward the pet-friendly side, her heart swelling.

Honestly, the four-legged treats are what put Pastries & Paws on the map. Not even a week after opening, Riley realized having her pet-friendly goodies was the thing that made her stand out among the other bakeries in the area. And even though she'd only been open for almost two years, she was well on her way to making an actual profit.

The tip of her tongue darted out from behind her lips as she scanned through her display case. "Okay, let's take a look."

Riley made a quick mental note to make an extra batch of her *Smoochies*, a dog bone-shaped biscuit, her, *Howl at the Moon,* doggie cupcakes, and her *Bow Down to Me* cat treats.

"That's not too bad."

Thank the Universe she didn't have to stock up on her *CatCrack,* a catnip-glazed bite-sized treat. They took forever to make, and right now, it already looked like she would have to get up before the butt crack of dawn to get everything done in time.

Riley's eyes instinctively traveled to the fancy clock on the wall as she attempted to calculate the time she'd need to make everything.

A sharp exhale escaped Riley as she moved her neck from side to side. "One of these days, I'll be able to hire someone to help. Maybe then I won't have to wake up as early as I do, run the register, or go through the bookkeeping, and I'll be able to spend all my time baking. It'll happen. It's called manifesting." She sharply nodded.

Riley knew she was close to that point, but not quite there yet. Besides, everyone that came into her little hole-in-the-wall bakery never made her feel rushed. Sure, she would get the occasional asshole customer, but it was rare.

She'd lucked out with most everyone's understanding. Maybe it had something to do with the items she made. Or her bubbly personality. Who knew? Regardless, she was still grateful it hadn't been an issue.

In reality, though, what's so bad about sacrificing sleep when it was your dream career that was the cause of it?

Plus, she never got *too* far behind on everything that needed to be accomplished.

Early on she decided to keep Pastries & Paws closed on Sunday.

Originally, she thought she would get a day off during the week, but it soon turned out she needed Sundays to catch up on paperwork and balance her books. Not to mention it gave her a jumpstart on the baking for the week, like feeding her starters for the bread or experimenting on whatever creation grabbed her attention.

But at least she didn't have to watch the front at the same time.

As Riley's mind raced with the calculations to figure out the time she'd need to get everything ready the following day, she pulled her bottom lip between her teeth. Sleep was important, but so was having adorable treats for all her furry customers.

And her four-legged friends would *always* win out. Even if that meant no sleep for her.

Who cares if you don't get enough sleep? You can sleep when you're dead.

"What in the world am I doing?" Riley shook her head,

her smile still on her face. "All this thinking is wasting time."

She chuckled to herself as she made her way toward the back. However, just as she was about to walk into the kitchen, her eyes caught the front window and noticed the sun had already begun to set.

Crappity crap.

Riley's face scrunched. Okay, it wasn't super dark out. Just, you know, that twilight kind of dark? The dark that would quickly turn to dark-dark soon.

Riley worried her bottom lip as her brain raced to come up with a plausible excuse for why she didn't have time to wait for Patrick or Liam to escort her home.

It was a stupid rule anyway. It wasn't like the house the three of them shared was *that* far from the bakery.

She'd walked it a thousand times with no issue.

"If it's dark out, me or Liam walk or drive you home. This isn't up for discussion." Her brother's words echoed through her mind for the millionth time.

Riley didn't know whether to laugh or cry at the situation. Part of her understood why Patrick and Liam were always so adamant about one of them walking her home. But at the same time, the reason behind their "rule" happened *years* ago.

She didn't even think about it anymore, or at least she tried not to. At the time, she was just a teenager, and it was the night before her *graduation*. That's how long ago it was. Yet, somehow that one day, even though she handled herself perfectly. It made Patrick, and in turn Liam extra protective of her. Okay, there was that *one* other time she'd had an incident...

But damn it, Riley was older now. She could handle herself. She sure as shit did *that* night, too.

Blahhhh, let's not think about it right now. Focus on the important things.

It was only a ten, maybe fifteen-minute walk tops to get home. Even less if she had a car...

Riley's brows dented at the center at the thought of a car.

If she had a car, she could come and go as she pleased; no more waiting around to be escorted back and forth like a child.

Then again, having a car would mean putting money into something that wasn't her bakery.

Riley shuddered at the mere thought.

That wasn't an option.

Besides, walking was fine by her. She enjoyed it. And if she really needed a car, she'd just borrow Patrick's or even Liam's.

Liam... Riley pinched her eyes shut. Ugh. She'd been nursing a *crush* on him for as long as she could remember. It was pretty pathetic. Not only was he her older brother's best friend, but they definitely had some rough patches growing up.

Rough patches. Riley scoffed. If by rough patches, she meant a solid year where he'd treated her like either she wasn't there or somehow was on the receiving end of his annoyance. It hadn't lasted long, and after her first *incident,* Liam pretty much went back to normal. He was still grumpy and annoying at times... *and* a little too protective, which agitated Riley to no end, but he wasn't usually like that.

Besides, what could she do about it? Nothing. Absolutely nothing. And, if she were being honest, her *crush* had a pretty intense chokehold on her.

Liam Kelly was in her life and it looked like he'd be in it for as far as she could see. *Strictly in a platonic, only her brother's best friend kind of way,* she forced herself to believe.

"Fiddlesticks." Riley shook her shoulders, attempting to push away any and all thoughts revolving around Liam.

It was better that way.

Riley quickly switched gears back to her to-do list. The sooner she got home, the sooner she could get into bed and *actually* get some sleep before turning right around to do it all over again.

She pulled out her phone as she always did when she was ready to text them that she was done for the night.

But for the life of her, she couldn't bring herself to hover her fingers over the keypad.

She had two options:

Wait for one of them, which could take a while. Or walk home and hopefully slip in undetected.

After all these years, they still weren't the best at communicating which included who was on pickup duty. She flicked her eyes to the ceiling.

It might've been wrong, but Riley may or may not have used that flaw to her advantage on nights she really didn't have the time to wait for them.

Kind of like tonight.

What's that saying? It's better to ask for forgiveness than permission? Honestly, what's the worst *that could happen? Nothing, really.* Riley pulled her bottom lip in between her teeth. *That's it. I'm doing it.*

She was a big girl and she damn well could take her curvy butt home.

Quickly, Riley grabbed the batch of brownie-fudge creations she'd been experimenting with and placed them in her bag along with the buttercream frosting she'd made.

Riley: one.

Dimwitted brother and his best friend: zero.

Riley's lips twitched into a smirk as she finished closing her shop. This was a win-win in her book.

If she got caught, she'd give them a sample of her newest creation to distract them. And if she didn't, she'd mosey out of her room as if she'd been there the entire time and then casually offer them the treat.

Another point for me!

Either way, she was coming out on top. She'd get home early and get a new taste test out of it.

Even though Riley hadn't been too thrilled about their living situation when it first came about, especially since it meant living with Liam, she was grateful they were always there to try out what she'd made.

The corners of her mouth quirked up, turning her crooked smile into a full-blown grin as she thought about the time she made them try one of her top-selling dog biscuits. Riley swore she did it under the pretense of: *if it wasn't good for human consumption, it sure as hell wouldn't be good for her furry friends.*

Her brother, bless him, tried his best to not hurt her feelings when he mentioned they were a bit bland and dry for his taste. Liam, on the other hand, spit them out and yelled how she'd tried to poison him.

To this day, it still made her laugh. Once she finally confessed they'd eaten dog treats... hoo-boy, it might've erupted into chaos, but it was well worth it.

Riley did another shake of her hips at the memory, her laugh even louder as she clapped her hands together in excitement.

Damn, she loved her job.

With her smile firmly in place, Riley walked around the kitchen and made sure all the appliances were off. The dough was proofing and would be ready in a few hours. Her starters for her bread were fed, and everything else was set for her return.

Riley really had gotten good at all of this. Sure, she would love some extra help, but until then, damn she was proud of what she'd accomplished.

With one last look around, Riley grabbed her stuff and stepped out of the backdoor that led to the alley behind Pastries & Paws.

Once the door was locked, she pushed the strand of her chestnut hair that had escaped the messy bun from on top of her head to behind her ear. She then hiked her bag higher onto her shoulder, spinning around on her heel to head in the direction of home. "Look out world, one badass bitch is coming your way." Riley shook her hips again, doing another little dance as new determination swelled through her.

She might be plus-sized, a little too opinionated, and a whole lot of 'not society's norm,' but she didn't care. Riley gave zero craps what the world thought. She was here living her dream and was damn well going to enjoy it.

A lopsided grin appeared on her face as she took off toward home. However, Riley only made it a few steps before a faint noise caught her attention, making her pause. She scanned the area, straining her head in the direction she believed the noise came from.

Only a few seconds passed before Riley heard the noise again, this time without a shadow of a doubt, knowing it was an animal.

A cat, if she wasn't mistaken.

And a tiny one, if the cry was any indication.

Being as quiet as she could, Riley waited for the sound again. As soon as she heard it, she was able to pinpoint it coming from the dumpster behind her bakery.

Abandoning her original plan, Riley dropped her

belongings to the ground before slowly making her way toward the dumpster.

Without even a second thought, Riley fell to her knees.

Please don't be hurt.

She worried her lip as her eyes searched the area, coming up empty. "Pspspsps. Come on out." Riley continued her search, but still nothing. "Come on, little one. I know you're still here. You're safe. Trust me, I'd rather cut off my left boob before I let anything happen to you."

Riley paused for a second, pulling back as she realized what she'd said. "You probably have no idea what a boob even is." She sighed, rolling her eyes. "Basically, what I'm trying to say is, I'd rather hurt myself than hurt you."

It was faint, but Riley heard another tiny cry.

At least it was still there, right?

"Okay, my little friend, I get it. You're scared. We all get scared sometimes. It's okay. It's a part of life. But just so you understand what I'm doing here to help you, I'm *right* next to a dumpster and it's *really* starting to stink. Like really bad—"

Riley heard the cry again, cutting off her ramblings, her heart clenching as she really hoped the little guy wasn't hurt.

Another cry echoed from under the dumpster, making Riley strain her neck further under the metal box as she held her breath. "I'm one of the good ones. Animals can sense when it's good people, so you're gonna grace me with your presence, right? That way, I can help you before I vomit."

After hearing the cry once more but Riley still not being able to see anything, she sat back on her knees as she grabbed her phone from her back pocket. She then quickly flipped on the flashlight and returned to her mission.

Carefully, Riley lowered herself onto the ground.

However, since she was more focused on the cat, she missed what was lying beside her. As she braced herself on her hands, she moved slightly to the left, causing something to squish under her palm.

"Ahhh!" Riley jumped back, her eyes honing in on her hand. "Ewww." She gagged as she looked at what she hoped was a rotten banana peel.

As she flicked it off, she glared up toward the darkening sky. "That better have been what I thought it was, Universe. I get I'm a joke to you, but can you cut me some slack? All I want to do—"

Riley snapped her mouth shut the moment she heard the small cry. Forgetting about the gloppy mess on her hand, Riley dropped back down, her flashlight illuminating the underside of the dumpster. "Sorry about that," she whispered. "I got distracted. I didn't mean to scare you." As she moved the flashlight, her heart stopped when she finally saw two small glowing eyes staring back at her. "There you are!"

Her heart hammered against her chest as she watched the very tiny kitten. "Hi, little one. I'm Riley," she murmured, trying not to scare it further. "Aren't you a cutie? Come here, kitty. Pspspsps. I'm gonna help you."

The kitten slowly blinked but didn't move.

"Is pspspsps offensive?" Riley asked, her lips pursing. "I apologize. It's probably offensive. No one wants to be catcalled. Especially not a cat. Wait, is that what I just did? Did I catcall you?" Riley groaned. "Good goin', Rye."

Screw it.

Drastic moments called for drastic measures.

Pushing the fact she was crawling under a dumpster out of her mind, Riley laid on her stomach, doing the best she could to maneuver toward the kitten. As she reached with all her might, she held her breath, cursing her larger figure as it stopped her from going further under the dumpster.

Body, don't fail me now. We're on a mission. We're almost there. Just a little further.

Riley was less than an inch from the kitten. She just needed to reach a litt—

Thunk.

A loud bang echoed through the area from the other end of the alley, causing the kitten to jump. It stared at her for the briefest of seconds before it took off in the opposite direction.

"Gahh!" Harrumphing, Riley crawled from under the dumpster and sat back on her knees. "Shit." As she stood, she wiped her hands down her jeans. "Double shit."

Riley's eyes searched the area, but the kitten was nowhere in sight.

"Damn it all to hell."

With a new sense of urgency, Riley rushed back into her bakery. As quickly as she could, Riley grabbed some dry cat food she kept on hand, a cardboard box, a bowl of water and some towels. Once she was back in the alley, Riley placed the box right outside the backdoor and put two towels inside. She then put a bowl of water and the plate of food next to it.

"I was so close. Dang it."

Worrying her bottom lip, Riley glanced around, her heart bottoming out when she realized the kitten must be long gone.

"Freaking great." She sighed, her shoulders slumping, as her eyes moved to the box, her heart clenching again. At least there was food and water now. Hopefully by morning, the kitten would be back and Riley could figure out what to do then.

The moment Riley pocketed her phone, she got a good

whiff of herself. "Good Lord. Ew." Her eyes narrowed toward the sky again. "You really just needed to add insult to injury here, now, didn't ya?"

Throwing her hands in the air, Riley huffed as she picked up her bag from the ground. With one last scan of the empty alley, Riley's stomached bottomed out, her heart clenching even further.

"I'm gonna go now. I'll be back in the morning. There is a nice warm box for you to sleep in and some food and water. Please, *please* be safe."

Riley's gut twisted, but there was nothing she could do about it. She could only hope for the best once she got back to the bakery in a few hours.

With that, Riley headed in the direction of home.

CHAPTER TWO

Since Riley was in a hurry to get home and into a shower, her walk only lasted around ten minutes. Although, with each step she took, her worry for the kitten continued to gnaw at her.

She couldn't help it.

The little guy looked so helpless under the dumpster, and the fact Riley couldn't do anything about it made her stomach twist into knots.

Doing her best not to focus on the what-ifs, Riley told herself she'd have better luck tomorrow and walked up the front steps to the home she shared with her brother and his best friend.

At this point, she was just glad to be home. More so, since at this rate, she was looking at maybe—if she were lucky—getting in a power nap before having to head right back to the bakery.

That was fine by her. She'd lose every bit of her sleep if it meant helping someone or something.

Sleep didn't matter when there was a poor tiny kitten in need.

Riley did a quick nod of her chin, agreeing with herself.

However, in the process, her eyes caught the sight of her hand, making her grimace.

Sleep was definitely gonna be an issue. Who knows how long I'm gonna have to shower to get all the smell off?

"Better get a move on. Time's a-wastin'." Riley grabbed her key from her pocket to open the front door. However, before she even had a chance to insert it into the lock, the door swung open, causing her to jump back.

"Ahhh! Holy shit!" Riley's hand flung to her chest as she lost her balance. Thankfully, a firm hand pulled her back right before she hit the ground.

"Please fucking tell me you did *not* walk home alone, Riley?" Patrick, her brother, snapped as he righted her.

Crap. She'd been so focused on the kitten she'd forgotten her master plan.

As Riley stared at her brother, her mind racing to come up with an excuse, her heart pounded against her chest. "Geez, Patrick. For Pete's sake, you could've given me a heart attack."

"I'm Pat, not Pete." His face contorted with his brow lifting, but his classic playful attitude still shined through, even if he was pissed. Then, out of nowhere, his lips pursed as his nose wrinkled. "What the hell is that smell?"

Dang, he didn't have to look at her like *that*. Gritting her teeth, Riley mimicked his stance, crossing her arms over her chest. "You come home smelling like shit all the time and I don't give you crap about it."

"Yeah, but I don't smell like I rolled around in something that died."

Riley gasped, her brows nearly shooting off her forehead as her hand jumped to her chest. "Rude."

Maybe it was her worry about the kitten, the fact she smelled like trash, or that Patrick scared the living daylights out of her, but right now, Riley wasn't in the mood for one of his "parenting" lectures.

Realizing it was best to ignore him, Riley tried to edge past her brother, only for Patrick to move, blocking her attempt.

"I don't think so. Explain. You know better than to walk home by yourself. We've had this conversation. A lot, might I add." There went his stupid brow, cocking again.

Okay, yeah, her last nerve was stepped on.

Riley's jaw firmed as she narrowed her eyes on her brother. "I'm a grown adult, Pat. I can walk home on my own. If I can own a bakery, I can sure as shit walk home."

His other brow lifted only further frustrating her. She loved her brother more than anything in this world, but right now, she really wanted to punch him in the nose.

Riley usually would've backed down by now, apologizing so she could move on with what she needed to do, but tonight was different. Against her better judgment, she continued, "I know you pretty much had to take care of me when we were kids, but I'm almost twenty-eight. That's really close to thirty. I'm an adult now."

Patrick stared her down, his gaze piercing right through her, making Riley's stomach flop. She hated fighting with him, but dang it. Sometimes it was just too much.

Even for the usually level-headed Riley.

"I don't know what crawled up your ass today, but this isn't an argument, Rye. Either Liam or I walk or drive you to and from the bakery when it's dark. Those have and will always be the rules. I don't care how old you are. You're my little sister and I'm always gonna make sure you're safe."

"How old *I* am? Patrick, you're *only* five years older than me."

"Which still makes me older."

"You don't need to protect me. I'm fine. I can protect myself."

"Riley..." Patrick pinned her with his glare.

"Gahh." She pushed past him, this time succeeding before dropping her bag onto the counter. She then spun in his direction; her hands propped on her hips. "Just 'cause you're my older brother and I have to live here doesn't mean you get to constantly boss me around."

"The moment me and Liam placed all our savings into opening Pastries & Paws, we became the rule-makers. Might I remind you that little fact is the reason we all have to live here together in the first place?"

How could she forget? Riley rolled her eyes. He constantly liked reminding her, as did Liam, for that matter. She crossed her arms over her ample chest again as she stared her brother down. She didn't ask them to front her the money. They offered. If she'd known then what a headache it would have been, Riley would've turned them down and gone ahead with her original plan of saving up half and then getting a loan for the rest.

"You know I wish it wasn't this way either. Don't you think it's about time I live on my own for once? It's always been me and you, and now it's me, you, and Liam. I'm older, Pat. I *am* an adult and I want to be treated like one. You don't need to keep protecting me. There is nothing to protect me from." Riley threw her hands in the air. "While I'm at it, I'm so freaking tired of always having to wait for one of you."

"If it's dark out, one of us comes to get you," he stated, matter of fact.

"Why?" Riley propped her hand on her hip. "Please explain it to me."

"Men are pigs."

Riley's brows dented at his words. Well, damn, Patrick had her there.

If her time on earth had taught her anything, it would be that men *were* pigs, and relationships were stupid. And love was nothing but a joke.

That's why Riley loved baking.

Baking was simple and safe.

You followed instructions and if you did it right, you'd get a masterpiece that tasted so damn good it was better than sex.

Not that Riley would know. The one and only date she'd gone on in high school resulted in her technically getting to third base, although it was more like base two and a half, and sadly, it wasn't by choice. Riley wasn't even sure how the simple date to the movies ended up with them making out in the back of his car, only for the jerk to push for more.

Riley instantly shuddered, her lips thinning as she remembered the night her date tried to force himself on her. Yanking up her shirt, touching her in ways she wasn't comfortable with as his hands pushed under the band of her jeans.

It all happened so fast.

Thank God she'd learned some self-defense from Patrick and Liam.

Before Riley knew it, she had her date pinned to the backseat after decking him in the nose, breaking it. Unfortunately for her, the moment the sleaze-ball got his bearings, he physically kicked her out of the car on the dark street, leaving a bruise on her hip. The jerk had even shouted some really awful stuff at her before driving away with zero remorse.

Geez, that night.

That freaking night. God... The night before her graduation.

It would have been one thing if she'd gotten to walk home, lick her wounds and move on, but no. *Liam* had to be the one to find her limping along the street, favoring the hip that was screaming out in pain.

At first, she'd been thankful someone was there to save her, but seeing who was behind the wheel was another sucker punch to her already bruised soul.

At the time, their friendship had been rocky. And to this day, Riley never really knew what happened. One day the fun-to-hang-around, caring, annoyingly attractive Liam, who made her laugh was gone, and in came the grumpy, grunting, always-seemed-to-be-glaring-at-her Liam. She couldn't help but wonder if it was her fault for his sudden change. Like he somehow figured out she had a crush on him.

It had been so freaking abrupt.

Riley got it, though. Who would want their plain-Jane, too curvy, best friend's little sister fawning all over them?

She blanched, thinking about how idiotic she'd been when she was younger, pining over her brother's best friend.

Give her a break.

But it wasn't all bad. When Liam had pushed her away, Riley found herself with his mom, Rhonda Kelly, more and more. And in that time, Rhonda introduced her to baking. It was more than that though, Rhonda taught her so much. Self-love, resilience, setting boundaries, and being true to who she was.

Riley could confidently say she was who she was because of Rhonda Kelly, and she wouldn't change that for the world.

Actually, both of Liam's parents were the reason Riley

and her brother turned out so well. Lord knew her biological parents were trash on so many levels.

Riley closed her eyes tightly as she attempted to force the memories to fade away.

That night had changed so much in Riley's life. And weirdly enough, it'd changed with Liam, too.

He wasn't as harsh with her anymore, and he'd made a point to be involved in her life. It was like a switch flipped inside him again.

Okay, normal wasn't the right term. He still had his hot and cold moments, but their friendship was back for the most part.

So much so, she swore he'd sometimes flirt with her, which never bode well for her *crush* that was supposed to be dead and gone.

But then again, what did Riley know about flirting? For all she knew, it could've been just normal behavior. And since she was *still* nursing that ridiculous crush on him even after all this time, she never knew what way was up.

Which was an understatement, because when it came to Liam, it was like her brain took a running leap off the nearest cliff.

It also didn't help he was always the one to somehow save her. From Liam being the one to catch her when she fell out of the tree in his parents' backyard, to him being the one to show up not only after the incident before her graduation but the one and only other time she'd gone out on a date—which also ended in a disaster.

He was there.

It was always Liam who stepped and picked up the pieces for her.

No wonder Riley was half-way in lo—*No*.

No wonder she had a crush on him.

Riley should've known love and relationships weren't in

the cards for her, but she never claimed she was smart in that department. Lord knew her supposed role models were a prime example of what not to do.

Riley shook her head as the night of her twenty-first birthday came rolling back to her. She'd met an attractive guy earlier that week at the library, and somehow, they got to talking. And before Riley knew it, after mentioning she was turning twenty-one on Friday, the handsome man insisted on taking her out for a drink and a nice dinner to celebrate.

A date.

A freaking *date*.

It was supposed to be her first real date, and Riley had been over the moon. Maybe this was the start of turning her love life around?

When she got home to tell Patrick, and inadvertently Liam since he was there as usual, they'd been pissed. Liam more than Patrick.

After arguing for a solid hour, they reluctantly agreed to let her go. She promised to keep her phone on her and be home early. She even agreed on meeting the guy at the restaurant versus him picking her up, for safety. Which if you asked Riley was stupid since she didn't need permission to go on a date, but seeing as it was her first date since that night, it was nice to somewhat get their blessing, even if they were iffy on the situation.

It was better than nothing.

Riley had been so excited. Not only was she going on a date with a drop-dead gorgeous hunk, she was also turning twenty-one. Honestly, at that moment, life couldn't get any better. And maybe if things went well, she'd finally be able to bury her crush on Liam.

When Riley and her date arrived at the restaurant and took their seats, she was damn near giddy when she told the waitress she'd like a glass of red wine, with her date quickly ordering the same.

However, the moment Riley ordered the steak since she remembered Rhonda telling her red wine went better with red meat, the guy suggested she should have a salad instead.

The audacity of him.

Riley's jaw hit the floor for only a second before she picked it back up, tossed her napkin on the table, and promptly told him to unkindly fuck off.

Yeah, it stung, but Riley felt empowered at the same time. As she walked home to the apartment, she tried calling Patrick first to let him know what happened, but he didn't answer.

So, with her tail between her legs, she called the other person she knew she could rely on.

Riley had been surprised Liam answered before the first ring finished. His voice held a panic she wasn't familiar with, and before Riley knew it, she'd told him what happened and how she was on her way home.

Then, to her utter surprise, Liam pulled alongside her within minutes, demanding she got into the car. He'd explained he'd been close by since he had a bad feeling about the guy and wanted to keep an eye on her.

If it were anyone else, or any other situation, she would've been pissed he was spying on her. But seeing as his gut feeling turned out to be right, she wasn't all that angry. She was just glad to be on her way back home to once again lick her wounds and solidify dating and the opposite sex was not for her... At least that was Riley's plan until she realized Liam was not headed in the direction of her apartment.

Nope.

Instead, he took her to a local pub where he bought Riley her first drink. The rest of the night was a blur, but she somewhat recalled Patrick storming into the bar, ready to murder not soon after they'd arrived. After calming him down, they all ended up drinking and having a good time celebrating her birthday.

Although if she remembered correctly, Liam only had one shot, so she'd be free to enjoy her birthday the way she was meant to.

It'd been sweet, minus the hangover the next day.

And as Riley nursed her hangover, cursing herself, she swore that would be the last time she'd let Liam show up as her knight.

Okay, fine, it might have happened a few more times, like when she'd gotten stuck in the bathroom when the door jammed, or other non-life-threatening issues, but never because of a date or a relationship.

Hell no.

And as she always said, feelings were ridiculous. They only caused more harm than good. And Riley would rather spend her life brightening other people's day than daydreaming about love and all that garbage. *Especially* if the subject of her head in the clouds always seemed to be Liam.

Riley's throat thickened, as she did her best to fight her asinine feelings once again.

Damn, it was pathetic.

She'd already resided herself to the fact she would be a twenty-eight-year-old virgin soon, and she'd probably end up dying before she popped her elusive cherry.

Riley snorted, her eyes flicking upward. Cherries were made for pies and to be topped on delicious sweets.

Nothing else.

Blahh.

Riley rolled her shoulders, desperately trying to release the tension. She was happy where she was in her life. And even though it annoyed her, she appreciated that her brother looked out for her. If it wasn't for him and Liam, she wouldn't be where she was right now. She was lucky to have them, even if they agitated her at times.

"Earth to Riley. Where'd you go?" Patrick's face softened as he got her attention.

"Huh?"

"Rye." He sighed. "You know I'm only a hard-ass 'cause I worry about you."

"I'm sorry, Pat. I know. You're right. I should've called. To be honest, it's been a night and I wasn't thinking," she mumbled.

When she glanced back at her brother's face, the concern she saw only twisted her gut further.

"Anything I need to know about?" he asked, his eyes scanning her as if to pinpoint what could've been wrong.

There he was again, ready to fight for her. She might've gotten the shit end of the stick when it came to parents, but Riley really did luck out when it came to her brother. Liam, too, if she were being honest.

"Does it have anything to do with why you smell like something died?" Patrick asked, jarring her out of her thoughts once again.

However, the moment Riley opened her mouth to answer, the front door flung open, revealing Liam Kelly as he stepped inside their home. He was still in his Kelly's Auto uniform, which had a grease stain right across the front of his chest, where the shamrock logo was.

Riley jumped back, her breath stalling in her throat as she stared at him, letting herself fully take in his presence.

Holy sugar biscuits.

Liam looked annoyingly attractive, as usual, which was agitating.

Even as a dirty mess, Liam still looked fan-freakingtastic. His work shirt clung to his broad chest, showcasing his muscles.

Hoo-boy those muscles. She swallowed as her eyes scanned him involuntarily. His normally perfect dark-brown hair was messy and out of place from a hard day's work.

And his jaw, his chiseled jaw...

Dear Lord, Liam should be illegal.

Riley might've been a virgin, but she wasn't an idiot. Okay, she was a little bit of an idiot, but that was beside the point.

Riley knew when someone had sex appeal. And Liam Kelly had more sex appeal than should be allowed. It was moments like this when the sheer masculine presence of Liam made Riley weak in the knees, and her crush would come rolling back like a punch to her solar plexus.

Even though Riley knew she wasn't supposed to think of him in that way, she couldn't help ogling him every once in a while.

Okay, maybe more than every once in a while.

Riley mentally shrugged, trying to justify it.

The years of working in his father's auto shop made Liam the perfect subject for the appreciation of the male physique.

That wasn't her fault. She was just doing the Lord's work if you asked her. You know, appreciating and admiring what was in front of her.

It would be rude if she didn't.

Although, with that same logic, Riley did her best to ignore the fact her brother worked right alongside Liam their whole lives, both filling out as they grew.

Oh, good going, now you're gonna vomit. Great job, Rye. You're winning the lottery tonight, aren't cha?

Riley focused on Liam's face, doing her best to keep her eyes from traveling up and down his body.

"I'm home," Liam announced, like they couldn't tell. His eyes focused on them before scrunching his nose in disgust. "What the fuck is that smell?"

Patrick quickly pointed a finger in her direction. "That would be her."

Instantly, Liam's eyes darted to Riley, his brows pulling together as he scanned her up and down.

Oh, geez.

Under Liam's intense scrutiny, Riley cursed herself the second her cheeks flushed. However, as Riley damned her body for betraying her, Liam's face quickly morphed into even more disgust.

It was an instant punch to her gut, as the foolish desire she had not only a second before turned into shame. It didn't matter if she knew Liam would never see her as anything other than his best friend's annoying, plus-sized little sister.

That shit hurt.

No one wanted to be looked at like *that*.

Wonderful. Absolutely freaking wonderful.

As Riley did her best to push down the hurt, she straightened her shoulders, refusing to let him see what his reaction did to her.

Liam's nose wrinkled as he continued his scrutiny. "Did you fart?"

"For fuck's sake." Riley threw her hands in the air. "Ugh. Men really are pigs. Lesson learned loud and clear. Thanks for the reminder, Pat."

Doing everything she could to tamp down her pain, Riley snatched her bag off the counter to distract herself.

Freaking pathetic.

"What's with all the attitude?" Liam shut the door behind him, fully stepping into their home.

Crap!

Before Riley could stop him, she heard her brother.

"She walked home alone."

The bag Liam held fell to the floor with a loud thump, causing Riley to jump.

"You didn't," he growled, deep from within his throat.

Son-of-a-b-hole. Great, now he's gonna be all angry and annoying.

Riley knew with everything inside of her, she should've just gritted her teeth, agreed with them, and moved on. Instead, she spun toward them. "It wasn't a big deal."

"I don't give a fuck if it was just next door from the bakery. You don't walk home alone." Liam's eyes hardened as he glared down at her, his shoulders lifting, making him bigger than she wanted to admit.

"Holy moly. You're acting like I robbed a bank," she grumbled, propping her hands on her hips. "Fine, I'll say it. I shouldn't have walked home when it was dark out by myself. There, you happy?" She huffed. And before she could stop, she mumbled, "I don't know why you guys get like this. It's not like anyone would steal me. I weigh too much for that. I wouldn't fetch a high price on the market."

As her brain registered the words she'd said, her eyes widened. *Oh, crap. Crap, crap, crap. A million freakin' times crap.*

It was like her brain-to-mouth filter had taken a vacation.

"What'd you say?" Liam's voice was sharp.

Riley's eyes shifted throughout the room. "Depends on what you heard?"

Oh, shit. Riley, shut up. Abort now! Think fast, Rye. Fix this, distract them!

As fast as she could, Riley grabbed her brownie-fudge creations and shoved them between Patrick and Liam. "I brought home goodies!"

Liam cocked his brow, his arms crossing over his broad chest, his stare still pinning her in place. "You walked home alone, Riley. You know that shit isn't safe."

Riley had to figure a way out of this mess, get into the shower, and get to bed if she planned on getting any sleep. And as much as she hated doing so, Riley let her eyes round all doe-like as she poked out her bottom lip. With everything she could muster, she spoke in the sweetest tone possible, "I made buttercream frosting to go on top…"

Liam's eyes darted to the pan of treats and then back to Riley. However, as he honed his focus on her, the intensity in his gaze made a tingle shoot through her lower stomach right to her—

Not now, body! Ugh, can you get a grip on yourself?

Doing the best she could to ignore her stupid body, Riley swallowed past the lump that formed in her throat, waiting for any sort of reaction from Liam.

"Why do you always think food can get you out of everything?" he asked, his brows pulling together.

However, as Riley focused on him, she could see behind the anger in his eyes was also worry, which made her feel even worse. They cared about her, which she appreciated, but damn… sometimes it was just a lot.

"Because it does." Riley shrugged, the left corner of her mouth slightly rising, as she hoped her attempt at a lame joke would ease the tension in the room.

"She has a point." Patrick grabbed one of the treats from Riley, shoving it into his mouth. "Damn, these are good. Holy shit. What are these? You better put this on the menu." He grabbed another one.

See, food made everything better. Who needed relationships and all that garbage when you could defuse any situation with the right sweet treat or savory?

Riley wasn't picky.

She'd long since given up on her unhealthy relationship with food. There was no point in hating the thing that was meant to help keep you alive. Besides, it's not like you could stop eating altogether.

Smokers could stop smoking. Alcoholics could stop drinking. But you needed food to live. So why go your whole life hating something that you needed to survive?

Thankfully, Riley was saved from going down that train of thought once again when Patrick broke her trance. "Liam, here. Holy shit, it's like caramel, brownies, and maybe fudge, had a baby, then add in..." He stopped for a split second. "I don't know, all things good wrapped into one fuckin' little square. Eat it." He shoved the piece at his best friend.

However, instead of taking it, Liam kept his gaze glued on Riley. "You know it's not safe to walk home alone."

"We live in a pretty safe area, so I beg to differ." There went her no-brain-to-mouth filter again. Riley mentally hit herself on the forehead. *Shut up. We're trying to get out of this situation, not make it worse.*

Liam's brows nearly shot off his gorgeous, angry, growly face. "Excuse me?"

As the next words came out of Riley's mouth, there was no stopping her. "I'm just saying. It's not like we live in the crime capital of the world. I'm sure I'll be fine if I walk home by myself every once in a while."

"Riley," he warned.

"It's fine. I promise I was fine. Nothing happened."

"What if it did? What if one of us weren't there to help you?"

"Nothing would happen, okay?" Riley shrugged. Lord,

this was getting out of hand. "Now, try a piece before he eats them all." Riley grabbed a square and handed it to Liam before Patrick snatched the tin from Riley's hand.

"Mine," Patrick staked his claim, clutching the treats to his chest.

Leave it to her brother to always find a way to make her laugh. Instantly, her body relaxed. Thank God she didn't know how much more of this she could take.

Another grunt sounded from her side, causing Riley to pivot back toward Liam.

For freak's sake.

She cocked her brow at him. "Are you gonna try it or not? We don't have all night."

Something flashed across Liam's face and even though she couldn't tell what it was, he did as she requested and tossed the square into his mouth.

She watched Liam close his eyes, analyzing the taste, while she held her breath. Riley didn't know why, but she really wanted Liam to like this one. She'd spent weeks trying to perfect her recipe. And it had some of his favorite flavors in it.

After a few more seconds, her heart racing a million miles an hour, Liam opened his eyes. "They're good, kid."

Kid...

Riley's heart stopped as her stomach bottomed out.

Freaking-a, that hurt.

Like really hurt. More than she wanted to admit. "If you don't like them, it's fine." Riley's heart sank even further as she lied.

She wasn't sure if it was the fact she took a walk down memory lane, her brother yelled at her, the worry of the kitten, she smelled horrible, or now, the fact Liam didn't like what she'd made, but she wanted to crawl into a hole and stay there.

She'd worked really hard on those babies for nearly a month.

A month.

"Didn't say that."

"How could you not like them, Lee?" Patrick moaned as he plopped another past his lips. "These are the best brownies I've ever had. Wait, are they brownies?" Patrick turned to his sister, his brow arching.

Riley shrugged her answer, still feeling the sting of Liam's reaction.

At least her brother liked them.

"Whatever the hell they are, add them to the menu. They'll sell out every day. Make an extra batch tomorrow so I can bring them to the shop. I know the guys would love 'em." Patrick tossed the last one into his mouth, closed his eyes and released another moan.

"Will do." Riley's voice was small even to her own ears, but she still relished in the fact at least her brother liked what she'd created. "Now, if you'd both excuse me, I need to take a shower. I crawled under a dumpster for twenty minutes."

Their eyes sprang to her like she'd sprouted an extra head.

"Do you care to explain?" Patrick asked, giving her a once-over.

"Not really." Riley took a step toward the hall leading to her bedroom.

Shower and bed.

That's all she wanted.

Riley took another step in her escape, but Liam's hand grabbed her elbow, making her spin back to him. "They're good, Rye."

Liam's eyes were softer this time, but she didn't quite believe him. Doing her best to hide her disappointment,

Riley straightened her shoulders, pushing down her hurt as she nodded. "Thanks." She turned to her brother. "I have to go in at three tomorrow. Do you think you can take me?"

Patrick's eyes widened for a split second before he grumbled, "Yeah. Three is fine."

"I could walk myself, but after this lovely conversation we've just had, I'd rather not get yelled at again."

"Riley—"

"See you at three." She spun on her heel and headed down the hall. She'd only made it a few steps before she heard her brother's voice.

"Why're you such an ass? Those were some of the best things she's ever made and you know it."

Riley slowed for a brief second as she waited for Liam's response, her heart stopping as she hoped he'd say something positive.

However, when all she heard was Liam grunt, Riley's heart sank again.

With more determination this time, Riley hurried toward her bedroom. Once she made it safely inside, she closed the door, forcing herself to have only one thought racing through her mind.

I hope the kitten is okay...

CHAPTER THREE

Regret burned through Liam's veins as he watched the curvy figure of his best friend's little sister disappear down the hall toward her room.

The room that was right next to his.

All the feelings he tried to conveniently keep locked inside a box over the years came rushing to the surface, only causing his anger at the situation and himself to heighten. He couldn't help it. What if something happened to Riley...

Liam shook his head. No. That wasn't an option.

Yeah, they lived in a safe area. He'd give her that, but honestly, you never know. And the thought of Riley putting herself in danger... fuck him, that's something Liam couldn't handle. And instead of voicing his concerns like a grown-ass adult, he let his anger get the better of him.

"What the hell was that about? I know you had a fucked-up day at work, but did you really have to bring the assholeness home with you?" Patrick punched Liam in the arm. His eyes narrowed as he scowled at him.

"What?"

"I get it, trust me. You don't have to be a fuckface and let work shit bleed over here. You know she thinks a lot of our opinion when it comes to her experiments. Yeah, she walked home when she knows she shouldn't have. You could've just bitched at her about that. You didn't have to make her feel like shit."

Fuck. Patrick was right. Yeah, he was pissed she walked home, but he didn't mean for his shit day to add fuel to his anger.

"You gonna say anything?"

With Liam's feelings right at the surface, he knew he needed to tread lightly. He didn't mean to be an ass about it, but he couldn't help it. When it came to Riley, everything was more intense. With all the years watching on the sidelines, there were times he couldn't control himself.

"I wasn't trying to be an ass. Although it is fun to rile her every now and again." At least that was only partially a lie.

Nevertheless, he didn't want her upset, and that's exactly what he'd done.

It's like he could never do the right thing when it came to Riley O'Neil. Fucking Lord knows he'd been trying, and look how well that'd turned out for him.

Patrick shook his head, exhaling sharply as he grabbed the tin that once held Riley's newest treats. He looked under it, then around it, and then under it again, hoping he'd find more. "Now she's gonna sulk in her room, or worse." Patrick moved his attention from the tin to him. "The next time she brings something home for us to test, we won't know if she put rat poison in it."

"Riley wouldn't have rat poison. If she'd found a rat, she'd probably convince it to be her friend." Which was true. During all the years he'd known her, she'd sneak anything into her room, claiming the creature was now her responsibility. He couldn't even count the number of times he found her with a box full of snails, giving each one a name.

Liam rolled his eyes at the memory. Thank God they'd convinced her not to bring any pets home since they started living together. Although he'd be lying to himself if he thought their rule of no animals actually held any substance.

Liam knew without a doubt the only reason their home wasn't full of pets was because the bakery took up all of Riley's time.

And, well... fuck, even admitting it made Liam want to punch himself in the gut. But he knew if Riley brought a pet home, it would make everything too real.

Too much like they were actually together.

Too white-picket fence, two point five kids, and a pet to go along with it.

Liam knew, he *knew* he couldn't have that. No matter how bad his mind begged for it.

Craved it.

Demanded it.

No matter how much it killed him, he would never cross that line.

Patrick thumped the tin on the counter with a chuckle, jarring Liam out of his thoughts. "You're probably right, Lee, but you could've pulled back on the asshole part."

"I wasn't that much of an ass," he grumbled. "I was pissed she walked home alone and it got the better of me. This isn't new and each time she does it, she gives us something she's made and we forgive her."

"I know." However, as Patrick said the words, Liam watched as his best friend's eyes honed in on the tin once again, looking for any crumbs, negating his words. "She's little miss independent. She has been since we were kids. Riley's never gonna change. She's always assumed she had to take care of herself. I blame our parents. She grew up too fast 'cause of that, and Riley thinks she can handle everything on her own. She feels she has to."

"She doesn't," Liam stated as a matter of pure fact. "She has me, my mom, dad, and more importantly, Riley has you." He knew where Patrick was coming from, but Riley knew she wasn't alone.

Patrick closed his eyes after a brief flash of pain ran across them. "I know that, and you know that. But deep down, she still thinks she can do it all on her own..." Patrick's shoulders turned in like he knew he'd failed her.

"That's not—"

Patrick held up his hand. "She didn't call me when that fuckface—"

"We took care of it. Don't blame yourself for that night." Liam stopped him. Although, he needed to tell himself that as well. The guilt he held on to still wreaked havoc on him even after all these years.

Liam didn't know when his feelings for his best friend's little sister changed, but they had. And once he realized it, he knew he should never go there. It was better for both of them, so Liam did what any sensible, responsible guy would do.

He took the coward's way out and kept her at a distance. And before he knew it, he had no idea what was going on in her life, when he used to know it all.

Even her pet rocks' names.

It all happened so fast.

And for what, his own self-preservation? That's all it was. He didn't know how to handle the new wave of feelings she'd sparked in him, and instead of figuring it out and dealing with it, he'd pushed her away.

Just thinking about it made him want to punch himself.

He'd been blindsided the night he found her walking

home alone, limping, with her eyes red as tears streamed down her cheeks.

Talk about a fucking punch to the gut.

That night was still burned in the back of his mind and it was never going away. When he'd asked her what happened, all he got was the brush-off and mumblings about a date.

Liam didn't even know she'd had a date.

Patrick did.

His mom did.

His dad did.

Everyone but him knew.

Liam pinched his eyes closed as the memory washed over him for the millionth time. He never wanted to see Riley hurt again. He might not have been able to protect her at the beginning of that night, but he swore on everything inside him he'd do whatever it took to keep her safe going forward.

And he had.

No matter what it was, he was there for her.

And the worst part, she forgave him for being an asshole. Plain and simple. But that was Riley. She had a heart of gold.

The world was better because she brightened it.

It was just more reason for him to want her more. Riley's kind heart *always* won out. She really was a bright light in an otherwise shitty world.

And with all the crap thrown at her, from her parents to the shit-tastic dates, hell, even to how he treated her when he was sorting out his feelings, Riley still found the good in everyone. She would give the shirt off her back if it meant helping someone. And because of that, she'd forgiven him, and he'd never been more grateful.

Because having Riley in his life, even if it wasn't in the context he dreamed of, was better than not having her at all.

Liam's eyes quickly darted to his best friend, his fists clenching at his sides in order to stop himself from punching Patrick. "I *assumed* you'd picked her up since you went home from the shop early." At Patrick's raised brow, Liam glared at the ceiling in pure frustration. "You know what? I should've known better."

"What's that supposed to mean?" Patrick squared his shoulders. "Newsflash, Lee, *I* assumed you were getting her since you got off at the same time she'd be closing. It's not my fault we got our wires crossed. It's been ages since she tried to walk home on her own. When she didn't text the group message, I figured *you'd* called her to let her know you'd gotten off work and were picking her up."

Liam grunted as more annoyance raced through him. He should've known better. Fuck, he did know better. You never assume anything when it came to Riley or Patrick, for that matter. He'd long since learned that lesson.

The events of the night crawled at Liam's skin as he worked to control his emotions. His shitty day started when he'd gotten the sloppy seconds of another mechanic shop whose shit service almost caused a battery to blow up in his face.

Thank fuck the hood had been down.

Once he'd gotten the battery dealt with, the amount of other shit wrong with the SUV had been a cluster-fuck, to say the least. The other shop's pure negligence could've cost the customer their life, or his if he hadn't been more careful. And clearly, he'd brought that agitation home with him, even if he didn't want to believe it.

All Liam *wanted* to do was go home, eat, drink a beer, and if he were lucky, somehow convince Riley to watch something with him in the living room. That way, in his own fucked-up mind, he could continue the charade of Riley being his. That he was coming home to her welcoming arms and he could get lost inside her.

But, no.

That wasn't reality and it never would be.

Liam shook everything off. He didn't know why he bothered with his farfetched fantasy anyway. It was the number one rule written in the Bro Code.

You never go after your best friend's sister.

Especially their younger sister.

That was a huge fucking no.

Even knowing that, Liam still couldn't stop his mind from pretending it was different. He'd even gotten damn lucky when most of the nights she agreed to watch something with him, she'd end up falling asleep.

And rightfully so. She worked hard. Harder than anyone he knew.

Again, cue his screwed-up mind, since Liam used that to his advantage. The moment she'd fall asleep, he'd take the time to watch her. Memorize the curves of her body, and commit to memory the soft sounds of her sleeping.

Over the last God knew how long, she'd occupied every part of his mind. Her smile, her laugh, her unique amber-colored eyes. And don't even get him started on her curves.

Fuck, her curves.

Liam's body immediately tightened as he thought about her body.

Pinching his eyes closed, he took in a shuddering breath. He was constantly on edge. Anyone would be when their perfect wet dream was inches from them, only to never be allowed to act on it.

He'd give anything to feel Riley in more than just a platonic hug or accidental touching. Although, to be honest a lot of the *accidental* touching wasn't very accidental on his part.

Liam craved Riley, and he couldn't help it.

But no matter how intense Liam's desire was for her, you don't mess with the best friend code. Besides, Patrick was more than a best friend to him. He was like a brother, which should mean Riley was supposed to be his little sister.

Too bad his brain never got the memo.

It wasn't ideal, but it was better than nothing. Having her in his life in any context was better than not at all.

So two years ago, when Riley told Patrick about her dreams of one day owning a bakery, and then Patrick let it slip in the shop, it was the perfect excuse to get what he wanted without getting what he wanted in a roundabout way.

Before he knew it, he jumped at the chance and began to set his plan in motion.

After working his whole life in his dad's shop, he'd accumulated a pretty hefty savings. He knew Patrick did too. It only took Liam merely dropping the hint of them funding her bakery for Patrick to be on board and run wild with the idea.

He knew his best friend would move heaven and earth for Riley. Liam would too. And this is where he admitted he was selfish. Liam knew for a fact if they helped Riley, the only way to survive would be for them to all live together.

It would be a win-win for him. He'd get to be near her every day and be a part of her life. He'd get to see the more intimate side of Riley O'Neil but never cross that line.

There was only one problem with Liam's plan, though, and everything had already been set in motion once he realized it.

Having Riley so close to him and not being able to act on his true desires was miserable.

Actually, miserable wasn't the right word. It was fucking torture. To have the person you desire more than life itself so close and yet so fucking far was unbearable.

He was hanging on by a thread.

But he'd suck it up if it meant he got to be near Riley. And he did. He made a point to be involved in her life and make time to be with her when she wasn't at Pastries & Paws.

As if on cue, Liam's ear perked as he heard Riley's bedroom door open and close before the bathroom door did the same. He stilled, his breath catching in his throat as he waited. The moment the shower turned on, he closed his eyes, swallowing, willing his body to not react.

They had a small, modest, three-bedroom, one-bath home. It would've been a little easier on him if it were at least a two-bathroom house, but the Universe wasn't on his side.

"Why do you look like that?"

Liam snapped his attention to his friend. "Like what?"

"That." Patrick's face lit as his mouth twitched. "You look like you're thinking really hard about something. Should I call the fire department?"

"Fuck off." Liam punched him in the shoulder, a little harder than he should have but, in his defense, he considered it payback for not picking up Riley from the bakery. Although, with that logic, he should punch himself too.

"Ouch, jackass. What the fuck? I'm just calling 'em as I see 'em."

"Whatever," Liam sighed, before heading to the couch and plopping down, exhausted. "Tonight's shit."

"At least you aren't the one that has to be up at three."

"You know I will," Liam grunted, his eyes honing in on him. "But I don't think she'd be happy with that."

Although, that could be fun...

Riley all mussed with sleep still in her eyes, her softness as she'd just woken up from her slumber, the intimacy of seeing the real her before she got her first cup of coffee.

Liam *loved* those moments.

It always took everything inside of him not to walk up behind Riley, put his hands on her hips, and box her in with his body before leaning down to kiss her exposed neck.

It only ignited his fantasies more.

"Nah," Patrick grumbled, drawing Liam back. "It's fine, I'll do it. Let's not piss her off more. Who knows, maybe we'll get our investment back in a few years and move out of here. I for once would like the chance to bring someone home rather than having to go to their place or a hotel," he griped.

"Yeah," Liam attempted to agree.

Patrick still got laid whenever he could. He, on the other hand, hadn't touched a soul in God knows how long. The nights his best friend would pick someone up at the bar, Liam would pretend he did too, only to make sure Patrick left first. Once he was in the clear, Liam always turned down whoever he'd been chatting with in hopes he'd end up back at the house, praying Riley was still up so he could see her.

He was absolutely pathetic and he knew it.

Liam snorted as he pushed off the couch. "Night, man. I'm going to bed. I'm exhausted."

"Same." Patrick stood. "Especially now since I gotta be up at three."

Liam nodded as Patrick moved to the kitchen.

As he headed toward his room, Liam's body involuntarily strained to hear Riley in the shower. The moment he passed the bathroom, he heard the water turn off. Damn, if that didn't ignite him all over again.

Liam could picture it now, water dripping down her curves, her skin damp. What he would give to dry her off...

Fuck. Liam did his best to hold back his groan as his lower half stirred to life. The fucker longed for her. He was so close and yet so damn far. Every. Single. Night.

Marching into his room, Liam grabbed his sleep shorts, his ears listening for the sound of Riley leaving the bathroom as he gripped the edge of his dresser with his hand.

It was only a few moments before he heard the bathroom door open, then Riley's bedroom door open and close.

Fuck.

Shutting his eyes for a second, Liam did his best to push aside the fantasy of Riley, freshly showered, warm and waiting just for him—

Shit, he needed to get a grip.

Without another thought, Liam grabbed his clothes and headed toward the shower. With any luck, it would still smell like her.

CHAPTER FOUR

RILEY ATTEMPTED to rub the tiredness out of her eyes, doing her best to stifle yet another yawn. Even though Patrick had dropped her off at the bakery over two hours ago, she still felt like she was only half awake.

She hadn't slept a wink, and when Riley had finally managed to fall asleep, the first image that popped into her mind was Liam.

It was like the Universe was trying to screw with her.

Thank everything her alarm went off when it did, otherwise, she'd be subjected to Liam slowly unbuttoning his work uniform, leaving him in—

Nope. We are not going down that road again. Stop it right the hell now.

A groan slipped past Riley's lips as she dug the palms of her hands into her eyes again. Maybe her mind had crossed wires or something and she should see a neurologist? Maybe they'd be able to rewire her delusional brain when it came to her deep-seated crush on Liam Kelly.

It would never happen.

End of story.

Riley stretched her arms over her head, rotating from side to side, desperately trying to lessen the stiffness in her shoulders. It annoyed her to no end that she was still hurt by the situation with Liam. Then add in the worry about the kitten, and it was the perfect storm for her mind to go haywire.

No wonder she'd barely gotten anything done.

It didn't help that when she'd arrived at Pastries & Paws that morning, the kitten was still nowhere to be found.

That only left her more on edge.

Riley couldn't count the times she'd gone out there *pspspspsing,* looking for the little guy, worried it was cold and hungry, or worse, hurt.

On her third time checking the backdoor, Riley swore she'd seen something by the dumpster but when she attempted to get a closer look, it was gone, making Riley's heart hurt even more.

"Gahh." Riley shook her head, trying to force the thoughts away. If it wasn't the kitten occupying her mind, it was Liam.

Why did it matter if Liam liked what she made? He wasn't the be-all and end-all. So why did she always treat his opinion like it was?

Because after all this time, you still want to impress him, dumb-dumb. You really need to get this under control. You preach how you're an adult and yet—

Riley groaned to herself. "Rhonda taught you better than this, and you know it. Stop being an idiot. It's annoying. You're annoying." Riley glared at the ceiling. "Any day now, Universe, I'd really appreciate if you'd zap these ridiculous feelings away. It's been long enough to have a crush on a guy that will never feel the same way. Please, do me a solid."

As Riley stared above her for any sign, her phone pinged. Taking it out of her pocket, she saw a text from Liam.

Riley's eyes snapped back to the ceiling. "Really? Freaking really?"

As a grumble escaped her throat, she opened the message.

LIAM

Sorry about last night, Rye. I had a shit day and took it out on you when I found out you walked home alone. Please don't walk home when it's dark out on your own. It's not safe. It worries me. And, whatever the thing was I tried last night was good. Damn good. I think you should add them to the menu. I'm sorry for not saying it last night. Maybe I can make it up to you by suffering through a baking show marathon with you?

Riley's heart fluttered in her chest for a second before she darted her eyes back to the ceiling. "Didn't I just ask you to take away the feelings? No, have him do something that makes my stomach flip. Do you think this is a joke? Am I your only source of entertainment?"

She waited a beat before sending back a message.

RILEY

It's all right. Sorry I walked home alone. I've got a lot to do, but maybe we can watch something Sunday if I get home at a decent time. And it wouldn't be 'suffering'. The baking shows are better than the crap car stuff you and Pat always have on. Have a good day at work. Please tell your dad I said hi.

Quickly, Riley closed the message thread and tossed her

phone on the counter. No matter what happened between them, Riley was always drawn to Liam. Even if she didn't want to be. There were just people you connected with in your life. Kind of like a bond you didn't know could be formed, one you had no control over.

And that's what she had with Liam.

She blew out a strained laugh. For some twisted reason, the Universe gave them the stupid bond. Maybe *them* wasn't the right choice of words since it was clearly only one-sided.

"Gahhhh," she groaned, pinching her eyes together with pure frustration.

It was safe to say he'd become the bane of her existence.

A hot, sexy bane, but still a bane, nonetheless.

And the worst part was you can't help who your mind and body were attracted to.

Ugh.

Pushing away her thoughts, Riley forced out a sharp sigh as she triple-checked her display case to ensure she was ready for the bakery to open. She had her last batch of croissants in the oven and a batch of blueberry muffins on her cooling racks.

"You're doing good," she told herself, pushing her shoulders back.

Lord, she was tired. Normally doing all the work didn't get to her as much, but damn, days like today, she'd give anything to have some help. Someone to pick up the slack when she was lacking.

Doing it on her own was a lot. Not that she was complaining. Riley loved her career. She loved Pastries & Paws.

Holy moly, sometimes she really needed an extra hand.

Riley took a deep breath as she pinched the bridge of her nose.

Today her body hurt, her heart hurt, and her mind was all sorts of messed-up. The fact she'd gotten as much done as she had was honestly a miracle, not to mention the number of times she'd found herself at the backdoor looking for any sign of the kitten. Each time she checked tugged at her heart further when the little one was nowhere to be found.

Thankfully, though, the food she'd left out had been eaten. She'd added more food and did her best to concentrate on the day's tasks, which were proving to be more challenging than normal.

Riley moved into the kitchen from the front room for what felt like the millionth time that morning. With one glance to the backdoor, she stopped herself from checking again as she reached for a pile of dough that'd been proofing.

As Riley's hands fell into muscle memory while she kneaded, her mind wandered.

She'd usually be better at keeping her disappointments in check and her thoughts from going all over the place, but for some reason, the Universe really wanted to poke her.

Lord knew she'd had enough disappointment in her life already.

Starting with her so-called parents.

Riley punched the dough a little harder than she needed to as she let out a sharp grunt.

Having kids seemed more like a requirement to them after they'd gotten married, rather than something they wanted to do.

Their parents were always too wrapped up in themselves. Either going after their next get-rich-quick scheme or taking off for weeks at a time on 'vacation' which was really only screwed-up 'business meetings' where they tried luring unsuspecting people who were down on their luck into their 'business opportunity.' They did so freaking well hanging the golden ticket over people, making them see stars and dollar signs.

Riley cringed thinking about how many people her parents had sunk their claws into. How many families they put riffs between.

Hell, they were the main reason Riley never had any friends growing up. As soon as she'd have one her mom and dad would sweep in demanding to meet with their parents to 'make friends' only to ambush them, trying to convince them to join whatever it was they were into at that moment.

It was embarrassing.

And in the end, it only hurt the people they were supposed to love, her and Patrick. It took years for Riley to come to grips with the fact her parents used them more than loved them. And they judged everything they did with a snide remark, or worse, false encouragement.

Of course, they'd pretend to be interested in whatever it was she'd been excited about. But it was all a facade. The whole time, they were actually searching for ways to help themselves.

When Riley told them about her bakery, they'd had the gall to laugh in her face, saying it would take her years before she made a profit and how much of a waste of time it would be. Only for Riley to find out, they were telling their new unsuspecting victims that she was some hotshot baker who owned shops all over the place.

Obviously, that was a complete lie and always made Riley feel even worse. Especially when her parent's new 'business partners' stopped in her bakery only to find out the truth, which left Riley trying to explain away her parent's actions.

Again.

Riley didn't fully understand it when they were

younger, but Patrick did. And at an early age, he'd been forced to step into the parent role.

And Riley was grateful for that.

Patrick never left her alone and always made sure she was clothed, fed, and protected. When shit really got bad, somehow Riley and Patrick found themselves spending more and more time at Liam's house.

His parents were nothing like hers. They loved Liam unconditionally and then extended that love to her and Patrick.

Hell, as of right now, Riley hadn't even seen her parents in probably over two years. The last time was right after she told them about the bakery. They'd made some remarks and then disappeared off on the trail of their next big scheme.

You'd think it would've bothered her more, but after years and years of their behavior, it was safe to say she was used to it. Holidays, birthdays, hell, even the grand opening of Pastries & Paws were spent with the Kellys.

It's all Riley knew at this point.

At least she wasn't alone on the holidays, but even so, it always left a hole in her heart. It was never fun to realize what you meant to the people that were supposed to love you no matter what. Not that she wasn't grateful for Liam's parents. Quite the opposite, actually.

Riley continued working her dough, a smile gracing her lips.

She knew the love Rhonda instilled in her was why she wanted to be a baker to begin with.

It was her happy place.

A place she understood. Riley followed instructions, received guidance, and before she knew it, she was inventing her own creations and putting twists on the classics.

When Riley baked, she felt loved. She felt like there

wasn't a whole world out there trying to scheme her out of something. Instead, it was her and the dough or whatever she was making at the time. Baking would never abandon her or put making money above her.

Riley blanched, her face slightly paling. "Oh God, way to be a downer, Rye. Urrgh." Rolling her eyes, she continued kneading the dough. "You don't need to be upset or even think about those things. You had a good childhood even if it wasn't with your parents. You had Rhonda. That alone is worth its weight in gold. Look at where you are now 'cause of her." A warm smile spread across Riley's lips. No matter what happened in her younger years, she'd always be able to look back at the memories of her and Rhonda and smile.

She'd learned so much from her.

And with that knowledge, Riley could grow and experiment. She took pride in coming up with all types of treats. She was damn proud of herself. Riley worked her ass off to create what she considered masterpieces.

Yeah, she'd willingly admit some of them had come out as disasters, but that was the fun part. Learning what flavors melded together and which didn't. It was like finding the correct pieces to a puzzle.

Riley loved it.

Being able to watch something she created go from the disaster-dumpster-fire stage, to the holy-shit-this-is-freaking-fantastic stage, was a feeling she never got over.

It was a process. And by the time Riley was at the point to bring her creations home for Patrick and Liam to try, she *knew* it was good.

As Riley worked her dough, she groaned, realizing that was the reason Liam's reaction stung more than she'd liked to admit. "For freak's sake."

Riley cleared her throat. "You pride yourself on knowing your worth. So why in the hell don't I do that when it comes to Liam?"

As soon as the words were out of her mouth, she pinched her eyes closed. *It's because you still have a crush on him and would give anything to actually have him look at you the way you've never had anyone look at you before...*

"Gahhhhh! Give me a break. What the heck? No. Stop being an idiot. It's a pipe dream that never is gonna happen. I already know this. I've known it for years. So please, for the love of all things stop embarrassing yourself. Besides, he'd never want an almost thirty-year-old virgin. Besides, relationships and love are stupid, anyway."

Riley punched the dough before pulling her hand back, her frustration getting the better of her. "Damn. I'm sorry that was rude. I shouldn't take my anger out on you," she cooed to the pile of dough. "It's not your fault. You're an innocent bystander in my annoyance. Do you forgive me?"

Riley chuckled with a shrug, realizing she was talking to the dough. Rhonda taught her a long time ago that if you showed love and kindness to your creations, they'd show you love and kindness right back.

Baking was a love language, and if cooing at her dough made her weird, then she'd own it. It's not like she had anyone else to show her love to.

"There you go again. Geez, I really am a ball of sunshine today, aren't I?"

Rolling her shoulders, Riley quickly shaped the dough and plopped it into the pan for its last proof before putting it in the oven.

As she looked around her kitchen, seeing everything around her, she closed her eyes and took a deep breath, her smile once again warming her face.

She'd come a long way, and here she was in her bakery, doing what she loved. Right where she always wanted to be. And one day, not only would she be able to finally hire some help, but she'd be able to pay back the money she'd borrowed from Patrick and Liam.

Riley's body tingled at the thought.

She'd get her own place, hopefully somewhere close to her bakery, and then she could finally start living her life.

The way she wanted to live it.

Making others happy with her baked goods and enjoying everything.

All in all, though, life was good.

And she was happy.

Riley glanced around the kitchen again. Everything was ready for her morning rush. Her glass display case with all her pastries and treats was restocked. And she'd left two fresh bowls of water out front for the dogs that would stop by.

She was ready for the day to start.

Plus, she'd made a few extra of her brownie-batter-bite creation things for her regulars to sample and get their opinions before officially putting them on the menu.

Wiping the flour off her hands, Riley's eyes darted to the backdoor one more time as she worried her bottom lip. She wanted more than anything to check if the kitten was there, but she knew she couldn't.

Pastries & Paws was about to open and Riley knew she had to get the coffee started or she'd have some angry customers.

And no one wanted to start their day like that.

Decision made, Riley spun on her heel as she let out another yawn. There was one thing she knew for sure, though.

It was going to be a long day.

Riley shimmied her hips, desperately trying to get into her groove as she headed to the front. "Let's get this party started."

CHAPTER FIVE

As Liam worked on the jacked-up SUV, his mind wandered back to the previous night when he'd let his feelings get the better of him.

His hand tightened around the wrench like it was his enemy. His lips thinned as he cursed himself for the hundredth time that morning. He was more annoyed with himself than anything else. Yeah, he was pissed Riley walked home, but his anger really came from his shit day and he took it out on her.

As soon as Liam rolled out of bed, he sent Riley a text apologizing. Regardless, though, he still felt like shit for upsetting her. The hurt that flashed through her amber eyes was like a dagger to his chest and yet he couldn't do much about it.

For fuck's sake, he wished he had a better grasp on keeping himself in check after all this time. He was a grown-ass man after all. He should be able to control his emotions and his urges. All of it.

Liam exhaled sharply as he closed his eyes.

He'd make it up to her. Maybe he'd bring her flowers or stop by the bakery and...

And what? Confess your undying love and that you were only a prick 'cause you were scared something could've happened to her and you wouldn't have been there to protect her? Which makes you lose your shit and lash out? He snorted. Yeah, that'd go over real well on an apology card.

Liam pulled back from under the hood, his hands bracing on either side of the front end, his mind completely lost in thought.

You aren't supposed to have feelings for your best friend's younger sister. Full stop. It's never gonna change. You know this already. So stop being an idiot. Get a fuckin' life. Move on...

The moment his brain said the words, his stomach recoiled. That wasn't an option.

Liam's hands tightened around the front end even further, giving him white knuckles. Just the thought of moving on or picturing his life without Riley sent a wave of bile up his throat. That wasn't something—

"You good, son? You're looking at the engine like it personally wronged you."

Liam groaned at this father's voice, his shoulders tensing. Right now was not the time.

Here it comes...

Liam grabbed the rag next to him and wiped his hands before glaring at his father.

"That's how he looks all the time," Patrick chimed in, walking up to stand next to James Kelly. "And here I thought you taught him better than that?"

"Me too." James chuckled before focusing his attention back on Liam, his left brow slightly higher than the other as he surveyed him.

"Both of you can fuck off." Liam tossed the rag onto the cart.

James's brows shot up, the corner of his lips twitching. "Someone's testy today."

"He's been like this all morning." Patrick slapped Liam on the back before leaning his hip on the car, crossing his arms over his chest, doing the same with his legs. "Maybe he needs to eat. He's an asshole when he's hungry."

"I'm right here," Liam clipped. "You don't have to talk about me like I'm not fuckin' standing here."

Patrick darted his eyes to James, the man he'd pretty much called his father with an annoying smile on his face. "Pops, I think we hit a nerve."

James's face twisted in amusement. "I think you might be right, Pat." James immediately narrowed his glare at Patrick. "If you call me Pops one more time, I'll level you to the ground. It makes me feel old, like I got grandkids or somthin'. And as much as Rhonda would like that, I on the other hand, need you to chill the fuck out. I still gotta lot of years left in me before little ones are runnin' around here."

"Are you telling me you don't want little Patricks and Liams running around this shop like we did as kids?"

"You're walking on thin ice."

Patrick's entire face beamed. "If you say so, Pops. Besides, she's only hounding on about grandkids 'cause she retired a few months ago. She's bored." Patrick scoffed a laugh, sending James a wink. "I guess you're not as fun as you thought you were."

At Patrick's wink, James stepped forward and smacked him behind the head. "The only thing keeping you alive is the fact Rhonda would murder me," James grunted, sending Patrick a death glare before turning his focus back to Liam. He crossed his arms over his chest, covering the Kelly's Auto logo. "What's got your panties in a twist? You've been over here cussing and banging all morning. You need some help? This job too much for you?"

"Fuck off, old man."

James's only reply was a raised brow.

"Ohh, yeah. We definitely hit a nerve." Patrick laughed, his face lighting with far too much enjoyment for someone who was up at the ass-crack of dawn.

"Don't you have work to do?" Liam snapped.

"Nah, I think I'm right where I'm needed."

After sending a glare to his best friend, Liam flipped toward his father. "Was there a reason you came over to harass me?"

"A day that goes by that I don't harass my son is a day wasted in my book."

"Glad to see you have your priorities in line." Liam rolled his eyes. "Remind me to tell Mom."

"She'd be proud." James straightened, puffing his chest as the corners of his mouth quirked.

"Seriously. Fuck off. Both of you. Can't you see I'm workin'?"

His father's eyes lit as his annoying smirk turned into a full-blown toothy grin. "I'm telling your mother you said fuck."

You've got to be kidding me right now.

Liam narrowed his eyes at his father, crossing his arms over his chest, mirroring his stance. "I'll tell her myself."

James shook his head as he placed his hand over his heart. "She'd be heartbroken."

"Pfft." Liam scoffed, with a flick of his eyes. "Yeah, right. Who do you think I learned it from?"

"True." James barked out a laugh. "Anyway, as much as I love this little chat, she's actually why I came over here. She's demanding you, Pat, and Riley get your asses to dinner this Sunday. Said it's been too long since we had a family dinner, so get your shit together and make it happen."

"Can't."

"The fuck you can." James eyed his son, his brow cocking.

"I mean it, Dad. I'm sure Pat and I can come by, but Riley can't. She spends most of Sunday getting ready for the week."

"Isn't Sunday her day off?"

"Yeah," Patrick answered with a grunt. "Actually, getting her to take the day off is another story, though. She's still there early as fuck, doing whatever it is she does to prepare for the week."

James's eyes narrowed on them as his jaw firmed. "Back the fuck up here. Are you telling me my little girl hasn't had an actual day off? And you two asswipes haven't stepped in to help her?"

His little girl... See, even Dad thinks of Riley as his kid. And I should only think of her as a sister. Nothing else.

"I'm—"

Liam groaned, cutting him off. "Dad..."

"Don't Dad me. My princess needs a damn day off and a good home-cooked meal. I doubt either of you fuckheads has cooked her anything worth talking about. She works ten times harder than the both of you put together."

He wasn't wrong.

"It looks like you two are just gonna have to get your asses up early on Sunday and help her so she can come to dinner." James's face hardened. "I can't believe you don't help her now. I raised you both better than that."

"She won't let us," Patrick defended, pushing off the front end of the SUV.

James snapped his eyes to him as he continued, "One of you should help her through the week so she can have a damn day off."

"She doesn't like us in her shop," Patrick repeated. "I've tried. Trust me. She kicks us out."

"That's probably 'cause you guys fuck it up somehow."

Patrick folded his arms over his chest. "We don't."

"I bet you do." James first stared Liam down, his gaze unnerving, before switching to Patrick.

"Okay, fine, yeah." Patrick was the first to break. "I might have mislabeled the flour and powdered sugar that *one* time, but it's not like it was that big of a deal."

"She didn't talk to either of us for a week," Liam grumbled, shooting his eyes over to his best friend. "I didn't do it and she still blamed me."

"I'm sure you deserved it," James interjected.

"He did," Patrick agreed.

When Liam shot his eyes to him, Patrick raised his brow. "He broke her favorite whisk." The asshole straightened like he was proud he was telling on him.

That bastard.

"I knew it." James moved his head from side to side as if he was disappointed. "Now, listen here. Help Riley so she's not working so hard. Don't fuck up her shop. And if I don't see all three of you at dinner on Sunday, there'll be hell to pay. "

"Dad—"

"See you at seven, Sunday. I'm taking off early. Your mother and I have shit to do." With that, James strutted away to his office.

"Well, guess that answers that." Patrick shrugged. "At least we get a home-cooked meal out of it."

"Shut up," Liam challenged. "You do realize Riley's gonna hate this?"

"Yeah, but Pops is right. She works too hard and she's supposed to have Sundays off, but she always goes in. If we help her out a little, she might *actually* be able to relax for once. She deserves it."

She deserves the world.

It was more than that, though. And the more Liam thought about what his dad said, the more he realized what an idiot he'd been.

Liam grimaced, wanting to punch himself in the face. They *should* help her more. Even if she didn't want them in her shop. They could follow instructions. They could lighten her load.

It was the right thing to do. The thing they should've been doing all along.

Liam pinched the bridge of his nose before his eyes focused on his best friend. Well, okay, Liam could follow instructions and he could try to not let Patrick fuck shit up.

God, he was an idiot.

And if he'd taken his head out of his ass, he might have seen it sooner, or at least had a clearer head to offer more help.

She did it all on her own. No wonder she was always so fucking tired.

"Besides," Pat remarked with a shudder, stopping Liam's train of thought. "I sure as shit don't want to be on the receiving end if your mother is pissed. Do you?"

"Not really."

"Then that settles it."

"Fine." Liam cocked his brow as he let out an exasperated huff, more annoyed with his realization than anything else. "You're the one telling Riley. Not me."

Patrick's face twisted, his upper lip rising for a second before he shook it off. "Fine, you coward."

In more ways than one...

CHAPTER SIX

Holy freaking crap on a cracker. It'd been a wild day. Fridays were usually more chill for Riley at Pastries & Paws, but for some reason, the day had been a whirlwind.

In her defense, though, it'd been fun. Filled with tons of laughs and smiles, but nevertheless, still wild.

Riley flipped the *Open* sign to *Closed* before she locked the door and did her regular end-of-the-night dance.

Even though it felt like she hadn't gotten a moment's break throughout the day, it still went way better than expected in her book. Especially with how tired she'd been earlier. Plus, everyone who'd tried her newest experiment raved about them.

Riley was one hundred percent putting them on the menu.

Another bright, sunny, successful day checked off in her book.

Hell yes!

Quickly, Riley scanned her inventory to see what needed to be stocked for the next morning and was thankful to find it less than the day before. As it came closer to the weekends, she always slowed down, which was nice. It's why she could close the shop on Sundays. There was always a pop on Saturdays, but it usually died down by ten in the morning.

Riley enjoyed it that way.

It was her time to experiment. Just her and baking. Nothing else.

Since Riley now knew her creations were a hit, she could move on to creating with something else.

Now to come up with a name for them. She chuckled, wiping the palms of her hands down her leggings. Deciding to deal with it later, Riley sent a text to Patrick, telling him she'd be done in about ten minutes.

Triple-checking she was ready for the following day, Riley walked past the backdoor, only to freeze the moment she heard a faint cry.

"Could it be? Please do not be messing with me right now." Riley's heart slammed against her chest as the hair on the back of her arms stood.

The kitten had been in the back of Riley's mind the entire day and whenever she had a chance, she'd run out and check.

Sadly, each time, the little one was nowhere to be seen.

As quietly as she could, to not spook the kitten if it was there, Riley opened the backdoor.

It took everything inside of her not to fist pump the air and do another happy dance when she saw the little black, gray, and white kitten on the ground next to the box, munching down on some of the fresh cat food.

Even though adrenaline and excitement raced through her because the kitten was back, her heart ached seeing the way it chowed down like finding food was an issue for it.

"Poor little guy," she cooed softly, tears welling in the corner of her eyes.

The kitten turned toward her when Riley spoke, its eyes rounding.

"Shh, it's okay. I'm not gonna hurt you. I promise. The yummy food filling your belly... I put it there." The kitten stared up at her, cocking its head to the side.

At the sight, Riley's warm smile spread across her face as she focused on the kitten's markings. "The black around your eyes kinda makes you look like a raccoon." Riley laughed softly. "You're so freaking adorable."

Doing the only thing she could think of not to freak the cat out, Riley plopped onto her butt in the middle of the backdoor and waited, observing the kitten the whole time.

"We'll go at your pace. I'll just sit here. Take your time." Riley held out her hand, hoping the kitten would be curious enough to sniff her.

Calm. Stay calm.

The kitten watched for a few seconds before testing the waters, taking a step toward Riley. The moment it did, Riley's heart tightened.

It's happening! It's happening!

She scanned over the kitten's body. Because of how small it was, Riley knew it could only be a month, maybe a month and a half old. As Riley surveyed the little kitten, she noticed its crusty ears and extended belly, making her stomach bottom.

Poor little one.

"It's okay. I'll make sure you're safe from now on."

As the kitten took another step toward her, Riley continued examining it trying to pinpoint anything that could be out of the ordinary.

Thankfully, she couldn't see anything.

And then, to Riley's complete surprise, the kitten walked over to her, bypassing her outreached hand and sniffed her knee instead.

Don't move. Don't you dare move a muscle, Riley. If you spook this kitten, you're dead to me.

Riley held in her breath as her heart slammed against her chest, letting the kitten explore on its own.

And that's when Riley heard it.

It was soft at first, but as the kitten explored, it grew louder.

Oh my God, it's purring!

If Riley thought her heart clenched before, she'd been wrong. As carefully as she could, she reached out her hand to touch the kitten's head. The second she did, the kitten surprised the crap out of her by brushing up against her fingers, like it wanted her love.

That was it.

Fate was sealed in Riley's book.

Can I love you already? 'Cause I kinda do.

The moment the kitten crawled onto Riley's lap, it took everything inside of her not to cry. "Aren't you just the cutest? Gahh, my heart's gonna explode. *Stopppp.*"

The kitten purred louder, almost as if it agreed about its cuteness. Riley scratched under its chin as the kitten crawled all over her. "Let me tell you something, little buddy. You just hit the jackpot. I hope you like being considered royalty?"

Carefully, Riley stood, keeping the kitten in her arms, which surprised her since it didn't seem all that interested in getting away. Instead, the kitten nuzzled into her, demanding more affection.

"It's too much. My heart."

Riley walked into the bakery and grabbed a fresh box.

However, the moment she tried to place the kitten inside, it cried, clinging onto her arm. "Aww, sweet thing. I just need to close everything up and then we'll head to your new home. Okay?"

The kitten cried as Riley tried lowering it into the box again. However, it was having none of that since it continued clawing up her arm, trying to stay with Riley. "Don't make me cry. It's only for a few seconds. I promise. Then I'll pick you back up." The kitten's protest echoed throughout the room, but this time it accepted being placed in the box. "Remember, I'm the one that crawled under a dumpster for you. Trust me. I'm not leaving you behind."

Riley looked into the box, the kitten's round eyes staring back at her as if it was trying to determine if she was telling the truth or not. "You're stuck with me for life." Riley placed her hand in the box to scratch under the kitten's chin again. "I'm so glad you came back. I was worried about you. And as soon as I can, I'm gonna take you to the vet to make sure you're not hurt. Now, we need to figure out a name for you."

The kitten purred, making Riley's heart somersault. How could she be so in love already? Well, that was a simple answer—it was a kitten. Who wouldn't love a kitten at first sight? Especially one this damn adorable.

"Let's see about that name. It's gotta be bakery related since I'm a baker and you were found out back." Riley thought about it as she looked around the kitchen. "Wait! I'm a freaking baker for humans and *pets*." She slapped her forehead with her palm. "I make treats for *cats!*"

Riley scooted to the container of *CatCrack* on her over-stock shelf, grabbing a few pieces before returning to the kitten. "Just to prove you've entered royalty status. Here. I made these."

After placing them in the box, the little guy smelled the treats, making a happy murmur as it began chomping away with its approval.

Yup, Riley was in love.

A tiny meow came from the kitten's lips, making Riley

shake her hips with excitement. "Yay! Okay, how about... Cupcake? No. Pumpkin? Nah. Cinnamon roll? Blah... Donut?" She scrunched her nose. Nope. None of those sounded right.

Think... use your brain and—

Riley snapped her fingers. "How about Snickerdoodle? That's the first thing Rhonda taught me how to make."

The kitten's tiny meow sounded before its purr filled the room.

"Yep. Even you like it." Riley reached into the box to scratch the kitten's belly pleased with their decision, just as the backdoor swung open to reveal her brother still in his uniform from the day.

"What the hell is that?" Patrick suspiciously eyed the box before glancing back at Riley.

"My new kitten, Snickerdoodle. Snicks for short," Riley stated matter of fact.

Both of Patrick's brows shot off his forehead. "I don't think so. No pets. We've already talked about this. Or did you forget? None of us have the time to watch it. Especially you with the bakery."

"Too bad. This is Snickerdoodle and he's now gonna live with us. If you have a problem with that, you can jump off a cliff." Riley crossed her arms over her chest.

As Patrick opened his mouth to argue, the kitten popped its head out from the top of the box and cried. "Did it just argue with me?"

"Probably."

Patrick stared at the kitten for a few seconds before a mischievous smile appeared on his face. "Liam's gonna *love* this."

"Funny enough. I don't really care what Liam thinks." *That's a lie...*

Refusing to let her brother see the truth, Riley straightened her shoulders as Patrick placed his hand inside of the box; the kitten instantly trying to crawl up his arm to be held.

"Well, aren't you an aggressive little thing?" Patrick laughed, before gently pushing the kitten back, turning his focus onto Riley, his eyes filled with enthusiasm. "C'mon, we're heading to the pet store before it closes."

A big, cheesy grin formed on Riley's face as her heart swelled. Damn, she loved her brother.

CHAPTER SEVEN

LIAM HAD BEEN HOME for the better part of an hour. It was a little weird Patrick and Riley weren't home, but he didn't think too much of it. He'd sent a text to Patrick and asked what the hold-up was, before he hopped into the shower. When he got out, he hadn't gotten a reply, so he made something to eat and took the trash out.

He knew his best friend had left an hour before him to get his sister. Honestly, they should've been home before he'd gotten there, or at least by the time he'd gotten out of the shower.

Unless... Liam's pulse raced as his skin pricked with nerves, his mind jumping to the worst. *Fuck.*

His eyes snapped to the door as worry assaulted his body. What if something happened at the bakery? What if something happened to them on the way home?

What if—

Liam's mouth dried as his heart hammered against his rib cage. *Fuck. Fuck. Fuck.*

They absolutely should have been home by now.

Liam snatched the phone he'd haphazardly tossed on

the counter when he'd gotten there. And seeing no missed calls or texts, he first tried Patrick, all while attempting to swallow past the lump that'd formed in his throat.

When his best friend didn't answer, he tried Riley.

Please, answer. Please fucking answer.

As his call went to voicemail again, Liam's hands shook.

"Fuck!" He grabbed his keys off the counter, already taking steps toward the door as his fingers dialed the emergency number. Before he got the chance to hit call, the front door slammed open, stopping him in his tracks.

Liam's pulse raced like he was only seconds from stroking out, his breathing rough and his eyes wide. It was like his body was frozen in panic. At least that was the case until Liam heard Patrick's voice sound through the open door.

The instant relief Liam felt was indescribable.

They're okay. They're home.

Patrick burst through the door, carrying a shit ton of bags and a—*Hold the fuck up? A fuckin' cat tree?*

"Nope, you're on your own there, Rye. You're telling him not me." Patrick laughed while talking with his sister, seemingly unaware of the panic they'd caused Liam.

"Hush your annoying face." Riley chuckled as she emerged from behind her brother carrying a cardboard box.

Seeing Riley in front of him caused Liam's body to nearly collapse on itself, knowing she was safe. Holy shit, he couldn't breathe. His throat thickened, and his arms and legs seemed weaker as his anxiety peaked.

Calm down, it's okay. Riley and Pat are safe. Nothing happened.

Liam swallowed, doing his best to calm himself even though his adrenaline raced, his body still on high alert.

Breathe. Take a fucking breath.

Once Liam was able to get some of his bearings back, he cleared his throat, trying to register what they'd been talking about. "Tell who, what?" he asked, shoving his hands in his pockets to control their shaking. Liam did his best to focus his gaze on Riley, scanning her up and down, more to prove to himself than anything that she was, in fact, safe.

He didn't know how much more his heart could take.

However, as Liam took Riley in, her mouth slightly parted. Fuck, even in his panic-filled mind, he was taken aback by her beauty.

There was no one quite like Riley. Her signature messy bun on top of her head, her curves hugged by a dark pair of leggings, which he could see had a few flour handprints on them. And a face that could bring anyone to their knees.

God, she was stunning.

His perfect woman was right in front of him.

Maybe it was the fact he thought he could have lost her or whatnot, but for once, he didn't hide watching her.

As Liam took his time, his eyes honed in on every part of her that wasn't being covered by the box. His heart continued to slam against his chest as he swallowed roughly.

Moving back to her face, Liam noticed the tiny hint of red on Riley's cheeks as she looked at her brother, her amber eyes sparkling with excitement.

As he watched them look at each other, a smirk mirroring both of their faces, he finally realized they were fine.

In fact, they were more than fine. Instead, they seemed to share some sort of secret brother-sister moment without a fucking care in the world, meanwhile he thought they were dead on the side of the road.

Liam couldn't stop the abrupt shift inside him.

Now he was just pissed.

They could've called or texted him. Or, you know, fucking answered *his* calls.

Doing his best to control the flood of anger that spiked through him, Liam cocked his brow, his arms crossing over his chest, as he tried to piece together the hurricane that was happening at their front door while actively holding his tongue not to lash out.

He already did it once this week, and he refused to do it again.

Was he pissed? Yeah, that was an understatement. But they *were* safe, that's what mattered. Liam's eyes zeroed in on the box, which he knew was the cause of them being distracted.

Whatever was in that box better have been worth his near heart attack, although Liam had a sneaking suspicion he already knew exactly what was in it.

Liam's eyes moved to the small cat tree his best friend held tucked under his arm.

"Stop stalling." Patrick nudged Riley's shoulder, making her stumble forward.

Liam growled as he darted his attention to Patrick. If he pushed her again, he'd break his nose.

"I'm not stalling," Riley huffed, her eyes shifting from side to side as she worried her bottom lip. When she finally looked at Liam, he saw her unease. "It's nothing." Riley waved him off like they didn't just send him through a fucking rollercoaster of emotions.

"This sure as fuck doesn't look like nothing to me," he clipped, his agitation in full swing. His attempt to keep himself calm was thrown out the window. "Where the hell have you two been? You should've been home over an hour ago."

Patrick shifted to him, his head cocked to the side.

"Aww, Lee, were you worried?" He turned to Riley. "I think we worried him."

"Yeah, you worried me. What the fuck?" He flung his hands in front of him, his blood pressure spiking. "I thought something bad happened. Neither one of you answered my texts or calls. There wasn't a damn thing from either of you. What was I supposed to think?"

Patrick's brows dented, his eyes apologetic as his shoulders turned inward. "Sorry about that, Liam. We didn't mean to freak you out."

"Well, you did. I thought the worst."

"I'm sorry, man." Patrick shook his head as he apologized, his voice filled with sincerity. "I'll keep you in the loop next time."

"You freaked me the fuck out, Patrick. Let's not let there be a next time, okay?"

"Deal." Patrick really had looked remorseful, until he held up the bags, a goofy smile on his face. "To answer your question, we were at the pet store." Patrick's eyes brightened even further.

Liam looked between the two of them, his brow cocking. "Care to explain?"

"That would be your cue, my dear sister." Patrick plopped the cat tree next to the couch and walked over to her attempting to take the cardboard box.

Riley glanced at Liam as she worried her bottom lip, her eyes soft and apologetic.

The concern he saw in her made him want to rush over and pull her into his arms and tell her everything was okay.

But he couldn't.

He wouldn't.

Not until they explained what the fuck was going on.

"We didn't mean to scare you, Liam." She held the box

tight to her chest but kept her focus on him, her eyes round and her voice soft.

"It's fine." He tried to keep the edge out of his tone. He was still agitated at the situation, but he didn't want to see her upset.

"He said it's fine," Patrick mused, with a stupid lopsided grin. "Now, are you gonna tell him?" He grabbed the box in her hands, making Riley shift toward him and shove him in the shoulder. "I'm getting there, geez. I wanted to say we were sorry. We should've called."

"Shoulda, coulda, woulda. Let's get this show on the road." Patrick waved one of his hands in the air, holding the box with the other.

He is your best friend. You cannot murder him. At least not right now. It'll upset Riley.

"You're acting like this is all on me." Riley shifted toward her brother, her arms folding over themselves. "You're just as much involved as I am. Don't act like you weren't in the pet store demanding to hold him. I didn't think I'd ever get him back. Besides, *you* were the one throwing everything in the cart. Not me. You love him just as much as I do."

Patrick responded with a shrug as the annoying, goofy grin appeared back on his face.

For fuck's sake, Liam really was going to murder him, but then his parents would be pissed and he was sure so would Riley. And Liam would never do anything to intentionally hurt her ever again. But damn, right now he'd love to deck Patrick right in the face. "Can someone please explain to me what the hell is going on?"

"Uhh, you see. Umm... nothing." Riley pulled her bottom lip between her teeth, her cheeks heating.

Fuck him if that didn't send a wave of lust through him.

If Riley only knew what she did to him.

Liam swallowed.

She'd probably punch him in the face and then kick him out of her life for good.

Patrick opened the box, drawing his attention away the moment Liam heard a tiny cry.

He raised a skeptical brow, his gaze moving from the now crying box back to Riley, whose cheeks were a deeper shade of red than before. "Doesn't sound like nothing to me."

"That's cause it's a cat." Patrick pulled out a tiny black, gray, and white kitten, holding him up for everyone to see.

"Where the hell did that thing come from?" Liam's eyes widened at the little guy as he watched the kitten fight against the air.

"It's not a *thing*. It's a kitten and it has a name," Riley announced. "Snickerdoodle, Snicks for short." She turned to her brother and took the kitten from him.

Patrick immediately argued, attempting to grab him back out of her arms. "Hey! Give him back."

"No." Riley nuzzled the kitten's head with her hand before looking back at Liam, her smile lighting the entire room. "This is why I was crawling under the dumpster. A loud noise spooked him off before I could get him."

"This is why you smelled like shit yesterday?"

"You don't have to say it like a jerk, but yes."

Liam's eyes moved to Patrick. "And you enabled her by going to the pet store and what..." His hand motioned to all the bags. "Buying out the fucking place?"

"What can I say?" Patrick shrugged, the corners of his mouth twitching like he was attempting to hold in his laugh. "Anything the little guy looked at, I threw in the cart."

"You're worse than she is." Liam chuckled as he rolled his eyes, his annoyance less at the surface as he watched the kitten cuddle into Riley's chest.

He couldn't blame the little guy. Hell, he'd give anything to do that himself.

Ignoring his remark, Riley held up the kitten in her hands showing him off, her smile brighter than before. "You can't be upset. I mean, I guess you can. We didn't tell you we'd be late. But look how cute he is! And he's so tiny." She brought the kitten to her face, giving it a quick kiss. "I already love him. You're gonna love him."

"We aren't keeping a cat." The words were out of Liam's mouth before he could stop himself. Sure, he knew they weren't true. He knew better when it came to Riley and her animals.

But still...

It would make it too real.

Riley clutched the kitten back to her chest, like his words would hurt the little guy. "Yes, we are. I live here just as much as you guys do. I'm keeping Snicks." Riley looked at the kitten purring in her arms. "You're Momma's little angel, aren't cha? Uncle Patrick bought you everything you could ever need. Ignore Uncle Liam, he's a dumb-dumb sometimes. Once the vet opens tomorrow, I'll call and make you an appointment." She scratched its tiny extended belly. "You're such a good boy. And this is your home no matter what the big scary, growly man says."

The kitten blinked at her a few times, nuzzling its head back into her arms.

Riley instantly shot her attention to Liam. "Do you see how adorable he is? How could anyone not love him?" Riley took a step closer to Liam.

"Someone allergic to cats."

Riley pursed her lips. "Good thing you aren't allergic, then." She smirked.

The kitten let out a pleased cry, almost as if it was

agreeing with her, then pushed his head back into Riley's side.

She gently took the cat from the crook of her arm before she shoved the kitten in Liam's hands and damn him if the thing didn't instantly start purring.

As Liam stared down at the little guy, his heart did this weird flip as it blinked up at him, making Liam notice the dark markings around its eyes causing his lips to twitch into a smirk. "You look like a raccoon."

The instant Liam said the words, the kitten butted its head against his hand and purred even louder.

Damn. Okay, that's fucking cute as hell.

"That's how he got me too," Patrick admitted. "The little furball is a lover. I couldn't say no."

"It's a cat."

"And you're being annoying," Riley grumbled, taking the kitten out of his arms as she scratched the little guy under the chin. "Those are just facts."

"Riley," Liam warned.

"Don't Riley me. This little guy was hanging in the back of the bakery and Lord knows what could've happened to him. I've been worried about him all day and night. I'm just grateful he trusted me enough to let me help him, and now he's mine."

God, Liam loved it when Riley was all fiery. Her passion. Damn, if he wasn't still trying to process everything going on, his dick would've taken notice.

Before she decided to spit more fire at him, which he *knew* would cause his lower half to stir, Liam gave up. He knew they were keeping the cat the second Patrick walked in with the cat tree, but he still needed to give them crap about it. After all, they'd nearly given him a fucking heart attack. "Fine. But next time, fucking call me. You both should've been home an hour ago. I thought something happened."

Riley's face softened as she looked at him. "We really are sorry about that. I think we got excited."

"I get you, but it still freaked me out." Liam scrubbed his hand down his face. "Next time let me know. I was about to call for help and go searching for you myself."

"Isn't that sweet?" Patrick cooed. "Love you too, Lee."

"Fuck off," Liam grunted, but his eyes were soft as he watched the kitten on its back playing with a piece of Riley's hair that had escaped the messy bun on top of her head.

Fuck me.

"I'm sorry, Liam." Riley's soft voice got his attention. "We didn't mean to worry you. It kind of just happened."

Damn if his heart didn't flutter at her apologetic voice. All he wanted was to pull her into his arms, feel her body against his and connect them like he dreamed about. Prove to himself that she was in fact here in front of him, safe and sound, not on the side of the road.

Now that his adrenaline began to dissipate, the line between his fantasy and reality was blurring.

Thankfully, as his fingers itched to pull her into his arms, the kitten grabbed Riley's attention, pulling on the strand of hair a little harder, making her tilt her head toward it. "Ew. You kinda stink. No more under-dumpster living for you, mister." She chuckled as the kitten reached out, spreading its toes to touch her cheek.

Okay, damn, that was cute. Even Liam had to admit it.

"I'm gonna have to break this to you. There is no way in hell I'm calling him Snickerdoodle or Snicks." Liam raised his brow, his mouth twitching into a smile with the amusement heavy in his voice. "His name's gonna be Trash Panda. Not only did you find him under a dumpster, he looks kinda like a raccoon... Wait? Are you sure it's not? And how do you even know it's a he?" He scanned his eye over the kitten, nodding his head sharply.

"I'm gonna throw *you* in a dumpster." Riley's eyes snapped to his, but they were full of playfulness. "You're *not* calling my little Snicks Trash Panda. And we checked, thank you very much."

"He's got balls." Patrick jutted his head to Liam. "Small. But they're there. Hey, you guys have somthin' in common."

"Pat, stop. Liam's already mad enough." Riley glared at him. "Plus, we can only assume he's a boy. We'll make sure the vet confirms it, though."

"But it's fun to fuck with Liam."

"*Patrick...*"

"Fine."

Oh, for fuck's sake, these two are gonna be the death of me.

Liam quirked his brow at his best friend. "Guess *you'd* know small balls when you see 'em." He focused back on Riley. "Rye, you found a kitten under a dumpster, and its name is now Trash Panda. It's the only fitting name." Liam's lips twitched into a smirk, his tone light and playful.

"Don't you dare, Liam Kelly. His name is Snicks."

"Or what?" He raised his brow, not holding back his half-smile.

Patrick burst into a deep round of laughter, his eyes shining. "I knew this would be worth it. Sorry we didn't call you, but, holy shit this had been amazing."

Liam rolled his eyes.

Figures.

This was Patrick, after all. Liam cocked his brow, staring at his best friend. "You tell Riley she's going to Mom and Dad's Sunday for dinner?"

Patrick instantly sobered.

"What?" Riley spun toward her brother. "I can't go anywhere Sunday. I have so much to do. I have to work on my books and—"

"Tough shit, Rye." Patrick stopped her. "We already promised Pops we'd be there."

"James doesn't like it when you call him Pops."

Patrick's whole face beamed as a boyish grin appeared. "I know."

Ignoring him, Riley shook her head. "Nope. I can't. Especially now. Not only do I have the stuff to do for the bakery, but I've gotta take care of this little guy. There's no way I can go over to the Kelly's. I'll call Rhonda tomorrow morning and let her know."

Liam's gut twisted again, hearing all the things Riley needed to do, his father's words echoing through his mind. "No can do, Rye." He cursed himself for the hundredth time.

At his words, Riley snapped her attention to him, her amber-eyes hard. "You don't get it. I have a lot of stuff to do. And Sunday nights are the only time I get to relax."

"You're supposed to have the whole day off."

"Maybe one day," she countered. "But not right now."

"Have no fear, Rye. Liam and I will help you get everything sorted in the bakery Sunday morning, so you'll have everything done and ready to go. Plus, this way, you'll still get some free time."

Riley's eyes widened for a split second before she shook her head vigorously. "Absolutely not."

"Why not?" Patrick demanded.

"Putting aside the flour and powdered sugar incident." Riley pointed at him. "Whenever you're in the kitchen, you eat all the cupcakes."

His best friend shrugged, the corner of his mouth tipping upward. "Flour and powdered sugar look a lot alike.

That's not my fault. And your baked goods are delicious. I can't help it. You're a damn talented baker. I'm proud of you."

Riley's face softened for a second at Patrick's words until she snapped out of it. "Thank you for saying that, but listen here, buster. Hell freaking no. I'm not letting you into my bakery."

"We won't screw it up," Liam promised.

"Yeah, right. You'd both cause me more work."

"No, we won't." Liam looked at her, trying his best to convey his words. "We'll listen to you. You're the boss."

Riley stopped for a second, the side of her mouth quirking as she tapped her finger to her chin. "Not gonna lie. I kinda like that. I am a boss lady if I do say so myself."

"Then use us," Liam rushed out, his brain flooding with other images he desperately needed to avoid coming to the surface.

Slow your roll. He swallowed roughly as Riley watched him, her eyes flicking up and down.

He'd give anything for her to look at him that way just in a different context.

As his mind raced, Riley's shoulders relaxed after a few seconds. "I guess it'd be nice to have some company..."

"Good. Then—"

Riley cut Liam off. "You're in charge of him." She pointed to her brother. "If he screws anything up, it's you I'll come after. Got it?"

Even with her threat, Liam saw the playfulness in her eyes and damn, he loved it. He loved it a lot.

Liam straightened and sent her a two-finger salute, making her laugh, and fuck if that didn't send a wave of warmth through him.

"Hey!" Patrick grumbled as his arms crossed over his chest, his brows pulling together.

"Not my problem." Riley nodded to Liam, her smile as bright as ever, as she turned to the kitten. "Come on, Snicks. I'll show you the best room in the house, and then I'm giving you a bath."

As Liam watched Riley head down the hall, he couldn't argue with that. Riley's room was the best room in the house.

Actually, wherever Riley was would always be the best.

As the morning sun seeped through Riley's curtains, she stretched, throwing the sheets off her body. Once she let out a deep yawn, she wiped the sleep out of her eyes, gathering her bearings to start the day. Sunday morning might have come around all too quickly for Riley's taste, but what was she to do?

At least she could sleep in.

Riley's eyes flicked to the sunbeam on her bed from the window. And of course, Snickerdoodle was conveniently smack-dab in the middle of it, making Riley's lips curve into a soft smile as she watched the kitten.

He'd settled in over the last two days, making the place his own.

Literally.

No room, corner, closet, or crevice was off-limits for him. He'd explored everything like he was some famous archeologist on a mission to uncover new treasures.

Riley laughed, thinking back to the tiny ball of fur running full speed toward her when she walked through the front door after closing up her bakery a little earlier than usual Saturday afternoon.

The bakery had been dead after her rush in the morning and even though she had a lot to do, she couldn't stop the urge to walk home to see her little guy.

And with the way Snickerdoodle reacted when he saw her, Riley knew she made the right choice.

"Hey, you're home early," Liam remarked the moment Riley walked through the front door, his brows pulling together as he surveyed her. "Why didn't you call me? I would've gotten you."

"Hi." Riley smiled at him. "It was nice out and I wanted to wa—"

Snickerdoodle came flying toward her as fast as his little legs could take him, cutting her off with his cry of determination. "Snicks! I missed you. Come give your momma kisses. Did you have fun today with Uncle Liam?"

Riley grabbed him from the floor and brought him to her face as she laid as many smacking kisses on him as she could before he cried again.

"Damn. If I knew all I had to do was run toward you when you got home to get a greeting like that, I would've started doing it years ago." Liam chuckled, his eyes bright.

However, his words had Riley snapping in his direction, her heart skipping as her mind raced with a fantasy she knew damn well would never happen.

Riley stood there, kind of frozen in her spot, not really sure what to say until she saw Liam smirk and send a wink her way as he turned back into the kitchen.

Well, there went her heart. One moment she could picture it all, the next she was crashing and burning.

Stupid feelings. Riley glared at the ceiling. Stupid Universe.

After taking a beat to right herself, she desperately tried to stop her heart and mind from battling against one another as they always did when it came to Liam Kelly.

Riley quickly tucked the cat into her arm. "Did you have fun while I was at work? Do anything exciting? Take over the world, or at least the house?"

Out of the corner of Riley's eye, she saw Liam lean against the doorframe of their kitchen watching her. His arms were folded over his chest, with a soft smile on his face, making Riley's body heat under his gaze.

Gahhh. Enough already.

"He had fun," Liam answered. "If his idea of fun is crawling up and down my body like I'm his personal cat tree. At one point, I thought I'd need to change my resume to professional stripper pole."

Riley's eyes jerked to Liam, her mind going somewhere it shouldn't.

"It only took two times for me to realize I needed jeans and a long-sleeve shirt while he's around." He laughed out a huff. "Fucker drew blood at one point."

Liam's smirk and playful eyes were the only reason Riley didn't yell at him for calling Snickerdoodle a fucker. Okay, and she had to admit, his jeans hanging low on his hips and his long-sleeve shirt tight across his body showcasing his form kind of made Riley's brain short-circuit.

Again, did he have to look so damn good?

Annoying.

Shoving her thoughts and feelings down, Riley cleared her throat. "Yeah, well, we can't blame him for having poor taste," she shot back, her smile matching Liam's. "He doesn't know any better yet."

"Ouch." Liam's hand went to his chest. "Daggers."

Rolling her eyes, Riley kept Snickerdoodle tucked into her arm. "The shop was dead, so I figured why not come home early and check on him."

"Didn't think I could handle it?"

"I wouldn't say those words exactly, but..." The right corner of her mouth quirked.

"Riley," he warned, but his playful tone made her body squirm.

She swallowed, desperately trying to tamp down the light, too relaxed, almost too perfect, making her want things she could never have moment between them. "What?"

Liam laughed, pushing himself off the frame before walking to her with purpose. Once Liam was right in front of her, he plucked the cat from her arms. "Mine."

"Give him back!"

"Nope." Liam placed the cat on his shoulders, which seemed to be exactly what the kitten wanted.

Riley watched in amazement as Snicks balanced with ease, happy as could be, perched up on Liam's shoulders.

"Did you call the vet about Trash Panda?"

"Don't call him Trash Panda," she snapped. "Yes. He has an appointment at Richman Veterinary Hospital Monday morning. It was the only time they had. I'm gonna see if I can drop him off or—"

"I'll take him." Liam waved her away as he moved to the couch before plopping down, the kitten instantly crawling onto his lap.

Riley walked over to the couch and sat right next to Liam in a daze as the kitten maneuvered itself right between them and went to sleep.

Then, to add one more tick in the Universe-loving-to-screw-with-her category, before she knew it, Riley had fallen fast asleep on Liam's shoulder right next to Snickerdoodle.

Her cheeks warmed as Riley desperately tried erasing the embarrassment from the previous day.

I just had to fall asleep on him, didn't I? She snorted, sending a quick glare to the ceiling, before pinching her eyes shut. *Okay, yeah, he smelled freakin' fantastic and his shoulder was super comfy—No. What in the hell am I doing?*

Freaking pathetic.

Taking a deep breath, Riley opened her eyes as she rolled her shoulders.

New focus.

Deciding to bring her attention to the middle of her bed, Riley scratched the kitten on the head, causing him to let out a surprised yip before he began purring.

"You are too damn cute for this world. You know that right, Snicks?"

The kitten glanced at her, his eyes wide before slowly closing them again.

"Course you do."

Letting the kitten snuggle on the blanket, Riley stretched her arms over her head, arching her back, enjoying her muscles loosening. Once she was done, she nibbled her bottom lip while she reached for her phone, checking the time.

A little after six-fifteen.

That wasn't too bad. It was more sleep than she normally got. Plus, the sun was out. If Riley played her cards right, she'd be able to sneak out of her room and walk to the bakery. This way she'd at least get some work done before they showed up.

Lord knew there was no getting out of them coming to *help*.

A part of her was excited for them to all hang out. Even if it could be at the expense of her bakery. It was going to be a wild ride today, that's for sure. Riley only hope she'd come out on the other end unscathed, her bakery and her heart.

Riley huffed out a defeated sigh. She didn't know what had flipped inside her, but everything with Liam had been more intense over the last few days. Maybe it was the fact her thirtieth birthday was two years away which was right around the corner, or that she'd stupidly brought up all those old memories from her past. Who knew, but something had made her feelings for Liam intensify.

She swore she was better at keeping herself in check when it came to him and her heart... and yet...

How's that going for you, dumb-dumb? Huh? Huh?

Yesterday, once they'd settled on watching one of her bakery competition marathons, that one-sided spark she had for Liam pricked at her skin the entire time.

In all honesty, it'd been hard for Riley to not fall into some screwed-up fantasy of them being more. They'd relaxed, joked, and played with Snickerdoodle. And when Liam ordered takeout for them, she realized how easy it was.

And, damn, she hated to admit it, but it felt right.

At least that was until Patrick got home and Riley was once again reminded of how much of an idiot she was.

Riley groaned causing Snicks to look at her, blinking his eyes slowly.

For the love of all freaking things sweet and glorious, it's now just ridiculous and annoying. It's never gonna happen. Riley wrinkled her nose. *I'm only annoying myself at this point. And setting myself up for heartache. All I need in life is my baking.* Riley looked over at the kitten. "And you, of course."

Snickerdoodle purred louder, brushing his head against Riley's hand, causing her to scratch under his chin. "Are you gonna miss your mommy when I'm at the bakery?"

The kitten blinked at her, but Riley took that as agreement.

She didn't know how it was possible to love something so quickly, but here she was.

Being careful not to disturb the little guy, she leaned over and grabbed her phone to check the time.

Six-thirty... crap.

Riley needed to get a move on if she planned on getting to the bakery to get work done before they showed up. She didn't mind seeing the Kellys for dinner, but it definitely threw a wrench in her plans.

A tiny cry came from her right, causing Riley to look over, only to see the kitten wide awake, kneading away on the throw blanket she kept on the bed.

"Aww, don't you look just like Mommy? You putting in an extra shift for me at the bakery? You making those biscuits?" Riley cooed, nuzzling the kitten's head. "I'd take you into the bakery any day to help me. You'd be the best little baker there ever could be."

She kissed his head, causing the kitten to cry once more.

"Stop, you're too much." Riley's heart swelled. "How about this? You keep baking those biscuits here, and when I get home we'll check your inventory and see if I can hire you on full-time?" She laughed, a full-blown grin on her face.

The kitten looked at her and meowed, purring even louder this time.

Oh God, it was too much.

"You be good." Riley kissed Snickerdoodle on the head, jumped out of bed, and quickly got dressed.

As she reached the handle of her bedroom door, she turned back to Snicks, still kneading away on the blanket. "Don't do anything stupid. You're in charge."

With that, Riley quietly tiptoed out of her bedroom, leaving the door ajar, and headed toward the front door.

However, the second Riley took a few steps down the hall, someone cleared their throat from behind her, making her jump and clench her chest. "Ahh. What in the buttery biscuit hell?"

"You sneaking out?" Liam asked, a chuckle in his voice as he watched her. His eyes raked up and down her body, instantly making Riley's cheeks flush.

Oh, for Pete's sake.

Doing her best to tamp down the rush she felt, she swallowed roughly. Damn, Liam looked good.

Too good.

His sleep pants hung low on his hips, showcasing his taut stomach. No matter how hard she tried, she couldn't stop her eyes from focusing right under his belly button to the line of hair that traveled down...

Riley forced herself to stop before her eyes followed the happy trail. Instead, she snapped her attention to his face.

Okay, well, she tried to. Halfway there she got distracted with his arms crossed over his bare broad chest. His right side leaning against the doorframe of his bedroom.

Geez, the sight took her breath away and made her body heat even further at the same time.

Liam pushed himself off the frame, making his way down the hall toward her. "You gonna keep staring at me, or are you gonna answer?" The corner of his mouth twitched as he chuckled. His eyes flashed with something Riley couldn't quite put her finger on.

I wonder if—

When Liam cocked a skeptical brow at her, she snapped out of her trance. "What?"

Liam's low laugh somehow went directly to her core, making her breath hitch.

The tension between them thickened.

Holy freaking crap on a cracker. Get yourself together, Rye. What the hell is going on? Didn't we just discuss these unhealthy reactions not only ten minutes ago? Good grief.

"You sneakin' out?" Liam asked, his eyes once again scanning her. "I thought we discussed this last night while playing with Trash Panda on the couch. We were—"

"That's not his name."

"It is," Liam stated matter of fact. "As I was saying. If I remember correctly, we were gonna ride in together and help you get everything in order. And we'd leave here at seven-thirty." His eyes moved to the clock on the wall. "Looks like you're trying to speed up the plan by forty minutes or so."

Riley's eyes rounded, her brows nearly shooting off her forehead. "That's not what I was doing."

"Wanna try another lie?" Liam stared at her, pinning her in her spot as her heart slammed against her chest. Oh, for the love of...

Giving up, Riley grumbled, pushing past the lump in her throat. "Uhh, no."

"That's what I thought." Liam's mega-watt smile made her weak in the knees.

Fudge her life.

For freak's sake. It's never gonna happen, so just go ahead and bunch all those feelings up, toss them into the nearest dumpster, and then set it on fire.

Riley forced a smile and cleared her throat, desperately trying to listen to herself and keep her haywire feelings in check. "I have a lot to do this morning. I have to—"

"I know. That's why I'm up. I'll be ready in two minutes." Liam tipped his chin toward her, his smile tempting which sent another rush through her. He turned, stomping down the hall back to his room, only banging on Patrick's door once. "Get your lazy ass up. Riley tried to make a run for it."

"Did not!"

Liam cocked his head back in her direction, his left

brow higher than the other. "You keep telling yourself that, Rye." His gaze seemed to pierce right through her soul. "You forget I know you. I can read you like an open book."

Riley's eyes widened as she sputtered trying to come up with words. However, before she could remember how words worked, Liam winked her way. He then turned back to his room, shutting the door behind him.

Riley stared at Liam's closed door, her heart leaping into her throat.

I hope to everything out there, you can't.

CHAPTER NINE

"Stop pouting, Rye." Liam glanced at Riley from the rearview mirror as they drove toward his parents' house later that afternoon. Her adorable bottom lip poked out as she kept her arms folded over her chest. Just the sight of her took everything in him not to laugh.

"I'm not pouting," she grumbled, keeping her focus out the window, refusing to acknowledge him or her brother. Which had been going on for the better part of ten minutes.

Again, absolutely adorable, if you asked him.

"Yes, you are." Patrick snorted out a laugh from the passenger seat.

That got Riley to snap her attention to the front, her expression pinched. "You'd be pouting too if you had two buffoons in your bakery screwing everything up." Riley huffed as her hands migrated to her temples and began massaging. "I knew this was gonna happen. But no, you both went in there and... You know what?" She narrowed her eyes toward Liam. "I don't even know everything you all did. But it's bad. I think I have a migraine."

"We didn't screw anything up." Patrick twisted in his seat with a smirk on his lips. "We improved the place."

"I no longer *think* I have a migraine. I *know* I have one." Riley harrumphed, directing her agitation toward Patrick. "And yes, you did screw everything up. Liam overworked two separate batches of dough and now they won't rise. And *you* ate everything you touched that wasn't nailed down. I think you might've even scarfed down a few dog treats."

His best friend barked out a laugh, his hand going to his stomach.

"It's not my fault you make everything look like human food. I wouldn't have gotten confused if you didn't do that."

"How is that my fault?" Riley's brows darted off her forehead. "I didn't even have time to look at my books since I had to keep going behind you guys to fix whatever it was you were doing the whole freaking morning."

"That's 'cause you're a control freak."

"Am not."

"Are too."

"Children." Liam chuckled, his fingers drumming on the steering wheel. "I'm trying to drive here. Stop bickering." He bit back his smile to keep from laughing harder which he knew would only aggravate Riley.

In her defense, though, it had turned out to be a shitshow. He tried following all of Riley's instructions.

He really did.

Fixing machines Liam could do. Kneading dough—but not too much, was a science. Who knew there was so much that went into baking? He sure as hell didn't. Although he'd try again for Riley.

If she'd ever let them in the bakery.

But after this morning, that was a huge *if*. At least for him. Patrick would never be allowed back. Liam glanced at his best friend, the edge of his mouth quirking. "She has a point. You did eat everything."

"Thank you, Liam." Riley darted her eyes to her

brother. "See, even *he* agrees with me. You both screwed everything up."

Liam's brow cocked as he glanced back at Riley in the mirror. "Didn't say that."

"I took liberty in your statement to correct it."

Liam rolled his eyes and snorted out a huff as he pulled in the corners of his lips to stop smiling.

These were the moments he enjoyed.

Let's be real. I enjoy all moments whenever Riley is involved.

As Liam focused on her in the mirror, he saw agitation but that wasn't all. There was also a mischievous twinkle in her eyes as she attempted to hide her smile.

Which made Liam's heart do a weird flip in his chest.

Since Riley walked in the door early Saturday afternoon, things felt different between them.

But in a good way.

In a way Liam shouldn't admit. Maybe that's why he relentlessly flirted with her that morning before they headed to the bakery.

And the way Riley scanned his body when he leaned against the doorframe, fuck him. His skin heated under her gaze, like he could feel every inch of it.

When Riley's eyes migrated lower... talk about an instant reaction. He had all of ten seconds to get his body in check or he'd be sporting a tent in his well-worn pajama bottoms.

Fuck him, he knew he shouldn't cross that line. The line Patrick would literally murder him for, but a man could only control himself for so long.

And as Riley's eyes ate him alive, a tiny spark of hope flashed through him, which made his brain say fuck the bro code and flirt even harder.

During the mess at the bakery, Liam found himself more often than not, resting his hand against Riley's ample hip to grab anything off the top shelf she needed, even if she insisted she didn't need or want his help. He also scooted behind her any chance he got, using the excuse she was too short, which Riley immediately denied, as he'd casually reach for whatever she wanted off the shelf.

He'd press his body against hers ever so slightly, each time only igniting him more.

It was like the dam holding him back, finally started to crack.

Which wasn't safe.

"Tonight sure is gonna be a blast if you insist on being all pissy. I said I was sorry," Patrick groaned.

"I was more than happy to stay home with Snickerdoodle. I love Rhonda and James, but leaving my little guy home alone hurts my heart. And what do you think he'll get into?"

"He'll be fine. He's probably sleeping as we speak."

"How do you know?"

"I do." Liam flicked his eyes to her. "It's a cat. He can't get into much trouble. He's got food, water, and a clean litter box. It's not like we'll be gone long. I think he'll be just fine." Liam watched as Riley rolled her eyes before looking out the window.

Liam forced himself to not moan. He didn't know why, but every time she did it, his dick took notice. It was probably because of her usually calm, easy-going nature.

The *only* people Riley ever spit fire at were him and her brother.

Call him a masochist, but he fucking loved it. That edge to Riley that no one ever saw.

The real Riley.

The Riley full of emotions and fire.

The Riley that wasn't afraid to put him in his place and do it with a fucking smile on her face.

Liam swallowed his moan, begging his dick to stay calm as he focused on the road.

Best friend code. You don't cross the best friend code. Remember that, dickface. Deep breath. Think of something else. Use your brain for once.

Liam expected his mind to jump to work or something mindless. However, the Universe loved taunting his perfect woman in front of him at all times, just to remind him he was a pathetic idiot.

He began replaying the morning. Hectic was an understatement.

Liam knew Riley did a lot, but holy shit, he wasn't expecting all *that*. And he only got a glimpse of her office. If you could even call it an office. It looked like her filing cabinet exploded.

Liam's brows dented in the middle as he realized just how much Riley did on her own. No wonder she was always tired. And fuck him if that didn't make him feel even worse for not offering to help sooner.

Although if today was any indication he'd cause her more issues than she needed.

Not entirely his fault.

He tried.

He really did, and he'd keep trying, if she'd be willing to teach him. Liam had to admit, even though it was a disaster, it'd been a hell of a lot of fun. Riley was constantly spouting off rules about what to do and what not to do. She'd shake her head huffing or throw her hands in the air every few minutes.

Then she'd hand him a recipe card to start, her eyes

pinning him in place, threatening if he screwed it up, she'd smother him in his sleep.

Sounds like a damn good time, if you asked him.

Hey, he wasn't averse to her in his bedroom at night, even if it was under malicious intent. He'd take her in there any way he could.

God, he'd loved every second of their morning. It'd been a playful, chaotic mess.

When he rolled up to a red light, Liam took the time to focus on her, his smile pulling at his lips. There was so much to Riley.

Her confidence.

Her beauty.

She was so fucking talented.

Watching Riley dance around the bakery, her hands in every project like a well-oiled machine, was something else. The whole time he'd been focused on observing her move with ease.

It'd been mesmerizing.

She was fast and efficient, and damn did it turn him on.

Liam knew he'd overworked the dough, but in his defense, he was distracted. Riley's apron had been pulled tight around her waist, emphasizing her curves.

The curves he'd give anything to sink into.

Liam's mouth watered at the sight. He swore he had to keep checking if he was drooling. Holy shit, he'd almost lost it more times than he could count. No wonder he'd over-worked the dough. Not once, but twice.

Riley was unbelievably beautiful.

And then she'd be yelling at Patrick over something he was doing wrong.

The fire she only reserved for them... She'd get all pouty before pushing them aside to show them what to do... again.

As he laughed to himself reminiscing over the morning, Liam focused on Riley, seeing the tiredness in her eyes.

Riley really did it all. Yeah, in the back of his head he knew that, but he never really thought how much that entailed.

First chance he got, Liam planned to hire his dad's bookkeeper to help with her godawful office. Then, he was going to do what he should have done a long time ago.

Liam would make it his priority to help Riley. Even if that meant learning how to bake from his mom so he could—

Wait. My mom.

Liam fought the urge to punch himself in the face. How could he have missed it before? His mom retired a few months ago and was bored out of her mind. It was the perfect solution.

For fuck's sake, he was an idiot.

Liam grunted low so no one would hear.

The first opportunity he had, he would ask his mom if she'd help out at Pastries & Paws. It was the perfect plan, since he knew his mom would be the only person Riley would really trust when it came to her bakery.

Plus, the second he'd ask his mom, he knew she'd jump at the chance. Even if she only managed the register in the morning, it would help Riley out a ton.

Liam's eyes flicked back to Riley for a second, this time the corners of his mouth turning up.

Riley would one million percent fight him on this, he had no doubt. But there was one thing Liam knew for sure. No one went against Rhonda Kelly and the moment he'd let it slip Riley needed help, it would be a done deal.

Although it could also backfire and Mom will threaten me and Pat for not helping sooner... He shrugged. *Whatever, it'd be worth his mom pissed at them if it meant Riley got what she needed.*

Liam's mouth curved into a mischievous smile as he drove to his childhood home.

Patrick was right.

Tonight was sure as fuck going to be a blast.

CHAPTER TEN

"MY BABIES!" Rhonda shouted as the three of them walked into the house.

Which, of course, soon erupted into pure chaos as it always did.

But Liam didn't mind. Whenever any of them were there, it always felt like coming home.

Hell, it *was* home.

Even though his dad, on more occasions than not, annoyed the crap out of him, Liam really did have a good relationship with his parents. And the fact they extended their love to Patrick and Riley had always been a plus. They were caring, loving, stern when needed, and always supportive of each of them.

The corner of Liam's lip twitched. Besides, whenever they'd arrive home, Liam knew for a fact it would only be a few minutes before his dad and Patrick would be bickering back and forth somewhere. And Riley would end up in the kitchen helping his mom with whatever she was doing at the time.

As for Liam, he'd somehow end up between them both,

either chiming into conversations with his dad and best friend or attempting to offer his help in the kitchen.

Usually, his mom and Riley would try to shoo him away. Sometimes it worked. Sometimes it didn't. More often than not, though, he'd end up sitting at the kitchen counter watching them work.

It felt right.

It always felt right.

Like clockwork, not even five minutes after they stepped through the front door, Patrick and his dad were bitching about something in the living room, while Riley made a bee-line directly to the kitchen.

And Liam was biding his time, searching for the perfect moment to bring his mom into his master plan.

In the meantime, as Liam stood next to his dad and Patrick, his eyes focused on the kitchen, watching as Riley and his mom worked in tandem, like it was second nature.

He'd be lying if he said he didn't enjoy the fact Riley was with his mother doing anything she could to help. It always seemed to send his fantasies into overdrive.

It was especially worse on the holidays when his mind would easily fall into what he dreamed of more than anything.

Riley as his wife.

Not much would change. Riley and his mom would still be in a knee-deep, joyful conversation as they cooked. Before he'd leave the room, though, he'd get to pull Riley into his arms, kiss her, and squeeze her hip.

Liam swallowed roughly, his fantasy once again nearly choking him alive as he stood next to his dad and Patrick.

He closed his eyes, taking in a staggered breath.

What he wouldn't give for it to be real.

To be able to walk right into the kitchen and pull Riley into his arms right now.

But it's not.

Liam shook himself out of his thoughts as he focused on his father and Patrick, who were bitching about something that happened Friday and put them behind schedule in the shop.

Which reminded him, Liam had more important things to do anyway than get caught up in a dream.

However, the moment Liam attempted to participate in whatever conversation his dad and Patrick were having, Riley's laugh rang out, causing him to snap his head toward the kitchen.

Liam's blood raced as his fantasy took hold again.

Damn, he loved Riley's laugh.

"What's that look for?" James asked, nodding his head toward Liam, breaking him out of his daydream.

Liam darted his attention to his dad. "What look?"

"Great." Patrick snorted out a laugh. "Here we go again."

"Fuck off."

James quirked his brow. "Your mother can hear you."

"So?"

James flicked his eyes and smacked Liam on the back of the head.

"Ouch. Fuck." Liam rubbed the spot. "Was that necessary?"

"You didn't answer me. Why the hell do you look like that?" James's nose scrunched as he eyed him.

This wasn't like his dad's normal scrutinizing, though. This time, there was a hint of knowing behind it, making Liam tense.

He'd done a damn good job of hiding his true feelings for years, and he wasn't about to let his dad in on his secret anytime soon. Or ever, if it were up to him.

Liam cleared his throat, folding his arms over his chest.

He may or may not have stood a hair taller, broadening his shoulders. "Just thinkin'."

James's eyes sized him up, his brow nearly jumping off his forehead as he crossed his arms over his chest, mimicking Liam's stance.

Damn.

Liam should've known better than a sorry-ass attempt at intimidating his father in hopes he'd leave it alone.

Thankfully, before James could confront him, though, Patrick took a step toward the garage. "Be right back. Gonna go grab the fire extinguisher."

Liam snapped his head to him, his lips thinning. "You want me to punch you?"

"Boys," James interjected with an annoyed grunt. His dad's eyes pinned him in place, his underlying questions there at the surface. "Not when we're about to have dinner. You can wrestle after."

"He started it." Patrick pointed at Liam.

"Did not." He turned to his dad, hoping to change the subject before he started asking questions. "Can I get the name of the guy who does the shop's accounting? I want to talk to him about helping Riley at the bakery."

Patrick slapped his hand on Liam's shoulder. "That's a great idea."

James watched Liam for a second before giving him a sharp nod. "Sure. I'll get you his info tomorrow when I'm back in the office."

His dad continued to analyze him, making the hair on the back of Liam's neck stand.

"Dinner's ready." His mother bounced into the room, carrying a tray. "Liam, dear, help Riley grab the rest of the food. Patrick and James set the table."

Thank fuck.

"Aye aye, captain." James's entire face lit as he beamed at his wife, his eyes holding so much love.

Liam wanted that.

He wanted that more than anything.

And he wanted that with Riley.

Too bad it would never happen.

Liam shook his head as he walked into the kitchen to see Riley balancing two plates on her arms. "Here, let me help you." He managed to grab the bowl of mashed potatoes just before it fell.

"Thanks." Riley's inviting smile warmed his soul, making his heart skip. "If you'll also grab the rolls, we should be all set."

"Sure thing, Rye. Whatever you say." He winked, grabbing the basket on the counter. "Your wish is my command."

"Hmmm?" Riley's lips twitched into a playful, almost seductive smile, nearly sending Liam stumbling over his own two feet as his dick instantly took notice. "I might have to put that to the test."

Holy fuck.

That familiar need rushed into him as his member pressed tightly against the zipper of his jeans, threatening to break through. He had to snap his eyes shut as his mind raced with all the things he dreamed of.

Liam knew Riley probably only meant making him clean the bathroom or fold her laundry... although he wouldn't be too hard-pressed with the latter. But damn, he wanted to believe Riley was on the same page as him. Even if only for a moment to fuel his fucked-up fantasies. "You name the time and the place, and I'm *all* yours."

Riley's eyes nearly popped out of her head as her cheeks turned a bright red before making a weird pained noise as she spun away from him. "Food's burning my arm!" She scrambled running out of the kitchen.

Fuck.

Liam wanted to punch himself. He went too far, and he knew it. But he couldn't help it. The line between them had been blurring and he couldn't stop it.

Good job, idiot.

Liam groaned, cursing himself as he reached down and adjusted his pants before picking up the basket of rolls again. Once he knew he was under control, he made his way to the dining room. His eyes instantly sought Riley who conveniently turned away from him the second he'd entered.

"What the hell took you so long?" James grumbled, reaching for the basket of rolls.

"Fuck off, old man." Liam placed the potatoes on the table next to the roasted chicken, cursing himself the whole time. Especially since Riley refused to look his way.

"I swear it's like you think you were raised by wolves. Respect your elders and all that shit." James jabbed his fork toward Liam.

"*Elder* is the key word there." Liam's lip quirked as he sat down next to his best friend and across from Riley, who was still conveniently not looking his way.

"Yeah, Lee." Patrick quickly added his two cents, not even attempting to hold in his smirk. "Get your shit together. Show Pops some respect."

James rumbled, glaring at Patrick. "You're fired."

Patrick's face beamed while he puffed his chest. "No, I'm not."

"If I say you're fired, I mean—"

Rhonda cleared her throat. "All of you knock it off. This is supposed to be a fun family dinner and so help me, if any of you fuckers mess this up, I will end you all." She stared down her husband. "I mean it."

"What'd I do?" James's brows shot up, his mouth open.

"What *didn't* you do?" Ignoring the laughs throughout the room, Rhonda turned to Liam.

The moment she did, Liam saw the fire in her eyes and he knew exactly what was coming.

Shit.

Liam knew better than to believe his mother *just* wanted a family dinner night. This was Rhonda Kelly, after all. She always had something up her sleeves. She wasn't just *the* master of guilt-tripping. She was so much more.

"Liam, my son, when are you gonna settle down?"

The forkful of food he'd shoved in his mouth was almost his death sentence as he coughed up a lung.

Since he was clearly occupied with not dying, Rhonda turned her sights on Patrick. "Same with you, Pat. When are we gonna get grandbabies? I'm not getting any younger and I'd like to still be able to chase after them for a few years before I need a hip replacement."

"Mom!" Liam finally found his words as he pounded on his chest, trying to dislodge the food. Damn, he knew she was up to something, but he thought it wouldn't be settling down and kids. Fuck him.

"Dear, you aren't gonna need a hip replacement." James winked. "We stretch those babies out every night."

Liam threw his fork down. "For fuck's sake!"

Patrick coughed, but his lips twitched into a smile.

"That's true, James, but you never know." Rhonda then moved to Riley. The red tinge covered her cheeks beautifully. "And you, missy? Seeing anyone special? Any chance of me getting any grandbabies sooner rather than later?"

It was an instant assault on Liam's mind.

Riley pregnant.

Rounded with *his* baby.

"I have a cat!" Riley blurted.

Liam coughed again, trying to gather air.

"A kitty cat. He's cute!" She yelled in a panic. Liam couldn't blame her, it was like an ambush and his mother had them all in her sights.

Thinking as fast as he could, still trying to keep the picture of Riley heavy with his child out of his mind, Liam snapped to his dad. "When are you gonna retire and give me the shop?"

The conversation needed to switch right the hell now. There was no way Liam could go down that road of Riley pregnant.

James scoffed as he slammed his hand on the table. "You really wanna try me today, don't ya? The shop is going to you *and* Patrick equally. While we're at it, why do you wanna push me out so fast? I can outwork you any day. You wanna go outside?"

Geez, his dad was a piece of work. "Not that I wanna push you out. You're just getting old. Might hurt yourself one of these days. "

"Son, I will level you to the ground so fast you never knew what hit you."

Liam rolled his eyes. "Talk about broken hips. We'd end up havin' to call the paramedics since that's exactly what would happen if you tried, old man." He laughed, his eyes shining.

"This is fun." Patrick smiled, shoving food in his mouth. "Family nights are always the best."

"And you—" James turned to Patrick, his fork pointed in his direction.

"So the cat I found!" Riley hollered, getting everyone's attention, her face beet red. "He was hanging outside the bakery and he was so tiny and cried a lot. I knew I needed to help him. I crawled almost all the way underneath the dumpster, but my hips wouldn't budge and then he ran off, but he came back the next day and now he's mine," she was out of breath, her eyes round as she looked everywhere and anywhere in the room.

"Yep, she came home smelling like shit." Patrick snorted out a laugh.

Riley glared at him. "You make it sound like I do it all the time. I heard him cry and I wanted to make sure he was okay. I'm just lucky he came back." She turned to Rhonda. "He's perfect. He's constantly kneading all the blankets and pillows in the house. It's like he's trying to be me. He's my little biscuit maker."

Rhonda held a softness in her eyes as she laughed. "Guess it runs in the family."

"Guess so. We're taking him to the vet tomorrow to make sure he's okay, but so far, he seems good. He's adorable and you'll fall in love as soon as you meet him."

"I recall you saying the same thing about the slug you found on the back porch when you were thirteen?" James interjected with a laugh.

"Howey," Riley corrected. "Wasn't he the best too? The kitten is a lover. All he wants is to be in your arms. It's like he was made for me. You're gonna love him. Unlike Howey." Her nose wrinkled. "I still don't get why you wouldn't let me bring him inside. I kept him in a shoebox."

Liam shook his head, pushing out a snort, as the whole room erupted into laughter.

"I'll tell you now, what I told you then..." James's eyes were bright and loving. "Slugs belong outside, not at the dinner table."

Riley shrugged. "Tomato, to-mah-toe. Anyway, he's sweet."

"The slug or the cat?"

"James," Riley whined. "The cat. Howey died years ago."

At her adorable pout, Liam's heart skipped. Lord, this woman could bring him to his knees even when she was talking about slugs or God knows what else.

"I can't wait to meet him," Rhonda remarked, reaching out to touch Riley's arm. With her gesture, Liam knew what his mother was about to ask...

"Trash Panda's pretty cute," Liam quickly added, knowing he'd get a rise out of Riley and keep the focus on her and the cat instead of what his mother wanted to talk about.

"You named him Trash Panda?" James asked, a clear chuckle in this voice.

"No! His name is Snickerdoodle. Snicks for short. Don't listen to Liam, he's an idiot."

Liam shrugged. "He looks like a raccoon, and he came from under a dumpster."

James slammed his palm on the table again, his smile going from ear to ear. "Trash panda it is," James agreed.

"No! His name is Snickerdoodle." Riley's eyes rounded as she lovingly looked at his mom. "It's the first thing you taught me how to bake."

"Aww." Rhonda placed her hand over her heart. "That's sweet, dear. I can't wait to meet him."

"You're gonna love Snicks. He's the best. It's like he'd just been waiting for someone to care enough about him his whole life. And that's gonna be me."

For some reason, Riley's words sent a pang through Liam like she was speaking from experience. But she should know she was cared for and not on her own. Far from it.

And he was about to prove it to her.

Now was his chance.

Liam quickly turned to his mom. "Hey, Ma, just so you

know, Riley's been working her ass off at the bakery. Did you know she's not even taking Sundays off? Which she promised you guys she'd do. Since you said you're always looking for something to occupy your time during the day when Dad's at the shop now that you're retired, why not spend a few days helping Riley? She does it all herse—"

"Liam!" Riley growled, her eyes shooting daggers his way. "Don't listen to him. He's a liar."

To add the nail in the coffin, he continued, "Her hours keep her at the bakery longer than she needs to be and instead of waiting for one of us, she's been walking home *alone.*"

The betrayal in Riley's eyes almost gutted him, but he knew it needed to be done.

"Riley!" Rhonda's hand flung to her chest as James roared.

"Missy," he warned. "You better not be fuckin' walkin' home alone when it's dark out. You promised us."

"I'm not—"

"She did it the other night," Patrick added, nodding his head.

"I'm gonna murder you both in your sleep tonight," Riley mumbled, sending him and Patrick death glares.

When Liam looked at his mom, he knew what was coming.

Rhonda turned in her seat, calmly placed her fork down on her plate, and sent Riley a pointed stare.

Bingo.

"Riley O'Neil, not only are you walking home alone after dark, are you telling me you're still doing everything yourself?" Her right brow cocked. "I swear you told me you were gonna hire someone. I thought you had. And if you had hired someone like you said *you* would, you wouldn't be forced to walk home when it's dark out."

"I will when I can."

His mom was too calm about this, and Liam knew it.

Rhonda shook her head, her chin dipping down as she let out a heavy sigh. "If I'd known, I would've been there every day helping you. And to think, my baby has been struggling? Please tell me they go in and help you?" She cocked her thumb toward Liam and Patrick.

"They don't," James answered before anyone else had a chance. "Bastards. You raised them better than that, dear."

"Hey! We were there today," Patrick defended. "Besides, Riley doesn't let us in the bakery."

"'Cause you fuck it up." James nodded. He then turned to Riley. "Did they fuck it up today?"

Riley still had a bit of panic in her, but as she looked at James, a playful smile tugged at her lips. "Yep." She popped the 'p.'

James swung back to him and Patrick, jabbing his fork at them. "I told you not to fuck it up."

Rhonda cleared her throat, louder than needed. "Are you telling me *you* knew they weren't helping her, James?" She eyed her husband and Liam had to hold in his laugh.

See, no one was safe from his mom's wrath.

"Rhonda, that's not—"

Her brow cocked. "Sounds like you knew to me."

Grumbling, James took his napkin and tossed it at him and Patrick. "Great, now you've both gotten me in trouble for your fuck-ups. I told you to help Riley more."

"We didn't fuck up," Liam answered. "We helped today."

"Yes. You helped so much by overworking the dough and Patrick eating half my stock," Riley grunted into her food.

"I told you not to fuck it up."

"We tried. I tried more than Pat." Liam pointed at his best friend. "Yell at him, not me."

"No one is yelling."

"Sounds like yelling to me."

"Everyone quiet down." Rhonda flipped to Riley. "Why didn't you tell me?" She held up her hand. "Actually, you know what? I should've known better when it comes to you three. I should've just shown up the day after I retired."

"No. That's not right. You should enjoy your retirement. You don't need to swoop in and help. I've got it under control," Riley pleaded. "I mean, I *did* have it under control until they screwed it up this morning."

Liam had to give it to her. Attempting to deflect the attention back on them versus her when it came to his mother was a golden tactic.

"Riley," James warned. "My little girl is not gonna work her ass to the bone."

"I'm not."

"Bullshit," Liam growled. "You're tired all the time."

"And whose fault is that?" James added, sending his son a pointed look.

Rhonda narrowed her eyes at Liam before turning her sights on her husband. "And I'll be dealing with *you* later."

"Fucking-a." After one last glare toward Liam and Patrick, James stared hard at Riley. "Well, this has been a cluster fuck of high proportions, and now that I'm wrapped up in it, Rhonda's gonna be at the bakery first thing tomorrow morning. Besides, it'll get Rhonda out of the house."

His mom shot a glare toward his dad.

"Not that she needs to be out of the house."

"Damn straight." Rhonda looked at Riley. "But it'd be good to see you more. I wish you would've told me sooner you needed the help. You know I'd do anything for you."

"But you've already done so much. I don't want to ask you for more."

Rhonda waved her off. "You aren't asking for more when that's what parents do. We take care of our babies."

At her words, the entire room fell silent for a brief second. Realizing her mistake, she sighed as she quickly spoke. "I want you to succeed and if you'd let me, I'd love to help. Maybe we can even do what we did when you were younger and see what creations we can come up with together?"

Riley's face softened as she watched his mom, her eyes swimming with unshed tears. "I'd really like that. It'd be nice to lean on someone every once in a while. It's a lot at the bakery to do on my own."

"I'm sure it is, sweetie. I'm sorry I didn't offer it sooner."

"How would you have known? I've been saying I've got it handled anytime anyone would ask."

"You'll have it handled in no time now that you've got me at your beck and call. How about I come in a few days a week and help you with the morning rush?"

"I'd... I'd really like that. There wouldn't be another soul I'd trust more than you at Pastries & Paws."

Rhonda's head tilted to the side, her soft smile on her face as she held Riley's arm. "Then that settles it." She then faced the rest of them. "You're all still on my shit-list, though."

Liam flicked his eyes up as he stabbed a piece of his chicken with his fork. "Thanks for letting us know."

"You're welcome."

Not soon after, the room fell back into its normal discussions, with Patrick doing whatever he could to annoy his father. Liam took the chance to glance at Riley to see what damaged he'd done. Her amber eyes held a slight hint of vulnerability, but yet still so beautiful.

More importantly, as he held her eyes, for the first time in almost two years, he saw relief.

The sight instantly made his stomach clench as his hand tightened around his fork.

He should have done something sooner and right then and there, he swore he'd make it his life's mission to do whatever he could for Riley.

RILEY'S MIND and emotions were all over the freaking place. She didn't know whether to laugh, cry, punch Liam in the face for bringing it up, or run out of the room screaming.

Maybe all of the above.

Oh, God.

What a freaking disaster on so many levels. It'd be one thing if she was only dealing with the fallout of the morning, but no. Her and Liam's impromptu conversation in the kitchen had sent her body into overdrive.

She knew he didn't mean it. But dang did his words make her stomach flip. It'd been like that all day. And there was only so much she could take. He constantly had his hand on her hip, or be close to her, and well damn it, she was sure he was flirting with her a few times.

Although, Riley didn't have much time to really pay attention or think about it since Patrick was at the display case more often than not, eating everything. So she had to keep a close eye on him and keep shooing him away.

But for a while there, whatever was going on between her and Liam felt real. And for the first time in forever, she wasn't in the all-men-suck club.

The problem was, Riley *wanted* Liam's attention to be real.

To feel what it could be like.

To... Riley thickly swallowed... *feel desired.* Maybe that's why she attempted flirting in the kitchen with him. Although she failed miserably, it's like every nerve ending in her body had been heightened by Liam's presence.

The way he said *all yours...* She gulped.

How embarrassing? Gahhh, you're ridiculous. Let's just say it never happened. Yeah, I can do that. Consider it done.

Riley did her best to calm her freaking mind as the room filled with its normal bickering.

Breathe and it will all go away.

After a few minutes of staring down at her potatoes, she glanced at Liam, only to find him watching her, his eyes holding something she couldn't quite figure out.

Whatever it was, though, made her breath stall in her throat, and her cheeks heat.

Well, there goes my plan of pretending it never happened.

Riley knew she just needed to chalk it up to Liam being Liam. He didn't mean anything by it.

But damn, it still got to her in ways she wished it wouldn't.

A part of Riley wanted to toss a spoon full of mashed potatoes in his face for mentioning it to his mom, but then there was an even bigger part of her that was relieved.

The idea of having someone else in her shop... and it being Rhonda. It was almost as if the stress of everything melted away for the first time in years.

Although she'd preferred if Liam had run it by her first but she knew she would have made some excuse to turn down the help.

Liam would have known that, too.

Riley pulled her bottom lip between her teeth as Liam's words, "*I can read you like an open book*," ran through her mind as he stared at her.

Darting her eyes away from Liam to focus on her food, she took a calming breath.

There was one thing Riley knew for sure: family dinners at the Kelly's never lacked entertainment.

CHAPTER ELEVEN

RILEY STILL TRIED to wrap her mind around everything
that'd happened the following Friday.

Five days had passed since the dinner at the Kelly's and
she was still a little lost. Although, Riley had to admit,
things were more manageable for her now that Rhonda was
helping at Pastries & Paws.

A hell of a lot easier.

And on top of that, the visit to the vet with Snickerdoodle turned out better than expected. Riley couldn't
thank Doctor Richman enough for letting her stay on video
chat while Liam took Snicks in for his appointment.

She might not have been able to step away from the
bakery, but with Rhonda helping, she was at least able to
run into the back, which she was grateful for.

As she chatted on the call, Riley hadn't been the least
bit surprised as she watched her kitten crawl all over Doctor
Richman, demanding as much love as he could get. Doctor
Richman had been more than willing to comply with Snickerdoodle's demands.

It was freaking adorable if you asked her. Riley ended

up with a boatload of screenshots of Snicks crawling all over him.

A-freaking-dorable!

Snickerdoodle received his shots during the exam, and was thankfully given a clean bill of health.

The relief Riley felt after the doctor had given her the A-Okay was indescribable. Just knowing her little baby had been out there on his own and came out with no serious issues was like a ray of sunshine on a cloudy day.

Afterward, Liam kept Riley on the call when he made his way to the front desk to talk with Holly, Doctor Richman's wife. And of course, Snickerdoodle demanded love from her as well, which the curvy woman was more than willing to give.

Riley burst out laughing when a Corgi, apparently named Lord Waffles, strutted into view giving the camera the side-eye of all side-eyes before inspecting the animal his mom was now doting all over.

She'd never seen anything like it. And whenever Riley cooed into the camera about how cute the dog was, it would turn its glare on her, as if to tell her he was anything but cute.

Too bad his fluffy Corgi butt said otherwise.

Even thinking about it still made Riley smile.

Overall, though, it'd been a good visit. The best part, hands down, was when Liam mentioned how Pastries & Paws also sold dog and cat treats that were handmade by Riley.

Holly's eyes nearly popped out of her head with excitement.

"No shit!" Holly turned in her seat toward her Corgi and somehow almost rolled out of her chair, causing Liam to jump to help her. "No worries." She'd waved him off. "Happens all the time. Now, tell me more about these treats?

"'Cause I might have to stop by and bring some to the clinic to put them on our counter."

Holy freaking moly! The idea of Richman Veterinary Hospital stocking some of *her* treats.

Heck to the yes. That would be a dream come true.

See, hard work did count for something!

A proud smile quirked Riley's lips.

Despite the fact Riley had to keep reminding them the kitten's name was Snickerdoodle and not Trash Panda, it was a great appointment.

Riley held her hand to her chest as she breathed a grateful sigh.

Rhonda helping at the bakery had been more than a godsend. Everything, and Riley meant everything, had ran more smoothly. The plan was for Rhonda to be at the bakery a few hours once or twice a week, but Rhonda Kelly swooped in and made herself at home, showing up an hour before opening and staying until the closing duties were done.

And after a few days of Rhonda getting the lay of the workload, before Riley knew it, closing tasks were done in half the time.

Actually, almost everything was done in half the time.

Riley had no idea what she'd been missing.

More importantly, Riley no longer felt like she was drowning. Sure, she was still exhausted, but not like before.

Hell, the past two days, Riley even managed to get home at a decent time.

But the best part, hands down, was that she got to spend her days with Rhonda. It was like old times when she'd been a tiny, chubby, round-eyed kid in the kitchen, learning everything she could from the woman she wished was her real mom.

Holy crap on a million crackers was she happy to have Rhonda there.

A mischievous smile played across her lips as Riley thought about the night of the dinner. As soon as they got home from the Kelly's Riley threatened to murder Liam more than once, and swore up and down the next treat she'd have him test, would be his last.

However, after a few shudders from him and a couple of apologies, and a, "*I only did it to help you.*" Riley forgave and even ended up thanking him.

She really did need the help but wasn't sure how to go about it. She sure as hell wasn't going to rain on Rhonda's new retirement and ask her. Riley loved that woman more than anything.

"Look at us!" Rhonda beamed as she wiped down the counter. "We'll be out of here in no time."

Riley spun toward her after flipping the lock on the front door. "You should've been out of here hours ago." Riley's smile spread from ear to ear.

"And miss out on time with my golden child? No, ma'am." Rhonda cocked her hand on her hip, causing Riley to burst into a deep laugh, her entire face lighting.

"I'm telling Liam you said I was your favorite."

"He already knows." Rhonda winked, her eyes twinkling.

"I love you."

"Love you too, child."

Riley took a step toward the counter.

"No, you don't." Rhonda held up her hands. "I look forward to this part every night."

A lightness seeped into Riley's chest as a mega-watt smile formed on her face. "Dance party?"

"Do you even have to ask?" Rhonda threw the rag on the counter. "It's tradition. You can't back away from tradition."

The love on the older woman's face had Riley's heart swelling. She didn't know how she'd done everything without her for so long.

"Once we're done, I'll drop you off at home."

Riley swung her hips with the celebration of another day completed with ease. "Deal."

It was because of Rhonda that Riley found herself relaxing on her bed with Snicks before the sun went down, and for the first time in forever, she wasn't tired.

Actually, she was excited.

She got to spend more time with her baby, and maybe if she was lucky read a book or watch another baking show.

It wasn't soon after Riley got home that she heard the front door open before Patrick stomped into her bedroom, asking if she'd need anything since he planned on heading to their local bar that night to unwind.

At first, Riley's heart clenched as that familiar pang of hurt ran through her. She wasn't an idiot. She knew exactly what happened when Patrick and Liam went out.

Not that she had any reason to be upset. She didn't really... at least that's what she kept repeating over and over again in her head.

Although just because relationships weren't for Riley didn't mean it wouldn't sting the nights she'd be home alone knowing Liam would be off with someone else.

Riley swallowed hard, her stupid freaking heart twisting with her ridiculous *crush* once again screwing her over.

Ugh...

Whatever. Relationships, sex, and love were stupid.

End of story.

Riley only had a few seconds to push the hurt down when she realized Patrick had other plans because he'd snuck farther into her room and tried to steal Snickerdoodle.

"Give him back!" She lunged for her brother, attempting to reach for the kitten he'd plucked from her bed.

Patrick shook his head, his boyish smile on his annoying face. "Nope. I don't think so. He's coming to hang out with me before I leave."

Her brother's words sent another sting through Riley but she managed to hide it. "He doesn't want to hang out with you."

"Snicks wants to hang out with anyone that'll let him bite their fingers."

Well damn, that was true. But more than ever Riley needed him as a distraction from Liam going out with her brother. She hopped off her bed, strolled over to her brother and snatched him from his arms. "And that'll be me, since you'll be getting ready anyway."

Patrick grunted. "Fine. You win this time, but I get him all weekend."

Riley rolled her eyes. "You can try, but I don't think you'll win."

"We'll see about that my dear sister." With that, he walked out of her room and toward the shower.

Riley couldn't really blame her brother for trying to take Snicks with him, though. What could she say? The little guy had stolen all three of their hearts.

Once she knew Patrick was gone for sure this time, Riley's shoulders sunk in on themselves as she tried to push away her hurt.

No! You know what? Nope. We are better than this. We've always been better than this. Tonight is our night to shine.

Riley sat up straight, pushing her shoulders back as she nodded to herself. She was going to take this unexpected freedom and enjoy it. For the first time in probably two years, she was home early enough to truly relax.

Plus, Riley sure as shit wasn't going to let the image of whatever Liam was bound to do rain on her night.

Nope. She was going to take this night as an opportunity for *her time.*

Peaceful.

Alone.

Relaxing.

Well, not really alone since she had Snicks with her.

Riley's smile quirked into a silly grin as she played with the kitten.

Not long after her brother's failed attempt at stealing Snickerdoodle, she heard Patrick call out from the living room, "Don't wait up and don't do anything stupid." Not even a half-second later, Liam hollered, "See ya," right before the front door slammed causing Riley to wince.

Guess it's only a matter of time now... Riley blanched instantly as the words rang through her mind. *For the love of all things. I am freaking pathetic.* Ugh. She annoyed herself. *Get over it. You're being a dumb-dumb.*

After a few more pep talks, Riley calmed down enough to relax into her night.

She ended up staying in her room for another hour playing with the kitten, focusing on how much better her life had become, before deciding to take a shower.

When she was done. She quickly donned her old robe instead of getting dressed. Why not? She was home alone, so it didn't really matter.

Plus, it'd be hours before they got back. *If* they got back to the house at all.

When Riley walked into her bedroom, a tiny cry caught her attention, making her look over at Snickerdoodle playing with a pillow.

"I'm not alone." Riley moved over to her kitten. "I've got you, my little biscuit maker."

Riley sat cross-legged on her bed while she moved her hands in the air, giving Snicks a chance to play.

Another thirty or so minutes ticked by before Riley's stomach growled. "Give me back my hand, Snicks, we're going exploring. I'm hungry."

The kitten cried as Riley pulled her hand away, but soon gave up and pounced back on the pillow.

Riley adjusted her robe when she stood. Normally she'd never leave her room in just her robe, but she knew the guys were out.

Food was more important.

As soon as Riley was off the bed, Snicks ran after her, swatting the hem of the robe as Riley walked.

"Knock it off." Riley chuckled, looking down at the kitten instead of where she was going as she pulled one of the long ropes up, only making Snickerdoodle jump for it again. "You're a little monster. Do I really need to be your personal play-toy?"

Riley was a few steps from the kitchen when Snicks finally achieved his goal and jumped high, grabbing the knot of her robe, effortlessly untying it, exposing Riley's naked body to the cool air as the material swung open.

It was at that exact moment Riley heard a loud crash followed by a pained groan.

In an instant, Riley snapped her head toward the noise. Her heart stopped with her eyes painfully expanding as she saw Liam staring at her wide-eyed with a glass shattered on the floor in front of him.

CHAPTER TWELVE

No matter how hard Liam tried, he couldn't get his brain to function as he stared at Riley's naked body in complete awe. The sight of her instantly went straight to his cock. He'd dreamed of this moment more times than he could count. Albeit not like this, but fuck him, beggars can't be choosers, right?

And at that exact moment, as he feasted his eyes on the most beautiful woman he'd seen in his life, he was seconds from dropping to his knees to give thanks for Riley's creation. Fuck, she was beautiful. More beautiful than he'd ever imagined. Her curves... oh God, the lushness of her body.

Again, holy fuck.

Liam's eyes hungrily took in every inch of Riley as his heart slammed against his chest, threatening to break his ribs. Dear God, she was perfect.

So fucking perfect.

Her breasts hung heavy in a teardrop shape, making Liam's mouth water. Her nipples a deep dusty pink, causing him to roll his eyes into the back of his head in pure pleasure.

He was going to die.

This was it.

He'd get a taste of what Riley was and boom: death.

Fucking figures.

Story of his damn life when it came to Riley.

Liam's eyes avidly moved down her body, seeking out what he'd dreamed of more than anything. However, he'd only gotten about halfway before something finally sparked in his brain, making his body catch up to what was right in front of him.

Liam groaned out in pleasure as the glass of water he'd been holding fell to the floor and shattered.

It all happened so fast, and yet, in his mind he felt like the world had slowed down.

Riley's scream rang throughout the kitchen as she covered herself, running out of there and down the hall like she was an Olympic athlete and going for the gold.

No! Fuck no! Come back!

Finally. Fucking finally, Liam's brain worked as he raced after her. However, the second he made it to Riley's room, he stopped in the doorway. His brows furrowed together as he watched her pace back and forth, her hands fisting at her sides before throwing them in the air.

"Holy fucking shit. No, no, no, no, no!" Riley continued pacing, Liam completely transfixed on her as she moved. "Oh my God, my brother's best friend just saw my fat, lumpy, *naked* body. *Liam! Freaking Liam* of all people just saw *me* naked. Not kinda naked. All the way naked. Like whoop-di-do, here is my hoo-ha, have a gander. I think I'm having a heart attack. Is this what having a heart attack feels like because I'm positive I'm stroking out."

Liam was tempted to move toward her, but his feet were frozen in place as he watched the curvy woman of his dreams have a complete and mental fucking breakdown. And fuck him, she was damn adorable while she did.

"I need to move out. That's the only option. There's no other choice. I need to leave. Pack my bags and get the heck out of here." Riley glared at Snickerdoodle, who was happily playing with her comforter like he hadn't just ruined her life. "How could you? I thought you were my best friend. How could you do this to me? And for what? The string on the robe? You have a million toys. Why did you need my robe?" Again, Riley threw her hands in the air, frustrated. "Oh, God, oh my God. Maybe I can live at the bakery. I'm sure I can get a cot or something and squeeze it into my office. Yeah, yeah, that's plausible. I can do that." She snapped her head toward the kitten. "What I *can't* do is live here 'cause *Liam* saw *me* naked because of you," she groaned, the panic in her voice filling the room.

As Riley began pacing again, the bottom of her robe slightly lifted, giving Liam a glimpse of her thigh, making him snap, his dick already threatening to explode.

"You aren't moving out," he growled, his voice thick and raw.

"Ahh!" Riley screamed as she jumped back. "Don't fucking scare a person like that!" Her eyes rounded as she shoved her hands in his direction, telling him to stop. "Get out. Get out. Get out!"

Liam took a step closer to her, his feet heavy but full of purpose as his eyes honed in on Riley. "You *aren't* moving out."

"You can't tell me what to do!"

"You. Are. Not. Fucking. Moving. Out. Riley." He took the last few steps to stand in front of her. And while her eyes held panic, there was something more. Something that sent a fresh wave of desire to his dick.

The air thickened between them as Liam kept his eyes glued to hers.

"I—"

"You aren't moving out." Liam's voice was deep, sharp, husky, and full of raw desire as his body vibrated.

Riley's breath instantly hitched, as Liam watched her eyes dilate.

That's when he saw what he'd been waiting for in her eyes.

Need.

Before Riley could say another word, Liam cupped the back of her neck, pulling her forward as he slammed his lips onto hers.

Finally.

At Riley's shocked gasp, Liam deepened the kiss, pouring everything he'd fucking wanted to do for years into it.

It was hard.

It was raw.

It was desperate.

And he fucking wanted more.

The moment Riley kissed him back, he lost it again. His hand found the knot on her robe, quickly untying it before sliding his hand inside, moving to her rounded hip before squeezing it. He pulled her in close as she moaned into his mouth. Fuck him, he didn't give a shit about the consequences he knew would come because this, *this* was everything he wanted and more.

Being able to hold Riley in his arms.

Touch her.

Taste her.

Fuck!

Riley tasted better than anything he imagined. Each time she let a tiny moan escape her lips, his dick jumped, egging him on as he threaded his fingers through her hair, keeping control of their kiss.

He couldn't stop.

This was it.

His mind raced as he pulled her into his body, letting himself give in to the desires he fought with for years.

The fact Riley was kissing him back would be his undoing. Keeping their lips locked, with one hand on the back of her head and his other firmly on her hip, he walked them back to her bed, not stopping until they landed in a tangle of bodies.

"Fuck, Riley," Liam growled, tearing his mouth from hers as he placed open-mouth kisses against her jaw before moving down her neck.

"Oh," Riley cried, tossing her head back, giving him more room.

Fuck, she was everything he dreamed of and more.

He was one lucky son-of-a-bitch.

With Riley's robe mostly open, Liam let his hand skirt up her side before cupping her breast, enticing another moan from her.

Riley was so responsive to his touch, it sent another wave of fire through Liam. She was made for him in every way.

As he kissed down her neck, skimming the top of her chest, he poked his tongue out, tracing the rest of the way to her nipple.

"Liam," she moaned, her eyes rolling back in her head.

"Look at me," he growled, his voice rough as he bit next to her nipple, making Riley snap her head toward him. "Eyes on me."

"Liam—"

Riley didn't get to say anything else since he pulled her pert bud into his mouth, sucking the bud in earnest.

"Holy mother of God," she cried.

With a chuckle, Liam's other hand slid to her right breast as he flicked his thumb over her bud, making Riley arch into his hand.

Fuck yes... so fucking responsive. It was enough to unman him. He growled low in his throat, letting his tongue swirl around her nipple, making her shudder.

This would be burned in the back of Liam's mind for the rest of eternity.

Before he lost himself any further, he sat up and pulled his shirt over his head, tossing it behind him. His eyes honed in on hers as she watched him so intently it looked as if she was seeing him for the first time.

And well, damn if that didn't ignite him even further. He wanted that. He wanted Riley to see him this way.

And *only* this way.

As hers.

One hundred percent hers.

"Liam, please."

Her breathy words made his body tighten.

Liam quickly hopped off the bed, causing Riley to throw her hands up. "Wait. What?"

"Shh, I'm not going anywhere," he answered her panicked plea. "You couldn't drag me out of here even if you tried."

Liam placed his knee on the end of the bed as he crawled between her legs. His dick pressed painfully against his zipper as it begged to come out.

He couldn't blame his reaction. Not with Riley laid open in front of him, her body on full display with the sides of her robe bunched under her. Like every one of his fantasies coming to life.

Holy shit, it was a sight to be seen.

He would never forget it.

Fuck, she was goddamn perfect. Too many women raced to hide their bodies, but not her. Riley's confidence never ceased to amaze him.

With a deep growl from low in his throat, Liam wrapped his arms around Riley's ample thighs and yanked her close to him in one fluid move.

"Ahh!" Her hand flung to her chest. "Warn a person. Geez. I'm not some rag-doll."

Liam's eyes shot to hers. "Consider this your warning." He placed his hand on her lower stomach, squeezing as he growled out his next words. "You're mine."

Riley's breath hitched, her eyes rounding as her cheeks heated. "I—"

"If you tell me to stop, I will," he interjected. "But when I tell you I want this so fucking bad I'm shaking, I'm not kidding." He licked his lips. "I want you on my tongue, my face, my cock."

She whimpered.

He moaned. "I've always wondered if your blush went down your whole body." He raked his eyes up and down her, stopping at her lush pussy for a few seconds before moving back to her face. The image would be seared into his mind for the rest of his life. "Now I know."

Liam heard her breath stall in her throat, her all-over blush deepening as he watched her.

Licking his lips again, Liam lowered himself to her core, using his shoulders to push Riley's legs apart.

"Oh, God—"

Liam kissed the inside of her thigh, relishing on how smooth she was before moving to her center.

Fuck, her pussy was beautiful. Lightly trimmed and dripping with need, causing him to groan low in his throat, her scent intoxicating. He knew he was seconds from coming in his jeans as his body ached with need in a way he'd never experienced before.

"Liam, I—"

Riley didn't get to finish her sentence as he let out a shallow, hard rumble while he dragged the flat of his tongue against her core. Riley's flavor instantly exploded against his taste buds.

"Christ!" She bucked, her hands going to his head as she rutted against him. "Oh God, do that again."

Liam chuckled. "I plan on it." And he did. He let his tongue slide over her pussy, making Riley's legs shake. He was in pure fucking heaven. To finally have the woman of his dreams under him was more than he could take.

Riley's hands covered her face. "Oh, God, you need to—"

"I need to what?" he asked, his hand squeezing her leg as his other grazed her soft lower lips, causing her to jerk.

"Ahh." Riley fought her breath. "Wait. I—"

Liam's middle finger traced down her glistening core. "You need to come?" His cocky tone filled the room.

"Yes, no, yes, I—crap, this is embarrassing." Riley thrashed her head from side to side. "I can't think. You're making my brain dive right into a blender that's on the highest setting."

"Mindless pleasure." Liam chuckled, his finger sliding between her slit again. "Then I'm doing something right."

"Yes, but—" She stopped herself, her hands fisting the air.

He felt Riley's body tighten, but Liam knew it wasn't from pleasure this time. No, it was something else. As he pulled back briefly, Riley pushed up on her elbows, looking down at him before dropping back down, pulling the pillow over her face. "Oh God. This can't be happening." Her words were muffled, but he heard them. "There's no freaking way."

"It is."

Riley tossed the pillow aside, refusing to make eye contact with him. "You don't get it."

Liam cocked his brow as a rush of panic hit him.

Did she come to her senses and realized they couldn't cross that line in their dynamic? Had she realized it was *him* and had second thoughts? If Riley asked him to stop, he would, but damn, he'd die if she did.

Although at this point he was going to die, regardless. There was no turning back for him.

This was it.

No woman would ever compare and he wouldn't even try.

Riley was it for him, and this proved it. If she turned him away now, he'd live with that and survive off this memory alone.

"What?" he asked, begging his voice to sound neutral as the rest of his life rested on the balance of this moment. "Do you not want to continue?" He wasn't able to keep the fear out of his voice, even though he tried.

"What? Yes, holy shit, I want this. I think. I mean, it's you, so I've kinda always wanted this, but umm. I just... This is happening really fast and I have to—"

The relief that flooded through Liam's mind was instant. "Thank fuck. I'm so fuckin' turned on I'm about to come in my pants and you haven't even touched me."

Riley gasped, her mouth falling open as her pupils dilated.

"I'm so fucking hard. I think I could break something."

"Don't say that!"

"Why not? I want you." He squeezed her thigh again. "I want you so bad it hurts."

A pained whimper escaped Riley's lips as she shook her head. "It's just..." Riley took an audible breath.

Shit. Okay, something is up.

A wave of uncertainty cascaded around Liam as he pulled back. "Rye, it's me. You can tell me anything." His heart raced as he watched Riley bite her bottom lip, worry filling her face.

"I haven't. Oh, God." She sat up and waved her hand between them. "This."

Liam cocked his head to the side as he studied her, trying to make sense of what she was saying. "You've never had your pussy eaten?" His fingers trailed down her slit again, causing her to shake as she moaned, throwing her head back. If she hadn't, she was in for a treat. That thought alone made his mouth salivate further.

"Yes, no, more. Fuck me."

"I plan on it."

"I can't think. Geez, I really can't think."

It was on the tip of his tongue to tease her, but he could tell she was on the verge of a panic attack, and that was the last thing Liam wanted. Not when his dreams were finally coming true.

"This can't be happening. I have to be in some weird screwed-up food-deprived fever dream."

"If you ask me, I'm a little food-deprived." The flat of his tongue slid over her lush lips again.

She jolted. "Ahhh."

"Also, not a dream." Liam licked his lips, savoring her flavor as Riley's eyes snapped to his.

"My God, you can't keep doing that when I have to tell you something."

Liam kept his eyes focused on her, his fingers lazily drawing a circle on her inner thigh. "Tell me what, babe?"

"I've never..."

"Never what?"

Riley pinched her eyes closed for a second before opening them to stare directly at him. "This. I've never done this."

Liam yanked his brows together as she continued.

"*This.*" She waved her hands between them. "Sex. I've never had sex. There, I've said it." She flung her head back on the bed with an annoyed grunt. "I'm a virgin."

Liam's mouth fell open as Riley's words knocked him over. If he thought his brain had short-circuited when he first saw Riley naked, he'd been mistaken. This was... *holy fuck.*

But then again, it kind of made sense. Riley hadn't been on many dates that he knew of. Sure, there was that year they didn't really talk, so she *might* have crossed that line then but in the back of his head he subconsciously already knew.

She was a virgin.

His Riley.

His dream woman had never been with anyone. *Fuck.*

He was going to be her first...

And her last.

Something primal swept through Liam. More hungry and desperate than he'd ever been before.

A possessive growl took over his body. "Are you telling me no man has ever had the pleasure of being inside of your lush pussy?" He looked down at his prize, glistening with need as his heart slammed against his chest, blood rushing to his ears.

"Umm." Riley's cautious words had him snapping his eyes to her face.

"No." Riley shook her head. "I've never. I've never—"

"*Fuck!*"

When Riley's beautiful eyes rounded, Liam instantly saw the vulnerability in them, making him roughly swallow.

"I've never trusted anyone enough. Not after..." She stopped herself with another shake of her head. "I just... I never got around to it. I don't trust easy and..."

Riley stopped, the air around them thickening as Liam fought to follow her words.

"But I trust you."

CHAPTER THIRTEEN

R*ILEY COULDN'T THINK STRAIGHT* as *nothing* made sense. Holy freaking moly. Where would she even begin?

First off, she was supposed to be in the corner of sex and relationships were overrated, and yet here she was spread wide open, pretty much begging, yes, *begging* for Liam to take her.

Where in the hell is my screw-all-the-opposite sex attitude now? Huh? Huh?

And as she looked at Liam, a very sexy shirtless Liam, a Liam that was between her damn legs after he *tasted* her, she was seconds from her brain exploding.

Holy shit.

Liam saw her naked.

He *kissed* her.

Riley's anxiety raced, the gravity of everything falling around her. Not only was Liam, her long-time forbidden fantasy, between her legs... he tasted her.

Freaking tasted her!

What was even more mind-blowing was after that first shock in the kitchen, not once did Riley try to hide her body from him.

There was something about the way he looked at her that made her feel... safe.

Accepted for exactly how she was.

That's 'cause you do feel safe with him, dumb-dumb. Even naked, it's Liam. Your Liam. You would never feel unsafe with him, even spread open like a freaking three-course meal for him to see every inch of you.

Riley groaned, unsure which cliff her brain was taking a running leap off of, but it was happening. What in the hell was wrong with her? Besides, weren't virgins supposed to be all shy and meek?

Guess not, since I've got my hoo-ha a few inches from his face...

While she was at it, why not add in the whole *but I trust you* to the mix? Seriously, kill her now. Could she sound any more desperate?

Then again, could anyone blame her? This was Liam freaking Kelly. Her knight in shining armor.

Only in her deepest fantasies did Riley allow herself to dream of something between them happening.

And there went her brain again, taking a hard left from the *wow this is happening* to the, *oh my God, what have I done?*

It mortified Riley on so many levels.

However, the moment her mind and body got on the same page to get the hell out of there and pretend it never happened, her brain took another sharp turn in the opposite direction, making her heat and plead for Liam to keep going.

And damn it, Riley didn't want to fight her body.

She *did* want this.

Who wouldn't?

To feel desired.

To let her body open and be explored. That outweighed

any sense of shame she should have by being so willing, right?

It's not like this was a stranger. This was Liam. She wasn't out there at some bar, trying to pick up a random guy to lose her V-card with. No, actually, if the situation hadn't happened the way it did, she'd still be more than content living her life as it was.

Virginity and all.

Hell, she already had the cat...

But now that she had this chance, why not go for it? Why not say screw it and see what could happen?

Why couldn't she be allowed to experience sex? Liam was the only man she trusted other than her brother and James.

Besides, Liam didn't seem too hard-pressed to be where he was. He's the one who came after her.

He's the one that kissed her first.

He's the one that untied her robe, pulled her nipple into his mouth and... Riley gulped.

Yeah, he didn't seem too weirded out by the fact his best friend's little sister was the one he was with. So, maybe she could take this as a sign from the Universe.

Riley wasn't foolish enough to think this would start something between them. Or all her secret fantasies would come to life, but doing this could at least give her an experience she never thought was in the cards for her.

And one she'd never forget, that was for damn sure.

Maybe she'd get lucky and Liam would... she didn't know... teach her? Show her what she'd been missing out on?

Did that sound pathetic? It definitely sounded pathetic to her.

Oh, Lord, her brain seized as she tried to make sense of everything as her mind and body battled against each other.

The way Liam squeezed her stomach, growling out the words *you're mine,* sparked something inside of Riley she'd never felt or even imagined feeling.

Riley never thought she'd be down for that possessive type, but here she was, willingly spreading her legs further each time Liam growled or grunted.

Is this what sex is always like?

Her heart leaped to her throat as the heaviness in the room choked her.

She might never get this chance again.

On one hand, this was Liam and she *did* trust him.

And on the other, this was *freaking* Liam. Her brother's best friend. That was cause for the whole thing to end up in a disaster.

Good job thinking about this now, after Liam's already gotten acquainted with my va-jay-jay. The damage is definitely already done. There is no coming back from this.

Despite herself and the battle raging in her mind, she wanted this.

She wanted him.

Damn the consequences. Riley could deal with those later. She could make it out of anything. She knew that for a fact. Because she already had.

She was strong.

She'd always been strong. She could do this. Even if it meant her heart getting obliterated by the one person she promised herself she'd never indulge in.

Riley might never get this opportunity again. And would she really be willing to look back at her life and accept she let this pass her by?

No.

Hell no.

That wasn't her style. She was a fighter.

As Riley looked down at her body, there was the

smallest urge to cover herself to hide from Liam's prying eyes as he open-mouth stared at her.

Absolutely not. This was her. She wouldn't hide herself from Liam.

Not now.

Not when Riley was doing everything in her power to put herself out there with someone she trusted.

Besides, the lust she saw staring back at her in Liam's shocked eyes was enough to keep her in the present moment and not be afraid. And even though Riley knew doing this would more than likely destroy her heart in the end, it was fine by her. After this was all over, she had no plans of ever doing something like this again.

She might have tipped off her 'sex and all relationships were stupid' ledge at the moment, but she knew after Liam, there would never be another.

Argh...

Enough was enough. No more second-guessing.

Let's do this.

The best she could, Riley threw the barriers around her heart and prayed they'd hold together. "I trust you." She forced out a steady breath as her eyes searched his. "I trust you more than anyone."

Liam growled, the noise vibrating through her core, making her insides tingle.

"*Please.* I want it to be you. Show me. Teach me. You can be the one to teach me, right?"

"Fuck, Riley!" Liam's hand gripped tighter on her thigh as he stared her down. His eyes full of so much heat, she roughly swallowed as she watched him.

Am I making the right choice? I have to be right. This might be my only chance at this. She took another second for herself. *Yes, I am.*

Liam's eyes pinned her in place, making her breath stall

in her throat not really sure how to react. "I want to know," she rushed out. "And I want it to be you."

So much could go wrong. The consequences were endless.

What if she hated sex?

She doubted it. Well, probably not if it was with Liam. She might hate it with someone else, but not him.

Riley already knew that for a fact.

Her brother could find out...

She gulped. That would be a huge cluster and something she definitely wanted to avoid.

And when things ended, she knew it would be *her* heart shattered.

Riley bit her bottom lip, her eyes searching his. Was all the risk worth it? To finally be with the man she wanted for as long as she could remember?

Yeah... Yeah, it was.

Mustering all the courage Riley had, she chuckled desperately, trying to break the tension. "This is a hard conversation to have when you're inches from my hoo-ha."

"Your hoo-ha?" Liam quirked his brow.

"Uhhh, yeah."

He shook his head, but there was a slight smirk on his lips. "I don't know. I kinda like being this close to your *hoo-ha.*"

"Don't say it like that." She threw her arm over her eyes as Liam huffed out a laugh, the heat of his breath dancing against her core, making her all too aware of him being *that* close. Doing her best to ignore it, she continued, "I want to know what all the hype is about. I want to experience what it feels like to be intimate with someone. To come apart by another's hands. And I want that with you. I also know you're the only one I'd ever trust to do it." Riley groaned. "This is so freaking embarrassing."

"Babe." His soft word somehow felt like a warm hug, but simultaneously sent a shock wave through her as she heard it laced with lust. Which, if she were being honest, blew her damn mind. This was Liam Kelly. If anyone would've told her a week ago Liam would have lust in his voice directed at her, she would have laughed in their face.

"There is not a damn thing to be embarrassed about. I'm a little shocked, yeah, but fuck... you don't need to be embarrassed. If anything, you just made my dick harder."

Riley's eyes shot open. *Holy shit.*

CHAPTER FOURTEEN

Liam didn't know whether he'd won the lottery or was in some weird fever dream and was about to wake up to the worst fucking day of his life if this wasn't real. Every single part of him ached with arousal as he desperately forced himself to calm down.

Liam in no way wanted to scare Riley with how badly he wanted this. But fuck, it was hard.

While he perched himself between her thighs, his gaze raked over her lush curves. He'd never get the sight out of his mind, and he didn't want to.

He could die a happy man.

However, there was a nagging feeling deep in the pit of his gut that screamed Riley didn't truly understand the implications if they went through with this.

Yes, she was a virgin and she'd be losing that status, but it was so much more.

If they went down this path, it was a done deal for Liam.

Actually, it was already a done deal for him.

It always had been.

However, a pleading in Riley's eyes told Liam she didn't

fully comprehend the end game he was playing at now. And as Liam watched her, there was an unease almost as if she assumed this was her one and only shot at what... being with someone?

Fuck, that gutted him on so many levels. Sure, he was an overprotective dick when it came to Riley, but that stemmed from being in love with her and wanting her for himself. Not that she didn't deserve the world and all the pleasures that came along with it.

Because she did.

Fuck.

It nearly killed Liam to realize Riley thought she didn't deserve love, affection, and fucking fantastic sex.

She deserved it all.

As Riley laid beneath him, he could see her uncertainty. He could see her wheels turning. He could see the panic.

That's when it hit him like a punch to his stomach at full force. Something he didn't want to see bubbled inside of him and he knew.

Maybe she didn't feel for him the way he felt for her. He *knew* she was attracted to him.

But maybe in his delusional fantasy, he made it more, and those lines blurred for him.

Liam swallowed past the lump in his throat. If they did this, would it mean *nothing* to Riley? He would be just someone to get experience with? The thought nearly choked him as he searched her eyes.

No fucking way.

No.

He wouldn't let that happen. He couldn't let that happen. This was going to be all or nothing. It had to be. He couldn't be so fucking close to his dream just for it to be taken away.

But if she doesn't want that, I won't push her. I'd never

push her. I'd take what she'd be willing to give me and then I'd deal with the fallout afterward.

That thought alone pierced directly into his soul.

Liam's throat thickened as he searched Riley's face. He could always read her, and he knew it was on the tip of her tongue to dismiss what this really was.

What he wanted this to be.

"This could be a win-win, right?" she sputtered. "You get off, you uhh... I don't want to say teach me, but uhh, show me... you know?"

Liam's brows pulled in the middle as his suspicions were confirmed making his heart plummet.

A win-win?

A part of him wanted to get up and leave her room, pretend none of this happened and go back to his wayward fantasy. This wasn't how it was supposed to go. And it was never how he pictured finally being able to give in to his desires.

And now he was just... frustrated.

To be so fucking close to everything he ever dreamed of only to... what? How could it be going right and yet so fucking wrong at the same time?

Liam looked down at her body. The body he begged for and dreamed of. He was at a loss for words. And as his heart ripped apart, with his brain telling him to leave and save what he could before it got worse, he couldn't.

The bubble of unease he had switched over to pure frustration as his mind raced.

Liam watched her take a shaky breath. "Uhh. Your silence is starting to freak me out." She pushed herself to her elbows. "If me being a virgin is an issue, I get it. But if you're willing..." The words hung between them. "I'd never be able to repay you." Riley's voice was soft, almost painful to hear.

Repay me? Like I'd be doing her a favor?

Liam was no stranger to frustration during sex in the past. Usually it was on his part, since the person he was with *wasn't* Riley. But this was a new type of frustration altogether.

And if he was being honest, he didn't know how to handle it.

Liam closed his eyes, calming himself the best he could. How could he make her see this was the furthest thing from a favor anyone could think of?

God, he really should get up, put his shirt back on, and walk away. He really should... But there was one problem.

He could never tell her no.

"Liam?"

Instead of answering Riley, Liam shoved his feelings aside knowing he wouldn't be able to express what he really wanted and instead wrapped his arms around her thighs, yanking her even closer to his face.

"Ahh! What did I tell you about that?"

"I warned you already." Liam closed his eyes, swallowing down his frustrations knowing he'd figure it out later, as the tip of his tongue flicked against her clit. Her taste once again overwhelming his senses.

"Oh, God. That feels..." she trailed off.

Liam straightened his shoulders with a new flood of determination and purpose, pushing Riley's legs further apart. "It's about to feel a fuck-ton better," he rumbled as he glanced at her over her core, before he pulled her clit into his mouth, keeping eye contact with her the whole time.

"Oh, fudging-fudge."

Liam flicked his teeth against her nub. "Told you."

"Liam," Riley breathlessly panted as her hands fisted at her sides.

Fuck, he was going to commit her saying his name like

that to memory. Liam moaned against her core, his name falling out of Riley's mouth laced with need... yeah.

He'd never forget it.

Slowly, and as carefully as he could, Liam pushed one finger, then two, into her center, seeking out her spot. God, she was tight around him, causing his dick to instantly take notice.

Riley shuddered as soon as he reached her spot, her legs tightening around his shoulders.

Liam leaned into their intimacy, letting what they were doing rush through him, as he was determined to fix how they got to this point.

This was only the beginning.

He felt Riley's muscles strain as he pulled her clit into her mouth, this time sucking. Within an instant, Riley exploded, drenching his lower chin as he worked his fingers while she bucked against his hand.

"Oh my—"

Liam kept her steady, moving his other hand to her stomach to keep her in place as he drew out her orgasm.

"Garughhhh."

That's right... you'll always remember this. Remember it was me. Liam nudged his fingers against the spot inside her heat, only slowing for a second as he worked to build back pressure, determined to immediately roll her into another climax.

Liam knew there was a small part of him that edged her under his frustration, but there was a bigger part of him that needed Riley to remember this.

Remember *who* was bringing her this type of pleasure.

She squirmed under his skillful mouth as his fingers worked her core. His dick harder than it's ever been, as it leaked pre-cum into his boxers.

It took everything inside of Liam to hold back.

Fuck, just seeing *his* Riley like this was enough to have him shoot his load without even taking his dick out.

"Liam, Liam—"

"Say my name," he demanded as he felt her muscles clench around his fingers.

"*Liam!*" Riley screamed as he sucked on her clit causing Riley to skyrocket, his own release covering his boxers as he closed his eyes.

Fuck, he hadn't done that since he was a teenager. *Holy shit.*

Liam sat back more than a little dazed from the outcome as he focused on Riley as she panted, working on gaining back control of her body.

It was by far the most beautiful thing he'd ever seen.

Swallowing down his high, he nodded. "You did good."

Riley's eyes shot to his as a pleased smile cracked her lips. "Pretty sure you did all the work there. Holy crap. I..." she trailed off, still in her blissed-out world.

He did that.

He gave that to her.

As Riley laid there open for him, her legs still on either side of his shoulders, Liam crawled up the bed. When he reached her head, he brought his lips down to hers in a searing kiss.

A kiss full of promise.

A kiss full of hunger.

A kiss full of determination.

He might not like all the circumstances, but he wasn't going to back down. Not when he'd finally got the woman he'd always wanted:

Riley.

He retook her lips, pouring his need into their embrace before pulling away, only to kiss his way down her jaw. Carefully, not to hurt her, he moved off the bed and headed toward his discarded shirt. The same shirt the kitten was now rolling around in.

"Wait, that's it?" Riley sat up and watched him.

Liam turned back to her, his shirt and the kitten in his hands. "For now."

"But what about you?" Her eyes moved down his body. "What about the sex?"

Quickly, Liam walked back over to Riley, detangling the kitten as he went. He placed the little guy on her comforter. Then leaned over and kissed her softly one last time. "Don't worry about me. This was about you. Besides, I think Trash Panda wants to play."

Riley stared at him, her brows bunched together like he had two heads. "But?"

Liam shook his head and pointed toward the kitten who was crawling toward Riley. "Looks like he's demanding your attention."

"But, but... what about the sex?"

A low chuckle slipped out of Liam's throat. "We'll get there." He turned on his heel and headed out of the room to figure out his game plan.

CHAPTER FIFTEEN

The next morning, Liam still felt out of sorts. After *finally* getting a taste of his dream woman, you'd think it would've put him in a good mood, but no, instead he was fighting his own damn demons.

He'd spent the entire night replaying everything. And he meant everything, trying to pinpoint where he went wrong to make Riley think he'd only ever want her to get off, or that she'd be willing to settle for him taking her virginity and that would the end of it.

It took everything inside of Liam last night to walk out of her bedroom and not confess his undying love for her. His ego was a little bruised, but at least he had his pride...

Okay, kind of.

Coming in your jeans at his age was pretty embarrassing.

Whatever, though. *That*'s how much he enjoyed Riley and he was willing to accept he left her room with a sticky mess below his belt.

Now, he was stuck exactly where he was last night, desperately wracking his brain to come up with a plan to convince her this was more than just a one-time thing. Or even him teaching her about sex.

Liam was also ashamed to admit the number of times he forced himself *not* to run back into her room and lay it all out in the open right then and there.

It turned out to be a shit night as he tossed and turned, still not figuring out a solid plan of action. It's why he crawled out of bed before the sun came up and headed his ass to the shop on his Saturday off.

Call him a coward but the next time he saw Riley, he wanted to know exactly what his plan of action was to make her his. And in order to do that, he needed to get out of their house and figure it out.

He'd been at the shop for almost two hours and still hadn't gotten anywhere.

With a frustrated huff, Liam wiped his hands off on a rag after replacing the spark plugs in the SUV currently in his bay.

However, as he demanded his brain to concentrate on the task at hand, he couldn't stop his mind from replaying Riley's moans and pleasure-filled noises.

And when she screamed his name...

Fuck.

The way she responded to his touch.

The feel of her pussy clenched tight around his fingers as she exploded. She was more beautiful than he could've imagined.

The number of times he ended up jerking off last night as Riley's sounds replayed through his mind...

No wonder he hadn't come up with a game plan yet.

Liam's eyes closed slowly as he pulled his bottom lip into his mouth, imagining her taste for the millionth time. He never thought he'd actually get the chance to savor her. And to think he gave her shit about bringing the cat home.

As soon as Liam figured out how to win Riley over, he was going to make the little guy a steak dinner.

He'd never been so fucking thankful he turned down Patrick on his offer to go out in his life.

Liam squeezed his eyes tighter, his stomach recoiling at the thought that if he'd given in to Patrick's incessant begging, he could've missed it all. He could've missed his opportunity.

Best decision of his life.

Add in the possessiveness Liam felt knowing Riley hadn't been with anyone...

Maybe best decision was putting it lightly.

He shrugged. Liam didn't give a shit that the moment Patrick found out, he'd murder him. There was no going back for him, and he'd figure it out. Just add it to the list of stuff he needed to get in order before he saw Riley again.

But at this point, he knew there was no going back for either of them.

"Dude, why are you here on your Saturday off? I didn't realize your SUV wasn't in the driveway."

Speak of the devil. "What? You were too hungover to be aware of your basic surroundings?"

"I wish." Patrick barked out a laugh. He kicked a stool over to Liam's bay and plopped down on it. "The bar was a fucking bust. I was home before one."

The hair stood on the back of Liam's neck. He *thought* he heard something outside his bedroom door just after he'd gotten into bed, but he wasn't positive.

Holy fuck, that would've been a fucking disaster before he even got him and Riley started.

"Why're you here?" he asked, seemingly oblivious to Liam's new wave of panic. "I thought you wanted to get some sleep. Wasn't that your excuse for not going out with me last night?" Patrick cocked his brow.

"I did sleep. Not everyone needs to sleep eighteen hours to feel rested."

Patrick sent him a strange look. "You aren't wrong. No amount of beauty sleep would make you... beautiful."

Liam flicked his eyes to the ceiling. "Maybe you should try it sometime. Who knows, it might fix your ugly mug."

Patrick's hand flung to his chest as his bottom lip poked out in an overly dramatic way. "Ouch. Right through the heart."

"What? You can say it, but I can't?"

"No. You can't." Patrick folded his arms over his chest. "Especially since you left me hanging last night."

Turning to face his annoying best friend, Liam leaned against the front end of the SUV, crossing one leg over the other. He then waved his hand in a circle for Patrick to continue. There was no work getting done on the SUV in his bay or on his plan until Patrick took a hike.

"I struck out every single time. I couldn't even wallow in self-pity since I needed to drive home. I barely had a buzz. I *needed* my wingman," he started. "But no... my best friend wanted to rest. And to think, if he needed his sleep so damn bad, he would still be at home doing just that. Why the hell are you here? You're not on until like three Saturdays from now," he grunted, like a child who hadn't gotten his way.

I'm here 'cause I almost fucked your sister last night after she pretty much begged me to teach her what to do and before I drove headfirst into making her mine, I needed to come up with a solid way to execute that.

"I had to get this car out of my bay by Monday. Dad said he's got a *1967 Firebird* comin' in."

Patrick's eyes widened as his jaw dropped. "And he's giving it to you?"

"Why wouldn't he?" Liam puffed his chest. "I'm the best in the shop."

"Pfft. You keep tellin' yourself that." Patrick scrunched his face. "First, you leave me stranded last night and now this. I might as well call the funeral home and make my arrangements."

"Geez, you're fucking dramatic. It was one night."

"One night. Shrum night." He jumped up from the stool. "I'm disappointed."

"I can see that." A half-smile formed on Liam's face. "You tend to disappoint a lot of people. Look at it this way. You can say you saved the poor chick you were gonna end up with last night from waking up unsatisfied."

"Fuck you very much. No one leaves my bed without being thoroughly satisfied." Patrick wiggled his brows. "Multiple times."

"So you're saying you come before you even get your pants off and then you have to pretend?"

"And to think I call you my best friend and wingman?" The audacity on Patrick's face was enough for Liam to burst into a deep belly laugh.

"Glad I can amuse you."

"You always do."

"Yeah, whatever." Patrick waved him off. "I've gotta head up to the front to talk to a customer, but by the time I come back, I'm expecting an apology." He held his hand over his heart.

"Might as well call the funeral home while you're up there then."

"Fuck you."

"Only in your dreams."

"More like my nightmares."

Liam tossed his head back and laughed as Patrick stomped toward the office. That was exactly what he needed, some good ole playful jabbing to clear his mind.

As Liam walked over to his toolbox to fill out his ticket,

it's like everything started clicking into place. As quickly as he could, Liam added in his time and nearly ran toward the office to turn in his job.

He was a man on a mission.

Liam flung open the glass door to the office.

"Wow. Okay, that sounds like a lot of work," the guy standing in front of Patrick remarked. "Can I get a quote?"

Patrick nodded. "Sure. *Be yourself. Everyone else is fuckin' taken,* or some shit like that?"

The customer deadpanned, which made Liam chuckle. "I meant a car quote…"

Patrick tapped his finger on his chin for a second and then snapped his fingers. "How about, *Live free, Drive hard?* Or, *Keep Calm and Drive the Fuck On?*"

Liam shook his head as he tossed his ticket on the desk. "I'm out. See you later." With that, he moved out of the office toward his bay to pack up. His heart raced as excitement flooded through him.

If Riley wants me to teach or show her everything I know, I can do that. I'll teach her every fucking thing, and then just when she thinks that's all I've got, I'll teach her more.

An accomplished smile pulled at the corner of Liam's lips.

It wasn't going to be his problem. He'd make sure it took him over fifty years to teach her everything she wanted. And by that time, he'd make sure Riley was so damn in love with him, there was no going back.

Now, the only problem Liam had was to hide it from Patrick until he could figure out a way to tell him he was going to marry his sister.

CHAPTER SIXTEEN

THANK EVERYTHING IN THE WORLD, Pastries & Paws closed early on Saturdays, since it gave Riley time to figure out her next move or keep replaying the events, attempting to understand everything that'd happened. Because that's how her morning had gone.

Initially, Riley was grateful for the distraction of her customers, since it let her mind focus on something other than Liam. However, it only took a half hour into her day to realize Rhonda was all too aware something was up.

She wasn't wrong, but still...

Rhonda's eyes were glued to Riley with every move she made, which of course, had Riley fumbling more times than she'd like to admit. And whenever Riley chanced a glance at the older woman, Rhonda quirked her brow and gave her a once-over, only causing more panic in Riley.

Could she tell? Did she know? Is it written on my forehead Liam was all in her hoo-ha?

Gahhh!

The entire morning had been some weird standoff between the two of them that Riley wanted no part of. Who would? It's why it was Riley's only mission to avoid Rhonda at all costs as soon as she realized what was going on. Which worked... until now.

Riley stood in the back of the kitchen with a recipe card in hand as Rhonda closed the front. She worried her bottom lip since she knew it was only a matter of time before Rhonda joined her.

And they'd be alone.

No more avoiding.

And for the first time since Rhonda began helping at Pastries & Paws, Riley was nervous to have her there. And if she were being honest, it threw her for a freaking loop because it was Rhonda. The woman she loved like she was her own mother.

She *always* wanted her around.

Then again, that was before her son had gotten acquainted with Riley's downstairs area.

Ugh. Riley flicked her eyes upward, stifling her groan.

On one hand, she wanted the cathartic feeling she got when she worked on her creations and would let her mind process through whatever her current problem was. On the other, the idea of being alone with Rhonda right now made her shudder.

It took everything inside of Riley not to go to the nearest wall and bang her head against it.

Urrgh. That'd be real mature. But I guess my mature button took a flying leap off a cliff the moment I begged Liam to stick his dick inside me.

Riley's right eye twitched just thinking about the words.

And not just because you work with his mother. But 'cause you still don't know what in the ever-loving hell you're doing... and again... his mom is here! Why in the fudge did I not think this through more?

The wall was looking pretty damn good right about now. Maybe the orgasms had scrambled Riley's brain...

In her defense, though, they were by far the best orgasms she'd ever had in her life.

Hands down.

The hot pleasure that coursed through every inch of her body... hoo-boy. Riley thought she'd died.

Hold on... wait a minute, maybe she *did* die?

Holy moly, yes!

That would explain everything.

Yeah. This was all just some weird ghost hallucination. Liam clicked some unknown button inside my va-jay-jay and wham, dead. Either that or I'm in another dimension.

Riley wanted to pat herself on the back for figuring it out. It was the only logical explanation, right? It would also explain Liam leaving afterward like it was no big deal.

Damn, the other dimension was brutal.

One second he was between her legs going to chow-town, and then next... Liam handed her Snicks and went off on his merry way back to the correct universe.

It all made sense now because there was no way Liam would've left her like he did. Everyone knew leaving Riley to her own thoughts was *never* a good idea.

Or, or... hear me out, Rye. What if it was all a dream? Huh? Yeah, like one of those really freakin' realistic ones where you swear it was real.

Riley shifted, causing a pang of soreness on her inner thigh to hit her. In the exact same spot she'd woken up to see a huge bruise. A bruise left by one Liam Kelly when he... you know, *went to town on her lady bits.*

Argh. Banging her head against the wall sure as hell sounded appealing.

The thing was, if Liam *knew* Riley would freak out after he left, then why would he do it? Why would he leave her without answering her questions?

What did it mean?

What would happen next?

Were they going to continue?

Riley one hundred percent hoped they would if this wasn't some weird hallucination. Especially if last night was any indication of what else he was capable of doing.

Oh, God, what if he thought it was all a mistake?

What if she just wasn't what he was looking for in a partner to get off with? Riley's gut churned. She'd be lying if she said the thought of *her* being his reason for walking away didn't sting.

Riley bit her lip as her mind kept going. If that were the case, it would actually shatter her heart. Or what if it was the fact her being a virgin really was a turn off for him? Sure, he said otherwise, but actions speak louder than words.

And Liam's actions were leaving Riley on her bed without a care in the world.

Gahhh. Riley wanted to scream, cry, punch the air, anything to make it all make sense.

The worst part?

Someone really needed to help Riley because despite her mental breakdown, she couldn't help her mind harping on the fact she didn't actually get to see what Liam's hanging appendage looked like.

Riley really wanted to see it.

Like *really* wanted to see it.

Pfft. Couldn't Liam have thrown me a bone, and... I don't know, pulled down his— She stopped herself. *Oh, geez, a* bone. *Really, Riley? Really?*

A strained noise escaped her throat. *No wonder he left...*

Riley's cheeks flushed as she squeezed her eyes tighter, willing the whole situation to be some screwed-up dream.

Would you stop lying to yourself? It wasn't a dream. Stop. Deal with this like an adult. Riley wrinkled her nose like she'd smelled something bad. *An adult? Really. I lost the adult title when I begged Liam to do me like some horny teenager.*

Riley's self-induced tension headache was now in full swing as she opened her eyes.

Ahhhhhhhhhhhh!

Holy crap on ten million crackers, Liam, her fantasy man, her brother's best friend, went down on her and now knew she was a virgin.

And you asked him to teach you about sex! Don't forget that bit.

She was really winning *all* the awards for being an idiot.

Riley's eyes migrated to the ceiling. *Universe, I'd really appreciate if you did me a solid and took me out. I'm not picky. Lightning, a freak storm, a volcano opening under me... pick your poison.* Her face scrunched. *I'm serious. Any second now.*

She waited a beat before huffing out a sigh. *Fine. Be that way, you jerk.*

As Riley replayed everything once again for the millionth time, she cringed.

In her defense, what would you expect from a nearly thirty-year-old virgin? Almost two years to the big three-o and given the opportunity to explore a part of her she never thought she would... of freaking course, she went for it.

She'd be an idiot not to.

Although, she did kind of beg him... like really begged him. Not her finest moment.

Riley's brows knitted together as she shook her head. But then again, it was Liam. She trusted him with her life. Plus, he seemed like he enjoyed himself last night. Even if he didn't get anything in return.

Riley pulled her bottom lip between her teeth.

You know what? I put my cards on the table with

someone I trust. And there was an orgasm in it. Two, actually. Maybe instead of having a mental breakdown, I should... I don't know, own it?

Yeah. Riley straightened her shoulders.

Why can't I be confident and accept the fact I wanted to have sex and wanted it to be with Liam? What's the harm in admitting that? It's not like we already haven't crossed the line.

I love myself exactly as I am. This is all just another step in life. One I didn't think I wanted, but I do. At least with Liam. Just for a little while.

And for freak's sake, I'm a human being who also has urges.

There is nothing to be ashamed of... Unless Liam thinks it was a huge mistake... Wait. No. Absolutely not. I'm not going down that path. Even if he thought it was a mistake, I'm not gonna let this change who I am.

Riley puffed her chest and straightened. There should be absolutely no shame in what they did. And she refused to fall prey to her classic overthinking tendencies.

Nope.

Not this time.

Riley was going to hold her head high and put herself out there if Liam would take her up on her offer.

I got this.

Riley's stomach fluttered as their first kiss popped into her mind, making her lips tingle. It took everything she had not to trace her fingertips along them as she became lost in the memory. She'd never experienced anything like it. Yeah, she'd kissed a few guys here and there, but Liam's kiss...

Damn, it was... Wow.

After a kiss like that, of course her body's only natural reaction would be to throw herself at him.

It was biology or some crap like that? Maybe even

chemistry... although, at this point, her brain could probably argue it was calculus and physics as well.

Sex was human nature, and even though Riley still stood strong in the *relationships and love* were stupid corner. If Liam was willing to teach her, she'd learn everything she could.

Sure, Riley usually bunched Liam under the umbrella of her brother's best friend, and her knight in shining armor in most cases, but Liam was her friend too.

More than just her friend. He'd always been there for her.

And now, he'd just so happen to be her friend who also gave her orgasms.

A new determined smile spread across Riley's lips.

However, there was one problem. A kind of huge problem... Liam left their house before she'd even woken up, and she knew it wasn't his Saturday to work.

It's 'cause he didn't know how to deal with you.

Riley's eyes rounded at the thought. *No, that wasn't it. There has to be something I'm missing.*

If she were to look at the situation logically, she could see where he'd be hesitant. It only made sense since them sleeping together would complicate things. But maybe... all Riley needed to do was convince Liam she was an excellent and *fast* learner. And as soon as he was done, she'd swear it wouldn't change anything between them. Plus, no one would ever need to know.

It could be their little secret.

And they would leave it at that.

Sure, Riley would end up with a broken heart, but she'd get over it.

Relationships weren't for her. She knew that, and she was fine with it.

Whatever Liam and Riley ended up doing would be a

small blip in her life.

Nothing more.

Now to figure out how to get him to agree. I'm an outstanding student, and hoo-boy, he'd be an excellent teacher. That's one hundred percent already been proven.

Lust pooled in her lower belly as Riley thought about what he'd already done, and how he made her feel.

Before she could figure out her next step, though, someone cleared their throat behind her, making Riley jump. "Ahh!"

Oh, crap. How had Riley gotten so lost in thought, she'd forgotten Rhonda was there?

Riley swallowed roughly, her eyes bulging out of her head. What the hell was she supposed to say?

"Hey, Rhonda. We had a great day today, didn't we? Lots of happy customers. Oh, and by the way, your son had his tongue in my no-no square last night. Also, I pretty much begged him to show me how sex worked, 'cause I'm a virgin. Surprise. I've never done the deed. Which I'm fine with. Single club for life! But, yeah, I still want him to stick his part into my part. One problem though, he left last night after getting me off and he was gone this morning, so I'm kinda freaking out. But it's no big deal. Haha. Although I'd really like to lose my V-card and he's the one I want to do it with. Please don't hate me."

For freak's sake. Yeah, that word vomit would go over real freaking well.

"Either that recipe has got you stumped or something's on your mind?"

Riley's heart hammered against her chest at Rhonda's voice.

Uhhh. Maybe if I don't move, she can't see me...

"Riley..."

Of course she can see me, you dumb-dumb. Geez, Liam

really did scramble my brains.

Riley's eyes shot to the recipe card in her hand, glaring at it as if it was the card's fault for her being in her head. She attempted to play it cool as she kept her body turned away from the older woman. "Huh? What?"

"Something's off, missy. Has been all day. Finally wanna clue me in?"

Riley straightened her shoulders, doing her best to keep herself calm as she turned to face Rhonda, only to see the older woman's arms folded over her chest, giving Riley her signature stare down.

Crap.

"When I got here you had this dazed look, but since we were busy I let it slide. But not anymore, Miss Thing. What's going on?"

Riley's eyes rounded as her mind raced to come up with an answer which wasn't *I want your son to take my virginity and he ate me out last night.*

Sweat broke out on the back of Riley's neck as her eyes flicked around the room before focusing back on Rhonda. "Umm."

Her brain must have freaked out, since instead of coming up with a plausible excuse that might have been believable, Riley made a big show out of yawning and throwing her hands in the air. "It's nothing. I'm just tired."

Really? Just tired. That's all I've got? This is Rhonda, she's gonna see right through you, idiot.

Riley held back her wince the moment Rhonda cocked her brow.

Well, in Riley's defense, she *was* tired since she'd gotten exactly zero sleep after Liam left her room. But she didn't have to put on a dang fully orchestrated performance to prove her point.

"Call me crazy, but I don't think that's it." Rhonda

wiped her hands on her apron as she looked her up and down. "Did those idiot boys do something to piss you off? Leave the toilet seat up? Ruin your clothes in the laundry? Make a mess and not clean it? Did Liam or Pat upset you in any way? If so, you just say the word and I'll fix it."

"No!" Riley's eyes nearly popped out of her head.

"You sure?" Rhonda asked. "Liam can be a handful—"

He had his hands full of my va-jay-jay!

"And we all know how Patrick is. You never know what those two are capable of getting up to." She shook her head. "You're my golden child. They were the ones that put gray in my hair before there should've been."

Riley huffed out a strained laugh, her eyes dancing around the room. "Yeah, those jokesters. They're a lot to handle at times." Her blood pressure hit an all-time high. *Great, now I'm gonna have a stroke. At least it would get me out of this mess...*

Doing her best to rein herself in, Riley took a deep breath. "Everything is good. I'm just—"

"Tired?" Rhonda quirked her brow.

"Yes?" Riley squeaked and then cleared her throat. "I mean yes. Nothing is going on with them. All is fine. More than fine. I'm fine. You're fine. Patrick's fine. And I'm sure Liam is fine. Superfine. So fine, he could win the medal for the finest there is."

Holy fudge-muffins, I didn't just say that.

Riley mentally hit herself on the forehead as Rhonda cocked her head to the side while she watched her.

Crap on a freaking cracker.

"Okay, missy. I can see you don't want to talk about it." Rhonda being Rhonda, walked over to Riley, her eyes full of concern as she lovingly placed her hand on Riley's arm. "You know you can always talk to me, right? About anything."

Riley's heart jumped into her throat. Doing her best to keep herself composed, she attempted to place a soft smile on her lips.

If she only knew...

"Thank you. I know that. I'm really okay, I promise."

Rhonda cocked her head to the side again, her eyes slightly narrowing.

"Thank you for caring. I love you," Riley quickly added, hoping to convince the woman she was okay. All while trying to convince herself as well.

For Pete's sake. Riley, you are legit acting like a crazy person right now. Do you seriously have no chill, like ever?

There was only a beat of silence before Rhonda's smile took over her face as she winked. "Of course you do. How could anyone not love me? I'm amazing."

Riley huffed out a strangled, nervous laugh with a tiny shake of her head. She really did love the woman, and even though she could clearly see Riley was in a panic, she wouldn't push for more. At least not right now. "I'm gonna agree with you. Everyone *does* love you."

Rhonda squeezed her arm. "Let's get this stuff wrapped up for today and I'll drop you off."

"Sounds like a plan."

Rhonda pulled away grabbing a container of flour off the counter. "I'm meeting James in a little while." She turned back to Riley, the questions still in her eyes, but Riley knew she wasn't going to push, at least not right now. "Maybe we can have dinner with all of you soon? I'd like to get to know my grand-kitten better."

It took Riley a second, but she nodded. "I'd like that."

Rhonda sent her a smile as she moved into the overstock room while Riley released a long, pained sigh.

Great. One crisis somewhat averted, now to figure out how to convince Liam to take her V-card.

CHAPTER SEVENTEEN

THANKFULLY, Riley's ride home with Rhonda had been uneventful. Although, the constant fear the older woman would bring up what was going on kept eating at Riley's nerves.

Pretty sure living in a state of panic isn't good for my health... and yet, here I am.

Once they'd gotten a block from her home, though, a fresh flood of anxiety hit Riley, which had nothing to do with Rhonda and everything to do with Liam.

How was she actually going to bring up the subject? Or worse, what if he was home and acted like it didn't happen?

Gahh.

Either scenario made her anxious. What was she to do? Walk right through their front door, go directly to him, and be all, *"Hey, you left last night, which was a jerk move, but I think I get it. Anyway, can we get past it? And you know, figure out if we are doing this or not? Because I'd like to have your dick inside me. Or at least freaking see it."* And then what? Stand there with her arms crossed over her chest waiting for his answer.

Well, it could work. It might be a little brazen, but at

this point, there were no more lines to cross, since the line was obliterated the second he stuck his tongue in her pussy.

And at least she'd get her answer.

Riley could honestly say she never thought *this* would be a situation she'd find herself in during her lifetime.

Yet, here she was.

As they rounded the corner, Riley noticed Liam's SUV wasn't in the driveway, causing her to worry her bottom lip.

That was a good *and* bad thing.

Good, because it gave her time to come up with a more tactful way of asking him to take her virginity and teach her all the things he knew.

Bad, because she'd rather rip off the Band-Aid.

Dang it.

With a quick goodbye to Rhonda, and a promise to work out the details next week about dinner, Riley rushed into the house only to instantly be greeted by Snickerdoodle as he came to a screeching halt in front of her.

Riley glanced at the all-too-happy kitten, who seemed pleased she was finally home. "I don't know whether I'm an idiot, a genius, or both." Riley scooped the kitten into her arms. "Your mother has short-circuited her brain about fifteen hundred times today."

The kitten purred, rubbing its chin against Riley's hand.

"I'm glad you're concerned. Love you too, Snicks."

The kitten made a weird noise before jumping from Riley's arms and heading toward the cat tree.

"Wow. Really, thanks. I thought we could talk it out and you could advise me on how to convince Liam to screw my brains out."

Snickerdoodle looked at her, blinking his eyes slowly once before turning back to the hanging string on the cat tree.

"Figures."

Riley threw her things on the counter as she worried her bottom lip. She could do this. She had to do this.

She *wanted* to do this.

Liam was the only person she trusted to take her virginity.

She was brave, she could do this.

To make a liar out of her, though, the second Riley heard a car door slam right outside, she panicked. "Not yet, though! Crap, crap, crap, crap. Yes, okay, I'm gonna talk to him about this, but ahhh." She looked around the living room. "What am I gonna do? What if it's Patrick? Oh my freaking God, I haven't thought of seeing Pat after his best friend had a meal out of my hoo-ha. Fuck me!"

Thinking fast, Riley raced to her room, blindly grabbed her clothes, and ran full speed into their shared bathroom, not stopping until she had the water on full blast.

As soon as the noise filled the room, she slumped against the wall. "Holy shit." She then slammed her palm on her forehead. "What the hell was that? You're acting like a crazy person."

She banged the back of her head against the wall. *I guess I can live here until I've figured out what I'm gonna do or say to Liam, or get the courage to face Pat. It doesn't seem too hard... I've got running water. The tub could be a nice bed. Towels for pillows and blankets... I— Oh, for fuck's sake, I really am acting crazy.*

Riley rolled her eyes. "You really are a piece of work, aren't you, Rye?"

Grateful she had a few more moments to figure out her next move, she peeled her clothes off and hopped into the shower.

"Breathe, Riley, breathe."

As the steam melted away her stiffness, she couldn't help but wonder how she ended up here. Instantly, Riley's mind flooded with images of the night before with a semi-naked Liam reminding her exactly how she ended up here.

As the water warmed her body, she couldn't help how it matched the warmth she felt when Liam touched her. His hands moving around her curves, making her feel things she never dreamed possible.

Her body tightened in response as lust pooled in her lower belly as the scene ran through her mind.

The way he made her feel, the desire, the pleasure... Riley's body flushed. Only this time, Liam didn't leave after getting her off.

No, instead he stood at the foot of her bed, slowly undoing his zipper. His hands moved into his waistband as he slowly pushed his jeans down.

Oh, God.

Before she knew it, Riley's hand slowly descended down her soft stomach as she sought out her core. Her breath hitched the moment she touched her sensitive lips. Riley couldn't hold back her groan even if she'd tried.

It was risky if they'd just gotten home, but her body needed release. *She* needed release. And more than anything, she needed to change the ending of last night.

Mindful of her noise, Riley let her fingers slide between her folds, the sensation rocketing through her as she found her clit. Her one hand pushed against the shower wall keeping her upright, as her other fought for her release.

As pleasure engulfed her body, setting her on fire, she bit down on her bottom lip, begging herself to keep quiet.

Riley might not be versed in pleasure with a partner, but she damn well knew what to do for herself.

Her fingers worked her core, causing her legs to tremble as she panted, her muscles tightening as another moan escaped her.

Riley was seconds from her peak when the shower

curtain flung open. She screamed as she fell backward onto the tile, desperately trying to cover her body with her hands. "Gahh! What the fuck?!"

"You don't touch yourself." Liam's voice was hard as he stared down at her, making her body heat.

"Oh, my God. Liam get out! What the hell are you doing?"

Ignoring her, Liam's eyes traveled up and down her. "You wanna get off, you come to me."

Riley stared blankly at him, her mouth opening and closing, her hands still covering herself the best she could. "What?"

"You heard me. You wanna get off, you come to me."

"I—" Her words died as her heart leaped into her throat while she watched Liam pull his shirt over his head, tossing it to the floor behind him. His hand went to his belt, just as he did in her fantasy that he rudely interrupted. "What're you doing?"

"Getting clean." Liam sent her a cocky smile as he winked. "Seems as though you need to get clean, too. Especially since you've been dirty."

Liam's words sent a shock wave through Riley as her core tightened. Did this mean what she thought it meant? She swallowed roughly, begging her brain to function. "Where's Pat?"

"Still at work. I wasn't scheduled today, so I left as soon as I was done. He'll be home soon, though so we don't have much time."

"Much time?" she squeaked, her eyes round as she stared openly at his chiseled chest, much like she did the night before.

"Yeah, we gotta be strategic."

"Why were you home last night?" Riley had no idea where that thought came from, but she wanted to hit her forehead on the tile. Did it really matter? No, and right now was *not* the time to ask.

"I didn't want to go out with Pat." Liam's eyes raked up and down her body. "Best fucking decision of my life."

Riley's breath caught in her throat. "Does that mean you want to... umm? You know?" Holy shit, was it hot in here because it sure as hell felt like Riley was about to be boiled alive. And here she thought she would have to convince him to be her teacher.

She should've known better when it came to Liam. He'd always been there for her when she needed it. He'd never let her down in the past. Why would he do it now?

Liam licked his bottom lip as he took her in, the arousal heavy in his eyes. "More than you know." He unhooked his belt before undoing the button of his jeans.

In one fluid move, Liam unzipped and pushed them toward his ankles, causing his dick to spring free, making Riley's eyes painfully round as she watched his cock bob up and down. "Holy mother of freaking-a."

Liam's deep chuckle went directly to her core. "Now that's the reaction I like to hear."

A strangled sound fell from her lips as Liam palmed his dick.

"Oh my, whoa." Forgetting about covering herself, Riley leaned forward, getting a better look. "I've... Holy—"

Liam's laugh filled the room as he stroked his thick dick, Riley's heart sputtering against her chest. Before she could do anything stupid, she flicked her eyes to him. "I thought you might be packing, but I didn't know for sure." Her eyes slowly moved back down.

"Have you thought about my dick a lot?"

"No." Riley's cheeks flushed.

"Liar." To prove his point, he stroked himself again, Riley's eyes following every minuscule movement he made.

"I'll never admit it," she blurted, her eyes twinkling as she scrunched her nose. "You already have a big enough head as it is."

Liam's brow quirked. "Big head above *and* below the belt."

"Please don't." She rolled her eyes. "Your ego doesn't need inflating. You know what? Just for that remark, I think I'm having second thoughts about this."

In a flash, Liam was in front of her in the shower, pushing her against the wall with his dick pressing into her soft stomach. "You sure about that?"

Her damn body betrayed her as she shuddered and moaned her response.

"Thought so." Liam stepped back and then it hit her.

Holy crap, she was naked in the shower with Liam. Full on, zero clothes, naked as the day you were born with his dick hard and pointing directly at her.

After he caught her touching herself.

The strangest part? Riley had no desire to question anything. Instead, she was more than willing to be there and learn. Her eyes moved down his body, only stopping on his abs for a moment before honing in on the appendage she was dying to get better acquainted with.

"You have seen a dick before, right?"

Riley's eyes snapped to his. "Yes, I've seen—" she hissed, but Liam held up his hand.

"On second thought, I don't want to know." He widened his stance. "Lesson one?"

Holy fucking crackers. This is happening.

Riley nodded, trying not to look as eager as she felt. "I'm ready."

"Knees."

Blood rushed to her ears as her heart slammed against

her chest. The only other time she'd done this, she hated it. Plus, it hadn't turned out well for her.

But right now... Damn, right now, Riley wanted nothing more than to sink to her knees and try again.

As carefully as she could, she lowered herself to the floor of the tub. Once she was there, she glanced up at Liam, who was still a few inches away from her. "You'll have to tell me what you like. I don't know."

"Fuck." A pained groan came from Liam's throat.

Was that a good groan or a bad groan?

Riley kept her eyes on him as she waited for his instruction. She didn't have to wait long, since Liam took a step forward, causing his dick to be level to her face.

Holy—

Riley bit her bottom lip as she looked up at him. The moment she met his eyes, he nodded, and that was all the encouragement she needed to move her face forward. However, try as she might her nerves still wreaked havoc on her.

"Explore." His voice was soft and encouraging. "Do what feels good for you."

"I want to make *you* feel good. What would *I* get out of giving you a blowjob? Isn't this supposed to be about you?"

Liam reached his hand under Riley's chin, cupping it so she'd keep her eyes focused on him. "Pleasure always goes both ways—"

"It didn't last night."

The look Liam gave her set Riley on fire. "It did."

How? I'm the one that saw freaking stars and I didn't even get to see—

Riley didn't have much time to ponder it since he pushed her chin closer to the head of his dick, letting her know time for thinking and talking was over.

Well, here goes nothing.

Still a little nervous, she moved the hand that'd been resting on her thigh and took hold of Liam. As she gripped him, she did everything she could to memorize the moment. How soft he felt, the thickness, the heaviness. Cautiously, she stroked him. Once and then twice. When he let out a hiss, her eyes darted to Liam's face to make sure she was doing it correctly.

"Good," Liam grunted.

Riley's body shuddered hearing his praise. Okay, so she liked that. She liked that a lot and wanted to hear it again.

Hoping to do just that, she gave his dick a few more strokes before she brought her lips closer, gently grazing them against the head of his cock.

"*Fuck,* yes."

That was all the encouragement Riley needed to envelop him into her mouth. At first, it was a foreign feeling as he stretched her lips, but she soon relaxed into it. It's not like she hadn't seen porn before. Doing her best to recall things she'd seen, she tried mimicking them on her own.

Swirling her tongue around, she worked her hand simultaneously along with her mouth. She figured she must have been doing something right since the noises Liam made above her kept going directly to her core.

With each noise he made, Riley's arousal grew. She spread her knees as far as they could go as her other hand moved between her legs.

"Yes, fuck yes, touch yourself, Rye," Liam growled as he pushed into her throat with more force.

What surprised Riley was how much she liked it. How much she liked all of it.

There was something about this that thrilled her. *She* was the one drawing these noises from him. *She* was the one bringing him pleasure.

Fuck yeah, she liked it. She liked it a hell of a lot.

This was… Damn, this made her feel powerful.

Riley yanked her hand from between her legs and placed it on Liam's hip as she continued her exploration while she worked him with her mouth.

She wanted to draw out every moan and gasp she could from him.

No, she *needed* to.

However, the moment Riley was really getting into it, finding her rhythm, Liam jerked himself out of her mouth with a groan. "Fuck, Rye, you're *too* good at this. I thought *I* was teaching you? Aren't you supposed to be a virgin?" he gasped, his hands on her shoulders as he steadied himself.

"I've seen porn."

"Fuck me," he grunted, his fingers digging into her flesh. "I'm trying to go easy here, Rye."

"Why?" Not waiting for an answer, she moved back to his dick as she leaned forward and took the head of his cock into her mouth, making him moan.

He kept one hand on her shoulder to hold on, as the other went to the back of her head. She stiffened for a second, trying to decide if she liked it or not, but the moment he moaned again she decided she did.

"You've got to pull back." He gripped her hair, attempting to pull her off him. "I'm gonna come."

Why would she pull back? Wasn't him coming the point? And, if she were doing this, she was going to do it right.

She wanted to experience it *all*.

As Liam moved to take a step back, Riley stopped him, her hands on the back of his thighs as she yanked him closer.

The moment she swallowed around him again, Liam's body tightened.

The sound he made as the first string of the salty

substance hit the back of her throat would be forever burned in Riley's mind.

Doing her best, she took all of it down as Liam's dick pulsed inside her mouth as he emptied himself.

"Fuck, Riley." Liam shuddered, his groans echoing off the walls.

Wow. Okay, yeah. I'm definitely doing this again.

Once she was sure he was done, Riley sat back on her heels as she watched Liam come down from his high, all while her body vibrated with need.

She closed her eyes, savoring his taste still in her mouth, instantly sending a bolt to her pussy.

Now she got it. Pleasure *did* go both ways. Although, if she were being truthful, she felt if she didn't get some sort of release soon, she'd actually die.

Holy moly.

Riley screamed at Liam's determined growl when he yanked her to her feet, the water from the shower splashing her in the face as he sank to his knees. "What're you doing?"

"I haven't been able to get the taste of you out of my mind." Liam tossed her thick thigh over his shoulder, making her brace herself on him as she stood on one leg.

"Ohhh." At his first lick of her core, Riley's knees wobbled. "Geez. Wow. Oh my..." She was already turned on from listening to the sounds Liam made. It only took him a few seconds before she found herself on the edge again. And the moment he flicked her clit with his tongue, she was done.

Riley came with such force if Liam weren't holding her up, she would've collapsed onto the floor in a puddle of goo.

Holy fucking shit. Is the fact I came so fast embarrassing? I feel like I should be embarrassed, but I can't find it in myself to care.

Maybe that's why it took Riley a full minute to realize

Liam had shut off the water, pulled her out of the shower, and was now drying her off. "When did—"

Liam wrapped her in the towel and pushed her toward the bathroom door with a swat of her ass, cutting her off. "Hey!"

He chuckled, grabbing the other towel and tying it around his waist, before handing her the clothes she'd brought in. "Go get dressed. Pat will be here any minute with dinner."

Her brother.

Riley's eyes bulged as her heart jumped. The last thing she wanted was for Patrick to find them both walking out of the shower together. That thought alone sure as hell got her to move her ass, regardless of the questions she still had.

Doing her best to push everything away for the moment, she ran to her room and threw on some clothes. Holy crap on a million crackers. The moment Riley tied her hair into a wet bun on top of her head, she heard the front door slam open, making her heart actually stop.

That can't be him! There is no way we were that close to being caught. Nope. Absolutely not.

Her cheeks flushed as a new wave of panic hit her full force as her pulse raced.

Holy shit.

"Pizza's here!"

Riley shook her head. "Absolutely freaking not. I live in my room now." There was no way in hell she was going out there. Not on your life. She'd rather starve to death than face either of them.

Especially with how close they were to being caught.

Instead, she walked over to her bed and plopped down, Snicks instantly climbing up her comforter. "Maybe I can send you out like a homing pigeon and you can bring me back food?"

The kitten purred, flopping onto its back, throwing his paws in the air. "Figures."

However, Riley's master plan of hiding out for the rest of her life was taken away the second her brother started banging on her bedroom door making her heart stop. "Give me the kitten! I've been waiting all day."

"I'm getting dressed," Riley lied.

"I want my kitten," Patrick grunted.

Any other time she would've thought it was sweet he wanted to play with Snickerdoodle, but right now she one million percent didn't want to see him.

"Pizza's here and it's gettin' cold. Get your ass out here and bring me Snickerdoodle or I'm coming in there to get him myself."

Oh, for fuck's sake.

Well, the sooner she got this over with, the better. Shaking her head, Riley scooped her kitten into her arms and walked out of her bedroom door with her cheeks on fire.

She took a giant breath before righting her shoulders and mustering up all the confidence she could.

Game face. You got this.

Stomping down the hall, counting her breaths, Riley avoided everyone's gaze as she handed Patrick the kitten and grabbed a plate. Which she was conveniently going to take right back to her room once she had her pizza, that way, she could avoid everyone until she got her mind back in working order.

"Nope. Family night." Patrick stopped her as she took a step toward her room. "I've barely seen you all week. And since fuck-face bailed on me last night, I'm lonely."

"I didn't bail on you. I told you I didn't want to go out. To bail, I would've had to agree and then didn't follow through."

Riley's cheeks heated at Liam's voice as she cast her eyes

down. *Why did his voice make my body tingle? That's not normal. I should probably get that checked out.*

"You pretty much bailed just like you did today. One second you were at the shop, and then you weren't. I got a text to bring home pizza and then nothing. The fuck?"

Riley finally looked up to see Patrick glaring down Liam. The same Liam who wasn't wearing a shirt as he leaned against the counter, his jean-covered legs crossed like he had zero cares in the world.

She instantly swallowed as she forced her eyes to focus back on her brother. *For freak's sake.*

"Anyone ever tell you that you're annoying as shit? 'Cause you are," Liam grunted.

"At least once a day. Now take pity on me and let's have dinner together." Patrick moved his gaze to Riley who closed her eyes, willing herself to function like a normal human being.

Not one who just had Liam's dick in her mouth.

Clearing her throat, she looked behind her toward her bedroom.

"Sit," Liam's voice rattled, making her shoot her attention to him.

His eyes moved to the table in front of her, and before she realized it, Riley found herself obeying his silent command.

Oh Lord, was this how it was going to be now? Was Liam going to bark and she was going to comply just like that? Geez, yeah, orgasms are great and all, but they shouldn't render a person helpless.

Breaking away from Liam's stare, Riley looked at her pizza, praying she'd make it out of the conversation without spilling her guts.

Or worse...

Liam grabbed a plate before dropping it onto the table to sit across from her making Riley jump.

Okay, this is awkward.

Very awkward.

"So how was your day?" Patrick asked.

When Riley didn't respond, he nudged her leg under the table. "What, now you're not talking to me just cause I asked to have dinner together?"

Riley flicked her eyes. "I didn't know you were talking to me."

"Of course I'm talking to you. No one gives a shit what Lee did."

He would if he knew…

"Fuck off, man," Liam grunted.

"My day was fine," Riley squeaked. "I didn't do much of anything at the bakery and Rhonda took me home. That's it."

Patrick nodded as he shoved a slice of pizza in his mouth. "No new experiments?"

Only one and that included me giving Liam a blowjob. "No. I might go in tomorrow and experiment."

"Riley," he grumbled. "It's your day off."

"I know. I'm not talking about catching up or making sure I'm ready for Monday. That's all done. I just wanted to get in some experimenting. That's all. I'd do it here, but I like my kitchen better." *And I need to clear my head.*

Patrick narrowed his eyes at her. "Why don't I believe you?"

"That sounds like a *you* problem rather than a me problem."

"Want me to come in and help?" he asked, his eyes shining.

"Only over my dead body." Riley shook her head. "I'd

rather gouge out my eyes than let you buffoons back in my bakery."

"Hey," Liam grumbled, the noise making her belly tighten. "I believe I already told you I'd be more than willing to help you out. In fact, maybe you can *teach* me all your ways."

Riley's jaw hit the table as she stared at Liam. She didn't know whether to smack the smirk off his face or run.

And since smacking him would raise questions, she did the latter. "I think I'd like to keep my bakery in working order." She stood.

"But Rye, you could be a fantastic teacher. I'd kill for a slice of your cherry pie. Just think if I could make it myself."

She was going to kill him.

"Only one baking my cherry pie is me." This was a nightmare. "Now, if you'll excuse me, this *family* time was riveting, but I think I need to hit the hay. I'm exhausted." Riley turned on her heel and headed toward her bedroom.

"I'm keeping Snicks tonight," her brother called after her.

She spun back to him. "You know he only tolerates you, right?"

"That's not true!"

"Keep telling yourself that, Pat." Her eyes moved to Liam who had a shit-eating grin on his face.

That's it.

She was murdering him.

Ignoring them both, she flung open her door, walked into her room and did her best not to slam it shut.

Once inside, she let out a shaky breath as she leaned against the door. "Holy freaking cake balls." After a few moments of composing herself, desperately trying to get a handle on her body, she marched over to the bed and fell onto it.

Oh God.

What in the hell was she going to do now? Flipping over, she closed her eyes for a second before opening them as her mind raced.

Riley's brain wouldn't shut off no matter how hard she tried. Which she fully blamed Liam for. It would be one thing if she was thinking about their shower time, it was a totally different thing adding in his comments.

She really was going to murder him.

After he took her virginity, of course, but once that was done, he was being pushed off the nearest cliff.

RILEY HAD no idea how long she'd been staring up at her ceiling fan, attempting to count the blades as they passed. So when she heard the door make a noise, she jumped.

Her first instinct was to check her phone. It nearly knocked the wind out of her when she saw it was just past eleven.

How in the hell was it so late?

When Riley heard the noise again, she shot up only to see Liam walk into her room before silently closing the door behind him.

As he stood there, the low light of her lamp hitting him, Riley's breath stalled in her throat.

"Riley," he whispered as he shook his head. "I can't—" He stopped himself for a second. "I can't get you out of my fucking mind," he growled. "It took everything inside of me not to grab you earlier and fuck you on the table."

Holy shit.

"All I want to do is crawl in behind you, toss your leg over mine and sink deep inside you."

Blood rushed to Riley's ears as her heart slammed against her ribs while Liam moved closer.

"Tell me no. Tell me to go back to my room and we'll never bring this up again." His words were laced with pain, making her heart clench. "Tell me to go, because if you don't, there's no going back."

Without a second thought, Riley's hand reached for her comforter as she pulled it back, inviting him in.

CHAPTER EIGHTEEN

"Fuck, Riley." Liam took the remaining few steps toward her, grabbing her face, pulling her into an earth-shattering kiss, like if he didn't get to taste her again, he'd die on the spot.

That's all he could do that this point. Sure, he waged a tiny war within himself after Riley escaped to her room. The nerves he saw in her, especially when he threw out some teasing, had Liam questioning everything.

He knew *he* wanted this. Fuck yes, he wanted this. He wanted to be with her more than anything, but he needed to know for sure Riley was okay. It might kill him, but he'd pull back if she had second thoughts or needed time... whatever it might be. Because Liam knew with every ounce inside of him, she was it for him.

There was no going back. Even if it meant losing Patrick.

Riley was his life, no matter how convoluted that sounded.

The emotions raged inside of Liam as he moved back from their kiss, causing Riley to whimper.

"Shhh. You can't make any noise," Liam whispered into

her mouth. "It was fucking torture waiting for Pat to go to bed so I could slip in here." Riley watched him as he crawled over her, tucking himself in behind her body. "Thank fuck he sleeps like the dead."

"Wh-what?" Riley stared back at him, her eyes round, with her mouth opening and closing slightly, which Liam thought was damn adorable.

With a quick shake of his head and a small chuckle, he easily maneuvered Riley so she was on her opposite side, facing away from him. He then snaked his arm around her waist pulling her back, tucking her into his body. "I'm tired. Time for bed." He kissed her exposed neck. "For some reason, my shower earlier seemed to take everything out of me. Wonder how that happened."

As he moved to nuzzle her neck again, Riley pushed herself onto her elbow as she looked over her shoulder. Her eyes narrowed as she glared at him. "Hold up. Wait a freakin' second here," she whisper-shouted at him, her brows knitting together. "You can't come in here and be all *oh-em-gee I'm gonna throw your leg over mine and sink into you* and then just what, crawl in next to me and..." The look she gave him had another round of laughter bubbling from Liam. "... go to sleep? No, that's not how this works."

"Yes, that's exactly how this works." The fire he saw in her eyes was enough to make his dick twitch. Liam wanted to pat himself on the back, since his plan was now in full swing. He'd draw this out for the rest of his life if he needed to. "I can see where my words could have been misconstrued—"

"Misconstrued?" Riley flipped over. "You know what? I'm going back to my theory that I'm actually dead. That's the only way any of this would make sense."

Liam pushed his hard cock along her back. "You aren't dead, babe."

The strangled noise that escaped Riley was a mix between pleasure, awe, and surprise, had Liam forcing himself not to do it again.

"Then why the hell aren't you sticking your thingy into me?"

"*Thingy?*" Liam quirked his brow in amusement. "I think our next lesson is gonna be dirty talk. Here, let's start. First I'll say it, and then you."

"Liam," Riley growled.

"Shh. School's in session. First word: dick. Now your turn."

"I will murder you."

"It's not that hard, I promise..." Liam looked down at his tented pajama pants. "Okay, that's a lie. I'm fucking hard as hell. But we need to focus on *your* education. Just like this. Di-ck. Then put it together and you get *dick*."

"Liam, I swear to everything in the world I will flip you over and suffocate you with my pillow."

His eyes flashed with lust as his body tightened. "Babe, you can flip me over and do whatever the fuck you want." He groaned, his eyes rolling to the back of his head before he focused on her again. "Fuck, yes, I can't wait for you to ride me. Actually, I can't wait to pin you to this bed and fuck you so hard you'd remember me for days. Feeling I was inside you with every move you make." He opened his eyes and focused on her. "But that's gotta be another lesson."

"It's impossible for me to forget you."

Riley's mouth hung open as Liam heard the words slip past her lips. The way her eyes widened in shock told Liam she didn't mean to say it but fuck him, that was exactly what he needed to hear. The primal possessive feeling urged him on as he flipped them so Riley's arms were pinned above her head as he straddled her waist, making her yip.

He leaned down biting her bottom lip. "What did I tell you about noise?"

"Then don't yank me around."

Liam nuzzled his hips into her so she could feel him again. "You gotta get this straight now. I'm possessive and in charge—"

"But—" she loudly grunted.

"I think I'm gonna have to gag you." Liam did his best to hide his smile. "What've I said about making noise? You're not being a very good student right now."

"What have *I* said about me suffocating you with a pillow?"

"Fair." Liam's eyes brightened as he chuckled. "However, I think I have the upper hand since you're pinned under me. As I was saying, I'm what you call a passionate lover and I'm gonna teach you what that means."

"Rough and dirty." Riley scrunched her nose for a second. "Okay, I understand. Got it."

Liam shook his head. "No. I don't think you do. But, you will."

"Then get on with it."

Riley really *was* perfect for him in every way. He hadn't had this much fun in the bedroom for as long as he could remember. The back-and-forth banter, the playfulness, the wave of fucking possessiveness that raced through him.

Yep, it only confirmed Riley was made for him.

He leaned forward, stealing her lips in a kiss. "Pretty sure I'm the teacher here and you're the student."

"You're being a crap teacher."

Liam moved her right hand to her left easily pinning them with one hand as his other trailed down the side of her neck, flowing effortlessly between her breasts. "That so?"

He watched her swallow.

"As I was saying earlier before someone rudely interrupted me a second time. I might fuck rough, but that's not all there is to sex. It's about a connection."

"Yes, you connecting your *dick* into my va-jay-jay."

Holy shit, she was going to be the death of him. It took everything inside of Liam not to laugh at her eagerness. "Good girl. You said dick. I'm very proud of you."

"You're a *dick*."

Ignoring her, Liam continued, "Now we need to work on *va-jay-jay*. Can you say pussy?"

"I can say I'm gonna kick you out of this room."

Liam brought his lips down to hers as he traced his tongue across the seam of her mouth. When he pulled back, Riley raised her head off the bed, attempting to follow. "I fucking love that you're only fiery with me. Fucking turns me on. The fact I get to see the real you..." he groaned as he thrust his hips once more, causing Riley to let out a stifled moan.

"You're learning." He rewarded her with another swift kiss. "But you're still too loud."

"Am not."

Liam arched his brow as he shimmied down Riley's legs, still keeping her pinned. As soon as his waist was at the perfect angle, he pushed his hips forward, bumping against her pussy making Riley gasp. Thankfully, he was quick as he covered her mouth with his hand before she made any more noise. "See?"

Riley's eyes widened as she stared at him.

"You're very vocal. I'd like to say we'd work that into our lesson plans, but honestly, I fucking love it. I love hearing you express how much *I'm* the one who drives you fucking wild. What *I'm* doing turns you on."

Riley mumbled something under his hand, but he shook his head. "Shh. You don't want to wake Pat, do you?"

Her eyes rounded even further as she shook her head.

"Exactly. That's why even though I want nothing more than to remove this thin barrier between us"—Liam touched the bottoms of her pajamas and then his—"I know we need to wait until you can scream your head off. And your first time shouldn't be me trying to shush you every few seconds. I want to hear you. I want to experience all of you."

He wanted—no *needed* to hear every moan, gasp, and whimper that came from Riley.

"Since you seem to be having difficulty with the dirty talk lesson, I'm gonna table it for right now."

Riley narrowed her eyes on him, her brows pulling together.

"Are you gonna argue with the teacher?"

Riley mumbled something, this time he swore it sounded like fucker, but he ignored it. "Yes, I am an exceptional teacher. Thank you for saying that. I appreciate you acknowledging all my hard work."

When she moved her head from side to side, he laughed.

"And because I'm such an excellent teacher, I'm gonna help you out." His other hand cupped her pussy. The warmth he felt on his palm nearly had him coming.

Fuck, she really was perfect and he couldn't wait to finally sink into her. No matter how badly he wanted to do just that. He knew he'd have to wait until they were alone. Not only because she liked to be vocal—and thank fuck for that. But for Riley's first time he would do whatever he could to make it special and he couldn't be focused on her if he constantly had his ear to the door listening for any sign of his best friend.

The heel of his hand pushed against the top of Riley's lush pussy, making her squirm. "Do you want me to help you out?" he asked, his gaze heated.

Riley nodded, her eyes pleading with him. "Anything

you want, I'll always give you." He pushed harder. "But I need to keep my hand on your mouth to help keep you quiet. You okay with that?"

Riley nodded, thrusting her hips against his palm.

"My eager little student." The corner of Liam's mouth turned upward. "Do you need to get off, Riley? All this talk about fucking make you hot?"

She whimpered against his hand.

Liam moved his fingers to her waistband before sneaking his hand inside to seek out her core. As soon as Riley's wetness greeted him, he growled, gritting his teeth. "Fuck, you're soaked."

Even in the low light from the lamp in the room, he saw Riley's cheeks flush. "Don't be embarrassed. That's fucking hot as hell. *I* did this to you." Liam tossed his head back with a moan. "Trust me when I say this, it goes both ways. The fact I can turn you on as much as you turn me on..." His eyes snapped to hers as he growled. "Fuck me."

What sounded like, "*I'm trying*," came from beneath his hand making him chuckle. "We'll get there." He circled Riley's clit with his finger making her jerk her hips.

"Yes. That's it. Take what you want." Keeping his eyes glued on Riley he worked her over as she moved her hips pushing into his hand as she attempted to grind against him. The muffled noises she made spurring him on.

Thank fuck he'd kept his hand over her mouth or she'd no doubt would've woken her brother, and maybe the entire neighborhood.

Seeing Riley like this was almost too much. He already felt the wet spot in his pants and he swore he wouldn't embarrass himself again like he did the first time. Forcing himself under control, he worked Riley harder with a new plan in place.

It only took a few more flicks of his fingers for Riley to

shake, her body tensing as she tipped over the edge. He kept his hand clasped against her mouth as she roared out, his body on fire as he watched her.

Beautiful.

When Liam assumed it was somewhat safe, he quickly let go of Riley's face and jumped up the bed. Once he was near her mouth, he yanked his bottoms down, his dick bouncing out of the material an inch from Riley's lips. "Open." His jaw clenched as sweat coated the back of his neck, his muscles tight.

With zero hesitation, Riley leaned forward and took the tip of Liam's cock into her mouth, like she'd been dying to taste him just as much as he wanted to taste her. No matter how sad it was, it only took one stroke from him to find his release.

Once he'd emptied every drop into Riley's willing mouth, Liam flopped onto the bed next to her, panting as his body came down from his high.

"*Holy shit.*" He couldn't even begin to fathom how intense things were with Riley. He hadn't even fucked her yet, and he swore each time he got off with her, he took years off his life.

"Wow." Riley wiped her mouth with the back of her hand like she'd spilled something, making Liam chuckle.

"Wow sounds pretty accurate to me." As carefully as he could to not waste his remaining energy, Liam shuffled under the covers, pulling Riley with him. "That, babe, is a lesson in a kind of foreplay." He moved her so her back was nestled to his front.

"Dirty talk that leads to orgasms?"

"Anticipation... I had every intention of stopping before getting off happened, but fuck... when it comes to you, I lose all my sense."

Riley yawned. "I guess there could be a worse way to

lose your senses?" Her eyes were half open with a lopsided grin on her face. "Is our next lesson going to be *dick* in *pussy?*"

Liam barked out a hearty laugh as he kissed the top of her head. "You're a quick learner."

"I guess it's 'cause I have an excellent teacher." She smirked, her eyes shining. "But I'll never admit that again, so you might want to lock it away and replay it whenever you want an ego boost. Although I don't know if your ego can get any larger."

Liam's smile spread across his face as he let out another chuckle. Oh, he planned on a repeat of those words over and over again. "Whatever you say, my prodigy. Now, let's get some sleep. I've gotta sneak out of here before your brother gets up, but I'd like to get a few hours lying next to you first."

CHAPTER NINETEEN

As Riley somewhat expected, she woke up alone the following morning. Which was fine. Liam did say he'd be going back to his room right before they'd both passed out. But it still felt... she didn't know.

Weird.

Off.

Actually, if Riley were being honest, *what* hadn't been weird since they started their... *lessons? Teaching, mentoring...* She didn't know what to call it. Riley refused to second-guess herself on it, though.

It was Liam. Her brother's best friend. The guy who on more than one occasion, swooped in and saved her. The guy who was *never* supposed to see her naked or... do the things they'd already done.

She gulped.

The guy who starred in her secret fantasies which she'd rather be caught dead than admitting.

But that had all changed now.

And she'd be lying if she said the new development didn't thrill her. Holy smokes, did it ever. Although the waking up alone *did* give her a weird feeling. Which was stupid, since she knew exactly what this was.

Liam teaching her about sex.

That's it.

Nothing more.

Riley just needed to remind her heart of that fact.

So instead of dwelling on the hollow feeling that seeped into her when she realized Liam wasn't beside her, she threw her shoulders back, gave Snickerdoodle a quick kiss, made herself some breakfast and got ready with her head held high.

And she kept it that way her entire walk to Pastries & Paws.

Riley swore she wasn't lying when she told Patrick she wanted to head to the bakery and experiment for the morning. Especially since she hadn't gotten in any the day before.

Experimenting with treats was Riley's own brand of meditation, and more importantly, her time to work out her thoughts. Lord knew they needed organizing after everything.

She was still excited about the turn of events, she wouldn't deny that. Her body was sure as hell excited about it as well, but she still needed alone time to sort out her mind and figure out a better way to keep the walls around her heart in place.

Everything was so new to her. The closeness, the desire... you name it. It was hard not to overthink.

Then throw in the way Liam took control... geez. No wonder people loved sex. Riley now understood what all the hype was about.

And they hadn't even *had* sex yet... Just imagine when they did.

Hoo-boy.

As Riley moved around the kitchen of Pastries & Paws,

she grabbed some odd-ball ingredients off the shelves and placed them on the countertop with zero idea of the direction she wanted to go. Which was exactly how she liked starting every new project.

"Human or animal? That *is* the question." Riley's nose scrunched as she drummed her fingertips on the counter. The moment her eyes drifted shut, she let her brain wander. Usually, she'd go with whatever she was drawn to most when deciding on her next creation.

It took Riley all of five seconds to realize she was making a human treat. Something that spoke to the primal need she'd experienced with Liam.

Riley swallowed roughly, her cheeks heating as images of what they'd done danced in her mind.

"Human it is." She worked hard to keep her blush down as she grabbed the granulated sugar. "Maybe I can create something like, *orgasm in your mouth*." She stopped for a second, her cheeks on fire. "Okay, not the best name, but something that feels the way I feel when I'm... I don't know, tipping over the edge?" She shook her head with an embarrassed laugh. "Now, I just sound like an idiot. But it could work. The name will need adjusting, though. If I nail down the flavor, I can come up with some secret name to call it. A name no one would ever know what it really means." A wicked smile appeared on her face. "Yep. I'm doing it."

With a wave of excitement and determination flooding through her—as it always did the moment she started a new experiment—Riley began reaching for ingredients. Maybe she'd come up with something that enticed an explosion of pleasure when you bit into it.

Maybe add a hint of salt...

Then it really would be her little secret.

Before she knew it, Riley had a pot of sugar simmering on the stovetop and was knee-deep in experimenting with whatever it was she was creating. Her only goal was to somehow recreate the feelings she felt when she was with Liam.

"Someone's been busy."

Riley screamed at the top of her lungs as she flung around with her spatula in her hand, ready to smack whoever the intruder was.

"Down, babe," Liam purred with his hands raised as he made his way toward Riley.

"Holy shit crackers. Don't scare me like that." She placed her hand on her chest. "I have hot sugar melting. Geez."

"I'll show you some hot sugar." Liam pulled Riley into his arms, kissing her like he hadn't seen her in days, which was silly since he saw her last night.

Regardless, it made Riley's stomach flutter.

Once he pulled away, Riley straightened herself, trying to get her bearings. "What are you doing here?"

Liam cocked his brow as the right corner of his lip turned up. "You're here. Why would I be anywhere else?"

Riley's stomach flipped again, but instead of melting into it, she took a deep breath, doing her best to remind herself she needed to keep her walls up.

This was *just* Liam teaching her about sex.

Don't they say men are always horny or something like that? She wiggled her nose. *That's probably why he's here.*

"Uhh, so another lesson?" She cleared her throat. *Hey, if I get another orgasm out of it, I'm not gonna complain. Even if it's my heart in the shredder in the end.*

"Maybe..." Liam boxed her in, effortlessly trapping Riley against the counter with his arms. "Or maybe I wanted a sweet treat?"

Riley gulped as Liam moved closer, his hot breath

grazing her skin. "The display case is up front and the fridge is full of overstock for Monday. Have at it."

The air around them thickened as Liam's eyes heated. "Do you have anything with cherries?"

Oh God, her body *actually* shivered. Like full on shivered at his words. How in the hell did he do that?

Riley cleared her throat. "Liam?"

"Yeah, babe?"

She closed her eyes at the endearment. Geez, it really was a weird battle she was having with herself. Of course, she wanted to jump his bones, why wouldn't she? But at the same time, she knew she needed to keep herself guarded, which was turning out to be much harder than she anticipated. "What are we doing here?"

"Already told you," Liam stated matter of fact. "I wanted a sweet treat and *you're* here, so I'm here." He licked his lips. "Maybe you can *teach* me a thing or two about baking?"

Riley's breath hitched as excitement hit her.

Call her crazy, but the idea of being all *alpha* and teaching him a thing or two sounded like a hell of a good time.

"Okay." The corners of her lips quirked in enthusiasm. "Lesson one."

"Babe, I'm all ears." Liam's tone was light and playful as he leaned in to nuzzle her neck.

"Hey!" Riley shouted but didn't try all that hard to pull away. "That's not lesson one."

"It's *my* lesson one for the day." Liam's mouth found the nape where her shoulder began and lightly bit down, making Riley's body come to life.

"My God..." He licked along her exposed skin. "You taste good. Sweet, like candy." His hands moved to Riley's hips, hoisting her onto the counter. The ingredients she had out scattered all around them.

"Whoa. Hold on." She pushed him back, the amusement heavy in her voice. "First, this isn't very sanitary, and second, you're making a mess."

"I plan on making *many* messes with you." As Liam stared into her eyes, the arousal she saw nearly choked her.

Is this what all sex and chemistry was supposed to be like?

"Do you know how many times I've fantasized about bending you over the table and sinking into you while you work on your creations?" Riley's eyes almost popped out of her head. "Fuck, that day we helped you... it took everything in me not to bend you over."

Riley's breath caught. "Is that... is that why you kept moving in behind me?"

Liam tapped her nose, the corner of his lips tipping upward. "You are a smart one."

"But that was..." Riley trailed off as she stared at him. "Liam, that was before we star—"

He cut her off with his lips as he grabbed her hips, pulling her closer to the edge, locking them together so she could feel his hard dick pushing against her core. "Wrap your legs around me, babe," he demanded, which Riley seamlessly complied with instantly.

Oh, God.

Before she knew it, Riley was following Liam's every move as he repeatedly pressed against her in the perfect rhythm. The friction causing her body to tighten as her skin to heat.

At this rate, she'd be seconds from tipping over the edge if he continued.

But would that really be all that bad?

Which kind of blew her mind since they both still had

pants on. How could Liam ignite everything inside her so easily? And he hadn't even taken her V-card yet... Holy freaking smokes.

Liam's face pushed into the crook of Riley's neck as he continued to rock against her.

Hold it together. Hold it together. You can't come when you still have your pants on. There has to be a rule about that...

Liam must have felt her change since the moment she tensed, he bit down on her neck causing her to explode.

"Argghh!" Her legs shook as she thrust her hips into him, begging to prolong her release. However, just as every ounce was about to be taken from her, a faint burning smell hit her nose causing her to freeze. "What the hell—"

Oh, no!

Riley pushed Liam with all her might. Holy shit, she'd been so wrapped up in him she'd forgotten about the sugar.

Liam immediately jumped into action and grabbed the smoking pot before tossing it into the nearby sink. However, the second he flipped the faucet on, smoke filled the kitchen. In Riley's panic trying to make sure everything was okay, she didn't notice the open bottle of pure vanilla extract had tipped over and poured toward the lit burner.

It was only seconds before a tiny fire erupted.

That's when it happened.

The fire sprinkler on the ceiling only a few inches from the stove opened, causing the fire alarm to sound.

"No!" Riley jumped off the counter, the fire officially dying out a few seconds after the sprinklers turned on.

She did her best to save what she could. "Oh, God. This can't be happening!"

Thank everything she'd only pulled out a few ingredients and everything else was still put away. "Make it stop, make it stop!" she screamed.

"Where's the valve? I need to turn off the water." Liam hollered back as everything around them got soaked.

"How the fuck would I know?"

Liam rushed to the supply closet that housed her boxes and pantry items as the alarm bellowed throughout the room. Riley, on the other hand, ran around the kitchen, her adrenaline rushing with so much force she was sure she was seconds from stroking out.

"This can't be happening. This can't be happening."

"Got it." As Liam yelled the words, the water finally stopped.

Riley spun toward the supply closet to see Liam walking out. Her stomach churned as dizziness flooded her brain. "Oh my fucking God!"

"It's okay. It's all okay." He took a step toward her.

"It's all okay?! My kitchen! Oh my God, my kitchen!" Her head darted back and forth as she attempted to survey the damage as her pulse raced, threatening to kill her on the spot. "I can't breathe." She clutched her chest. "Oh, *God*. I can't breathe."

Liam jogged over to her, pulling her into his arms. "You're having a panic attack. You're okay. I promise. I'd never let anything bad happen to you. You're safe."

Riley melted into his embrace for a split second until her brain caught up. Instantly, she jumped out of his arms as her whole body shook with rage.

"Babe, breathe for me. It's gonna be okay." He nodded toward the ceiling. "It looks like one, maybe two, went off. It's not as bad as it seems."

"As bad as it seems?" She snapped her head toward him causing Liam to hold his hands up.

"Babe—"

Anger replaced her fear as she glared at him. "Don't you fucking dare."

"Riley."

She stormed past Liam to the front of the bakery. Right now, she'd give anything to turn back time.

As she swung open the door, her eyes scanned the front, once her brain realized nothing was wet, her shoulders turned in. The relief hit her like a punch to the gut.

Seeing as the front was fine, she turned back, her stomach churning at the sight of the back half of her kitchen soaked, the damn alarm still blaring.

At this point, she had no idea what the extent of the damage was. Yeah, the ingredients would all need to be tossed. Luckily, she only had a few out. But she didn't know if her stove top was damaged or her proofing oven right next to it was.

Thank the Universe her two other ovens were on the opposite side.

The next thing she knew, Riley was hurled into Liam's arms again. "It's okay, babe."

Riley shook her head as the faint sound of a siren hit her ears making her wince.

"Everything is fine," Liam reassured her.

Everything was not fine.

It was far from fine, which was proven when the back-door to the bakery flung open not even a minute later and two firefighters stormed in. "Is everything okay?"

"Oh my God!"

Liam only half let go of Riley as he nodded to the guys. "Yeah, there was a tiny accident. But we took care of it." He then cocked his brow. "How'd you even know?"

"I'm gonna shut off the alarm," one of the guys remarked before disappearing. Where to? Riley had no idea.

The other muscular firefighter standing to the right jerked his head toward the ceiling. "The system is set up so if the sprinkler goes off, we get the call. These are older buildings so we don't take a chance even if it's by accident or already taken care of. We'd rather save a building than let it burn down."

"Burn down! *Burn down!*" Riley cried, clutching her chest.

"Ma'am, are you okay?" The firefighter took a step toward her. "Name's Hank Parker." He jutted his thumb over his shoulder. "This here is my buddy, Lucas. Do you need medical assistance? The paramedics are right outside."

Riley hyperventilated as her whole world fell apart around her.

"She's okay," Liam answered. "She's having a panic attack."

The firefighter nodded. "That's normal. We can get some oxygen on you—"

Riley shook her head. "No. No. I'm…" She swallowed, not sure what to say because she was anything but fine.

"We'll go at your pace," the other guy, Lucas, chimed in just as the alarm stopped. "There, that should help calm you down a bit. No one likes how fuckin' loud those things are. But it's needed."

Riley nodded, some of her sense coming back now that the alarm was off, but only slightly.

"It looks like everything is under control. You'll have to get someone in here to replace the sprinklers that triggered, but that looks like about it. We'll look around just in case, though." Hank nodded at his friend, who tipped his chin once before going off a second time. Riley hadn't realized he'd even come back.

"Wanna tell us what happened? Appears you guys thought fast and were able to keep the damage to a minimum."

At the word damage, Riley's heart jumped again, her

breath shortening causing the man to give her the eye. "Are you sure about the oxygen?"

Riley's face heated. "I'm sure. I'm just..." Again she couldn't finish her sentence.

Liam must have realized she couldn't answer since he spoke up, still keeping Riley pinned to his side with his firm arm wrapped around her. "We got sidetracked and the sugar burned. Instead of throwing a lid on it. I put it in the sink and turned on the water and poof, smoke."

Hank nodded. "Funny enough, we have a regular who does that a lot." His teasing smile made Riley somewhat relax, but only somewhat.

"Holly," Lucas added. "It's been a month or so since we've been to the Richman household. I think we're overdue. This was great practice." The guy winked at her. "Thanks."

Riley swore she heard Liam growl, but was too preoccupied to care. "Richman, as in the vet and his wife?"

"That would be her." Hank smirked. "They keep us on our toes."

"Understatement of the year." Lucas huffed out a laugh as he focused on Liam. "But smoke alone wouldn't have caused the sprinklers to go off."

Riley worried her bottom lip. Could you get in trouble for starting a fire, even if it was an accident and no one was hurt? She tried stepping out of Liam's grip but he held her tighter. "Umm, well, I guess somehow in the chaos the vanilla extract tipped over and poured toward the gas stovetop."

Lucas whistled. "That would do it."

"That accompanied by the smoke would be the perfect storm," Hank nodded. "Let us just double-check everything is okay, then we'll write up our report for your insurance company and we'll be on our way for you guys to start cleanup."

One of the firefighters Riley hadn't noticed came in through the door that led to the front of the bakery. "Everything out there is good to go. Looks like it was only this room that sprung. And the back corner at that."

Hank smirked again. "Good. Less work."

"For who?" Riley asked. "This seems like it's gonna be a lot of fucking work."

"All of us. Less paperwork for me, and you only have one room to clean. Trust me. It could've been a lot worse."

Riley pulled out of Liam's arms as she closed her eyes, trying her best to calm down. Liam must have gotten the picture that she needed a moment for herself, since he didn't try to keep her at his side again.

As she heard the commotion of everyone moving around her, she forced herself not to cry.

She could have lost it all.

And all because she'd been so freaking reckless. Liam came in and she threw all her common sense right out the freaking window.

Riley couldn't solely blame him, though. This was just as much her fault. More so. She knew better than to not recap and put away her ingredients right after she used them or at least move them out of harm's way.

If anyone was at fault, it was her.

Riley didn't know how much time had passed before she found herself in Liam's arms again as he wrapped himself around her. "Pat's on his way. So are Mom and Dad."

"You called them?"

"Yeah."

"Why?"

"Because that's what family does." He kissed the top of her forehead. "When one of us needs help, we all come."

Riley stared at him blankly, not ready to process his words as a fresh flood of panic hit her. "What if they ask how it happened?" Her eyes widened. "Oh my God, did you tell that hunky firefighter you were getting in my pants and that's why the sugar burned?"

"*Hunky?*" Liam growled.

Someone cleared their throat causing Riley to snap her head toward their direction. "I think he left that part out, ma'am."

The amusement in the firefighter's voice had Riley groaning as her cheeks flushed. "Kill me now."

"Don't worry." Hank chuckled. "I'll leave that little part out of the report."

Before Riley had a chance to say anything, Patrick exploded through the backdoor with Rhonda and James right behind him.

"Are you okay?" Patrick hollered, pushing his way through everything and everyone.

As if her body had a mind of its own, she removed herself from Liam and stepped toward her brother, who pulled her into his arms.

The second Riley was there, she burst into tears.

CHAPTER TWENTY

WATCHING Riley walk into her brother's arms was like a sucker punch to Liam's gut. Add in the fact that she went from *his* arms only worsened the sting.

Even though a part of him wanted to be upset, Liam got it. Patrick had always been Riley's rock. No matter what the situation was, they always had each other.

Riley always had him too. He was just as much as her rock as Patrick was. And one day he hoped instead of leaving his arms when she needed comfort and going to Patrick, she'd stay.

Liam knew that made him a selfish asshole. But he wanted to be the one to always comfort her. He wanted to be the one who took her into his arms and convinced her everything would be okay.

Fuck. Stop it. Now isn't the time.

Liam's stomach twisted as he fought back the flood of emotions coursing through him. Usually, when Riley turned to her brother, he'd be fine with it and he'd be there for when she needed him, but after starting what they had... he just...

Fuck.

Adrenaline moved through every inch of him as his heart pounded against his chest. How the fuck had he been so stupid? Thank everything in the fucking Universe there wasn't more damage.

If things had gotten more out of hand...

He'd like to say he didn't know what came over him, but that'd be a lie. Whenever Riley was involved, it's like all his common sense took a running leap off a cliff.

It was just... Liam *finally* had her. He was getting what he'd dreamed of for years. He couldn't stop himself even if he tried. It's why the second he realized Riley had left their house that morning, he'd hauled ass to Pastries & Paws.

He needed to be with her.

To see her.

Fuck, to just be near her.

He'd dreamed of them together for years, and he was going to take every opportunity he had to be with her.

Pathetic.

But he owned it.

Wherever Riley was, he needed to be.

In his defense, Liam had every intention of showing up and *actually* helping Riley with whatever she planned on doing. He wanted to learn the ins and outs of what she enjoyed while baking. What she loved about it. What made her excited when she created something new.

Truthfully, he could swear on everything he didn't mean for them to mess around. However, the second he saw her in the kitchen, slightly bent over the counter as she worked, the fantasies he'd had with her in the bakery hit him like a punch to his solar plexus.

He lost his mind and if he didn't taste her, he'd die.

Which was becoming Liam's natural state around Riley.

Their relationship might not be exactly how he wanted it, but it would get there. As soon as Riley realized they *were* in a relationship. Not just some teacher and student arrangement.

She only needed a little time to catch up to the truth.

"Looks like we've got all we need," Hank interrupted Liam's thoughts as he handed him a carbon copy of a makeshift report. "You'll be able to get the full report online in a few days for insurance."

"Thanks."

Liam watched as Hank glanced at Riley who was still cradled in her brother's arms as she silently sobbed. "We can stay longer in case she wants oxygen?" Hank gave Liam a knowing look, one almost of *I've been there and it sucks to watch the person you love hurting*, which made Liam's stomach knot. Was he that obvious?

Liam cupped the back of his head, a little embarrassed he'd been so obvious before he straightened his shoulders. "I think we'll be good, but thanks."

Hank lifted his chin, his eyes still holding what he suspected. "If you need anything, let us know."

"Will do."

Once the firefighters left, it was only them.

Him, his mom and dad, Patrick, and Riley. The five of them. As Liam stood there, the room's air hung thick as the events replayed over and over again in his mind.

"What happened?" James asked, breaking the silence.

"It's my fault," Liam was quick to answer. "Riley was trying to teach me something and since I was being an idiot, we got sidetracked."

James cocked his brow. "Sidetracked?"

The moment Liam opened his mouth to answer, his mom burst through the door that led to the front of Pastries & Paws. He'd been so focused on Riley, he hadn't even seen her leave.

"Looks like only the stuff on the counter back here was

damaged. Everything up front and the overstock fridge is fine." Rhonda waved her arms around. "It really doesn't seem all that bad."

"I wouldn't say that if I were you," Liam stated. "Every time I've said it, Rye's wanted to murder me."

Riley snapped her head from her brother's chest to glare at him. "That's 'cause when you said it, it wasn't true."

"But when Mom does, it is?"

Riley curtly nodded. "Yes."

"Sounds about right," James remarked, humor filling his voice.

Liam cocked his brow at Riley... *oh, really?*

Rhonda being Rhonda, swept her hand across the room, tsking, grabbing everyone's attention. "It's gonna take at least a day to get this cleaned up." She glanced at James. "You think you can bring one of those huge fan de-humidifier thingies you have at the shop to help dry everything out?"

With a twinkle in his eye, James puffed his chest. "Already on it, dear. I texted a few guys as soon as we got here. They're bringin' two over. Should be here soon."

"Good." Rhonda winked at him, taking charge as she always did. She quickly took the few steps over to Riley and pulled her out of Patrick's arms and into hers. "Now, sweetie. Dry those tears. Worse things have happened."

"I don't see how. What if the stove or something else is broken?"

"Good thing you have three mechanics at your disposal," Patrick answered, rubbing her back making Liam's eyes twitch. "If you wanted an upgrade, all you had to do was ask. You didn't need to set fire to the place."

"Hey!" Riley jerked her face to him, her eyes hard while she flipped him off. As soon as she started, though, it stopped as her bottom lip wobbled.

Fuck.

Liam took a step toward her, but his mom must have realized Riley's change since she pulled her in tighter.

"Knock that shit off, Patrick Seán O'Neil."

"Damn boy, she used your whole name." James crossed his arms over his chest. "I think you just ended up on her shit list."

Rhonda spun her head around. "You wanna join him?"

James sobered. "No, dear."

"Thought so." Rhonda focused back on Riley. "This isn't a big deal, sweetie. It's a quick cleanup and we'll be back to experimenting in no time."

Riley hiccuped. "But—"

"No buts," Rhonda stopped her. "You should've seen the things James got into when he first opened the auto shop before Liam was born." The older woman lifted her chin toward her husband. "Fire department, electricians, plumbers. What else?"

"You name it, it happened."

"We've heard a shit ton of stories growing up, 'member?" Patrick chuckled. "Didn't you start an electrical fire in the bathroom? I think that's what Ma always said."

"She'd like for you to believe that," James huffed with a flick of his eyes toward the ceiling. "*She* was the one who said it needed an upgrade for the customers. Next thing I know, there was a fire..." James's eyes zeroed in on Rhonda. "Funny how that happened."

The room fell silent for a brief second as Rhonda's brows shot off her forehead. "Are you saying I purposely committed arson to upgrade the shop's bathroom?"

"I'm not sayin' anything." James held up his hands.

Riley pulled her head from his mom's chest as she cracked a small smile. "It is a nice bathroom."

Liam could see the pride swelling through his mother as

she straightened her shoulders. "That's 'cause *I* was able to redesign it."

"Arsonist." Patrick coughed, instantly causing Rhonda to snap her head toward him.

"Smoke. It's the smoke... pretty sure it's the smoke." Patrick took a step back from her.

"You like the grave you're in, don't cha?" James laughed, then shrugged it off. "Better you, than me."

While Liam watched the scene before him unfold, he noticed a look his dad and Patrick shared. That's when it all clicked into place. They'd somehow started their everyday banter to lessen the tension in the room.

Damn, he loved his family and his best friend.

They were perfect.

Liam shifted as he forced a swallow past the lump in his throat as another realization hit him. He just hoped, somehow once everything was said and done, Patrick would still love him enough not to murder him.

He already knew as soon as it was out in the open, all fucking hell would break loose.

"I feel stupid." Riley's murmur broke through the room, along with Liam's thoughts.

His mom held her shoulders at arm's length so she could look into Riley's face. "Why?"

It was only for a split second but Liam saw Riley's eye shift to him, before flicking to his mother. "I just do. I should've been paying more attention."

"Shit happens," Patrick grunted. "Nothing seems too bad. I'm sure we'll get it all fixed by the end of the night, then we'll let the dryers do their magic. I'm positive you'll be back in here by midday tomorrow."

"Then why does it feel like everything is falling apart?"

"'Cause you were scared." Rhonda pushed Riley's head into her chest. "But we've got this. We'll close the shop tomorrow since it'll need a day to dry out then we can test everything and make sure it's safe. But really, sweetie, it's not that bad. I've burned dinner worse than this. We'll be open in no time."

Liam watched as Riley took a deep breath, stepping out of his mother's embrace. It was one of the things he loved about her. She might have her moments, as everyone does, but she never let them get her down.

At least not for long.

Riley was a fighter. Always had been and always would be.

Liam loved her. All of her, exactly how she was. And to think he could have lost—

"You feel better?" his mom asked, cutting off Liam's thoughts.

"I guess. I just..." Riley stood there for a few seconds, her bottom lip wobbling before she turned to him. The moment she took a step in his direction, Liam's heart stopped.

Without a second thought, he opened his arms as Riley walked into them.

She came back to me...

Liam closed his eyes, his arms tightening around her as he did his best to fight everything inside of him to stay as neutral as possible.

Once he'd gotten himself together, Liam rested his chin on Riley's head and opened his eyes, only to see his dad staring back at him with a cocked brow.

"Sidetracked you said?"

CHAPTER TWENTY-ONE

Monday morning rolled around and since Riley didn't have to set her alarm, she somewhat let herself sleep in. Okay, that might have been a lie. She'd barely gotten any sleep, but she at least laid in bed longer than usual.

What else was she going to do? She couldn't go to Pastries & Paws until at *least* early afternoon while the fans worked their magic.

At least, that's what James told her. The fans would dry everything out and she'd have nothing to worry about.

"Pfft." The no worrying part was really working out for her, if you counted the bruise she'd given herself from biting her bottom lip.

It was more like what *couldn't* she worry about? There was her bakery, the fire, the water damage, the staying out half the night getting things cleaned... and *Liam*. The last one is what got her the most.

Liam... Riley forced out a strained breath.

She didn't know how to act around him anymore. Half of her wanted to jump his bones, and the other half wanted to punch him.

It'd been less than a week since they started their

lessons and look where that'd gotten her? Maybe this whole thing was a bad idea.

Geez, don't even get her started on the weird looks James kept shooting her way while they cleaned and sanitized the kitchen.

It was like he *knew* which was impossible. Nonetheless, it still made the hair on the back of Riley's neck stand up, like she'd been caught with her hand in the cookie jar.

"It was probably nothing," she mumbled to her empty room. Okay, it wasn't empty since Snickerdoodle was at her side, but close enough.

Riley mindlessly scratched under the kitten's chin. "I think I'm seeing things that aren't there," she groaned. "Makes sense, since that's what overthinkers do."

What a freaking mess, and no matter how hard she tried, she couldn't help but blame herself. Even though no one else seemed to.

Rhonda, the amazing woman she was, disappeared for about an hour only to come back with replacement items for everything they'd thrown out.

Everyone helped. Even James was on his hands and knees at one point scrubbing the floor.

Honestly, by the time they left the bakery, it had never looked better. Well, minus the two giant fans.

Riley's eyes followed the blade of her ceiling fan as a warmth seeped under her skin. Yesterday, no doubt showed her what it was like to have a family. A real one with parents who gave a crap.

They'd all been amazing, even when she had another tiny meltdown around nine o'clock at night when the oven wasn't working right.

It took the guys all of ten minutes to fix it.

James had been the one that pulled her into his arms, telling her to buck up and as soon as the place was back in working order, he wanted a batch of blueberry muffins. Enough for everyone at the shop, which he conveniently announced he'd not share with a soul.

Something about over his dead body would he let Patrick or Liam's grimy hands near them, which made Riley laugh and relax again.

Through it all, though, even when she knew she shouldn't, Riley couldn't stop stealing glances at Liam. Lord knows she tried. Seriously, she really did. It was just... *ugh, why did she have to be so drawn to him even in the wake of a disaster?*

That's why you are *drawn to him, dumb-dumb. It's Liam, the guy who rides in to save the day a million and a half times. Just now you know what his dick looks like.* She gulped. *And what he tastes like.*

Shaking her head, Riley pushed the thoughts away, as she once again pulled her bottom lip between her teeth.

Around eleven, right before they were about to leave, Riley had to make a sign and hang it on the door letting everyone know she'd be closed until Tuesday and how sorry she was.

Not until she saw the sign hanging in the window did she realize how bad it actually hurt.

Losing money from her Monday morning rush sucked, but it was more than that. It was the first time since opening Pastries & Paws that she truly felt like she'd failed.

This wasn't one of her creations she screwed-up and ended up tasting horrible.

No, this was letting people down.

Her regulars.

Patrick and Liam who both put all their money into her bakery.

Her.

Tears pricked behind her eyes.

Sure, she might have been somewhat drowning before Rhonda stepped in, but she'd never felt like a failure. Hanging that sign was exactly that.

Maybe Mom and Dad were right... Owning a bakery was a stupid idea.

And while she was at it, so was asking her brother's best friend to take her virginity.

Riley scrunched her eyes closed as pain lodged in her throat at the heaviness.

For freak's sake, they hadn't even had sex yet...

Snickerdoodle batted her hand distracting Riley. "You rang? What can I do for you?"

The kitten stretched his paw, spreading his toes. "Would you look at those toe-beans? How can I be upset when I get to look at those babies every day?" She tickled him, causing Snickerdoodle to kangaroo-kick her hand.

"Just so you know, that shit hurts. You have claws."

The kitten didn't seem to care as he did it again. "You know what, owning a bakery isn't stupid. They're stupid." Riley snapped her fingers. "I'm gonna do a half-off special tomorrow to make it up to everyone for today. That's not stupid. It's good business."

Snicks let out a tiny cry.

"See, you agree."

Snickerdoodle hopped onto her chest and began purring. "Why are you looking at me in that tone of voice?"

The kitten cried again. "Are you trying to back sass me?"

He started kneading. "Hey, you don't need to bring up the fact that I need to work out the Liam stuff now that I've got the bakery kinda sorted out. I thought you were on my side?"

Snickerdoodle blinked at her. "Why, yes, I am having this made-up one-sided conversation with you, hoping to put things in place. Nice of you to ask." Riley blew out a huff, flopping her head onto her pillow.

"Now you're having a made-up conversation with your cat to figure out your brain. Good going, Riley." She glanced at the kitten to see him blink slowly at her. "All right, here's the deal. Don't get me wrong. I *love* the lessons we've done already. Hoo-boy have I ever. When we were in the shower... Oh, man, I don't think I've ever felt so empowered."

Snickerdoodle cried.

"Exactly. That's what I'm saying. There's definitely been an added risk. A part of me likes it, 'cause it's a rush, you know? But another part freaks me out. Pat almost caught us. We almost set the bakery on fire... and after all that, we *still* haven't had sex. The heck, right?"

Snickerdoodle agreed with another cry.

"Liam's supposed to be showing me what I've been missing out on... so far it seems like a lot of freakin' headaches." *And orgasms. Can't forget the orgasms.*

The fear she'd been trying to keep down hit her like a pile of bricks. "What's all this gonna do to us once it's over if it's already this much of a mess?" She gulped. *But do you want to stop?*

At the mere thought her body tightened in panic. "No. Not at all. Even with an almost burned down bakery."

Riley groaned, she was already in too deep with her heart and there was not a damn thing she could do. If almost burning down her bakery didn't have her end it, nothing would.

And dang it. She wanted to have sex with Liam.

Really freaking badly.

Worrying her bottom lip, she contemplated texting him... maybe even sexting him. That's another thing she hadn't done.

Great. Here she was again, her mind full of sex and Liam when she should've been more focused on the bakery.

What in the hell was wrong with her?

More importantly, why had she grabbed her phone and pulled up Liam's text messages?

Riley sat up, forcing the kitten off her chest and onto his back. "I'm gonna do it." Her fingers hovered over the letters. "I'm gonna do it. Yeah. Uhh. I'm gonna just text him something sexy because I've lost my freaking mind and I've... I really have no other explanation or reasoning."

Before she lost her nerve, Riley's fingers flew over the letters and then hit Send, instantly smacking her forehead with her palm.

"Oh, God. I didn't!" Her pulse skyrocketed. "I didn't really just say that, did I?" She slammed her eyes shut with a groan.

After a few seconds, she peeked, only opening her right eye slightly. "Yep, I sent it."

As she read back her message, she winced.

RILEY

> I like your dick. It's pretty. *Wink emoji*

"Kill me now." She threw her phone to the end of her bed, Snickerdoodle happily chasing after it. "I'm pretty sure that's not sexting... that's probably not even classified as texting. Great. Now that I've made a fool of myself, might as well get some breakfast, or at least coffee. Maybe add some arsenic in for *flavoring*." Riley threw the covers off her and crawled out of bed with a groan.

Standing, she stretched her sore tired muscles from the day before, which somehow must have been all the invitation Snickerdoodle needed, since the kitten took a flying leap from attacking her phone to somehow throwing himself onto her back.

"Hey. That hurts." Riley bent. "I'm not your cat tree."

Ignoring her, the kitten purred as he climbed Riley's clothes before perching himself on her shoulder exactly as he always did with Liam.

"Are you a parrot now? You do know you're a kitten, right? Plus, can't you see I'm having a mild panic attack at my failed sexting?"

Snicks balanced himself with ease as he rubbed against Riley's cheek. "You're lucky I love you and I need the distraction. Let's go get Momma some coffee."

The kitten purred louder as he somehow kept balanced.

Rolling her eyes at the little guy, Riley moved throughout their house and into the kitchen, not bothering to find her robe, instead walking out of her room in her nightshirt.

Once she'd finally started the coffeepot, she focused on it, praying she had some sort of magic powers to make it brew faster.

Come on, pot. You can do this. Give me the sweet nectar of the gods and maybe I can survive that I lamely tried to sext Liam.

Snickerdoodle, still perched, somehow began kneading Riley's shoulder, almost falling down her collarbone, but was able to stop himself using his claws making Riley wince. "Now you're just adding insult to injury. Are you *really* gonna try to make biscuits when you know I can't? All while being very aware of what I just did?"

The kitten cried digging his claws in harder.

"Hey! That hurts."

Snicks stopped for a second and looked at Riley before bumping his head against her chin.

"Don't do that. I can't stay mad at you if you're being all cute." The kitten rubbed against Riley's cheek this time. "Argh. Why are you so freakin' adorable? You're supposed to help me find something to add to my coffee so I can't remember almost burning down the bakery and sexting Liam."

"It's the game he plays when he wants something."

"Ahhh!" Riley flung around, her hand flying to her chest. "Holy fudge on a fucking stick. I think I just had a stroke."

In the process of Riley jerking around, Snickerdoodle jumped from her shoulder and gracefully landed on the floor, giving her the stink-eye before running off toward the cat tree in the living room. "Geez, thanks!"

It took Riley a few seconds to get her bearings and when she did, her eyes nearly popped out of her head as she came face to face with a shirtless Liam, still in his pajama bottoms as he leaned against the kitchen entrance.

"Uhhhhhh..." Her brain malfunctioned.

"Mornin' babe."

"W-why are you here?" she sputtered.

Liam pushed himself off the wall and stepped toward her. "You're here. Why would I be anywhere else?"

CHAPTER TWENTY-TWO

Liam loved when he rendered Riley speechless. It didn't happen very often, but when it did, it always thrilled him.

Not to mention the fact he was able to sneak up on her. That wasn't his original game plan when he stayed home. As soon as Patrick left, he wanted to crawl into bed with her and hold her like his life depended on it, but for some reason, the voice inside his head told him to wait.

Fuck, was he glad he did.

Not only did he get to see Riley in her rumpled night-shirt, the one that said *my morning is only puurrrfect once I've had my coffee* with a sleepy cat on it, but he also received a very interesting text.

Liam wanted to laugh at her attempt at sexting. Only Riley would call his dick pretty and then run away.

Damn, did he love it.

Riley's eyes scanned up and down his body, making his dick take notice. Fuck the things she did to him and she didn't even know it.

"What?" Riley's eyes widened as he took another step toward her.

"Told you, babe. You're here, so I'm here." Liam boxed her in with his arms as he did at the bakery.

Not being able to help himself, he leaned forward, stealing a swift kiss, causing Riley's breath to sputter.

"You know that's not what I meant. Why aren't you at the shop?" Her eyes shifted back and forth, a twinge of pink coloring her cheeks. "Did you..." She cleared her throat. "Have you looked at your phone this morning?"

"Why?" A wicked smile appeared on Liam's face.

"Uhh, just wondering. No big deal." She visibly swallowed as the red on her cheeks deepened. "Why're you here? Shouldn't you be at work?"

"Told dad I'd stay home so I can help you when it's time to go back in the bakery."

"You could've just met me there. That's what Rhonda and James are doing."

Damn Riley was adorable when she was nervous.

He leaned forward sealing his lips with hers, making sure to pour all he could into it. Truth be told, he was still rattled from the day before, and the fact that he couldn't crawl into bed with her when they got home last night bothered him.

He needed to be near her, feel her, kiss her, taste her.

It's why right after midnight, he ended up calling his dad.

"Is everything okay?" The worry in his dad's voice made Liam's stomach clench, feeling like shit for calling so late, especially after what happened earlier. "Was there another fire? Is Riley okay? The shop? Patrick? You?"

Fuck. *Liam shook his head, more agitated at himself than anything. "Glad to know I'm last on your list, Dad."*

"Fuck off and tell me why you're calling me after midnight? After what happened today, how do you expect me to not freak the fuck out? When you called us earlier I damn

near had a heart attack. Don't ever lead with 'there was a fire.' For fuck's sake. I'll never be able to unhear those words."

More guilt ate at him. "I'm sorry. I should've led with everyone is fine, but there was a fire."

"Yeah, you should have, idiot."

"While we're having this chat on what you should say first, don't you think your son should've been the first person out of your mouth?"

"Pfft." Liam could hear the eye roll in his dad's voice. "You're fine." There was a pause. "Actually, depending on why you called my ass so late after all the shit we did today, if it's not good I might kill you, be damned what your mother says."

Liam heard rustling through the line.

"Speaking of which, hold on, let me go to the kitchen. If I wake her, she'll kill me before I get to kill you."

"No one is killing anyone, Dad." Other than Patrick when he finds out what he and Riley have been doing.

"I'll be the judge of that. Why in the fuck are you calling me? And it better be a good reason or I'll drive over there and kick your ass. We've had enough excitement for the day."

That was an understatement. Blowing out a deep breath, Liam's shoulders tensed. "That's why I'm calling. I think I'm gonna take off tomorrow. Riley seemed really out of it after she put the note on the door saying the bakery would be closed. I don't think she should be alone."

There was a silence on the other end, making Liam's skin prick with unease. Clearing his throat, he quickly continued, "You can give the Firebird to Patrick. He was pissed you were giving it to me, anyway."

"That so?"

"Yeah, he was annoyed."

"I'm not talking about Pat. I'm talking about how you

227

feel the need to be with Riley since she's upset." The silence hung heavy between them. "Your mom could go over—"

"No," Liam cut him off. "It's fine. Let Mom sleep in. She can meet us at the bakery to prepare everything for Tuesday when the fans are removed. I'm already here and..." He froze for a second, trying to make sure he didn't sound like he was giving himself away. "I'll make sure she eats breakfast, and attempt to keep her relaxed until we can get back into Pastries & Paws."

There was another long pause. "You want to keep her... relaxed?"

The way his dad said the word 'relaxed' made Liam's body tighten.

Shit.

"Son, are you—"

"She was really shaken up. I'm worried about her." Which wasn't a lie.

Silence greeted Liam again. "She is an overthinker."

"One of the best."

"Liam," he stopped. "Just be careful, okay? That girl means the world to me and—"

"Dad, I'm just concerned about her."

"So much you'd give a '67 Firebird to Pat? Somethin' he's gonna gloat over for years..."

It'd be worth it to be with Riley.

"I can out re-build an engine him any day. Let him have this. It'll make him feel like he's worth something."

"Liam," he warned. "You know Pat and you are fuckin' neck and neck in the business. You're both second best. Under me, that is."

"Of course." Liam rolled his eyes. "I'm gonna go. I wanna get at least some sleep tonight before we have to get back into the bakery."

James grunted. "I'd be sleeping right now if my stupid

son didn't call me in the middle of the fuckin' night after spending all day fixing up the bakery because somebody *got sidetracked."*

Liam's nerves gnawed at him. "That's why I'm gonna let you go get your beauty sleep, old man. See you tomorrow."

"Liam, just be careful."

"I'm always careful." Before his dad could say another word, he disconnected the line. He knew he'd get shit for doing it, but he had no choice. His dad was already catching on. He might be an old man, but he was a smart old man.

Liam pushed away the conversation to focus on Riley. "Babe, you and I both know while you're waiting to go into the bakery, you're gonna be a panicked mess. I wanted to be home to comfort you."

"Comfort me?" Her eyes flashed with something he wasn't sure of. "Like you've always been there for me." She nodded her head. "Like when you showed up and made my twenty-first birthday something worth my while or when you found me walking down the street—"

"Don't," he growled, rage moving up his spine. "Don't bring that night up."

Riley watched him, her head cocking to the side. "You've always been there for me when I've needed it most."

The air between them heated.

"And I always will be." Liam leaned forward, taking her mouth in a kiss as he tried his best to pour what he wanted to say into it.

When he pulled back, Riley's whimper sent a shiver through him as he rested his forehead on hers.

"I guess that's why you agreed to help me lose my virginity and teach me about sex?" The flash of... was it uncertainty... ran across her face again, making him wince.

Jesus, he needed to figure out a way to explain to Riley

this was anything but helping her lose her virginity. But he also didn't want to scare her.

Fuck.

Riley was so much more than that to him. She'll get there.

Eventually.

Like he said, he'd drag this out eighty years if he needed.

The coffee machine beeped, breaking their moment as Riley flipped around in his arms, grabbing her mug. As she moved through the kitchen, Liam realized he'd be able to fulfill another one of his fantasies.

One he'd had for years.

He walked up behind her, his hands gripping her lush waist, as he pulled her back to his front.

"Liam..."

He pushed her hair to the side as he leaned forward and placed an open-mouth kiss on her neck, causing Riley to shudder.

Fuck him, the real thing was better than *any* fantasy he'd had.

His hands squeezed her sensitive flesh as he ground his dick along her ass. "Riley..." A flood of possessiveness ran through him as the moment he'd dreamed of came to life. Quickly, he spun her so she faced him.

"Riley," he growled, his hands firmly on her hips. He couldn't think straight. "I know you're probably still frazzled with yesterday, but, I just..."

Riley's mouth hung open, her eyes full of arousal, which only made him grind his hips into her harder.

"Next lesson?" He knew this was exactly what they both needed.

Riley's eyes widened even further as Liam watched her visibly swallow. "Do you mean..."

"Yes." Liam grabbed Riley's waist hoisting her into the air. "Lock your legs around me, babe," he demanded.

As soon as she did, Liam pushed his cock against her core, making her toss her head back with a moan.

Christ. The sound she made was fucking music to his ears.

Quickly, Liam turned them and headed toward his room with Riley's arms clinging around his neck.

"Whoa, whoa, whoa, hold on there. You're not supposed to be able to carry me."

Liam froze in his tracks. "Are you questioning my strength?"

"Uhh, no. I mean—"

Liam hiked her higher, securing her with one hand before smacking her ass with the other.

"Ouch. What the hell?!"

"Don't doubt me."

"I wasn't. I was jus—"

He did it again, this time harder.

"Liam," Riley warned.

"Don't Liam me. You need to trust your partner. And you know damn well I can carry you. I've been doing it my whole life. After you've gotten hurt and sprained your ankle—"

"I was ten and a hundred and fifty pounds lighter."

He arched his brow. "I threw you over my shoulder and got you in the car last Christmas when you were trying out your new holiday rum cake and put too much rum in it."

"Don't bring that up!" She narrowed her eyes at him, her cheeks heating. "Who the hell gets drunk off food? That should've been impossible."

Liam's toothy grin spread across his lips. "You put three bottles in it. I know you wanted to make it special, but damn. It's kinda like you wanted people to get hammered."

"I was only experimenting."

"And you did a good job. Gave me an excuse to toss you over my shoulder and get my hand on your ass to steady you. Don't know how many times I've jerked off to that."

"Liam!"

"Shut up and don't question my strength, it's an insult." To prove his point, Liam pushed her against the wall outside of his room and brought his lips to hers in a kiss that should've been illegal. When he moved back, he bit her bottom lip, pulling it with him. "Now, can we please continue without you insulting me?"

"I didn't insult you."

"I think you did. You're gonna have to make it up to me."

"You're the one that smacked my ass. If anyone has making up to do, it's you."

"I plan on kissing your ass all better. Don't you worry your pretty little head about it." Liam kissed her nose, which made her growl.

And fuck him if that didn't make his dick twitch.

"I should smack *your* ass."

Liam barked out a laugh. "Who knows, maybe I'd like it. I have a feeling with you, I'd like anything."

Riley's eyes rounded further.

Liam took that as a sign to pull her off the wall, taking the remaining steps into his room. Once inside, Liam tossed Riley onto his bed, and damn, he loved seeing her bounce. Especially since she wasn't wearing a bra.

Liam growled at the sight of her tits bouncing. Fuck him, he was a lucky bastard.

"Hey, don't throw me around. I've already told you this."

"I know. I chose not to listen to it." Liam placed his knee on the bed as he crawled toward her like she was his prey.

"That's rude."

"Rude, efficient. Close enough." Liam straddled Riley's legs as he reached for the hem of her nightshirt. He yanked it over her head in one swift move, causing a tiny yip to escape from her lips.

Another possessive growl ripped from him the moment he realized she didn't have on any panties. "Fuck, if I'd known you weren't wearing panties earlier, I would've explored more in the kitchen."

"I never wear underwear to bed."

"Fuck!" His hand flew to her soft stomach as he squeezed. "You're tellin' me all those times you'd come out in just a nightshirt or your pajamas, you never had anything on under them?"

The twinkle in Riley's eyes almost undid him. "Never."

"Keep it that way."

Riley cocked her head to the side, the corner of her mouth tipping upward. "Why? What's in it for me?"

"You damn well know what's in it for you." He captured her lips, his cock painfully hard as it strained against his bottoms.

"Oh, yeah? That so?"

"Fuck, Rye, you like to test me." He looked into her eyes. "I always knew you'd be a spitfire in bed."

"You say that like you've thought about it."

The air thickened between them. "I've thought about it a lot."

Riley's mouth opened, but instead of letting her say anything, Liam kissed her again. Once she was withering beneath him, he pulled back and pressed his forehead on hers. "You think you're ready for your next lesson?"

"If it's you finally putting your *dick* inside my *pussy*, then yes. I've *been* ready."

"Feisty."

"Impatient." She quirked her brow. "I thought the day I asked you to teach me we would've already gotten to this part."

Both of Liam's brows shot off his forehead. "Then you don't know me very well."

Riley watched him, her eyes scanning around as she chewed on her bottom lip. "I guess I'm about to know you a whole lot better?" she remarked, but even through her playfulness, Liam could hear her panic.

Closing his eyes, he did his best to calm himself. He needed to make this a good experience for her. And the last thing he wanted was for Riley to be nervous.

"You good?" Liam sat back on his heels.

"Yeah, why wouldn't I be good?"

"Riley?"

"What, I'm fine. It's not a big deal."

"Babe, losing your virginity *can* be a big deal. You've gone this long—"

"Not by choice."

That made a weird enraged feeling bubble inside him. "What do you mean not by choice?"

"Okay, yes, kinda by choice, it's just... You know we already talked about this. I wanna get it over with."

Liam shook his head, moving off Riley's lap. "This isn't something to just *get over* with, Rye. You always remember your first time."

"Do you remember yours?"

Liam hesitated for a second. "Yes. But it's different for guys."

"How so?"

"It just is. Besides, since you've waited this long, I wanna make it feel good for you and make sure you feel safe."

"You always do. I've never once felt unsafe with you, Liam. That's why I want you to be the one."

The one...

"I'll admit I'm a little, uhh nervous, but that's because I'm scared it's gonna hurt. Not because it's you. I've always wanted it to be you."

The words hit him hard as his heart slammed against his ribs. Did that mean... Fuck.

"I'd really *really* like it if we'd stop having these heart-to-hearts while I'm naked and you have clothes on. I might be secure in all my extra curves, but being on full display while you're still clothed is kinda weird."

Liam chuckled as he jumped off the bed and in one swift move lowered his pajama bottoms. "Better?"

"Damn."

"Pretty, isn't it?"

"Aargh." Riley flung her hands over her face. "So you *did* get the message. My God. Kill me now!"

"Might have." Liam crawled back onto the bed before removing her hands from her face, and kissed the tip of her noise, then smirked. "No need to be shy. I liked it. Not the normal sexting I've experienced in the past, but that's what I liked about it. It was you."

"Yeah. I called your dick pretty. Only thing that could've made this worse is if I waved at it, like ohh, hello. Nice to see you again."

Liam tossed his head back with a hearty laugh. "Fuck me, Rye."

"I'm trying and failing miserably."

"You're not. You turn me on like a fucking light switch. Bet you could wave at my dick and it'd try to wave back."

"Please stop."

"Nahh, I think this is too much fun." He kissed her. "You ready?"

Riley nodded. "I think so."

Liam kissed her again before trailing kisses down her body. First over her jaw, then her neck, chest, being sure to kiss each nipple causing Riley to hiss as he carried on with his journey down her soft stomach before stopping at the top of Riley's plump pussy.

Over her mound, he caught her eyes.

"That's the wrong part of your body that's supposed to be down there. I think you're backwards." She scrunched her face. "Wait, is this your way of telling me you're also a virgin and you have no idea what you're doing? The thing under your waist is supposed to go—"

Liam barked out another deep laugh. "Babe, God, you're fucking perfect in every way."

"I agree. I'm amazing. But I'd be more amazing if you stick your dick inside me."

A massive toothy grin appeared on his face. "No arguments here. Before I do stick my dick inside you, though, I want to make sure you're ready."

"I already told you I was. It's you. Of course, I'm ready."

Her words barreled through him. She had no idea what she actually did to him.

"Riley." He looked her in the eyes. "You said you didn't want it to hurt. Although I can't stop it from actually hurting, I can help make it hurt less by preparing you."

"Preparing me? Like basting a turkey for Thanksgiving? What do you mean preparing..." She stopped. "Oh... *Oh.*" She cleared her throat. "You mean, my downstairs area—"

"Pussy," he corrected.

"Yeah, my *pussy* isn't dry." The red on her cheeks nearly lit the room. "I can assure you I'm fine. As soon as I saw you with your shirt off, it was like a slip and slide down there."

Liam's face lit. "You saying just the sight of me makes you wet?"

"Is that gonna go to your big-ass head?"

"Probably." His eyes twinkled. "So you tellin' me you don't want to come from my tongue."

She shot up. "No, I mean yes. I mean..." Riley waved her hands in the air. "Sorry for interrupting. Please, carry on."

Liam chuckled moving back into position over her core. "How nice of you."

CHAPTER TWENTY-THREE

*W*ELL, *this is weird.*

Okay, what *hadn't* been weird since they started their lessons? It all kind of happened so fast. One second Riley was living her life, accepting she'd be one of those old women with a million cats, and the next, Liam was seconds from taking her virginity.

Riley looked down her body to see Liam hovering over her core, his eyes full of heat instantly making her gulp.

This is it.

Liam Kelly was about to take her virginity. The thought alone sent a shiver down her spine as her hands shook at her sides.

She was going to do *it*.

With Liam.

Weird was probably an understatement.

Here Riley was naked, as the day she was born, all her curves, lumps, bumps, everything on full display, all while desperately trying to keep the walls locked around her heart intact. And every time she tried to remind herself Liam was only doing her a favor, he'd say something that would make her head spin and her heart ache for what they were doing to be real.

For them to be real.

As real as the fact that Liam Kelly was about to take her virginity.

Holy crap.

Since they'd started, she'd caught herself more than a few times melting into his words, fighting her own head.

It was all about the process, nothing more. Sweet nothings, promises of tomorrow and fantasies of the past were only a part of the package.

Liam never did anything half-assed, so it made sense. Everything was a part of the experience of losing her virginity and to learn a few things along the way.

Riley wanted this. She wanted this more than her next breath, and with her emotions still raw from yesterday, she needed this.

For once, Riley was going to put herself first and let her misguided fantasies become reality. Even if only for right now.

Swallowing down her nerves, Riley shifted, letting her legs fall further apart, giving Liam the space he needed to position himself comfortably between them.

No going back now. You're literally *open for him. Like va-jay-jay in the face. No hiding. There wouldn't even be a place to hide.* Riley closed her eyes, demanding her body to calm down. *Breathe, Riley, breathe. This is Liam. He's gonna take care of you. You want this. You've always wanted this.*

She worried her bottom lip as she blew out a shaky breath.

This was it. She was about to lose her V-card to her older brother's best friend.

"You always smell so fucking good," Liam purred, the

vibration from his voice hitting her core with force. "I could eat you every fuckin' day and never get tired of it."

Riley's eyes shot open, her breath stalling. She liked that... Maybe too much.

"You're so fucking responsive," he growled, brushing his knuckles against her clit causing Riley to jump.

"Relax, babe."

Relax, yeah... I'm gonna relax. Let me just go grab a mojito and a book and pretend I'm at the beach instead of having you an inch from my hoo-ha.

Liam's hand gently caressed her inner thigh, making the spot quiver under his touch.

"God, you are so fucking perfect. Every single inch of you."

Liam's deep commanding voice had Riley's stomach somersaulting as she watched him, her mouth opening and closing, as she begged her brain to work.

"And you're all fucking *mine*."

Riley gasped as Liam took a long lick up her seam, his tongue circling her nub.

The sensation was too much.

She tossed her head back onto the pillow, her back arching as she squeezed her eyes closed.

Holy biscuit maker.

A sharp pain on her inner thigh had Riley snapping up, her eyes shooting to Liam. "What the heck was that?"

Liam jerked his mouth from her inner thigh and bit down on the opposite side from where she already had a bruise from him.

"*Liam...*" Riley wanted it to come out as a warning, but it sounded more like a plea.

"Eyes on me, babe." His words hovered over her pussy, the heat from his voice setting her on fire. "Or I'll do it again. Give me any excuse to leave my mark on you and I'll take it."

"Wha—" Riley's voice fell as she watched Liam go to her center. The flat of his tongue dragged from the bottom all the way to the top. He then curled the tip, flicking it over her clit once, before rising off her mound, his eyes scorching her.

A whimper escaped her when she saw the line of spit glistening from his tongue to the top of her pussy.

Holy fucking shit.

The sight before her was beyond one of the most erotic things she'd ever witnessed. The way Liam kept his eyes glued to hers as he licked his lips, groaning as if he was savoring her flavor. *Universe, kill me now... wait, no, don't. I take it back.*

Riley's mouth hung open, her body on the verge of splitting at its seams, and he'd *only* just begun.

"Mine," Liam's possessive growl bellowed throughout the room.

"Yours," Riley answered without missing a beat.

A part of her wanted to take it back, but she couldn't... because it was true. She was his for however long he'd have her.

She had nothing to worry about though, the second she answered, it was like a switch flipped in Liam as he dove, literally dove back into her pussy, like he was starved and her essence was the only thing that would save him.

With every flick, bite, and swirl, the pleasure shot through Riley's body filling her with need. She buried her fingers in his hair as Liam expertly worked her. And when his teeth grazed against her clit, it made her see stars.

"My God." Her hips thrust into his mouth.

"Yes. Fuck yourself on my face, babe."

And she did. Riley ground her pussy against him like she was a pro.

"That's it, Riley." His voice sent another shock wave through her center. "Come on my face. Drench me," he demanded with a growl. "I won't fuck you until you do." His hands squeezed around her thighs, his eyes primal. "Don't you dare fucking look away."

Liam's harsh words filled with more passion than Riley ever knew was possible, broke her in that instant. Her legs snapped shut around Liam's head as she exploded, her entire body breaking apart.

Their eyes locked together as Riley rode out her wave, her jaw clenching.

"Holy—" As she came down, her body flicked with aftershocks, not really sure how she got over the edge so fast.

"Good girl."

His praise sent another instant shock through her. *Holy shit.*

Liam pushed himself onto his elbows while keeping his gaze connected with Riley as she desperately tried to regain her breath. Then she caught the sight of his wet chin, making her jerk her face away as her cheeks flushed. "Oh, God."

"Eyes," Liam demanded.

His commanding tone had Riley swallowing hard, but nonetheless, turning her head to face him. He made a big show of wiping his lips with the back of his hand, and then licking off the essence, moaning as he did.

Holy fuck. She'd never... *Oh, my God.*

"Liam..." she panted, while pleading for her mind to function. It felt like someone had taken an egg beater to it and went to freaking town. "I-I..." she trailed off, still at a loss.

"Best breakfast I've ever fuckin' had." Liam winked as

he sat back on his heels. Doing so, instantly put his dick on display making Riley's eyes flew to it as he stroked himself.

She couldn't look away even if she wanted to. Her pulse raced, her heart slamming against her chest. She was locked in on Liam and nothing could tear her away.

The way he moved his hand up and down his shaft with such ease made her mouth salivate.

Was that even possible? Guess so, since I'm drooling.

Liam nudged Riley's legs further apart with his knees as he inched closer. "Riley."

Her breath caught, as her body tensed, the high she'd just had, leaving her body as a wave of anxiety replaced it.

"You're in charge." Liam's right hand went to her lower belly before trailing down along her sensitive skin, gently brushing against the top of her lush pussy. "I promise I'm gonna take care of you. You have nothing to worry about."

Liam's words soothed her soul as they always did. Which she knew was good and bad. He must have seen the worry in her eyes. "Am I that easy to read?" she whispered.

"To me?" His face softened. "Always."

Riley nodded, not really trusting her voice.

"I haven't been with a soul since my last annual physical," Liam's words held a twinge of pain, almost like he was holding back. And if his face was any indication, he was. "I was negative for everything. I *always* wear a condom, Riley. But with you..." He stopped, his pupils dilating. "If you want me to, I will. I'll never put you in harm's way or make you feel uncomfortable. But, I'm not gonna lie. I want you raw."

Riley sucked in a sharp breath, her eyes bulging as the blood rushed to her ears.

"I wanna see my cum drip out of you."

Holy fuck.

Riley wanted that too.

She *really* wanted that. There was something so… primal about it.

She wanted that with Liam. No, she *needed* that with him.

Obviously, she didn't have any STIs, and she'd been on birth control for her PCOS for years. So the chances of her getting pregnant were slim.

Riley's breath quickened as her heart pounded against her ribcage while she searched Liam's face.

She wanted to feel him.

To feel all of him.

Riley trusted him. She trusted him more than she trusted herself.

She spread her legs. "Yes."

A deep possessive growl came from Liam, the noise vibrating through her entire body. "There are so many fucking things I want to do to you *and* with you."

Riley vigorously nodded. "Yes. Yes, me too."

Keeping their eyes locked, Liam's thumb flicked over her clit, making her squirm. "You're my perfect dream come to life."

Riley couldn't argue since Liam's hand moved from her back to his cock as he stroked himself again, fully hypnotizing her. The mushroomed head looked swollen, almost purple, with a bead of cum at the tip.

"Does this turn you on?" He stroked himself again.

Unable to speak, Riley nodded, her eyes following his every move.

"Good. 'Cause you fucking turn me on more than I ever thought possible." He grabbed the base of his cock and lined the tip up with her opening.

This is it…

Riley stiffened, feeling Liam at her entrance.

"Relax," he cooed, his eyes holding hers. "Let me get it

started and we'll go slow. I promise if it's too much, we'll stop."

"Okay." She swallowed, her body tensing at the feeling of being stretched as he pushed his way in. After a few seconds, Liam must have been in the right position since he let go of his dick and braced on his forearms, lowering himself to capture her lips.

"You're doing good," his words echoed in a whisper as he kissed the corner of her lips, slowly pushing himself further inside.

The sensation was intense, the feeling of being stretched, of being full…

And then there was the pain. Riley's breath came in quick pants while she braced herself, as Liam slowly, ever so freaking slowly, inched his way into her core.

With another deep thrust, Riley squeezed her eyes shut as a sharp pain hit her. "Ahh."

Liam was instantly there, grabbing the sides of her head as he brought his lips down. "That's gonna be the worst of it. Relax." He peppered kisses along her jaw as she begged her body to listen to his words and relax at the foreign feeling. "I'm all the way in. Let your body accommodate to me."

"I'm trying," she grunted.

"You're doing amazing, Riley."

His words sounded far away as the blood rushed to her ears. "It hurts."

"I know." Liam's voice dripped with pain. "It'll be better soon. I'm so fucking sorry I'm the one hurting you. Next time it'll be better."

Next time? If the pain didn't subside, there would never be a next time.

Riley slowly opened her eyes and found Liam staring back at her. Her pain almost dissipated the second she saw how hurt *Liam* looked. The face he made, it was like... She stopped.

It was like the fact he was the one causing her pain was killing him.

Riley searched his eyes, trying to make sense of it.

"I'm going to move. Relax." Liam pulled out a little, the sensation sending a tingle through her as the pain seemed to lessen.

"That wasn't so bad."

"Good." He carefully pushed his way back in, this time there was almost no pain.

Instead, a new sensation settled in her lower belly. He did it again, causing the feeling to grow. "Oh, wow." Riley gripped his biceps as she pushed her hips into his thrust. "Move, please. I want to feel that again."

Liam circled his hips, causing the sensation she felt to build even more. "Again." She swallowed.

It'd taken her body a few minutes to adjust, but during that time, something changed inside her.

She wanted more.

No. Needed more.

Liam must have read her face, since he pulled all the way out, making her feel hollow, before he pushed back in, bottoming out making her full again. There was a dull ache, but it wasn't anything she couldn't handle. Not to mention, the other feelings coursing through her overshadowed any hint of discomfort she still had.

Liam's movements were slow and steady, and with each thrust her body craved more. His slow shallow movements were almost too much to take.

Before Riley knew it, her back arched, as her legs wrapped around his waist. She needed to be closer to him, to feel him on her skin. The pleasure seeped into her body as she clung to his back.

"Riley, fuck."

She rocked with Liam, raising her hips to meet his, as she let the pleasure take her over. "This, oh, God, Liam. I..."

"Yes, baby," he growled, his hands digging into her as he pulled her into a searing kiss, their tongues battling. This was nothing like they'd shared in the past. This was more.

More everything.

White-hot pleasure exploded through her as she tore her mouth from his. "Liam, Liam." She panted, her body on fire. "I— *Arrgh.*"

"I know," he grunted. Liam's hand slinked between them until he reached her clit. It only took one pinch for Riley to tip over the edge.

"*Urragh—*"

Liam's lips silenced the scream that ripped from her lungs as the stars exploded behind her eyes while he swallowed her euphoria. His movements increased, his thrusts falling out of rhythm until he threw his head back. The deep roar escaping him filled the entire room as he stilled, his body jerking as he came.

"Fuck, *Riley!*"

Liam fell on top of her, nearly crushing her as they gasped for air.

She did it.

Riley was no longer a virgin.

CHAPTER TWENTY-FOUR

WHILE THEY LAID THERE in his bed, Liam mindlessly circled his finger against Riley's arm as he watched her stare off into the distance. There was a part of him that still felt on top of the world. Even now, curled alongside the woman he loved as she was naked was everything he could have dreamed of and more. If he could stay this way forever, he would. But Riley's usual silence had his throat tightening. "You okay?"

Riley kept her head turned toward the ceiling. "I think so."

Concern punched at Liam, twisting his stomach into a knot. Had he hurt her? Was she okay? What happened? Forcing himself to get control, he cleared his throat. "Wanna tell me what's goin' on in that pretty little head of yours?"

Riley shifted her head so she was looking at him, her bottom lip slightly between her teeth. "I umm..."

Shit.

Liam waited patiently, but with each passing moment, his pulse raced while everything inside of him was on the verge of collapsing. Was Riley having second thoughts?

Fuck, fuck, fuck. I must've hurt her.

Liam's heart slammed against his chest as he lifted onto his elbow. While he half-hovered over Riley, he searched her face for answers. If he hurt her in any way... he'd... Fuck. "Talk to me, Riley. What's wrong? Are you hurt?"

"No." Riley immediately shook her head, her eyes pleading with him, almost a little shocked he'd asked. "I'm not hurt. Sore, but not hurt. You didn't hurt me, Liam."

Riley's words should've calmed him in some way, even just a little, but the knot was still heavy in the pit of his stomach.

"It's just... over, you know?" she continued.

Over?

Nothing was over. Not if he had anything to do with it. This was just the beginning, there was no way in hell this was *over*.

The knot in his stomach thickened, nearly pushing bile up Liam's throat. This couldn't be happening. Not after finally being together. Finally feeling all of Riley in the ways he'd only let himself dream of.

Keeping himself as neutral as he could, Liam looked into her eyes. "I don't understand."

"I mean..." Riley huffed out a shaky breath. "Like it's over. I lost my virginity. It's gone."

Fuck me. She's not talking about us. She's processing what we've done. Okay, breathe, Lee. Fucking breathe. This is normal, you gotta put your feelings aside and be there for her. Any way she needs.

Liam knew it could be a big deal for some as he tried to imagine where Riley was coming from. Especially since she'd waited so long.

He gently placed a kiss on her cheek, hoping to comfort her. "Are you okay with what happened?"

"Yes," Riley answered right away. "I wanted this. I

really did. I don't regret it at all. I guess it's..." She paused. "Weird? My whole life everyone's always talked about how losing your virginity was such a big deal. It was kinda beaten into my head it was supposed to make me an adult or something. Like it's this coveted thing or some crap like that. How it's monumental. Blah. Blah. Blah." Riley snort-laughed. "I guess before we started all this, I never thought sex was something I'd ever do. I mean yeah, I wanted to—"

"But?"

Her nose wrinkled. "After the pain went away, it felt amazing. So I get why people do it all the time."

"You're ignoring my *but,* Rye."

"Turn over and I won't ignore it." Riley's playful smile lit her face. "I still want to learn what you're willing to teach me. Turning over can be another lesson."

Liam's brows shot off his forehead. *Fuck, he loved this woman.* "For you. Maybe not for me." He laughed. "And I plan on teaching you everything I know and more." A lopsided grin appeared on his face before he gently pushed a piece of hair behind her ear. The moment between them softening. "I promise the next time, it won't be as scary."

"I wasn't really scared now." Riley's eyes held his. "It hurt, but I wasn't scared. It was you, Liam. I could never be scared with you."

Her words went straight to his heart, causing his eyes to close. As the wave of emotions choked him, he attempted a deep breath. Once he finally got a hold of himself, he opened his eyes, focusing on the woman that held his heart. "Thank you."

"For what?"

"Trusting me."

"I'd trust you with my life."

Liam's heart leaped into his throat. Fuck, hearing her say those words... he couldn't breathe. "Same, Riley," he managed to get out doing his best to keep himself steady. He wanted nothing more than to finally confess his love for her at that moment. It felt right, and keeping it inside damn near killed him.

But Liam knew he couldn't. Even though he'd do anything in the world for her, he wouldn't be so fucking selfish to drop that bomb after her first time.

So instead, Liam swallowed down the words that were on the tip of his tongue, begging to come out.

Riley shifted, drawing his attention from his thoughts back to her as she moved onto her side to face him. "It's just..." Her words came out shaky, which worried him. "It's not that I didn't think losing my virginity was in the cards for me or whatever, it's just... that night when you found me on the road after my date. I didn't—"

A jumble of emotions ran across Riley's face, sobering Liam instantly.

Even after all these years, he was still fucking pissed about that night. Seeing Riley limping toward him...

Rage ran up his spine.

That night. That fucking night. Knowing right now wasn't the time to let his anger take hold, he pushed it down, once again forcing himself to remain steady. "I still don't know what happened. You never told me."

Riley pushed herself onto her elbow, her brows pulling together. "Didn't Pat tell you?"

"No." Liam shook his head. "He said it wasn't his story to tell, and even then he didn't have all the information, but he knew enough to know he needed my help."

Riley's eyes rounded. "And you just went? That's it. No questions asked?"

"Yeah." Liam's face hardened as the haunted pain he saw in Riley's eyes all those years ago hit him in the gut all over again. "Someone hurt you, Riley. That's all I needed to know."

"Liam..."

"No, you don't get to Liam me. I'd do it again in a heartbeat."

"Please don't. I still can't believe you both beat him up. At least that's what Pat told me when he got home with his hand wrapped in a bandage." She narrowed her eyes at Liam for a split second before throwing her arm over her face. "I'd already taken care of it. I didn't need either of you to do anything else."

"There really wasn't any other choice, babe."

"Liam..."

"We'll agree to disagree."

"Fine," Riley grumbled with a flick of her eyes toward the ceiling. And damn, did that send a spark of desire through him. He ignited every time she showed him the real her, the one with fire.

Even during a serious conversation like the one they were having, Riley still got to him. She always would.

She's sore, you fucking idiot. And we're having a serious conversation here. Control yourself, asshole. Riley does not need to feel your dick hardening against her thigh...

"Wait a second," she broke through his berating. "So you beat him up and didn't even know why?"

"Pat showed up at my front door and said something happened to you and we needed to take care of it. After you refused to tell me what happened, I knew it was bad when I dropped you off. I didn't question it. It was you. I'd murder someone if it was to protect you, Riley. You should really know that by now." To prove his point, the arm around her waist tightened as he pulled her closer.

"You didn't murder him, did you?" she squeaked. "I never saw him again. Oh my God, you murdered him! And now that I know, I'm an accessory to murder. Great, I pop my cherry and now I'm gonna go to prison. I can't survive in prison. I'm not even allowed to walk to and from the bakery on my own in the dark."

"*Riley.*" Liam barked out a laugh with a shake of his head. Leave it to her to go from zero to a million in two seconds. "No. We didn't murder him, at least not yet. Depending on what you tell me next, I might find him and finish the job, but at *this* moment, he's still breathing."

"Then I'm not telling you."

Riley crossed her arms over her chest, causing his eyes to hone right onto those beautiful globes. It took Liam a few seconds, but he eventually looked back at Riley, his lips in a hard line. "I know what you just did."

"What'd I do?"

"Distract me with your tits." He tsked. "Well played. But it won't work. At least not right now. Spill your guts, pretty one. Do I need to get my murder overalls on?"

"Liam, it was a long time ago."

"And it shaped who you are."

"Yes, but in a good way." Riley placed her hand on his arm. "I wouldn't change a thing about my past."

Liam cocked his head to the side as he watched her. "Really?"

"Not my parents, not him, or the other guy. Hell, even almost burning down Pastries & Paws. Although the last one still gives me the heebie-jeebies. I can't believe how close I was to losing what I've worked so hard to build."

Liam moved to reassure her, but Riley held up her hand. "I'm not done. I wouldn't change anything I've been through because it's led me to right here... to you."

"Riley," Liam's voice caught in his throat.

"I know that sounds pretty stupid." A nervous laugh

bubbled out of her. "But it's true. I'm glad I got to experience my first time with you."

With each word out of Riley's mouth, Liam found himself falling more and more in love with her. She was by far the bravest, strongest, most stunning woman he'd ever laid eyes on. Having to keep his love locked away to not freak her out damn near killed him.

The fact he was her first...

Instead of telling her how he felt, he brought his lips to hers in a tender kiss. Every single emotion that ran through him, the love, passion, pain, the belonging, he poured into it, hoping she'd understand.

He loved her and would love her until his dying breath.

Liam pulled away when the emotions became too much and rested his forehead on hers. "I'm glad it was me."

He'd never forget this moment for as long as he lived. He thanked God he got to be the one for Riley. The one to help her explore a new side of her. He'd spend the rest of his life thanking the Universe, and never be able to truly express his gratitude.

It's gonna be me and you, Riley. Always.

The room fell into a comfortable silence as Liam tucked Riley in closer while he rested his head back on the pillow.

"It was the moves you taught me for self-defense that saved me that night."

Liam jerked back, his eyes narrowing, while his brows pulled together. "What?"

"That night. I used the uppercut to the nose, like you taught me." She huffed out a laugh. "Guess you teach me a lot of things."

"Riley," Liam's voice hardened. "That's it. I can't keep going on not knowing. What actually happened?" Liam didn't know if he could handle the truth. He suspected he knew what went down, but he needed to know for sure.

The guilt still ate at him. The only saving grace was now knowing what he'd taught her helped. He might not have been there to stop it from happening in the first place, but at least she used what he'd taught her.

"We started making out after the movie in his back seat—"

Liam growled, a pain running through his jaw with how hard he clenched his teeth.

"He started getting too handsy. I didn't like it and asked him to stop."

Liam's hand fisted at his side.

"He tried to force more—"

"I'll fucking kill him." Liam bolted up, his legs flinging off the side of the bed as he reached for his pants. "I'll find that motherfucker and kill him."

"Stop!" Riley grabbed his arm halting him. "It's okay. It was years ago, and I took care of it. I gave him an uppercut and broke his nose. I did what you taught me to do before it got too far."

The *only* thing that stopped Liam from storming out of the house to find the fucker was the panic in Riley's eyes as she pleaded with him.

It also helped she was naked... Liam couldn't stop his eyes from appreciating her form, with a quick glance down her body. Shaking his head, he grunted. "He doesn't deserve to live." His nostrils flared as his lips flattened into a thin line. "He tried to hurt you."

"But he didn't, and I broke his nose."

"You were limping."

"Okay." Riley waved her hand through the air. "Maybe a little, but it was a long time ago. It's okay now." She patted the bed. "Will you please sit down?"

Liam's eyes narrowed, his body still on edge, but he

obliged, as he plopped down with a huff. *I'm still gonna find him and fuck him up... I just won't tell her about it.*

"Thank you."

"If I ever see him again—"

"I'm sure you won't. But thank you for wanting to defend my honor."

Liam's grunt echoed from deep within his chest. "While I'm at it, I should find that other guy and beat the shit out of him, too."

"*Liam,*" Riley warned, making him snap his face to her.

"Can I at least beat the shit out of Patrick for not telling me everything?"

"No." She laughed with a shake of her head. "No one is beating anyone up. Besides, Pat doesn't know the whole story. You're the only one that does."

"We probably would've murdered him that night if he did."

"Men." Riley rolled her eyes again, making a spark zing through Liam. If she only knew what that did to him.

Riley was wrong, though. There was definitely going to be a fight as soon as Patrick found out what they were doing...

Liam let out a heavy sigh as he moved back to his spot on the bed. "You're no fun."

"Not everything can be fun." Riley kissed his cheek. "But I know what *was* fun." She winked.

"There you go, trying to distract me again." Liam's brow quirked. "That gonna be your new thing when you wanna change the subject?"

"Depends."

"On what?"

A playful smile engulfed her face. "If it'll work or not?"

"I guess we'll have to find out now, won't we?" Liam

pulled Riley under him, making her laugh. "You're gonna push all my buttons, aren't you?"

"Maybe. There are some things I'd like for you to teach me as long as this isn't over."

"Babe," Liam growled. "This is far from over."

"Good. 'Cause I'd like to try a few other positions. And figure out the sexting thing." She closed her eyes with a groan. "I can't believe I called your dick pretty."

"I kinda liked it." Liam's body ignited. "What other things do you want to try?" His hand caressed down her skin, being mindful he couldn't go too far since she'd still be sore.

Riley's face beamed as her eager smile brightened the room. "I've seen a lot of porn and I've got a list of things I'd like to try. Different positions, places, other *things*."

Liam stared at her open-mouthed as his mind processed what she'd said. The images that hit him... Holy fuck.

Riley really was the *perfect* woman for him and there was no way in hell he was going to let her go.

Now all he had to do was convince her.

CHAPTER TWENTY-FIVE

It'd been four freaking days since Riley and Liam had sex. Four. Freaking. Days.

Riley wanted to pull her hair out, and at this point, she might.

Liam had been the perfect gentleman after they'd finished their talk. He'd ran her a bath, telling her it would help with the soreness. At first she didn't want to leave his bed, but when he promised her he'd assist in cleaning her, making sure to spend extra time on her more sensitive parts, she couldn't really refuse.

It was probably one of the most kindhearted moments of her life.

The way Liam cradled her in his arms, the patience he had, his tenderness. Just thinking about it had Riley's heart clenching.

Which wasn't freaking good.

How in the hell was Riley supposed to keep her heart out of their *teachings* when Liam did things like that?

It was like asking someone not to breathe.

Every second that went by, the walls around her heart cracked more and more.

At least that *was* the case. Four motherfreaking days.

Riley should've known something was up when Liam pulled her out of the tub, dried her off, handed her some panties, and told her to get ready so they could meet his parents at the bakery, then left the bathroom to go back to his room.

He'd been so gentle and caring, all Riley wanted to do was run after him throw herself into his arms and stay there.

Forever.

Riley could punch herself in the head. She knew better than to keep letting her heart get involved.

Of course, he went back to his room. What did you think he was gonna do? Throw you over his shoulder and then what? Huh?

Ugh. Your stupid freakin' heart. What exactly did you expect to happen, dumb-dumb?

She put her idiotic feelings aside, as she should, since she knew exactly how this would end when she started. It was more than that, though. It was everything. It was the fact they hadn't so much as kissed since doing the deed.

It's like something changed and Riley couldn't figure out what it was.

The worst part, every night he'd wait until Patrick was asleep then crawl into bed with her, snuggling her close.

But that was it. He'd kiss her on the forehead and then go to sleep.

Freaking sleep.

Wasn't Liam supposed to be mentoring her? Well, he was doing a crap job. Four freaking days. Riley didn't know whether to laugh or cry.

Gahhhhh!

Other than Liam sneaking into her room each night, and being a little more hands-on with her, it was like nothing had changed.

While at Pastries & Paws, Liam laughed with his dad, while his mom talked to him about anything and everything, and Liam just... carried on with his life as if he hadn't stuck his hanging appendage inside of her hoo-ha a few hours earlier.

Okay, that was somewhat of a lie. Riley noticed him watching her more intently, and each time he did a nervous, yet excited thrill shot down her spine. Plus, he always seemed to be near her in one way or another.

Even though it felt a little rocky, at least on her part, she'd be lying if she said she hadn't enjoyed it.

It was like having a secret only they shared. True, they'd had the secret for a few days now, but it was more. They'd actually had sex now.

Sex-sex. Not just fooling around.

And she liked it. She liked it a lot. Damn her stupid heart for losing its mind.

But then the jerk had to go and ruin everything by not freaking touching her again. She'd finally gotten a taste of what everyone raved about and boom, he took it away.

Each night since, Riley's breath stalled in her throat the moment she'd hear her bedroom door open. Liam would then crawl in behind her, usually having to move Snicker-doodle to the end of the bed, which the kitten was *not* a fan of. Liam would then nuzzle her neck, kiss her forehead, and then tell her to go to sleep.

And when she woke up he'd be gone.

"Gahhh!"

The frustration that welled inside of Riley was liable to make her pop. Which led her to her current situation.

It was Friday night. She'd gotten home early from the bakery since Rhonda had been there to help...

Riley shuddered.

Rhonda definitely knew something was different about

Riley, but thankfully, she hadn't pushed. She'd instead, of course, stare Riley down multiple times a day, giving her the *look*. Which only added to Riley's never-ending frustrations. It honestly felt like she was lying to Rhonda.

Riley's gut churned at the thought. She hated that. Freaking hated it.

Not that it'd be worth it, but if her and Liam were at least still participating in their lessons, she wouldn't feel as bad.

Riley rubbed her temples as she plopped onto the couch in the living room. A part of her wanted to stay in her room, but the thought of going in there didn't appeal to her.

Neither did being in the living room.

What was she to do? At least out here, Snickerdoodle had his cat tree and toys. Although the little guy was far more preoccupied with a straw wrapper than any of the fancy things he had.

Besides, Liam was home, and they were alone.

Riley hadn't expected them to end up alone in the house, but her brother insisted on heading to the bar to brag about the *Firebird* he worked on all week.

She'd held her breath as he'd asked Liam to go with him.

Liam had looked at Riley over Patrick's shoulder, the corner of his mouth slightly quirking upward as he declined her brother's plea.

That had to mean something, right? Right?

Guess not, since as soon as Pat left, Liam headed into the shower.

Trying not to focus on it, Riley flipped on the TV and put on some baking competition. When she heard the bathroom door open, her heart stopped.

Stay calm. Stay calm!

A few seconds later, Liam padded into the room before plopping down next to her. Instantly, she was hit with the smell of a freshly showered Liam, which made her stomach tingle. It only worsened the moment he placed his arm around her shoulder.

Riley fidgeted under its weight. The flutters in her stomach making her nauseous.

"You good?" Liam asked, a half-smile on his face.

"Uhh, yeah," she lied. What was she supposed to say? *Hey, why'd ya stop with the sexy times stuff? Huh? Huh?* That would go over real well and make her feel like even more of an idiot.

Liam cocked his head. "You don't sound convincing."

"I am." Riley focused on the TV. After a few minutes she couldn't take it anymore. The tension between them made it hard to breathe. Mustering all the courage she had, she cleared her throat. "So, how was your week? Anything exciting?"

Really? Is that what we're going with?

"Pat was annoying as shit, but that's normal for him. He wouldn't shut up about the *Firebird*. It's why he wanted to head to the bar tonight to impress some chicks." A low chuckle slipped past Liam's throat. "I don't think he gets no one is really gonna care. Maybe some of the guys will, but I doubt anyone he wants to hook up with will."

Riley shoved her fingers in her ears. "I don't want to hear about him hooking up. Ewww." She shook her head. "Take it back!"

Liam barked out a hearty laugh. "My apologies, babe."

Babe... Riley's stomach somersaulted. *Stop it.* "I think you're wrong, though. I'm sure there are girls out there impressed with old cars. He just needs to find one."

Liam cocked his brow. "Are you impressed with old cars?"

"Eww." Riley scrunched her nose. "I'm not his target demographic. Blahh. So no."

"You're *my* target demographic," Liam growled, the noise sending a shock wave right to her core.

Aargh. It sure as hell didn't feel that way. Instead of becoming more annoyed, Riley changed the subject. "Rhonda and James are coming to dinner tomorrow."

Liam cocked his brow. "I know."

"Your mom wants to play with Snickerdoodle."

Liam nodded once. "Trash Panda should meet his grandma."

Riley stared at him with her mouth opened wide. *The audacity.* Not only did he call her kitten Trash Panda, *again,* but he also seemed to be completely unfazed.

Liam's eyes focused on her mouth as he licked his lips. "You better close your mouth or I'll give you something to fill it."

The sudden flirting had her cheeks flushing for a second before she remembered what happened or hadn't happened. "I doubt it," she mumbled.

"What's that?" Liam grabbed her chin, forcing her to look him in the eyes.

"You heard me." Were they really going to do this? She guessed so. "We had *sex* and then you stopped everything. Why haven't you touched me? I thought you had more lessons for me."

Liam stared at her like she'd grown an extra head. "Riley, you're sore."

"Am not." She folded her arms over her chest. "And how would you even know? It's not your va-jay-jay."

"Are we back to calling it a va-jay-jay rather than a pussy?"

Ignoring him, Riley continued, "You got into my hoo-ha and then nothing. You sneak into my room every night and the most I get is a kiss on the head. What gives?"

"Now it's hoo-ha?"

"Liam," she grumbled.

He had her pinned to the couch in an instant, her arms over her head. "Ahhh!"

"What'd you want me to do, babe? Fuck you every second of the day? I knew you'd be sore. You had sex for the first time. I was waiting for you to come to me and say you were ready."

It was Riley's turn to look at him like he'd lost his mind. "What do you mean come to you? You sneak into my bed every night and all I get is a freaking kiss on the *head*. Then you roll over and go to sleep."

"My kisses aren't good enough for you?"

"You know they are. They turn me on," she answered without thinking. "Wait, no. No, they don't. I'm mad at you."

Liam smirked. "I'm happy to hear my kisses turn you on."

"Liam!"

"What?" he asked, that stupid lopsided smile still on his face. "I've been waiting for you to tell me it's okay. We were pretty rough for your first time."

"What's hurting me is not doing it again, or anything for that matter. You can't give that to me and then take it away. Every single night you fall asleep like its nothing. I've been laying there wondering what the hell was going on. Was I not good enough? Have you changed your mind? And if you haven't changed your mind, aren't you *supposed* to be teaching me everything there is about sex?"

"I am," Liam stated matter of fact. "Which includes knowing your partner's needs."

"My needs are for you to *fuck* me."

Liam's deep growl filled the room. "I love it when you cuss. You only do it when you're so raw with emotion you can't stop yourself." His heated gaze hit her with force. "You want me to fuck you?"

Riley laid there frozen as he thrust his hips, hitting her exactly where she wanted, causing her breath to escape from her lungs in a whoosh.

"I plan on it," he growled. "But, my prodigy, the needs I'm talking about are knowing when you have to pull back and make sure your partner is safe, so whatever you plan on doing next won't hurt them."

"You letting me lay there all night without you touching me is hurting me."

Liam kissed her lips. "No one died from not getting off."

"I might."

"Glad I'm that good."

"Shut up."

"Seriously, I'm taking care of you, Riley." He nuzzled her neck, placing wet, open-mouth kisses on her skin.

"Then why haven't I gotten off in four days?"

"'Cause you're a good girl, and listened when I told you that you only get off with me." He bit the side of her neck. "All you gotta do is ask, Rye."

When Liam faced her, Riley glared at him.

"I need the words, babe."

If he wanted the words, then I'll give him the words. "Fuck me, Liam, or I'll find someone else."

CHAPTER TWENTY-SIX

"You LIKE to play with fire, don't you?" Liam's voice was stern and husky as his eyes dangerously darkened. "*No one touches you, but me.*"

Instantly, Riley's eyes widened, her breath hitching as her mouth fell open.

Good.

It'd nearly fucking killed Liam having to wait to be with Riley again. Seriously fucking killed him. However, two days after finally sinking into the woman of his dreams, he realized Riley *itched* for more.

He could see it in her eyes every time she looked his way. How her cheeks heated, even in the minuscule shifting she'd do when she was near him.

Others wouldn't have been able to tell, but he could. He really did know her better than she probably knew herself. Which was why he chose their next lesson to be one of patience, along with using your words.

Of course, he'd initially waited because he wanted to make sure Riley wasn't sore. He'd be an asshole not to.

It'd taken everything inside of him to wait.

And the instant Patrick asked Liam to go to the bar, he

knew tonight would be the night Riley did in fact learn to use her words.

Liam only needed to bide his time a little longer before Riley snapped. And fuck did she ever.

Call him a bastard, but he didn't care. This was about Riley getting everything she wanted, she only had to ask for it.

Using his knees to spread her legs apart forcing one of them to hang off the couch so he'd have room, he seated his hard cock against her pussy.

When he jerked forward, Riley gasped, her eyes snapping shut. "You sure you're not sore?"

Riley's eyes instantly opened as she glared at him. "If you ask me that one more time, I will *fucking* murder you."

Liam's hand moved to her hip, gripping tightly. "There you go cussin' again, babe. I don't think you know what that does to me. Only thing that gets me harder is when you roll your eyes."

Riley's mouth fell to the floor as she gawked at him.

"That fucking fire." Liam threw his head back with a groan as he jerked Riley forward forcing her to sit up. With one hand, he yanked her shirt over her head. Her bra was next as he effortlessly discarded it behind him. "I think I know your game here, though, babe. You're a fucking genius for tempting me. Pushin' me to snap." Liam's mouth flew to the nape of her neck as he traced his tongue along her shoulder.

"Liam," Riley whimpered.

He flipped them so Riley had no choice but to straddle him

"Gahhh! I told you to warn me!"

Ignoring her, Liam's hand moved to the waist of her leggings, pushing inside, until his fingers were greeted with her wet core. His eyes closed at the feeling, a heavy groan falling from his lips.

"Oh, God," Riley cried, thrusting her hips into his hand.

"Not God, but you can worship me any day, babe." He swirled her clit with his index finger. "I know I worship you."

Riley's hips thrust forward, making her nub press against the heel of his hand as she moaned.

The sound she made set him on fucking fire. "Fuck it." Much to her protest, Liam yanked his hand from her core before grabbing the top of her leggings with both of his fists.

It only took one hard yank for the material to give way, splitting right down the middle. His eyes instantly zeroed in on her pussy, and when he noticed she wasn't wearing panties, his dick twitched.

"Liam! What the hell!"

He silenced her, grabbing the back of her head, yanking her down so he could smother her with his kiss. "I'll buy you more," he growled against her lips as his hand sought out her center. His fingers moved through Riley's sticky slickness with ease. "Don't ever fucking say you'll find someone else again."

"I was—"

Liam grabbed her waist, flipping Riley again so she was now on her back. "Never. Fucking. *Again*." He jumped off the couch, ripping his clothes off as he glared at her. "Naked. Now."

"I can't get much more naked. You ripped my favorite pair of leggings down the dang middle." She jutted her hands to either side of her glistening pussy. "This is pretty much it."

"Riley," he growled, his voice hard, dripping with dominance.

She must've seen his fire, because Riley's eyes nearly

popped out of her head before she yanked the tattered remains of her leggings off her body.

"Good girl." He fisted himself a few times as he sat back on the couch spreading his legs wide. "Straddle me."

"W-what?" Riley's eyes rounded full of arousal as she glanced at his dick.

As she watched, he stroked himself slowly, her eyes following every twist he made with his hand. He stopped and waited for her to look at him again. When she did, her eyes were full of arousal and need.

"Next lesson." Liam helped her move to his lap. "Tonight you're gonna ride me."

Riley visibly swallowed as she shimmied above him, his thick dick a mere inch from her lush, perfect pussy.

Liam held her in place by her hips, keeping Riley right above him. "You sure you're not sore?"

Riley's eyes flashed with annoyance before they shifted back to need. She nodded, biting her bottom lip. "I'm not, but uhh..." She swallowed. "What if I do it wrong?"

Liam was so taken aback, his brows practically jumped off his forehead. "Do it wrong? Babe, I can guarantee you aren't gonna do it wrong."

"How do you know? I've never—"

He stopped her with another kiss. "Not possible."

Keeping Riley above him, Liam grabbed the base of his cock, lining it up to her core. The willpower it took to not thrust upward and enter her should've been award-winning. However, he knew even though she said she wasn't sore, there was still the possibility and her being on top controlling the pace and movement would be the best option.

Liam's nostrils flared as he rubbed the tip of his leaking dick against her clit, instantly causing Riley's breath to hitch.

"Does it always feel this..." She closed her eyes, her head falling forward. "Intense?"

"Eyes."

Riley's gaze instantly met his, filling him with pride as she listened to his command. "With us. Yes." Keeping his attention on her, he put the tip into her pussy. "Lower yourself slowly," he commanded. "Eyes on me the whole time."

Riley did as he said, as she slowly sunk onto his dick, taking him inch by fucking delicious inch. Liam's jaw tightened as her pussy clenched around him, sending a white-hot burst of pleasure up his spine. "That's it, baby. Slow."

Riley panted, her eyes glued to him as she lowered herself, carefully bottoming out to fully impale onto his dick.

"How does that feel?" Liam asked through gritted teeth.

"Full."

"Sore?"

Riley shook her head as she swirled her hips, the sensation like an ocean wave crashing over him, sending pleasure throughout his entire body.

"No. Not sore." Riley did the move again causing Liam's body to twitch.

"I think you know exactly what you're doing, Riley," he ground out through gritted teeth.

When Liam was greeted by her half-smile, it nearly knocked the wind out of him.

"I already told you I watch a lot of porn."

"Fuck me," Liam growled, his hand tightening around her plump hip. "You're gonna have to show me what you watch, babe. I need to know what turns you on."

Riley's eyes seemed to pull him in, like he was being granted the ability to stare into the depths of her soul.

"You," she stated with confidence.

Fuck him. That was it. Liam couldn't take it anymore.

He held her in place, thrusting upward, making her moan. "Ride me, babe. Now."

At first, she was slow as she moved up and down his length, Liam helping her keep her balance while Riley found what worked best for her.

Then, out of nowhere, her body jerked. "That. What's that? Oh my *God*."

Taking the cue from Riley's face, Liam realized the tip of his cock had brushed against her spot. Keeping her at the same angle, he took over the movements while Riley lost all control. Her arms clung to his as she threw her head back, exposing the curves of her neck.

"Liam. My God. Oh God!" she cried as he continued to hit her spot with every thrust.

"That's it, fuck yes. Ride me. Feel me inside of you hitting what drives you fucking wild. Hitting your every need, Riley. That's it, baby, fucking feel me."

Her fingers dug into his shoulders as she bounced with vigor, using his body to help her achieve her peak. "Please, *pl*—," she ground. "I need... I need—"

"Give it to me," Liam ground out with a force that threatened to shake the walls. "Now. Give it to me. *Now*."

One last thrust, hitting her in the perfect angle and Riley screamed, her head falling back as she shook, her pussy clenching around his aching cock.

Liam couldn't hold off even if he tried. Gripping her hips, knowing he'd be leaving bruises—that thought somehow driving him even more wild, knowing he'd be marking her again, Liam pulled her down, her warm spasming pussy only stopping when the base of his cock slammed against her skin.

Liam emptied every last drop in her as a grunt tore from his lungs that came straight from the bottom of his soul.

As he came down from the most intense orgasm of his

life his heart pounded against his chest, threatening to break his ribs.

Riley fell forward, her body sticky with sweat as she damn near hyperventilated. "That was *way* better than last time."

"Told you it gets better." He held her lower back, keeping them connected as she rested against him.

"The first time was good, but this..." Riley pulled away to look him in the eyes. "I—wow. I definitely want to do that again."

Liam's heart skipped, the emotions shooting through Liam.

As he observed every single thing about Riley, from the flush of her cheeks, to the post-orgasmic glow that hung heavy around her, to the way her half-hooded eyes seemed as though they spoke directly to his soul, he couldn't handle it.

He was seconds from losing his composure, and he knew it.

Fuck, they were still connected in the most intimate way possible. Riley was by far the most beautiful thing he'd seen in his life.

It took everything in him not to scream the words he desperately wanted Riley to hear.

Before he did something stupid, Liam took hold of Riley's chin pulling her to him, their lips only a whisper apart. "I will *always* give you what you need, Riley. No matter what it is. All you ever have to do is ask."

CHAPTER TWENTY-SEVEN

RILEY PACED AROUND the kitchen like it was her first time cooking. Her anxiety was at an all-time high. which was stupid, since Rhonda and James had come over for dinner countless times in the past. Yeah, they normally ate at their house, but it wasn't so unusual to have dinner nights here.

This was however the first time they'd be having dinner after Riley and Liam had... She swallowed, her cheeks heating.

It wouldn't have been so bad if Riley hadn't been a fumbling mess at Pastries & Paws that morning. She dropped almost everything she'd touched, burned two separate batches of cookies, and overworked the dough for bread.

At one point, Rhonda had even made Riley go sit in her office and *relax*. Geez, it'd been humiliating. She hadn't been this much of a wreck since the first week after opening the bakery. It's like something overtook Riley's brain and no matter how hard she tried, she couldn't function like a normal human.

Was this what sex did to you? Yeah, it's amazing and I really really like it, but this... For freak's sake I've almost burned down the bakery at least five times and I can't blame Liam at all for it. This was all on me. Not to mention, I'd given the wrong order to at least three people.

Blahhhhh.

Riley grabbed the homemade garlic butter spread she'd mixed when she got home from the fridge and tossed it on the counter. Worrying her bottom lip, she stirred her pasta sauce and focused on her breathing.

It wasn't that she'd had sex, screwed-up the orders or being a mess-up at the bakery that had her on edge.

Nope.

It was the fact she felt like she was lying to Rhonda.

Each time she looked into the older woman's eyes, it was like a kick to her stomach.

It was *Rhonda.* The mother she wished she had.

It ate Riley alive.

Plus, there was the constant fear she'd disappoint her or James with Liam being the one to teach her all the things she wanted to learn.

Which then made Riley worried if she was doing a good enough job at hiding the recent development in their relationship.

It was all a mess, an absolute freaking mess. And now she was panicked as she tried her best to cook some of her favorite people a meal they'd all enjoy. All the while attempting to not blurt out Liam had taken her virginity and he'd also graciously agreed to be her teacher of all the deliciously dirty things they could do.

Wait no. Stop it. No one is gonna find out, and I'm not giving anything away. I'm not gonna be an idiot and scream it out when James takes a bite of his garlic bread. I have more self-control than that. No one knows anything. I'm blowing all of this out of proportion. See that's my problem, I'm overthinking this yet again and keep running around assuming

274

everyone knows and is about to call me out on sleeping with my brother's best friend and being a virgin.

Although I guess I can't call myself a virgin anymore. Blahhh.

As Riley was in the throes of another panic attack someone grabbed her waist making her scream. However, the sound she made was muffled by a hand causing her eyes to round as she looked to her side and saw Liam smirking.

"Shhh."

Shhh, shhh? Did he just shush me after almost making me pee my pants? I should kill him. This is all his fault anyway.

Liam gripped her tighter, making Riley's ass grind against the front of his jeans, and damn if that didn't send a thrill through her.

"If I take my hand away, are you gonna scream?"

No, I'm gonna stab you with a butter knife, so it hurts more.

Liam lowered his hand, skimming his fingers down her neck, easily grazing over her chest before stopping at her waist to pull her into him.

"Don't freaking scare me!" Riley attempted to dislodge herself from him but failed when Liam's grip tightened. "Get off. Patrick's home! What are you thinking?" she whisper-shouted over her shoulder with a glare.

"That I needed to touch you." Liam kissed the corner of her mouth, his tongue poking out to flick over her lips.

"Ahhh! What the hell are you doing? Patrick—"

"Is in the shower."

"Oh." Riley stopped, her brows denting for a second before she shook her head. "Doesn't matter. He's home and your parents are gonna be here soon."

Liam spun Riley so she faced him. "We only have a few minutes before he's out and they get here. Let me have this."

"Let you have this? Are you insane?"

"For you?" He smirked. "Yes."

Liam's lips were on her before Riley could respond and damn if his possessive kiss didn't melt her right on the spot.

More importantly, how could one gesture as simple as his kiss calm her? It's like with one look, Liam could take away all her worries and more.

"That's better." Liam pulled away, but as he did, Riley's lips chased after his seeking more contact. More intimacy, more peace of mind.

Just the simplest of Liam's touches gave her what she needed.

He's your rock. Aargh. Stop. Can I knock out my own heart? 'Cause I think at this point I'm gonna have to just take it out since it's not getting the damn clue to knock it off.

"I love that you always want more," he grunted, a pleased smile spreading across his face. "But you'll have to wait. We can't start something we don't have time to finish."

"But—"

"No buts, babe." He tapped her nose with his index finger, his smirk firmly in place as he spun her around to the counter and smacked her ass.

"Hey!" She turned back and glared at him.

Ignoring her, Liam moved to the stove. "What can I help you with?"

"Putting me out of my misery."

Liam turned, resting his back against the counter, his arms folded over his chest as he watched her with a cocked brow. "What's got you so worked up? It's just my parents."

"I know."

"Then why're you stressing?"

"Because your mom keeps giving me the *look* all the damn time. I don't know how to act around you with other people. What if I burn the sauce or the garlic bread? And you just scared the daylights out of me and also somehow turned me on. Plus, my brother is a few feet away." Her whisper was louder but still a shout, nonetheless. "What if I put too much salt in the sauce or not enough? What if I go to stick my fork in my mouth and instead blurt out I've seen your dingdong?"

Liam threw his head back with a hearty laugh.

"Don't laugh at me!"

He pushed off the counter and pulled Riley to him, cradling her in his arms. "It's all gonna work out."

"What if Snickerdoodle scratches your dad?"

"Then it'd be fuckin' hilarious." He placed his chin on her head. "Besides, you and I both know Trash Panda would never hurt a soul. He doesn't even attack me when I move him to the end of the bed. It's all gonna be fine." He kissed the top of her head. "I'm never gonna let anything bad happen to you."

Riley melted into him, begging herself to believe his words. He was right, though. No matter what happened, Liam had always been there for her. She knew this, because he always had been.

"Somethin' smells good."

Riley catapulted from Liam's arms tripping over her own feet. Before hitting the ground, though, Liam pulled her up as he laughed.

"Geez, you look like you've seen a ghost." Patrick quirked his brow at Riley for a second before focusing on the stove. Like a man who hadn't eaten in years, he grabbed the nearby spoon and scooped some sauce.

Riley blankly stared at him as he shoved the food in his mouth.

What the freaking crap? Is Pat blind? Did he miss it? Oh God, do I need to call the eye doctor for him? He's probably got metal in his eye and doesn't even know it. He's gotta be seconds from going blind.

"Damn, this is good. I know you like baking more, but you could've easily been a chef."

"You've never found a food you didn't like." Liam laughed, making Riley's wide eyes dart to him. Okay, something was wrong. Very wrong. She must have hit her head and was passed out on the floor because there was no way in hell this was happening.

"True. This shit is good, though. You try it?" Patrick sent Liam a cocky grin.

"Nope, I came in here to see if Riley needed any help and she was having a panic attack."

Liam's brows knitted together as he looked back at Riley. "You good now?"

What in the freaking hell is this?

Realizing she'd been staring at Patrick without answering for far too long, she cleared her throat. "Just nervous."

"She's scared my parents won't like Trash Panda or he'll bite my dad."

Patrick burst into a laugh. "Yeah, right. That cat doesn't hate anyone. *But* if he did bite Pops, it'd be..." He kissed the tips of his fingers in a chef's kiss. "Puurrfection."

"Puurrfection?" Liam cocked his brow. "Really?"

"What?" He shrugged. "It would be. So Rye's havin' a bit of a meltdown?"

"A tiny one."

"Hey!" Riley jerked her arms over her chest. "Can you guys stop talking about me like I'm not here?"

Liam winked her way, making her stomach flutter. "We know you're here."

Oh geez, why wasn't he freaking out? He should be

freaking out. *She* was freaking out. They were almost caught *again*.

Although Riley had to admit Liam covered it up remarkably well. Plus, he wasn't really lying. She was having a panic attack. He just left out the other stuff.

Gahh.

Riley huffed out an exhausted sigh.

"Stop freaking out. Trash Panda's gonna love them," her brother mumbled over another spoonful of sauce.

"Can you stop eating it? It's weird. You're sitting there drinking the sauce like it's lemonade. You do know that's not normal, right?"

"Whoever said I was normal? And people do it all the time with bread."

"*With bread.*" She gestured to the loaves on the counter. However, when Patrick took a step toward them, she growled. "Don't you dare. Those are for garlic bread. I made the spread when I got home."

Patrick's eyes lit. "You made garlic butter?"

"With cheese."

"My God, I love you." He closed his eyes, letting out a deep groan. "Homemade garlic bread. *Yessss.*" In an instant, he snapped his eyes back to her. "Please fucking tell me you brought home ten loaves."

Riley laughed with a shake of her head. "Three. You need to share."

"Only three!" He focused on the bag that held the bread she'd brought home. "Fine, but one of them is mine."

"You'll have to fight James for it."

"Pops wouldn't stand a chance."

"Oh for the love of all things." Riley laughed, flicking her eyes up as the three of them worked together finishing up the dinner. With each moment that passed, she found herself more relaxed. Liam was right.

Riley had nothing to worry about.

Snickerdoodle kept running from the kitchen to the cat tree and back again like he'd invented his own game, making her smile. How could anyone be nervous when they got to watch a kitten in his element?

"We're here!" James hollered as he burst through the front door, making Riley jump.

"Fudge balls!" Riley's hand shot to her heart. "Don't do that."

"You should've knocked." Rhonda trailed in behind him. "You can't go around opening doors like you own the place."

"Why not? They do that to us," James huffed. "Now, where is this kitten I have yet to meet?"

Liam chuckled, scooping the kitten into his arms before handing him over to James. "Dad, meet Trash Panda. Trash Panda, meet my father. He's going to be a pain in the ass. I hope you bite him."

"Liam!" Riley yelled, her jaw hitting the floor.

Liam turned to her with a wink. "It'd be funny."

Ignoring Liam but locking what he said away in the back of her mind so she could get him back later, she rushed over to James. "He doesn't bite. He's perfect and his name is *not* Trash Panda. It's Snickerdoodle, Snicks for short. We already talked about this." Riley jerked her head toward Liam with a growl before she turned back to James. "Your son's an idiot."

James flicked his eyes between her and Liam a few times then held the kitten in the air. "Trash Panda, I'm your granddad."

Riley's groan filled the room.

"At least that's what that crazy old woman over there informed me that's what I call myself." James moved the kitten so Snickerdoodle looked at his wife.

"Wanna repeat that?" Rhonda's hand flew to her hips.

"If I do, will you promise to punish me later for it?" James winked at her.

"For fuck's sake." Liam threw his hands up. "Can you not? Thank fuck we haven't eaten or I would've just upchucked all over your feet."

"Interesting you say that." James's eyes snapped to Riley, making her palms sweat. "Not my fault, Lee, you're jealous I can get some—"

"That's enough of that." Rhonda stormed to her husband, snatching the kitten from his arms.

"Hey. I wasn't done."

"You lost your turn when you talked about our sex life."

"Mom!" Liam dry-heaved. "You don't have a sex life. *Stop*."

Rhonda walked over to her son and patted his shoulder. "Oh, sweetie, I thought your father told you about the birds and the bees years ago and how you were born. I didn't realize he hadn't explained how you got here."

"He knows about the birds and the bees, dear. Remember when we caught him and Pat looking at porn?"

"Why're you bringing me into this?" Patrick yelled from the kitchen, sounding an awful lot like his mouth was full of food.

"If one of you is getting shit, you both are getting shit," James stated matter of pure fact.

"Stop eating the garlic bread!" Riley was about to lose it... Seriously, how did it always end up like this? "And for the love of my sanity, can we please change the subject?"

James cocked his head. "I thought you'd be interested to know what Liam was int—"

"James, leave them alone." Rhonda hip checked him. "We're here to meet our grandkitty, not traumatize our kids."

"Where's the fun in that?"

Ignoring him, Rhonda focused on the kitten cradled in her arms. "Aren't you a cutie?" She nuzzled his head. "I've heard a lot about you. I'm Grandma and I'm gonna spoil the ever-loving daylights out of you since none of these buffoons have given me grandbabies yet."

"*Mom.*"

Rhonda glared at Liam. "Don't you dare Mom me. I'm taking what I can get here." She turned to Riley. "My perfect child, you wanna be the first to gift me with a grand-baby to spoil?"

"I gave you a cat!" Riley screamed at the top of her lungs, her brows shooting off her face. "He already loves you!"

Oh God, oh God, oh God.

"It might happen sooner than you think, dear," James added, his brow quirking even higher.

Riley's heart stopped as she went into survival mode. She damn near sprinted to the cat tree. "This is where he plays most of the time. Pat bought all these toys for him." She swung her hand to the toys scattered around the floor. "Snicks prefers paper though, straws, receipts, recipes. Anything that's paper he wants to play with. He purrs really loud. Sounds kinda like a car. Vroom vroom. He also does this thing where he climbs up your arms to sit on your shoulders like he wants to look over his kingdom," she rushed out on the verge of a heart attack.

"That's a lot of information, sweetie." Rhonda softened. "What's got you so anxious? You've been like this all day. How many batches of cookies did you burn?"

"I'm..." Riley trailed off as her cheeks flushed.

"She's afraid you won't like Trash Panda."

Rhonda clutched the kitten to her chest. "Missy, is that

why you were a mess today? Why wouldn't we like this precious little baby? He's so cute I might just eat him alive."

Snickerdoodle cried and then knocked his head against Rhonda's arm.

"Not sure if that was protest or acceptance?" James asked.

"It was, *give me love right now*. He's very demanding." Liam's eyes caught Riley's as he winked, making her breath hitch. "Thankfully, he's learned to use his words. Or his head should I say, to let us know what he needs."

Blood rushed to Riley's ears. *Ground, please swallow me whole. Right here. Right now. Poof.*

Thank freaking everything the timer on the oven beeped. It might not have been the ground eating her, but Riley would take it. "Dinner time! That's the last batch of garlic bread."

"Or is it the only?" Patrick popped his head from around the corner, munching on a piece of crust.

"It better not be."

"And what if it is?" he challenged.

"I wouldn't if I were you," Liam remarked with a chuckle. "We both know she'd take you in a heartbeat."

Patrick's shocked gasp filled the room as his hand went to his heart. "That hurts. I thought you were my best friend."

"Maybe I'm Riley's best friend now."

Oh, for the love of everything!

"That's enough." Riley threw her hands in the air as she stormed past everyone, her cheeks on fire. "Food before it gets cold."

Laughing at the antics everyone moved into the kitchen, grabbing plates of food off the stove as they found their seats around the table. Once they'd gotten their food, Riley stood in front of the stove, doing her damn best to calm her nerves.

Liam moved in behind her, making her jump. "Relax, babe, you're doing great."

Riley's sharp eyes hit him. "Go away," she whispered.

He held up his empty plate. "I'm getting my food."

"Are you serious right now? Back up. This is a disaster. I'm an idiot for ever agreeing to this."

"Don't call yourself an idiot," he growled. "That's your only warning."

Riley almost dropped her plate, her breath stalling in her throat.

"Pick your jaw up, babe. We both know if you don't, I'll fill it with something."

Holy fudge crackers. See! This was bad, very bad. And damn my hoo-ha for taking notice of his growl.

Riley's eyes snapped to the other end of the kitchen where the others were deep in conversation. Clearly paying zero attention to her or Liam. *Thank the Universe.*

James and her brother were complaining about something and Rhonda was talking about all the things she planned on buying to spoil the kitten.

Good. Good. Looks like no one saw.

Riley jerked her face to Liam. "Knock it off."

"If you can make it through dinner without freaking out, I'll make sure it'll be worth your while tonight." Liam winked, pushing her out of the way to grab his food as she stood there dumbfounded.

This night was going to be the death of her.

She could feel it.

Doing what Riley could to center herself and not dump her food over Liam's head and call it a night, she headed toward the table and realized the only two seats left would put her between Patrick and Liam, making her gulp.

Normally, that wouldn't have been an issue, but it was always a tight squeeze around their tiny kitchen table.

It's fine. Super fine. You'll just have to pretty much sit in Liam's lap. It's great. Wonderful.

Controlling her breath, Riley squeezed into her spot, Liam doing the same next to her. *He* seemed to have no problem with it, since he took to opportunity to lean into her.

Which was fine, until the heat of his leg seeped into Riley, making her all too aware of how close they were.

In the throes of what was sure to be another panic attack, Snickerdoodle grabbed Riley's attention as he cried before attempting to jump into Rhonda's lap.

"I can see you love your grandma best, now don't cha? Aren't you a little lover?"

"It's the worst," Liam joked.

"Liar."

"Maybe."

"Okay, now that you're all here," Patrick began. "Let's talk about the *Firebird.*"

Liam and James both groaned.

"I'm never giving you a classic again." James smacked the back of Patrick's head. "Do you ever shut the fuck up?"

"Nope." Patrick popped the *p.* His hand then went to his heart, his bottom lip jutting out. "Pops, you wouldn't deny my right to work on old beauties like that, would you? I'm your favorite."

"If you call me Pops again, I *will* shoot you."

"Can I choose where you shoot me?"

"*Pat.*"

"James, when are you gonna learn not to take his bait?" Rhonda jabbed her fork at her husband.

"When I'm dead."

The entire room burst into laughter as everything felt easy, while their normal banter echoed around.

"S'good," James mumbled around his garlic bread.

Riley's shoulders pushed back as pride swelled through her chest. "Thanks."

"That's the only piece you're having, the rest is mine," Patrick grumbled, his hand reaching for another piece.

"Says you and what army?"

Rhonda grabbed the basket. "How many have you had?"

As Riley watched the chaos, Liam reached under the table and squeezed her knee, causing her eyes to widen.

Holy fudge balls. What the hell is he doing? She side-eyed him. *This is fine. Just don't move and no one will know. Although as soon as they leave, I'm going to strangle him.*

Riley stabbed her pasta, hoping no one would notice her hand shaking, or that she looked out of place. While she focused on her breathing, Liam's hand pushed its way between her thick thighs, closer to her center.

Oh, no.

Oh fucking no.

"Only a few," Patrick lied, giving Rhonda a puppy dog look.

James scoffed. "You've never been a good liar."

Riley's heart raced, the blood rushing to her ears as she attempted to shift. But not too much or she'd bump into Patrick who was on the other side of her.

Desperately trying to push Liam off and failing miserably, Riley tried again. However, Liam must have taken her movement as an invitation since he squeezed his hand, his pinky brushing against her core.

A strangled noise escaped her lips the moment she felt it.

In an instant, all eyes shot to her. Thinking fast, she coughed, grabbing her water. "Choking. Just choking."

"You okay?" Rhonda asked, while James only cocked his brow at her.

Now in a full-on panic, Riley pinched her lips in a tight line. "I'm fine. Who needs to breathe anyway? It's a stupid thing we do. We should've evolved past it by now," she rambled.

Liam removed his hand from her thigh and covered his mouth to hide his smirk.

Bastard.

Oh, yeah, he was a freaking dead man.

"Riley, are you *sure* you're okay?" Rhonda asked. The concern in her eyes was like another sucker punch to Riley's solar plexus.

Okay? She was absolutely not okay.

Before Riley had a chance to come up with another lie, the doorbell rang, making her jump.

Who the heck could be here? And for freak's sake. Why am I so jumpy. What in the hell had Liam done to me?

"I'll get it." Liam stood. He made it look casual as he placed his hand on Riley's shoulder like he was helping himself from the table, but Riley knew his squeeze was one of reassurance.

That was Liam.

Although he caused her unease, he somehow was also always the one to calm her. Riley's shoulders turned inward as her body relaxed now that she had some breathing room.

Taking the opportunity, she picked up her forkful of pasta and brought it to her mouth.

However, the moment Riley heard the voices from the front door, she froze, her fork clanking to the plate as everything crashed around her.

CHAPTER TWENTY-EIGHT

LIAM WALKED to their front door, curious about who could be there. However, the moment he pulled open the door, the hair on the back of his neck stood as he was greeted by none other than Riley and Patrick's parents, Doug and Julie O'Neil.

Fuck. This isn't gonna end well. It never does.

"Liam, it's good to see you, my boy," Doug, Riley's dad chirped as he pushed his way inside, slapping Liam on the shoulder.

"Nice to see you again." Julie, their mom, barged in right after her husband. "We came as soon as we saw the news."

"What news?" Liam asked. A bad feeling hit the pit of his stomach as he stood back crossing his arms over his chest. For some reason, he glanced over his shoulder only to see Riley making her way into the living room. All he wanted to do was pull her behind him and protect her from whatever the fuck these assholes were about to do.

Because that was their game. Always had been, and always would be.

As the O'Neil's forced themselves further into his

home, Patrick, James, and Rhonda made their way into the living room.

Out of the corner of his eye, Liam saw Trash Panda run at full speed toward him, as he always did when someone entered the house. However, the second the little guy was a foot or so from the front door he skid to a stop, his back arching as he turned himself to his side to look bigger.

He then did something Liam never thought he'd see in his life.

Trash Panda hissed.

Not only once, but twice before the kitten ran like hell toward Riley's room.

Smart fucking cat.

"Well, that little guy doesn't seem too friendly," Doug grumbled.

Liam sized him up, his anger inching up his spine. "Must not like you." His eyes moved to Riley to see her worrying her bottom lip.

Fuck...

"Just keep it away from me. I don't want its fur on my skirt." Julie waved the cat off like him being there was an inconvenience.

Funny. Liam thought the same thing about them.

"Julie, Doug, long time no see," James greeted, his tone sharp.

Liam understood one hundred percent. His parents had been around long enough to know this wasn't going to end any other way than Riley and Patrick getting the short end of the stick. Which left him and his parents always picking up the pieces, reminding the two they were loved and cared for just as they were.

No stipulations.

Although Patrick had hardened when it came to his parents, it still got to him whenever they turned up.

And then there was Riley. God damn. Liam's heart clenched knowing what this would do to her. Whenever they'd shown up in the past, it took Riley and Patrick a while to get through whatever asinine shit they tried to play at.

"Mom, Dad, why are you here?" Patrick straightened, but Liam could see his unease which only pissed him off more.

Why couldn't they just leave them all alone? Everyone would be better off.

"We saw the news about our little girl's bakery burning down," Doug answered with a shake of his head. "We knew she'd be devastated." He turned to Riley. "We told you owning a silly little bakery was going to be too much for you."

Riley's jaw hit the floor. "It didn't burn down."

"That's not what Gladys said on social media," Julie stated. "We saw her post. What a shame. You all lost all that money."

"Bet you both feel foolish now giving Riley what you'd saved." Doug laughed it off, pointing to him and Patrick, before he turned back to his daughter. "You should've just joined the family business and never started your bake—"

"Family business?" Riley growled, cutting her father off. "You mean the one where you scam everyone you meet to join your bullshit pyramid scheme? Then, after it falls through like it *always* does, you blame your recruits for not doing a good enough job, hoisting all the blame on them when it was never going to work in the first place. You mean that *family* business? Which one are we talking about? The supplements, the fashion clothes, the energy saving power company, the makeup?"

Julie gasped, her hand flying to her chest. "Riley, that is no way to talk to your father."

"What?" She cocked her brow. "You mean the truth?"

Fuck. Liam had never seen Riley this intense when it came to her parents.

And damn him, his dick twitched. He'd never been so proud. Usually, she'd take whatever they threw at her and deal with it later, but this time...

Fuck yes. Damn did Riley shine right now. Although, being able to read her as he could, Liam saw the slightest crack in Riley's boldness. It wasn't easy to stand up to your parents, especially ones like Doug and Julie. And he *knew* Doug would zero in on it.

Taking the cue to step in and help, Liam moved a hair closer to Riley, hoping to give her some comfort. "Why are you guys really here? If you were both so concerned about the bakery or Riley, you would've shown up on Monday. Not four days later. Or, I don't know, *called* her?"

Doug's eyes narrowed on him with a shrug. "We had to make our way back here."

"You could've called to see if everyone was okay if you really thought the place burned down. But you and I both know, if it had, there would have been more news about it. And you probably wouldn't have come at all."

Doug took a beat before ignoring Liam and moved through the room over to James. "We're here now. That's all that matters. Glad to hear it didn't burn down." He looked past James into the kitchen. "Looks like everyone's having a good time. What's that? Pasta and garlic bread?"

"That's a lot of carbs," Julie instantly stated, looking directly at Riley.

Oh, fuck that. However, before Liam could rip Julie a new one, though, his mom jumped in.

"Really? I think we could use some more." Rhonda squared off with the woman. "We should bake a cake once we're done. Maybe add some red wine to the mix. You know, really bring up those calories."

The pure fire Liam saw in his mother's eyes was nothing short of terrifying. Yeah. He'd seen her pissed before, but *nothing* like this.

"It was an easy meal." Riley's voice broke through. "I've been working a lot and I knew pasta and garlic bread was easy."

No, babe, don't.

The fact Riley was trying to explain away her choice to her shit parents gutted him. There was not a thing wrong with what she made *or* her.

"Always going with the easy route? I see." Her dad's uppity laugh annoyed him. "Typical Riley."

"Excuse me?" Did this man have a death wish? Because Liam would make sure he regretted those words. "Riley's never taken the easy way her whole damn life. And you'd know that if you were around."

"That's not very nice of you," Julie clipped.

"Never said I was nice."

"Liam," James got this attention.

"What?"

Doug waved away everyone as he focused back on his dad. "How have you been, old friend?"

"We were never friends."

Riley tensed next to him, they both knew what was coming next.

"How's the shop? Still working with cars?" Doug asked, the predatory gleam heavy in his eyes.

Riley stood there next to Liam in shock having a hard time believing her parents were actually there after not seeing them for years. Hell, they hadn't even called. But here they were back to their old habits.

To make matters even worse, not only had they used the incident at her bakery as their way in, which Riley still didn't fully comprehend how they found out.

They insulted her *and* made a shitty comment about what she'd made for dinner in front of everyone.

Riley's eyes darted to Liam, her heart leaping into her throat.

How freaking embarrassing.

And now, she knew exactly what was about to come out of her father's mouth.

"If the shop isn't holding up, I've got this great business opportunity—"

"Fuck right off." James shook Doug's hand off his shoulder. "Don't touch me."

"No need to be rude." Julie walked over to her husband. "Doug's just trying to do you a favor and help—"

"The only favor you could do for me is leaving us the fuck alone."

Patrick stepped between James and his dad, his shoulders pushed back as he glared down at his father. "Did you really come here under the pretense of the bakery burning down to try and guilt us into your next business *opportunity*? I knew you guys were shit, but I didn't think you were *this* shitty."

"That is no way to talk to your father, young man," Doug hollered. "I raised you better than that."

"Raised me better than that?" Patrick's eyes hardened, his lips a thin line. "I think you've got history distorted in your narcissistic piece of shit mind. You didn't raise me. *I* pretty much raised myself and Riley." He jutted his chin to

Rhonda and James. "With the help of real parents. One's who gave a shit about us."

Doug took a step back. "What are you trying to say?"

"Exactly that." Riley moved forward. "You were never there for us. If it wasn't for the other people in this room who knows what could've happened to me or Pat, and neither one of you would've given a shit about us."

"That's not true."

"Why are you here?" Rage burned inside of Riley. "Multiple people have told you my bakery didn't burn down, but you've yet to ask what happened. Instead, you slimed your way in took one look at James and tried to sink your claws in."

"Young lady."

"Fuck off and get the fuck out. You lost the right to *young lady* me years ago." Her hands shook at her sides as the years of neglect bubbled over. This was it. This was fucking it. How dare they show up and pretend to care when all they really wanted was new lackeys for whatever the hell they were attempting to do now.

"We should've kept you away from them," her father sneered. "Seems as though the Kelly's have been nothing but a bad influence on you. Should've known since Liam was always getting Pat into trouble when they were kids—"

A powerful growl ripped from Riley's lungs. "Rhonda and James are a million times better than you in every fucking way. They took care of us when we were sick or needed money for school. James helped me with my homework and Rhonda taught me to bake. They gave me everything I ever could have wanted." *Including Liam.* "Because of *you*, Patrick had to work at the shop at fifteen to make sure I had clothes on my back when you were off on your *business trips*, pretending to be hot-shot millionaires when you couldn't even keep our lights on."

Riley took another step closer to them, her eyes hard. "And Liam." She paused, her voice dripping with anger. "Liam protected me like it was his job. He's come to my rescue on every single occasion I've been in over my head. He takes care of me in ways I didn't know were possible. He makes me want to be a better person."

Riley's throat thickened as her entire body shook. "Liam is the best fucking thing that's ever happened to *me* or Patrick."

Everyone froze as spots formed in the corner of Riley's eyes, the years of pain and hurt finally breaking through the surface.

Her head spun as she stood there panting, her angry tears pricking the corners of her eyes. They might be shit parents but how fucking dare they go after the Kelly's and especially Liam.

Over her fucking dead body.

"I think it's time for you to leave," James broke the silence, his chin jutting toward the front door.

"They're my kids. You can't tell me to leave."

"Get the fuck out." Patrick stormed toward the door, yanking it open. "We don't want you here. Seriously, get the fuck out and never come back."

Her dad made a strangled noise but kept his mouth shut.

"Doug, I think it's best if we leave. Clearly, *our children* have decided they're too good for us."

"They are." Liam grabbed Doug's arm and shoved him toward the door. Julie, getting the hint, was right behind him. "If you come near Riley or Patrick again, you'll regret it."

The second they scampered out the door, Riley watched in shock as Liam kicked the door shut and stalked over to her, his eyes full of more passion than she'd ever seen in her life.

What is he—

In one fluid move Liam grabbed the back of Riley's head and pulled her into a searing kiss.

CHAPTER TWENTY-NINE

"What the fuck!"

Liam was dragged backward as Patrick yanked him off Riley. Since he stumbled, he didn't have a chance to dodge the fist that connected directly with his jaw.

"Get the fuck off her." Patrick went in for another hit, but Liam saw it coming and was able to side-step the blow.

When Patrick lunged again, Liam swept his leg from underneath him, causing his best friend to fall to the floor. He hoped the distraction would have given him a chance to stop the fight from continuing, but Patrick grabbed a hold of Liam's arm, dragging him down as well.

In Liam's surprise, Patrick got in another hit, this time to his stomach, making him grunt. "Fuck."

"Stop! Oh my God!" Riley screamed, but it was too late. Patrick was pissed and he was out for blood.

Liam's blood.

Even though he'd been hit, Liam refused to fight back. Instead, he attempted to calculate every move Patrick made in order to avoid whatever his best friend had planned next.

"Boys!"

They both ignored his mother's plea as Patrick rolled

them with another hit to Liam's jaw, forcing him onto his back. Patrick hovered above him, his normally blue eyes were almost black. "That's my fucking sister."

"I know." Liam grabbed his best friend's waist, flipping them again as he pinned his arms to the floor. "I fucking know who she is."

Patrick used his heels to kick off the ground with such force it flung Liam over Patrick's head and onto his back. "She's my fucking sister!"

"That's enough." James yanked Patrick up, giving Liam the chance to jump to his feet. The intervention only lasted a split second, though, as Patrick lunged past his dad. Thankfully, James was quick. He grabbed Patrick's collar, hauling him backward before James shoved him away. "Enough."

"I'll fucking kill him."

"Stop, please, stop!" Riley cried.

Patrick made a grab for Liam, but James kept him back, his arm slamming across his chest to hold him steady. "I said enough."

"Fuck that." Patrick's eyes dripped with rage as he glared Liam down. "What the fuck are you doing?"

Liam knew he shouldn't.

He fucking knew he shouldn't say it, but with the adrenaline coursing through his body, his brain-to-mouth filter took a running leap off a cliff. "Your sister."

Patrick's nostrils flared as he bared his teeth.

Fuck.

It was only a beat before Patrick attempted to lunge at Liam again, only being stopped by James with another shove.

"You're sleeping with my *sister*?" he sneered.

In the heat of the moment, James snapped his eyes to

Rhonda while he kept Patrick back with his arms across his chest. "You owe me a hundred bucks and a blowjob."

The entire room froze. Even Patrick, who was mid-grab for Liam, stopped as all eyes shot to Rhonda.

What did he just say?

Liam threw his hands in the air, snapping toward his mother. "The fuck! Are you kidding me?"

Rhonda grunted out a huff, her arms folding over her chest as she cocked her hip. "Fine. You won fair and square, James," she grumbled, side-eyeing Riley. "I *really* thought since they've been sleeping together she would've told me about it. It's the only reason I agreed to the stupid bet to begin with."

"Not my fault you picked the losing side." James winked.

The color drained from Riley's face making Liam's protective side kick in. He took a step toward her but was stopped when Riley threw her hands in the air.

"This isn't happening. This isn't *fucking* happening." She shook her head with her eyes wider than he'd ever seen. "I must have ingested poison from dinner and now I'm dead."

"You're fine, sweetie," Rhonda cooed. "I'm a little annoyed you didn't talk to me since James won't ever shut up about the bet now. But you're not dead."

"Not dead. Just doin' the horizontal tango with our son," James added in, making Patrick lose his shit all over again.

"You're fucking my sister!" His lunge was warded off by James, who must've known it was coming.

"Yes." Liam jerked back toward Patrick. "I just told you that. Apparently everyone in this fucking room just told you that." Liam glared at his parents knowing he'd deal with them later.

"Get over here and let me beat the shit out of you," Patrick sneered.

For fuck's sake, this was worse than he thought it would be. Then again, he hadn't expected his parents to be there, or for them to have fucking known.

"I already let you get a few hits in." Liam waved his hand to his jaw. "Don't you think it's weird I didn't fight back? I know how screwed-up this is."

"I should fucking gut you." Patrick snapped his head toward James. "And you knew? All of you knew?"

"Suspected," Rhonda corrected.

"Enough that you made a fucking bet?" Liam growled toward his mother. Patrick being pissed he understood. This, though? Fuck, Liam saw red. "We aren't something you can bet on."

"Too bad," his dad remarked. "Been doin' it for years. How do you think we got the new coffeemaker at the shop?"

"You've *got* to be fucking kidding me right now."

Patrick attempted to shake out of James's grasp. "Who gives a flying fuck about the bet? Can we circle back to what's important here, like you sticking your dick inside of my sister? You're supposed to be my best friend. How fucking could you?"

This time, when Liam caught Patrick's eyes, they weren't as full of anger as they were before. No, it was much worse.

Liam's gut churned as the betrayal he saw sliced right through him.

It was never Liam's intention to hurt his best friend. Fuck, he'd rather die than cause Patrick any sort of pain.

But it was Riley. The love of his life. The woman he knew was made for him. She superseded everything and everyone.

She always would.

How had everything gotten so messy and so fucking fast? Fuck, they still needed to deal with the O'Neil's showing up... and now they were adding in him sleeping with Riley to the mix.

Fucking-a.

Liam's eyes jumped to Riley, her face a crumpled mess as she held her chest. He shouldn't have kissed her like he did.

He *should've* waited.

And if he were a better man, he might have.

Liam swallowed, the gravity of his actions hitting him with force. But he knew without a shadow of a doubt, if he could do it over, he wouldn't change a thing.

The way Riley came to his defense. The things she'd said. He wouldn't have been able to stop himself even if he tried.

He loved Riley.

He loved every single thing about her and there was no way he could hide what she meant to him a second more.

Liam ripped his gaze from the woman he loved and turned back to his best friend. "Pat..."

"Don't Pat me. That's my *sister*. You were supposed to protect her when I couldn't. You're the only one I've ever trusted with her. You were—"

"I do," Liam answered. "I would give my life for Riley. I'd never let anything happen to her."

"Except sticking your dick inside her. How is that protecting her?"

"Patrick, don't."

"*Don't?*" he hissed, his brows shooting off his forehead. "You don't get to tell me what I can and can't do. You lost all right the second you screwed my sister. And for what? A piece of ass."

"*A piece of ass?*" Liam's jaw clenched as anger erupted

throughout his entire body. "Don't ever call Riley a piece of ass like that's all she'd ever be to me. I haven't hit you yet, but I fucking will. I know you're pissed at me, but don't you fucking dare."

Patrick grimaced, his head snapping to his sister with the apology written all over his face. "I'm sorry, Rye. I didn't mean it. You know I'd never purposely hurt you. *Fuck!*" The strangled noise falling from Patrick's pained voice was another slice to Liam's gut. "You aren't just a piece of ass. For fuck's sake, you're my sister. You're way better than he deserves. *He* should've never taken advantage of you. This is on him. He's the—"

"*Stop!*" Riley's arms swept in front of her as she commanded the attention of the room. "This is fucking unreal. First, everyone needs to stop acting like I'm not in the damn room. I'm right fucking here. I can speak for myself." She glared at her brother. "Liam didn't take advantage of me, you asshole. *You* know us both better than that. He's your best friend, he would never betray you." She cocked her brow. "I *deserve* better than him? How? Please tell me how *Liam,* your best friend isn't up to your standards when you just said he was the only one you ever trusted? Talk about deserving? *Pfft.* You and I both know Liam is the best damn guy out there. If anyone isn't deserving in all this, it's *me* for *him.* He could do a lot fucking better and *has.* So fuck right off with your deserving crap."

Patrick's mouth fell open with his eyes rounding like he'd been stabbed.

"And then there's me. *Me.* Your fucking sister. Do you *really* think I'm so weak that the second someone showed me attention I'd jump all over it? That's insulting. I get that you're upset right now. Newsflash, so the hell am I. Out of everyone in this damn room, you know more than anyone I'd *never* let someone con me into something I didn't want.

I've learned enough from our shitty parents to let someone take advantage of me for *their* gain. Screw you for thinking that."

"Riley, I'm sorry. I didn't mean—"

"No," she cut her brother off. "Absolutely fuckin' not. How dare you?"

"Babe, you're shaking." Liam moved toward Riley, dread hitting him like a punch to his gut. As his panicked eyes searched her face, he reached for her but Riley took a step back.

"No," her voice was rough and commanding, stopping him in his tracks.

Liam's heart seized on the spot, his blood pressure skyrocketing as he watched the woman he was in love with so easily dismiss him. "What do you mean, no?"

"Exactly that, Liam." She gritted her teeth. "Do *not* fucking touch me."

Riley's sharp words were like a knife straight through Liam's soul as he saw everything they had fall down around him.

The pain in Riley's eyes as she stared back at him. The hurt, the embarrassment, the *regret*. He couldn't breathe.

No.

There was no way.

"Babe?" Liam's voice broke as he reached for her. However, the moment Riley took another step back, Liam's entire world collapsed.

"We're done." Riley flicked her hand between the two of them. "All of this is *done*. It was gonna end eventually anyway. We both knew it."

"No." Liam shook his head as the pain ricocheted through his body as if he'd been shot. Riley didn't understand. Liam hadn't had enough time to convince her this was more than some fucked-up mentor-teaching situation.

"Riley..." Liam froze when he saw a single tear fall down Riley's cheek, causing his stomach to bottom out.

He needed to make her understand.

He needed to—

Liam searched Riley's face as he ripped his heart open to bare his soul. "We can't stop this, Riley." He paused, choking on his words. "We can't stop this because I'm in love with you."

CHAPTER THIRTY

LIAM'S WORDS took the air right out of Riley's lungs like she'd been punched in the gut.

There was no way she'd heard him correctly.

However, as everyone around her stood impossibly still, she couldn't help twitching a little over their combined scrutiny of what she'd do next, making it clear he'd said it.

Maybe if I close my eyes really hard, it'll all disappear? 'Cause, how in the hell am I supposed to accept what he just said? Wait, go back. Accept? How about believe him? There is no way in hell Liam's in love with me. That's... Riley knitted her brows together, her brain racing a million miles an hour. *There is no freaking way.*

"I'm in love with you, Riley," Liam repeated, hope shining in his eyes as he searched her face. "I have been for years."

Riley's breath froze in her throat as every single muscle in her body tensed like she'd been hit.

That's impossible. No. There's no way. This had to be some weird screwed-up way to fix the catastrophe that's happening. A way to save face. Yeah, that has to be it, because there is no way in fucking hell Liam Kelly is in love with me.

"That's not... You're not." Riley's chest twisted as her heart hammered against her ribs. "You're not in love with me, Liam." He took a purposeful step, positioning himself directly in front of her, causing her throat to instantly dry.

"Yeah, you aren't in love with her," Patrick growled from the back of his throat. Thankfully, being held back by James.

With a growl of his own, Liam snapped his head toward her brother. "You don't get to tell me how I feel, fuckface. That's not how love works. You don't get to choose who you fall in love with." On his last word, he swiveled his head back to Riley. Reaching out his arm, he cupped the right side of her neck with his hand.

No matter how hard she tried to stop, Riley leaned into him. Even if she didn't believe him, Liam's touch never failed to soothe her when she was on the brink of a full-blown mental breakdown.

"I *am* in love with you, Riley. I've been in love with you for as long as I can remember."

She tensed, frustration making tears prick behind her eyes. "No, you're lying." Riley's heart lodged in her throat while she jerked away from him, instantly missing the loss of his warmth against her skin.

"He's not," James interjected. "My idiot son has been in love with you since you were kids. We saw it pretty early on. It's why I'd hit him upside the head all the fucking time when he *tried* to distance himself from you." He darted his eyes to Liam. "*Idiot.* Look how well that turned out for ya? A whole fuckin' year of everyone being miserable ' cause of you, you fuckin' twat."

"*James...*" Rhonda snipped.

"What? I've been waiting to say that to him for years. Fuckin' *years*, Rhonda." James pushed out a breath like he'd been holding it in for most of his life. "Feels good to finally say it."

"Not the time or place, dear. We can get back to that later."

"No," Riley's voice bounced off the walls, her breath coming in fast pants as she hyperventilated.

There was no way any of this was possible. *She* was the one who had a crush on Liam growing up. *Not* him.

He tolerated her. Hell, he stopped talking to her because... *wait, if James said... No!*

There was no love.

Liam protected her. He came to her rescue because he felt obligated. It wasn't out of love.

Liam was her brother's best friend, the one Riley somehow fell for even though she *knew* nothing would ever come from it.

And by happenstance when it did, and they started their lessons, Riley fully understood it was only physical. Liam agreeing to mentor her about sex, was only that... *sex.*

"It's true," Liam's soft voice broke through Riley's thoughts causing her unbelievably-round eyes to dart to him.

"You don't..." She froze, searching his face for answers, her breath stalling.

"I do," he stated matter of fact. "I have. I *always* have."

"But-but," Riley sputtered. "You go out to the bars with Patrick. You acted like I annoyed you. You stopped talking to me the moment you realized I had a crush on you when we were younger. It had nothing to do with whatever crap James just said. It had everything to do with you finding out your best friend's plus-sized, annoying little sister had feelings for you."

"Is that what you thought?" Liam's mouth fell open, his

brows shooting off his forehead. "You thought I stopped hanging around you 'cause I found out you had a crush on me?" Liam jerked his thumb over his shoulder to his dad. "He's not lying. I thought it was screwed-up to have feelings for my best friend's little sister, so I tried to stay away from you. Tried to keep you at a distance and force my attraction to go away." He huffed out a strained laugh. "It didn't fucking work. If anything, it made me want you more. It nearly killed me keeping you at a distance. And then when you got hurt? Fuck, I hated myself for it, still do. But, I knew then I couldn't stay away. I forced myself to lock away what I felt, 'cause I knew having you around was better than not having you at all."

Riley's eyes painfully rounded as each word hit her like a brick. "Liam, I—"

"Wait." Liam stopped her, holding his hand up, the corner of his mouth quirking. "You had a crush on me?" He straightened his shoulders like the mere idea of her pining after him had given him the world in that instant.

"Babe, are you telling me I've always starred in your fantasies?" His smirk turned into a wide, toothy grin.

"For fuck's sake. That's my sister," Patrick groaned. "Plus, she's right. If you were in love with her for all these years, why'd you go to the bar with me?"

"I never went home with anyone. I only went to shut you up," Liam answered not taking his eyes off Riley. "As soon as you'd leave. I'd wait a few minutes and leave, too. I'd always come home to Riley."

"What about the others?"

"What others?" Liam finally tore his eyes from her and looked at Patrick. "I might've fucked around when we were younger, when I fought my feelings for Riley. But there was no use. She always won out every single time. There hasn't *been* anyone else in years. I couldn't pretend anyone would mean more to me than Riley already did."

Patrick stared at him, his mouth half open like he was calculating something in his mind and Riley couldn't blame him, she was doing the same.

Patrick continuously flicked his eyes between her and Liam, finally stopping on his best friend after a minute. "You're in love with my sister?"

"Yes," Liam answered without missing a beat. "I love her more than anything in this world."

Riley's gut swirled with a gamut of feelings from nerves and disbelief, all the way to what could possibly be hope.

Swallowing roughly, her mind desperately tried to comprehend what was happening.

"Alright, now that we're doing this, let's get this out of the way. My arm's gettin' sore." James grunted, glaring at her brother. "If I let you go, are you gonna hit him again?"

Patrick gritted his teeth. "I won't."

However as James lowered his arm, Patrick lunged, hitting Liam in the jaw again.

The second James moved to grab her brother, Patrick took a step back, holding his hands up. "I'm done." He narrowed his eyes on Liam. "For now."

"Fuck, man." Liam rubbed his jaw. Can you stop hitting the same spot?"

"You're lucky I didn't castrate you."

Liam shrugged like he agreed. "Fine, but can you go for somewhere else next time?"

"James, why'd you let him go?" Rhonda scoffed.

"'Cause I knew Pat only had one more hit in him and he'd be good. We needed to get it over with. There is not a damn thing any of us can do. Those two have been in love with each other for years and like I said, my arm was hurtin'."

A strangled sound came from deep within Riley. "I'm not—"

Rhonda spun toward her. "Don't even try to deny anything, missy. You've been in love with Liam just as long as our idiot son has been in love with you. Did you not hear yourself? The way you defended him?" She cocked her hand on her hip. "Besides, you should see the way you look at him when you think no one is paying attention."

Heat flooded Riley's cheeks while a heaviness formed in the pit of her stomach.

Was I that obvious? No. I was always so careful after he'd stopped talking to me. I never let my guard down. I... Riley argued with herself before looking back to Liam. *Wait. He loves me?*

Riley's stomach somersaulted.

"Not sure when our son got his head out of his ass and took the chance, but there ain't no point in fighting any of this," James added with another grunt. "There's still a few pieces of garlic bread that have my name on 'em. So, can we get a move on?"

"I didn't," Liam answered honestly. "Riley was the one that came to me." He flicked his eyes to her, and the heat she saw in them made her stomach flip again. "Well, kinda."

Oh no!

Chills ran up Riley's spine as she telepathically begged Liam not to tell everyone she'd been a virgin. All this had already been embarrassing enough. They really didn't need to add her V-card into the mix.

Rhonda squealed, her brow quirking as a massive smile overtook her face. "Oh, really?" She spun to her husband. "Guess you owe *me* two hundred bucks and a new kitchen table."

James's annoyance filled the room. "Whatever. As long as I get a BJ on the kitchen table."

"Oh, for fuck's sake." Liam dry-heaved. "We are never

coming over again and we sure as fuck aren't eating at the table."

"We clean it," Rhonda dryly remarked.

Riley didn't know whether to laugh, cry, scream, or run away. Holy mother-of-pearl, this was insane. Every absolute second of this was insane.

"This part of the conversation is over." Liam dry-heaved again. "I could've gone my whole life without knowing that."

"And I could have gone mine without knowing you're screwing my sister."

"Fair point," Liam grumbled. "But can we please go back to the important part?" Liam caught Riley's eyes, and as he did it felt like he was staring directly into her soul causing her stomach to flutter.

She was still having a hard time wrapping her mind around everything, but with the way Liam looked at her... It was like everyone else in the room disappeared leaving only them.

Like he only could see her and no one else.

Liam took Riley's tear-stricken cheeks into his hands gently brushing her tears away with the pads of his thumbs. While he did, their eyes locked making Riley's heart pound in her ears.

"I am in love with you, babe. I've been in love with you for years. And nothing will ever change that. I know we started this on your terms, but you need to understand, I swore to myself I'd never let it end. I had every intention on dragging this out until I made you fall in love with me."

Riley's breath sputtered, her eyes filling with more tears as an unfamiliar warmth seeped around her.

"If I allow myself to believe my parents and what you said, it kinda sounds like you might already love me."

Her throat thickened.

"My mom doesn't say shit, just to say it."

"Damn right."

They both ignored Rhonda while Liam continued, "Maybe you don't realize it right now, but I'm pretty sure you're in love with me too." He pushed a strand of hair behind her ear. "Plus, you're wrong. I'd never be good enough to deserve you. You, Riley O'Neil, make the world a better place. You take all the shit thrown at you and flip it into pure light and joy. You've persevered through so much. You make *me* want to be a better person. A better person *for* you."

Another tear slid down Riley's cheek as the walls around her heart crumbled to the ground. "Liam..."

"I love you. I have loved you for as long as I can remember and I will continue to love you. Even if you don't realize it yet, I will do everything in my power to convince you that you already love me too. And, if by chance I'm wrong and you don't love me, I'll stop at nothing until you love me even half as much as I love you."

Riley closed her eyes, her heart tightening as understanding finally filled her.

Love...

Keeping her eyes shut, Riley started with a shaky breath. "I've tried so hard to keep my feelings locked away for years. I thought you'd never feel the same way about me. So I lied to myself and said my crush was only a crush when it was so much more. It's always been so much more. I'd fight myself every step of the way, because I knew you'd never love me like I'd assumed I'd already loved you."

She opened her eyes, tears falling freely. "I'll be honest and tell you I didn't know what I felt was love. There is no denying it, though. Every experiment I came up with, I did in hopes *you'd* enjoy it. Every shared glance, I dreamed there was more. Every time you left to go to the bar, my heart would ache. I can see now those all pointed to one thing. I thought love wasn't supposed to be for me, Liam," her voice cracked. "My parents never showed me what love was."

"You're wrong." Liam cupped Riley's cheeks in his hands as he brought his lips to hers, brushing gently over them. "You're supposed to be loved, Riley. You're supposed to be loved by me."

The dam holding the walls around Riley's heart broke as Liam kissed her. She didn't have to question what love was, because Liam showed her.

And even though everything inside her screamed she wasn't worthy enough, she knew with Liam by her side, teaching her what love was she could take on the world. Riley pushed onto her tiptoes, melding her lips to Liam as their kiss lit up the room. Everything she'd ever wanted was poured into their embrace.

And for the first time in Riley's life, she felt whole.

She felt accepted for exactly who she was.

She felt loved.

Not that her brother and the Kelly's didn't shower her with acceptance and love, but this was different. This was more.

This was Riley's heart finding its other half.

"Isn't this lovely?" Rhonda's voice echoed through the room causing them to pull apart.

"I *am* gonna get grandbabies after all." She danced on the balls of her feet, throwing her hands in the air like she'd won the jackpot.

"*Mom!*" Liam groaned, rolling his eyes. "Can you not? One step at a time. You have a grand-cat. That's gotta be good enough for now."

Riley laughed, her eyes meeting Liam's. "Let her have this. Maybe she'll stop talking about it."

Liam's half-smile raced across his face. "I doubt it. Come to think of it, it'll probably make her worse."

Riley's whole face beamed just like his. "You're right."

"Always am, babe."

"Pfft." She shook her head with a flick of her eyes to the ceiling. She was still having a hard time accepting everything. But she knew no matter what happened or whatever they got into, Liam would be there for her.

Just like he always had been. And she'd finally be able to express herself in the ways she'd only ever dreamed of.

Although she wasn't opposed to riling him up. "You keep telling yourself that, Lee."

Liam cocked his brow. The grin that spread across his face could easily light the night. He leaned forward, his lips brushing against her ear. "I think I've proven to you multiple times now how right I can be, babe. Or, would you like me to add that to our next lesson plan?"

Riley's mouth dropped, a thrill rolling through her before she snapped her eyes to glare at him.

Liam's deep chuckle bounced around the room as he kissed the tip of her nose. "Damn, you're always gonna keep me entertained, aren't you?"

She wrinkled her nose, failing to hide her smile. "What if I said maybe?"

He grabbed her waist, wrapping his arms around her, making Riley squeal in surprise. "Then I'd say I love you."

Riley took a second to let the words wash over her as they warmed her from the inside out. "I guess I love you too. I probably always have."

"You guess?" He cocked his brow.

"Ehhh. If I say I do, it's gonna go to your big as head."

Liam kissed her again before his dad clapped his hands together.

"Great, now that we've had this little heart-to-heart bullshit that was way too fuckin' overdue, and since no one ended up in the hospital, can we please get back to dinner before Pat eats the last piece of garlic bread?"

Riley looked over Liam's shoulder to see Patrick leaning against the doorframe that led to their kitchen.

Oh, no. The no hospital part might've been said too soon...

"Too late, Pops." Patrick held up his prize, sending a wink directly at James.

CHAPTER THIRTY-ONE

ONE WEEK LATER

"Babe," Liam whispered against Riley's ear as he brought her lobe into his mouth, nibbling gently. "You know I'll always take care of you. All you ever have to do is ask." Liam released her ear, flinging his right leg over Riley's naked waist so he'd be above her.

"I'm asking." Riley's lust-filled eyes, half-hooded with pure desire, pleaded with him.

"Anything you want, babe." Liam's growl tore from the back of his throat. He placed his hand on her lush lower stomach. After a possessive squeeze, he trailed his hand up her body, caressing between her breasts, before he reached the base of her neck. "Always." He grabbed her throat, tightening his fingers around her flesh as he stared deep into her eyes, his lips hovering above hers. "Good girl."

Liam swallowed Riley's gasp with his lips, their kiss so deep he doubted he'd ever recover from it. He kept his hand wrapped around her neck, tightening his hold as their tongues battled for control.

As she squirmed under his touch, Liam pulled back with a deep groan, his hand keeping Riley in place so she couldn't chase after him like she usually did. "Mine." He hovered over her, drinking Riley in like she was his one and only glass of water, and he was dying of thirst.

The pressure of Liam's hand kept Riley in place, but not enough to harm her, only enough to heighten the sensation.

He'd cut off his own arm before he'd hurt her.

Mine.

Liam's arousal pushed against Riley's stomach, his eyes dripping with heat as he stared down at the love of his life. "Next lesson?" He released her throat, his fingertips trailing down her soft skin, stopping between her breasts.

Riley eagerly nodded, lust flaring in the depths of her eyes. "I'm an excellent student."

"That you are, babe."

"It's 'cause I have a phenomenal teacher."

Liam pushed his face into the crook of her neck with a growl. "That you do."

Riley shivered under his lips as he bit the sensitive skin, marking her. He'd never get over the way Riley reacted to him.

There was no other person on the planet who was made for him like Riley was.

She was his equal in every way possible.

Liam pulled away, grabbing Riley's hips. "Hands and knees," he commanded, not waiting for her response. Instead, he jumped off her waist, flipping her around so her head pointed at the headboard.

"Down," he demanded, pushing her upper back into the mattress making Riley fall to her chest, her ass high in the air.

"Good."

"Liam," Riley whimpered, shaking her hips slightly. Fuck, she had no idea what that did to him. Her openness, her raw need, her trust in him to give her everything she needed and more.

"I'm a little disappointed we haven't tried this position yet," he stated, his right hand caressing from the middle of her back where he'd pushed her down, following the curves of her body until he reached her ass. "So fucking beautiful."

The tips of his fingers danced across her skin, causing goosebumps to appear.

Riley tossed her head back, her hair falling over her shoulders. "Fuck me, Liam. Now."

"Shhh, who's in charge here?"

Riley snapped her head over her shoulder to glare at him. And fuck him, the sight nearly made him come on the spot.

"In me now or I'll do it myself."

Liam cocked his brow. "That a challenge, babe?"

"It's a promise."

Liam's hand smacked the rounded globe of her ass before squeezing. "Always so eager, babe. Didn't I teach you already? Patience is key."

Riley pushed her ass. "I think that lesson was a stupid one. Your real game here is you like torturing me."

"Making up for lost time." He shrugged before he bit her ass cheek, causing Riley to moan and push back with force, her body begging for more. "I knew you'd like it, Rye. You just need to trust me." He kissed the spot he'd bitten.

"I always trust you."

Her words touched every inch of him, like waves crashing in the ocean. "Same." He scooted himself between her spread legs, lowering his head, positioning himself at her pussy.

"Liam, what are you—"

He took a long lick of her core, letting his tongue swirl around her opening. "I don't know how it's possible for you to taste better and better each time, but you do," his voice vibrated against her center. "Like pure fucking sugar."

"Well, I *am* a baker. It's probably in my blood."

With a heavy groan, Liam's eyes rolled into the back of his head. "*Mine*. My sweet fuckin' treat."

"Yours."

Possessive need rushed down his spine as he took another lick, savoring Riley's unique taste.

Once he got his fill, he quickly sat up, his hard dick already at Riley's entrance like it knew where its home was. "And it's always going to be that way."

He pushed in with one swift move, bottoming out instantly making Riley toss her head back in pleasure. Liam's hand moved to the base of her head, tangling his fingers into her hair before clenching, pulling her head back.

"My God, yes," Riley cried, pushing back as she met him thrust for thrust.

"Not God, babe, but your man."

As he thrust into her, something snapped within him.

This was the woman he loved. He needed more than just fucking, he needed her.

He needed Riley.

Liam jerked out, grabbing hold of her waist, and flipped Riley onto her back as he covered her body with his.

"Liam?" she questioned, but he shook his head, his emotions threatening to break through his skin.

"I've got you, babe." He shoved her legs apart, his dick easily entering her core. He rested on top of her, their bodies gliding together.

Liam's mouth sought out her skin, kissing every inch he came in contact with. Right now he needed Riley more than his next breath. Nuzzling his face into her neck, Liam pushed inside her warm heat, his movements more controlled when Riley wrapped her legs around him.

"I love you," he groaned into her neck.

"Love you too." She moved her head to the side giving him more room. "So freaking much. It's always been you."

Liam's heart pounded in his ears as he grabbed Riley's chin bringing her lips to his.

"So close, so close," she cried into his mouth.

Riley didn't have to say anything though, because he knew. Liam knew exactly what she needed as her pussy clenched around his dick. "Give it to me, Riley." Her body squirmed but wouldn't tip over the edge.

Knowing what she needed, Liam sat up.

Riley liked dirty and possessive. She liked unhinged and raw.

Fuck, so did Liam.

And the mere knowing he'd be the only one to ever see Riley like this made him fucking wild for her. Keeping them connected as he leaned back, causing Riley's legs to hang over his thighs as he pistoned into her, his movements hitting her with more force as his thumb found her clit to feverishly rub against it. "Mine, always mine."

"Always."

Liam's eyes focused on their connection, the sight making him lose control. He shot his face to Riley, ensuring he had her full attention.

Riley shuddered, her eyes rolling into the back of her head. "Why is this so hot? It shouldn't be so freaking hot." Her legs shook, her pussy clenching around him with force.

"Because it's us," Liam growled low, swirling his thumb around her clit as he pounded his hips into her.

"I'm so..." She gasped for air. "*Please.*"

Liam's pace quickened, his fingers flicking against her nub.

Instantly, Riley's back arched, her body losing control as she thrashed from side to side. It was like a chain reaction as Riley came apart.

"That's it, babe. Come for me. Come for your man."

She did.

Riley lost complete control of her body as she exploded around him, taking Liam with her.

The pleasure erupted from the bottom of his spine as he emptied every last drop of himself inside the woman he loved.

Once the room came back into focus, they both battled for air, still connected as they came down from their high.

As gentle as possible, Liam pulled himself from Riley's core, his cum instantly dripping out of her, causing Liam's body to jerk with another aftershock. "Fuck." His heated eyes hit Riley's as she nodded her head in agreement.

"Whoa, Liam, damn. I don't think I'd ever—"

"Oh, my fucking God! My eyes!"

Liam and Riley jumped apart in an instant, with Liam nearly being tossed off the bed as Riley yanked the comforter from under him to cover herself.

"Why the fuck was the door open? Where's the bleach? I need the fucking bleach!" Patrick screamed, his voice echoing through the house.

Even though Riley's face paled, her eyes bulged out of their sockets, Liam burst into a deep laugh.

"You're supposed to be at the shop!" Riley screamed at the top of her lungs before shooting a glare at him. "Stop laughing. This isn't funny! Pat just saw us..." She waved her hand between them, her cheeks flushing an even deeper red than Liam thought possible, causing him to smirk.

"It's kinda funny."

"I was at the shop!" Patrick hollered back. "I'll never unsee it. I'm scarred for life. Where the fuck is the bleach?"

Liam laughed harder as the cabinet doors opened and slammed shut.

"Why in the hell was the door open?"

"You weren't supposed to be home and we got a little carried away," Liam replied, his voice full of humor. "We forgot to close it. My bad."

"Your bad?" Patrick bellowed. "Are you serious right now? I accept you two are together, but for fuck's sake. I *never* need to see my *sister* and my best friend like that." Another door slammed. "Where the fucking Christ is the bleach?"

"Sorry, Pat," Riley's embarrassed voice attempted to shout through Liam's laugh.

"All I wanted to do once I got home was get Snickerdoodle and watch that new movie that came out. But no. Now, I need to gouge out my eyes with a fuckin' rusty spoon."

"We've upgraded from bleach to a spoon? Glad we're changing it up." Liam laughed harder.

"I can't find the damn bleach. And can you please stop talking to me without clothes on and *right* after you fuck my sister? Do you have no dignity? I'm your best friend!"

"Not my problem you came in here," Liam hollered back. "You should've known better. It's not rocket science. What the hell did you think we were doing if we weren't in the living room?"

"I wasn't thinking. That's the problem. This is still new for me. Damn. I just wanted the cat."

"And *we* weren't thinking about closing the door when we were otherwise preoccupied." Liam leaned over the bed and grabbed the kitten who'd been playing with his discarded pants before pushing him gently toward the door.

The kitten must have realized Patrick was home since he took off running. "Trash Panda's on his way out. Open a can of tuna and he'll get there faster."

"I'm not opening shit unless it's a bottle of bleach."

Liam laughed harder, his hand going to his stomach.

"You'd willingly deny Trash Panda tuna? And here I thought you loved him."

"Fuck you." The telltale noise of a can opening hit Liam's ears causing him to send a lopsided grin Riley's way.

"I'm never gonna look Pat in the eyes again." Riley covered her face with the comforter as she slid further under the covers.

With another laugh, Liam grabbed the blanket, ripped it off her head and dropped a kiss on the tip of her nose. "Sure, you will. Own your power, my sex goddess. He's just jealous. Walk out of here with your head held high that you can bring a man to their knees and have them damn near blackout." Liam's eyes narrowed on her, his lips thinning. "But only with me."

"Always, only with you."

"I can still hear you, for fuck's sake. That's it. I'm calling Pops."

"Why?"

"I don't know. He's always threatening to off me. Maybe he'll actually do it this time. And for the love of all fucking things, stop talking to me until you're dressed."

"Who said we're getting dressed? I'm not done." Liam jumped off the bed and made a dramatic show of slamming the door shut.

"Dude, that's still my sister!"

"I shut the door. What more do you want? You already got Trash Panda."

"For someone to run me the fuck over. We're going on a field trip to the shop, Snicks." The front door slammed, making Liam burst into a deeper belly laugh.

Riley scrambled off the bed. "He better not take my baby anywhere."

Liam grabbed her around the waist, hoisting her back

onto the bed with a bounce. "The cat will be fine. He'd never let anything happen to him."

"I don't care. The shop is no place for a kitten."

Liam crawled up the bed, his arms boxing Riley in as he moved over her. "It'll be fine." He lowered his head, taking her lips.

"I can't believe that just happened." Riley shook her head. "I was always nervous he'd catch us."

"It was bound to happen eventually. He never pays attention to anything. Maybe now he'll think twice before walking in here."

"True." Riley's nose wrinkled, but Liam saw a hidden grin on her face.

"What's that look for?" he asked.

"Oh, nothing. Just a little payback for him calling me a piece of ass."

Liam's mouth broke into a brilliant smile. "Why, my innocent little Riley? Look at you." Pride filled him as he puffed his chest.

"Liam." She side-eyed him, holding back her smirk. "Messing with Pat isn't something to be proud of."

"You're wrong." He gazed down at Riley. "Anything you do is something to be proud of, regardless of what it is." Liam pulled her close. "*You*, my love, are always something to be proud of. And us being together..." His smile brightened even further. "*We* are something to be damn proud of. It was always gonna happen between us, even if we didn't see it. The cards were already laid out. It was just a matter of time."

NERVES ATE at Riley's stomach as she worried her bottom lip. Today was the second anniversary of opening Pastries & Paws.

Two years of owning her bakery, and then the following weekend would be her birthday. Holy moly, so much had happened in the past two years. And honestly, if you'd told Riley she'd be standing in her bakery surrounded by people and decorations, *and* in a relationship with Liam, she would have laughed so hard she'd probably would've ended up in the hospital after breaking a rib.

What a whirlwind of a time.

Riley blew out an unsteady breath as she looked around the front of the bakery. Nearly every inch of the place was decorated.

She originally wasn't going to do anything special for the occasion. It wasn't really *that* big of a deal.

Rhonda, on the other hand, was having none of that. *She* was the reason the place looked like it did. And much to Riley's protest, there wasn't a thing she could do about it.

Riley learned a long time ago it was better to agree with

Rhonda than not to. The woman was downright scary when she needed to be.

Riley's eyes scanned the room, still a little shocked at how full it was. Holy fudge sticks, there were so many people there to help her celebrate. Which honestly blew Riley's mind. When she'd opened the place, it'd only been her, Patrick, Liam, and the Kelly's.

That was it.

Right now, though, the place was full of people. Some she knew and some she didn't. Speaking of which, Patrick was in the corner chatting up one of her regular clients. She'd have to ask him about it later, but right now Riley didn't quite care.

So she'd let him have his fun.

Riley and Liam *had* been torturing him a bit recently anyway. Although, after his first initial walk-in on them, he'd been a good sport, and *always* announced when he got home. Even if he walked in with Liam, he'd scream at the top of his lungs he was home and to put clothes on.

Snickerdoodle thought it was some weird game and apparently his new name... Riley rolled her eyes, before focusing back on the front of Pastries & Paws.

Holly and her husband, Doctor Richman, were nuzzled together right outside the bakery's front door that'd been propped open. Their dogs, Waffles and Ripley, at their feet.

There were even the firefighters who'd shown up the night Riley and Liam almost burned the bakery down, along with their significant others.

Riley nearly lost her mind the moment she found out Hank's wife was none other than Quinn Sparks, the erotic romance author she loved to read. The curvy woman's real name being Olive Parker.

Riley was *always* first in line to buy her next book. The woman was a goddess when it came to her writing, and now she fully understood why the firefighter series had gotten so much love. With a husband like Hank as her inspiration, no wonder Olive wrote as well as she did.

Riley laughed to herself as she continued to scan around the room, stopping on Rhonda and James Kelly, who were in front of the display case, handing out samples of Riley's newest creations.

Her *Just a Batter of Time* cake bites.

Riley's cheeks flushed, as she watched Lucas, one of the firefighters grab one and toss it into his mouth.

He moaned so loudly the entire room stopped what they were doing to stare at him, making Riley's cheeks heat further.

"Damn, this is good."

"Riley only makes the best." Rhonda beamed, shooting her a warm, loving smile.

"No complaints here."

Pride washed through Riley as she watched him grab another one, before flinging it into his mouth.

She'd worked damn hard on perfecting them.

They might not be exactly what she was going for when it came to recreating the feeling she experienced when she was with Liam, but they were damn close.

Or as close as food could get.

She'd crafted the perfect bite-sized treat. A mix of salty and sweet, just like Liam, and when you bit into them a surprise cherry filling exploded over your taste buds.

Of course, no one knew the inspiration behind them. That was a secret she would take to the grave. Especially the cherry filling part.

Okay, Liam knew. He was the only exception, though.

The night she'd brought them home for him and Patrick to try, he took one bite and *knew*. His eyes filled with heat as he scarfed down a few more before dragging her to their shared bedroom.

Patrick, being himself, had been so engrossed in eating them, Riley still didn't know if he realized they'd left.

That had kind of been her plan, though, since she brought home five batches knowing they would keep him distracted.

It also helped she'd brought home new cat treats as well.

What could she say? Riley knew exactly what she was doing.

Not even bothering to hide her smile when Lucas scarfed another one down, the woman he was with... Riley believed her name was Miranda, shoved him away from the plate, telling him he needed to leave some for others.

Everything really was perfect. More perfect than Riley could've ever hoped for. The entire room had an over-flowing feeling of love and acceptance in it, warming her soul.

Her eyes focused on James and Rhonda again, who were deep in laughter as they cuddled together. Riley really took the moment to appreciate who they were. She no longer needed to wish she had parents like them, because they *were* her parents, at least metaphorically. She was sleeping with their son, so there was that...

Riley huffed out an amused laugh.

Throwing that tidbit to the side, they'd pretty much raised her and Patrick like they were their own. They'd protected them and cared for them when no one else would.

Riley owed so much to both of them.

Hell, they gave her Liam.

Liam Kelly, the love of her life.

Riley's stomach fluttered as she looked at him.

This was family.

This was love.

This was what she'd been waiting for all her life.

A fresh flood of pride hit her as she glanced around her bakery again, taking in all that she'd accomplished. This was *her* bakery, *her* family, and standing right next to her was the absolute love of her life.

"I don't know what you're thinking about, babe, but you're glowing." Liam pulled her to his side, kissing the top of her head.

Riley gazed up at him, her smile spreading across her entire face. There was just something about Liam that soothed something inside of her like no one else ever could.

"It's nothing," she lied.

Liam cocked his brow. "Riley, are you asking for another lesson? Something along the lines of always telling the truth?"

Her eyes rounded for a split second before she laughed and sent him a wink. "Not right now, but maybe later." She turned her face back to the seating area. "I can't believe it's been two years since we opened the bakery."

"*You* opened the bakery, babe. We did nothing."

"That's not true. I wouldn't be here if it weren't for all of you." Her hand swiped across the room toward everyone. "This is family. Family works together and because of that, we were able to accomplish my dreams."

Liam smiled softly, his face lighting. "I love you, babe."

"Love you too, Lee."

"I'm glad you said that." Liam cleared his throat before stepping directly in front of Riley.

"What are you doing?"

He lowered himself to one knee as he pulled out a velvet box from his pocket, causing Riley to gasp as her hand flew to her mouth.

"Babe, Riley," he corrected. "Riley O'Neil. The love of my life. My partner, the other half of my soul." Liam took her hand. "I never dreamed we'd be here. At least in real life. When we first moved in together, I'd pretend we were married. Yes, I know that sounds like I'm crazy. But it's true. I'd pretend to be coming home from the shop to my wife. I know it was wrong, but I looked forward to the nights you'd be so damn exhausted you'd fall asleep on the couch next to me, or if I was lucky, on my shoulder. I let myself fall into that fantasy of you being mine. And now it's real. You are the most beautiful woman I've ever laid eyes on. You've had ahold of my heart for years. And if you say yes, you'll have my heart for the rest of our lives. Riley, will you do me the honor of allowing me to give you my heart?"

"Liam..." Tears spilled down Riley's cheeks.

"Riley O'Neil, will you marry me?"

Instantly, she jumped into his arms knocking him onto the floor. "Yes, yes. Yes, I will marry you!"

Cheers erupted around them with hoots and hollers as Riley kissed Liam with all the love she had inside her.

"Told you the party would be the perfect place to do it." Rhonda clapped her hands. "Now, about those grandbabies?"

"Looks like we might get a front-row seat to making them," James scoffed, but Riley could hear the joy in his voice.

"That's still my sister!"

Riley burst out into a hearty laugh as she pulled herself off Liam. Her heart overfilled with joy.

"She might be your sister, but she's gonna be my wife." Liam winked at Patrick.

"I'll still kick your ass. Plus, it's about damn time you make an honest woman out of her," Patrick huffed, making Riley glare at him with her brow cocked. "Not that you needed anyone to make an honest woman out of you," he corrected.

"Oh, look, he's learning," James stated. "Only took a million years."

Patrick's hand flung to his heart. "Pops! How could you?"

As James and Patrick fell into their normal banter, Riley turned back to Liam as he looked at her like he always did.

Like she was the only person in the world. Like she was the reason for his next breath.

"I love you, Riley. With everything inside of me, I love you. Thank you."

Riley grabbed the collar of his shirt, yanking Liam to her. "I love you too." She kissed him. "And even though it pains me to admit this... you were right."

"*Oh*, really?" Liam quirked his brow. "About what?"

Riley's smile lit the entire bakery as her eyes flicked to the cake bites before focusing back on the man she loved. "It was *Just a Batter of Time*."

THANK you so much for reading Just a Batter of time! I hope you enjoyed it.

Do you want to read more about the hunky Firefighter Hank Parker and the erotic romance author Olive Quinn? If so, check out their story in Teased by Fire. There is a sneak peak of chapter one on the next page.

Or, was it Doctor Richman, Holly, and Lord Waffles the Corgi? If so, read their story in Stumbling Into Him.

TEASED BY FIRE SNEAK PEAK
CHAPTER ONE

OLIVE QUINN GLARED daggers at her traitorous best friend, Miranda Parker, as the bane of her existence—Hank Parker—moved yet another piece of his furniture into her apartment.

"Stop trying to murder me with your eyes, Olive." Miranda sighed with a huff of annoyance as she pushed the hair out of her face.

That only caused Olive to glare harder in her friend's direction. "I will *not* stop trying to murder you with my eyes," Olive whisper shouted. "It's your fault *he* is moving into *my* apartment."

"What the hell did you want me to do, Olive? I knew I couldn't leave you stranded to pay the rent on your own. You're just pissed I'm moving."

"Damn right, I'm pissed. If I were you, I'd check every box you packed for surprises." Olive squinted her eyes harder in Miranda's direction trying to intimidate her.

"How many times are we going to go through this?" Miranda shook her head. "If I thought I had a chance of getting the job, I would've told you. I legit figured hell would've frozen over before they offered me the position."

"And yet here we are. Hell must be mighty cold right now."

"I'm sorry, okay. I'm freaking sorry."

At Miranda's defeated posture Olive softened. "No, I'm the one that's sorry. You've got your dream job now. I need to stop being angry and just be happy for you."

"It's a lot of things changing all at once."

Olive looked at Miranda, her eyes filling with tears. "I'm going to miss you. We've been stuck together since the first grade."

"Nothing's changing," Miranda tried reassuring her.

"Everything is changing. You're moving clear across the country and I only found out two days ago. I haven't had time to accept the fact my only friend is leaving me." Her eyes narrowed. "And, to top it all off, you went behind my back and gave your *brother* your room."

Miranda sighed before crossing her arms over her chest. "I don't understand why you are freaking out so much. Yeah, Hank is an ass, but if you both stay out of each other's way, you'll be fine. Plus, I've brought you the best research tool a romance writer could ever ask for. You'll be able to get up close and personal experience on how he operates. I brought you a gift."

"If you mean the gift of an STI infested manwhore? You can keep it." Olive's eyes widened as everything clicked into place. *Oh my God!* This wasn't her best friend. Nope. There was no way in hell *her* best friend—who she'd known for years—would actually be doing this. There was only one explanation. Miranda had been abducted by aliens and the person standing in front of her was an imposter.

This is it. This is the zombie apocalypse we've all been waiting for.

Olive quickly grabbed Miranda's arms, examining them for any sign of an implant.

"Jesus, Olive, what are you doing?" Miranda instantly snatched her hands back.

"Checking to see if you have a tracking device somewhere," she stated as a matter of fact.

Miranda rolled her eyes. "Do you ever live anywhere other than your fantasy world?"

Offended, Olive crossed her arms over her chest. "Hey, my weird brain is a masterpiece. How else do you think I come up with my stories?"

"I don't know how you function when all you think about is the zombie apocalypse or some strange alien race invading the earth."

Olive pointed at her head. "This imagination makes me money."

"How? Your brain makes zero sense. Besides you don't even write the shit that goes on in your mind." Miranda shook her head. "Olive, you write contemporary erotic romance. Please explain to me how a brain so involved in aliens and zombies writes hardcore romance with alpha males who make all women drool?"

Olive shrugged. "I don't know. I think it's a weird yin and yang thing. You know, balance to the Force and what not."

"Fuck!" They heard from the other room as a loud bang echoed throughout the space.

Olive's eyes narrowed back at her friend as her lips thinned. "He's a big oaf, and he's gonna use his big oaf muscles to make holes in my walls."

Miranda crossed her arms over her chest. "All right, Olive, I get it. You're fucking pissed. Okay. If I were you I'd be pissed too, but there is nothing we can do about it now. Hank is moving in. Right now, as we speak. He needed a place and you need someone that can pay half the rent. End. Of. Story."

Olive knew Miranda was right, but that didn't stop the betrayal and hurt from running through her. Within two days, everything she was accustomed to had been upended. That's a lot for anyone to take in.

"It's not like he'll be here often anyway," Miranda remarked. "He's always at the fire station, and when he's not, he'll be out with his flavor of the week."

"That isn't the point. With Hank the Tank..." Olive physically revolted. "I hate that nickname everyone calls him."

"I agree, it's stupid."

"Back to what I was saying," Olive started again after shaking the thoughts from her head. "With Hank moving in, I can't be me anymore. Olive Quinn: awkward, hates people, never goes outside or wears a bra. I'll be banished to my room or *forced* to wear a bra. I don't want to wear a bra. Bras suck and stifle my creativity. Oh God, don't even get me started on underwires. Who the hell came up with underwires for bras, anyway? I bet you it was a man. Yup, it had to have been a man. A woman wouldn't have invented something that after a little while a hard metal wire pokes out and causes you excruciating pain." She grunted. "All you want to do is walk to the store and buy some snacks. But *nooo*, instead I'm walking down the sidewalk discreetly trying to move the wire to a place where it's not trying to puncture through my skin and kill me."

Miranda chuckled as she shook her head. "You have a point about the bra, but you said the same thing about pants and you've grown accustomed to wearing them."

"*Not by choice!* I only wear them because you kept the air on 'cold as fuck.' If I didn't wear pants these thunder thighs would have gotten frostbitten."

"I keep it cold because you have that weird obsession with the holidays."

"I do not!"

Miranda's brow rose before she pointed to the corner of Olive's bedroom. "You have a freakin' Christmas tree up."

"Yeah, what's your point?"

"It's the middle of *June*. No one needs a Christmas tree up in the middle of June."

Olive held her hand to her chest as if she'd been shot. "How can you say that?"

Miranda instantly rolled her eyes. "It's the *middle of June*. That's how I can say that."

"Haven't you heard of Christmas in July? I'm just a few weeks early."

"Christmas in July," Miranda scoffed. "Olive, you haven't taken it down in the three years we've lived here."

"Damn, Scrooge much? Sorry, my joy of the holidays makes you a bitter humbug."

Miranda held Olive's shoulders. "Please leave this apartment more often and get some fresh air. I really am worried about you."

"Do not shit all over my love of the happiest time of the year. And, stop deflecting on the fact that *you* went behind my back and moved in your brother."

"Think of all the material you'll get for your books now." Miranda swiped her hand toward the bedroom door. "His friends are delicious. What more could you ask for? Hot firemen as your personal research subjects. You can save your computer from all the viruses from those porn sites you..." She made air quotes. "...use for research."

"Hey, don't knock it. Those sites are a golden tool for my line of work."

"Whatever. It's done. Now, let's go back out there and get the rest of my stuff packed away."

Olive huffed before following her friend. "Remember

those *research subjects* include your brother the next time you read one of my books." Olive couldn't help the smirk that spread across her face when Miranda's eyes widened. *Take that you, traitorous devil woman!*

"Oh shit, what have I done?"

Olive pushed Miranda's shoulder, shoving her toward the door. "Serves you right."

As they walked back into the living room, Olive's heart stopped as she saw a shirtless, sweaty Hank standing in the middle of the room. How in the hell was it possible to look *that* good? He had muscles for days. Her eyes went to his abs as she started mentally counting them. Sure, half the men in her books were described like him, but that was in her mind. Men did *not* look like them in real life. And why the hell was he looking at her like she was a tall glass of water and he was a man dying of thirst?

Her whole body shivered. She one-hundred percent stepped into an alternate universe.

"There you two are," Hank remarked. "I thought you'd left all the work to us." He nodded his head toward his station buddies who'd agreed to help move Miranda out and him in.

Olive looked around at the men scattered throughout the room. It was like a *Hot Fireman/Paramedic* calendar threw up in her apartment.

Maybe this wasn't such a bad idea after all.

She turned toward her friend and smirked, which made Miranda blanch for a brief second before she spoke. "No, we haven't left. We were just discussing something in Olive's room," Miranda announced before making her way to one of the many boxes in the living room.

"That so. And what did you and Olive Oil need to discuss?" Hank smirked in her direction.

"Do not call me that!" Olive glanced around the room for something to throw at his head. She'd grown up with Hank teasing her every chance he got, and if he thought she would just stand by and let him do it in her own home, he had another thing coming.

At her annoyance, Hank chuckled. "Oh, I think living with you will be lots of fun, Olive Oil."

Olive turned back to Miranda ready to demand she make him leave when Hank yelled out, "Any of you seen Dog?"

A chorus of *no's* rang out throughout the room which made Olive roll her eyes. "Let me guess, another one of your degenerate friends?" she asked, glaring at Hank.

His eyes brightened with laughter as his smile grew wider. "Miranda didn't tell you about Dog?"

Olive's eyes shot to her best friend who was now pretending to remove an invisible piece of dirt from her shirt. "No, I guess that tidbit of information escaped her," Olive sneered.

Hank disappeared out of the room leaving Olive with her brow raised and her arms crossed at his sudden departure. *Well, okay then. Clearly living with Hank was not going to be a walk in the park.*

A few minutes later she heard Hank shout, "Found her!" He then made his way back into the living room. That's when Olive spotted the largest Maine Coon cat she'd ever seen in her life cradled in Hank's arms.

"What is that?"

Hank scratched the cat on its head causing the ginormous creature to tilt its face in his direction seeking out more attention, or possibly meat from a small animal being used as a sacrifice. "This is Dog," he said with a grin.

That's when she snapped. "Who the fuck names a *cat* Dog?"

CONTINUE HANK & *Olive's story in Teased by Fire...*

ALSO BY MOLLY O'HARE

Stumbling Through Life Series

Stumbling Into Him

Stumbling Into Forever

Stumbling Into the Holidays

John & Emma's story – *Coming soon*

Teased by Love Series

Teased by Fire

Teased by Tinsel

Lucas & Miranda's story – Coming soon

Hollywood Hopeful Series

Hollywood Dreams

Risking It All (Danny and Lexi's Story) – *Coming soon*

Standalone Novels

Nothing But a Dare

Learning Curves

Tents & Tights

Just a Batter of Time - *This book*

Stay Connected

Sign up for my newsletter or check out my website.

If you just want to hang out, come join my reader group: Molly's

Badass Babes.

ABOUT THE AUTHOR

Molly O'Hare is a USA Today bestselling author of plus sized/curvy romance books.

She's obsessed with all things animals, mainly Corgis, and body positivity. She grew up with severe dyslexia: trust her, spelling is not her strong suit. Over the years, she's become a huge advocate of "just because you learn something a little differently than others doesn't make you less." To help herself fall asleep, she'd create stories in her head, always picking up where she left off the night before. Molly figured if she got enjoyment out of her imagination, others might as well. So here we are.

Stay Connected

Sign up for my newsletter or check out my website.